SECOND CHANCE ROMANCE

SECOND CHANCE ROMANCE

CAROL MASON

bookouture

Published by Bookouture in 2024

An imprint of Storyfire Ltd.
Carmelite House
50 Victoria Embankment
London EC4Y 0DZ

www.bookouture.com

ISBN: 978-1-83525-872-9
eBook ISBN: 978-1-83525-871-2

For Val Thompson, whose English Literature classes brightened my schooldays.

ONE

I've never been a person who loves surprises. Probably because I've got a history of them being horrible ones. So, when I get my daughter's cryptic little text this morning, *Lunch in Venice? Something to tell you...* my first thought is I'd probably look forward to meeting the Four Horsemen of the Apocalypse more than I'm looking forward to this.

Can't wait! I respond. *Exciting!*

I spot her already seated on the patio, essentially a converted parking lot just a stone's throw from the sand. Harriet is the only non-Instagramming nineteen-year-old I know who could waltz into a buzzy new bistro in Venice Beach, California, without a reservation and still manage to land the perfect table – in a shaded, semi-private corner against a backdrop of sand and palm trees. Close by on the boardwalk, an elderly black woman sits on a director's chair under a rainbow-coloured umbrella, singing a charmingly coy rendition of 'My Girl' that she's re-lyricised to 'My Guy', pausing to smile and thank the passers-by who throw a dollar into her canary-yellow hat.

'So, Mum...' Harriet tugs her ponytail over her shoulder, absently combing her fingers through its silky chestnut length. 'I really don't know how to say this, so I'm just going to come right out with it, if that's okay...' She draws a big breath in, then pushes it out. 'I've met someone. A guy. And, well, I think he's the one.'

'Very funny.' Harriet can have a quirky sense of humour at times. 'Now what's the real news?'

She gives me her steady, sanguine stare. The blue gaze of reason. The one that attracts a lot of truth-seekers and good friends. And then she says, 'Er... Mum... That *is* the real news. I've met a guy. We're in love. And it's quite possible I'm going to marry him.'

I play this back. Clearly, there's a blockage between my ears, and the information won't properly penetrate. 'Marry?' I repeat it like it's a death sentence. She didn't really say 'marry'? 'But you don't even have a boyfriend. You can't have. How can you be in love when we've only been in America two minutes?'

'I know!' she almost sings. 'I met him on my first day. Six weeks ago. I was at the campus taco truck. I'd just bought lunch, and then, oh my God, I dropped the thing! The whole taco just... splat on the ground.' She throws up her hands with delight. 'And there I am staring at it, and then I hear this voice. And this guy says, "You know, your face is priceless right about now."' She chuckles. 'He said I looked like the kid who drops their ice cream and is about to bawl tears. And then he said he'd actually snapped a picture of me! He said he'd send it to me if I gave him my number.'

My jaw has dropped so far it has practically become unhinged. 'Well,' I say. 'That's rather calculating of him. A little bit unscrupulous. Is it even legal? I don't think you can just go around snapping photos of people these days without their permission.'

He needs escorting off that campus in handcuffs.

'Oh, Mum! He's adorable.' She flutter-taps her chest like she might be having a cardiac episode – though if anyone should be having one, it's me. 'His name is Aiden Lewis, and he's the kindest, most mature, most insightful human being I've ever met, and I'm totally crazy about him.' She cups her nose and mouth with her hands like she's overcome by her own admission, her eyes tearing up on either side of her fingers.

I think I'm having a stroke. My face has gone numb and there's definitely something *off* about the world around me. My gaze is pulled to the stretch of buttermilk sand. To waves swelling and breaking in the distance. To cyclists on the beach path. Tourists lingering in front of tacky T-shirt shops and tattoo parlours. A homeless man playing a baby grand piano. The drifter towing a boombox with a twenty-pound mutt on the back of his bike. A kid in a shiny purple suit singing Michael Jackson's 'I Want You Back', complete with backslide, toe stand and robot. The sensory assault that is the Venice boardwalk. The frame freezes. My daughter's announcement has stopped time, and my heart.

'Seriously Mum, he's so bright – like, razor-sharp funny – but quietly funny, you know; he doesn't need to be the centre of attention. In fact, he hates that. But he's not shy either. You can take him anywhere. He's just so confident and classy, and proud.' She studies me with an overload of tenderness. But it's not really for me; it's just the ripple effect of her thoughts. 'It was insane. From the instant we met there was just this connection.' She presses an index finger to her lips, as though there's an acupuncture point there that can stem the tide of emotion. 'I looked at him, and he looked at me, and it was like we'd somehow always known one another. There was no surprise to it, no awkwardness, no sense of having to make a good impression or say the right thing. It was as though we'd said it all before.' She gazes off wistfully, into the sunset of her memory. 'It was amazing. Like a gift. Definitely the most incredible, most intense thing that's happened to me in my entire life.'

'Harriet...' I say, as delicately as I can. I barely recognise this twitterpated stranger sitting in front of me. 'I hate to point out the obvious, but you haven't had an entire life. You've had nineteen years of a life. You've been an actual, legal adult for only one of those years. I mean, you've barely even dated.' Harriet was always into more intellectual or artsy pursuits and hanging out with her mates. Boys didn't seem to really make it onto her radar. Very few got past a couple of dates.

'Do you remember what you once told me?' she asks, and I find myself wanting to repeal it before I even hear it. 'You said that when you meet "the one" there'll be so much right with him that even what you don't like about him will seem charming.'

Huh? I can't seriously see me telling her to aspire to liking someone so much that all the crap about them will come across as a bonus. She's making this up as she goes along.

The waiter freewheels over to us, bearing tap water that's been decanted to a glass bottle, and I quickly tell him I'll have a double gin and tonic with extra gin. So he says, 'A *triple* then?' And I tell him, no, I mean a double gin with an extra shot on the side, and he raises an eyebrow like I'm a suitcase short of a trip to the Betty Ford Center. Harriet says she'll stick with water.

'Harriet, darling...' I wait until he's gone. 'I think who you might have met is *the first one*. And that's lovely. But no one hooks up for a lifetime with their first boyfriend.'

She frowns. 'But Dad was pretty much your first, if you don't count that loser who never showed up for any of your dates. And you weren't much older than I am.'

At the very mention of Rupert, that bilious sensation is back in my stomach. 'And look how that turned out,' I say. I still can't think about what my husband did without floundering around in a giant wake of disbelief.

'Aiden is not Dad,' she says, tartly.

I don't want to tell her that I don't think her dad was even her dad when I met him. Nor do I want to get us back on that topic; not here, not now. So I say, 'But your dad and I were together for over a year before we even mentioned having a future together. You've known this... this person for six weeks. I've had bouts of constipation that have lasted longer than that.' I can't even bring myself to call him a boy because giving him a sex or a name just makes him too real to contend with.

Her face has steeled, and she's refusing to look at me. I suddenly feel bad for not being able to sound more excited for her. I fully remember what it was like to be nineteen. Your emotions are always up there on the surface; you can never fully absorb them. You're ready to erupt the second anyone puts doubt and negativity in the path of your ideas and dreams.

'I'm very happy you've met a great guy,' I say, 'but, well, this is not your home, is it? Our home is England. You're only here at UCLA for one semester.' Three short months.

'I know.' She nods, vigorously. 'You're right. But none of that changes the fact that we're in love.'

I gaze at the back of her pale, freckled hand, the white crescents of her short, bare fingernails; these graceful, expressive little hands that have fascinated me since the day she was born – which feels like three minutes ago. And I don't know whether I'm suddenly tongue-tied because I feel so cut out of the loop, or because I actually believe she's serious.

But then something occurs to me. Hang on. Didn't she call him *mature*? 'How old is he?' I ask. Surely he's not one of her professors? I can just see Harriet falling for a pontificating old paedophile in an acrylic sweater, with a thatch of messy hair. Jeff Bridges in *The Mirror Has Two Faces*. My dread surges. I'm already mentally lining up my legal team. I can practically taste the satisfaction of seeing him rot in prison for the remainder of his miserable little pervert life.

'He's twenty-two,' she chirps. 'You'd never think it, though. He's so wise and interesting for his years.'

A regular Socrates whose voice has barely cracked. Great. But he's not a paedo, so there's that.

The waiter returns with my drinks. He gives me the 'It's me again; your favourite person' thumbs-up. Harriet orders Hamachi crudo and some sort of high-protein salad with a side of truffle fries for us. I down the shot of gin a little too keenly. Harriet reaches for the water and pours some into her glass.

Wait...

I stare at her board-flat stomach in her black Lululemon top. Oh, heaven help me! I'm convinced something in there just moved. 'You're pregnant.' I can barely choke the words out. I wag a finger at her belly, inwardly wailing. 'I get it now.' My beautiful, intelligent girl who had the world as her oyster until we came to America, is going to be a teen mum?

At first, she seems bemused. And then she slaps a hand to her mouth. 'Is that what you think? That I'm going to have a baby?'

My eyes must be bobbing around on stalks. 'You're not?'

'Of course I'm not!' She chuckles, then lunges for her phone. 'Oh, Aiden's going to get a kick out of this.'

I watch as her thumbs fly out a message.

'Er... Harriet, please don't do that.'

But it's too late. It's gone. Moments later: Ping! He must have just been sitting there waiting for her to throw him a nugget of attention. She beams at me. 'He said that's the funniest thing he's ever heard.'

Well, maybe he needs to get out more. I cross my hands at my chest. 'Personally, I'm not finding this amusing,' I tell her. 'But I'm glad you are.'

'Mum...' She finally stops the frantic texting, complete with little private smirks, and puts her phone back down on the table. She gazes at me like I'm impossibly endearing. 'You don't need to worry. We're not having a baby. We want to focus on our careers, travel... But even if I were pregnant, guys don't have to marry girls for that reason nowadays, you know. It's not the year 2000.'

I can't keep the eye roll back. 'Sweetie, I hate to disillusion you, but even in the noughties you didn't have to marry a man if he got you up the duff.'

'But Dad got you pregnant. That's why you two married.'

I blink. 'Whoever told you that?'

'You did.'

'When?'

There's a loaded pause, and then she says a doleful, 'That day.'

Ugh! With the mention of *that day*, my world is upended again and my stomach lists.

'My whole life I thought you two were a match made in heaven, and then you told me you'd never have married him if you hadn't been *knocked up*.'

'I truly do not remember ever saying that or using that vile expression.'

'Your exact words.' She looks at me as though to say, *My family. The place where romantics go to die.*

'I was obviously very angry. Under the circumstances. But anyway, I believe you've taken us off the topic.'

The good thing is, she clearly doesn't want to talk about her dad right now either. She's back to looking dreamy again. 'You know, he's got the world's longest eyelashes. They're like... unfair.' She shakes her head at the mere marvel of him having hair in a place where pretty much every human being has hair. I mean, even our cat has eyelashes. It's like she's joined a cult. Someone has hijacked her brain. 'And he's got this ability to just see the world through a truly unique lens. Which is fitting because he wants to be a film director. And he's going to be *so* fantastic at it.'

Realistic career aspirations, then. Steady job. Always going to be able to pay the bills. 'That's wonderful.' I try to smile.

'How lovely for him. But I'm sure a lot of people have those dreams, but very few get to make them a reality.'

Her eyes suddenly blaze with hurt feelings. 'You know what? All those directors who are household names today started with those same aspirations. And if I'd been telling you I wanted to be a film director you'd have done nothing but encourage me. So why do you have to put down someone you don't even know?'

This slap hits hard. The roles have reversed; she's the forty-two-year-old, and I'm the kid with no filter. Not only has she hooked up with some 'gone Hollywood' accidentally hilarious genius with eyelashes like Clarabelle the Cow, but now she's making me feel awful. But she's right. I'm a jaded, old, criticising harridan; I should be ashamed of myself. And I am. I truly am. I hate the sound of my cynicism right now. 'I'm sorry,' I say. 'I really am. I didn't need to pass judgement on his career ambitions. He sounds like a fine guy. He really does...'

The waiter almost frisbees the plate of crudo onto our table, like he must have practised that for days. Then comes the salad and the fries, each making their own fuck-you entrance. I stare out across the sand to a group of surfers in their wetsuits walking towards the shoreline. But the view doesn't look so idyllic any more. I suddenly notice a homeless encampment on the beach, a bin spilling litter, with bags of rubbish piled up around it, graffiti all over the path. Even Ella Fitzgerald has moved on to some soulless number that can't do justice to her wonderful voice. I suddenly regret that we came to LA. Why couldn't Harriet have chosen an exchange programme in Europe instead? It's only in LA where people fall in love and talk about marriage in under six weeks. Only here where they make you feel like an alcoholic just because you want to order a drink for each hand. Only here where the waiters get to be cocky asses and still expect a twenty-per-cent tip.

When I glance at Harriet, she's back to looking at me fondly again – like I'm incorrigible, but she wouldn't have me any other way. 'Look, Mum, I'm sorry I never told you about him. I know that must feel a bit hurtful. It's just that, I was just so horrified of jinxing it until he told me he felt the same. Until... we knew.'

We knew.

I'm aware of this cataclysmic grief, this profound inability to accept. My daughter. My little girl. She's barely out of braces and now she's talking about being someone's wife? I watch as she tucks in to the food, spearing lettuce and fries; she always did have a hearty appetite. I, on the other hand, have lost mine, after she just dropped the atom bomb on my life.

'Look, Harriet...' I try not to focus on how she actually does look different – less weighted down by the extraordinary pressure she puts on herself to be sensible and make smart decisions, like she's got some self-imposed accountability to an imaginary life auditor. Harriet has always been a bit too serious, a bit too old for her years. A bit too like me in that regard. I think I saw it the minute I walked in. I think *I knew.* I try to inject a note of lightness and positivity into my tone. 'Even if you do think you might want to marry him, it's obviously not going to happen any time soon, is it? Certainly not until you finish your education. You've got your summer placement to look forward to at Heatherwick. You were so excited about it, and you've worked so hard for it.' She'd been elated when a top London architecture firm offered her an internship after she'd honed her portfolio, networked and hustled for almost a year. She'd gone out there and done the very thing I've never been able to do – asked for exactly what she wanted, because she *knew* exactly what she wanted.

'I never said we're doing it tomorrow,' she says, much to my spectacular relief. 'And of course I realise I've got my placement, and I'm not about to throw that away...' I can tell by the way her voice tapers off that reality is gaining a little access.

'Anyway,' she says, a mite more subdued. 'You're meeting Aiden next Sunday. And his dad.'

I almost cough up my sip of water. 'His dad? Why do I have to meet his old man?' The waiter hasn't yet cleared our plates, but he appears with the bill and the credit card machine. I slug back my last drop of gin.

'Because this is important to us,' she says. 'Because Aiden's only got his dad, and, well, I've really only got you.' She lowers her eyes, perhaps in recognition of the way she's just wiped her father clean out of the picture. I know she's taken what Rupert did hard, that she's chosen sides without my even asking, or wanting, her to. But I also know she's suffering because of it. More than she will say. 'His dad's some sort of writer,' she adds. 'He lives in Malibu.'

I don't care if he wrote *The Da Vinci Code* and lives on the moon; I can't muster a single word that won't sound like I'm asphyxiating on my own loss. I can't have come to America with a husband and a daughter and end up going home to a life by myself.

She slides the chair back, stands. I watch her slip the strap of her black leather tote across her tiny body. 'We have to be there by ten for brunch.'

I want to scream, *No way! I'm not doing it!* But I can't bear to rain on her parade again. She is looking at me as though our bond is being tested, and her faith in me hanging by a thread. So I find myself mumbling, 'Well, okay then. I'm sure it's going to be a bust.'

She cocks her head. 'Huh?'

I smile. 'I said, if I must.'

TWO

Only four messages from Rupert today. Not the normal thirteen. Or forty. I tend to keep him on mute all day then read them when I go to bed, which is an oddly masochistic way of ensuring I will lie awake for hours going over everything that happened and trying to decide what I'm going to do about it. With all this Harriet business to think about, I don't feel like opening another worm can tonight, but the evening text torture proves irresistible once again.

> *Just remembered... Isn't it Grace and Paul's wedding on 23 Feb? Assuming you'll be back for that??? Please confirm ASAP that attendance will be guaranteed.*

> *Saw our Mastercard bill. Almost had a purple fit! PLEASE remember to pay for your purchases in US$ not in £, otherwise we're getting crucified on the exchange. PS Not sure why you have to buy hypoallergenic pillows if your apartment is supposedly furnished. Assuming you're not going to lug them home with you? Which means other people reap the benefit of our expenditure.*

Any idea where you put Tiddles' anti-anxiety meds?
Poor thing's overgrooming again. She's practically as
bald as a Sphynx.

He has attached a close-up of our cat's nether regions, legs akimbo. As far as I can see, her fur is perfectly normal. Zero evidence of her licking herself to the bone, which is what happens if she's stressed. Talk about ways to gaslight someone!

Can we please just talk on the phone and have a civilised
conversation? You can't go on ignoring me forever!!!

'Sorry,' I chirp out loud. 'No can do.'

I click off, conscious that my heart is pumping a little harder. Telling him to essentially F off when he can't hear me is a short-lived gratification, though. There are no winners in this. My tiny triumphs are quickly replaced with the sort of crushing sadness that I hardly know how to handle.

Suddenly, I'm blazing hot. I kick the duvet off, stretch myself across the queen-sized mattress, gawk at the ceiling. Now what? Night-time is the worst as there's no distraction. Bed has become the enemy. I can't throw myself at copious activities to keep my mind occupied. Can't run from it; it has backed me into a corner and there is nothing for me to do but face it again. Relive every sanity-shattering detail of...

That day.

The flight over here from England.

Harriet about to embark on her big adventure of a study term at UCLA. Her first experience of being away from home. Rupert and I accompanying her on the pretext of the three of us having a little family holiday in California before we would say goodbye to her for three whole months. But we were really doing it because we didn't want her arriving in a strange country all by herself. Having to navigate setting herself up in residence; shopping for groceries, dishes, reading lamps... All that without us, without even a car. She'd been used to university being a twenty-minute commute from our house in Reading. She'd chosen, sensibly, to live at home to save some money, though I'd often wondered if she might have short-changed herself of a proper university experience, like the one I'd had. I still did her laundry and we still shared cups of tea while I talked her down from feeling overwhelmed when she'd said 'yes' to a few too many commitments and was about to crumble under the weight of all her good intentions. Secretly I had loved it; I could still be there for her, she still needed me. We knew she was capable of travelling to America by herself, facing whatever challenges that came with it. Harriet is strong, and strong-minded. But this way we got to make her feel like she totally 'had this', as everyone says in America, but we could keep a watchful eye in case she didn't. Deep down, I just wanted another of our 'three Musketeers' adventures for the memory bank. Another pristine page in the many chapters of our life that I would pore over at some later stage, perhaps when she truly had grown up and left us.

But I could never have guessed what I was going to get instead...

There we were. The three of us on the runway. Harriet by the window. Rupert in the middle. Me at the aisle. Row 18. The pilot announced we were fifth in line to take off. We didn't care. We were happy. We'd never done a long-haul holiday before. The stress of all the preparations was behind us. We'd even shared a bottle of Champagne in the airport. Rupert hadn't yet put his phone in flight mode because Rupert generally likes exercising his rebellious streak – but not in big ways that could get him into trouble. He was more relaxed than I'd seen him in ages. He was showing us some travel article he'd found of a scenic drive he thought we might do from Santa Monica to Montecito. Harriet was all into it. I could hear the giddy note in her voice; for the last few weeks she'd been like a kid on Christmas morning knowing this adventure was coming up. Rupert was going on about the ocean and the orange groves, and a famous resort where John and Jackie Kennedy supposedly spent their honeymoon, which enthralled her. We were leaning into him, flanking him, staring at the pictures, when up popped a text. A lightning bolt across the bottom of his screen.

You don't intend to read somebody's message. But it's there, and your eyes have gone to it without you even realising.

It was from someone called Dagmara.

And it said: *I really need to fuck you.*

THREE

'Did you know that people with weak chins secretly lack willpower and self-confidence, and often struggle to make it through when the going gets tough?' I say to Harriet as we bomb down the Pacific Coast Highway in the cherry red Mustang I've been renting for the last two months. Apparently only roller-coasters offer more thrills than a Mustang, said the rental guy about the last available vehicle left on the lot. I reckoned I'd done the rollercoaster, so what was there left to fear?

'What on earth are you talking about, Mum?' She looks up from her phone.

'I googled him. Lewis. Malibu. Writer.' I tell her there was a LinkedIn page for a bald, bespectacled Bob Lewis with atrophy of the chin, who lives in Malibu and writes entertainment media franchises in the film industry. 'We all know that chins run in families.' I send her the side-eye. 'I'm just saying it's highly likely that the children of this man's children will be cursed with that thing.'

We're approaching what looks to be an upmarket shopping and dining development that sits directly across the highway from the ocean, called Trancas Country Market. I spot a Star-bucks. 'Hurrah! Coffee.' I indicate to turn right.

'Can't you wait? Aiden's dad hates late people.'

'He's a writer nobody's heard of who expects people to be at his house by ten a.m. on a Sunday, and he hates late people. Could he get any more appealing?'

'Ooh!' She looks me up and down. 'I didn't realise you were hoping to find him appealing. This could be interesting.'

I cluck my tongue in disapproval. 'Firstly, you couldn't pay me to have anything to do with another man, as long as I live. But I've seen Chinless Bob, remember?' The satnav says I've gone too far. I try to see where I can safely turn around.

'If you call him Chinless Bob behind his back, you know it's only a matter of time until you call him it to his face, don't you?'

I titter. Okay. I'm going to try to stop being a bitch. For my daughter's sake.

'Oh look,' I say. 'It must be down here.' It's telling me we've arrived at Broad Beach Road. There's a turning off the highway that you wouldn't notice if you weren't looking for it. We follow it down an incline and it loops into a very long street of houses. The properties all occupy the same side of the road – the ocean side. Some of them are gawk-worthy mansions, others like cottages from a different time. Bursts of hot-pink bougainvillea climb the walls and overhang doorways, which is Mediter-ranean style pretty, but makes it virtually impossible to see the house numbers. And it's so very quiet, as though the highway just dissolved.

Harriet peers around like a curious meerkat: '7856... 58... We must be close.'

There is very little sign of life. A few guys working on a new build. Parked cars and workmen's trucks on a grassy verge. An obese, uniformed security guard stands beside his SUV tinkering on his phone. It all feels very *extra*, as Harriet would say.

'I'm going to text him we're nearly here,' she chirps.

I watch her out the corner of my eye, her lips curling into a cute little self-satisfied smile as she types, the chestnut-brown hair scraped back into her trademark high ponytail, the profile that is so much like her dad's. The way her elegant neck curves to her pale, pronounced clavicles in her boat-neck black T-shirt.

Ping!

'Okay. He says we're super close. He's coming out to meet us.'

'I think I see someone,' I say, slowing to a crawl. Yes. A guy is standing on the road. A tall, slim, dark-haired figure in navy shorts and a teal-coloured T-shirt. He spots us and waves.

'There he is.' She does a spontaneous little clap. 'It's him, Mum!'

'Really? You're sure it's not just some random Malibu millionaire who's excessively happy to see us?'

She chuckles. 'Nope. Just my Aiden.'

Oh my God, I can't unhear it. 'Harriet,' I say. 'He's nobody's Aiden. He's *his* Aiden. Just like you are *your* Harriet. You can't own another human being.'

She lets out a lustful, almost feral little noise, then she lowers the window and waves like her life depends on it. Even from this distance, I can see his face launching a great big, charismatic smile. She wasn't exaggerating. He is gorgeous. Fit, sporty, classily put together. The male version of her. And he somehow looks way more assured, and a lot less twenty-two, than I had imagined.

When we park and climb out, Aiden Lewis greets me like he hasn't dreaded this nearly as much as I have. 'Mrs Fitzgerald...' He looks me levelly in the eye and shakes my clammy hand. It's a genuine smile, a sincere display of affection. Everything about him shrieks *upstanding good guy*.

This is how I know I'm doomed.

He pulls Harriet in for a Kodak moment hug. I watch as her

arm slides around his waist, as though his body is her natural habitat, how she gazes up at him with so much adoration, almost pride. And it's mutual. The way his eyes lovingly orbit her face, Aiden Lewis is obviously just as besotted with my daughter. I am so deeply affected by their tender show of togetherness, that I forget – briefly – that this is a terrible thing. So much so that when they pull apart, my jaw is slightly hanging open and I almost can't snap out of my stupor.

We are standing on the blue-tiled driveway of a modest, shingle-style, white house that reminds me of those you read about in books set in Nantucket, kept real by the fact that it could use a fresh coat of paint. It is beachy and sun-blasted. Two pots that contain giant cacti flank double garage doors, their bases surrounded by dust and leaf debris.

'Let's go inside,' Aiden says, leading us into a lift.

'There's an elevator?' Harriet looks at me in astonishment. 'In your house?'

Oh my God, she's already calling a lift an elevator. Whatever next?

'Dad's house. Not mine.' He raises his hands in surrender, sending an apologetic glance my way. Then – to possibly downplay the fact that his family is clearly loaded – he gives us a benign engineering lesson, explaining how houses here are built on a slope and that many of them are six or seven stories below street level. Presumably that's why they have to be so massive. 'And besides, Dad's getting on,' he adds. 'He's going to need a way to get between floors soon.'

So Chinless Bob will have all his needs met in his old age. Lucky him.

When we land, however many levels down, and the door opens, it's hard even for me to contain a gasp. We have arrived in an enormous, open-plan, sun-drenched living room, with distressed, wide-plank, walnut floors, and a high, wood-beamed ceiling reminiscent of a well-kept country cottage. By contrast, a strikingly modern, U-shaped floating staircase sits centrally, dramatically separating the place into two zones: a comfy living area with a couple of easy upholstered sofas and a tall, stone-walled fireplace; and a sparkling, high-tech kitchen with a vast Carrara marble breakfast bar. The counter is bare except for an open newspaper with a pair of reading glasses beside it. A pushed-back chair gives the impression that its occupant just absconded. Straight ahead, ceiling-to-floor windows show off a breathtaking view of the ocean that looks like it's practically in the back yard.

'Good heavens,' I say. 'It's extraordinary.' Clearly there's a lot of money in writing entertainment media franchises – whatever they are.

'You're right on the beach!' Harriet trills. 'You never said.' She has wandered outside to a vast, paved patio with a collection of lounge chairs clustered around a sunken fire pit. Aiden follows, placing a hand in the small of her back. 'I can't believe you'd choose a shared house in Westwood with a bunch of smelly students, over living in this paradise. Do you own part of the sand, too?' She gazes up at him dotingly, and a little bit cockily.

He sends her a fondly scathing look. 'Come on. You can't own the actual beach.'

She grins, then glances at me, like she quite loves him giving her a little telling-off.

'Why *didn't* you tell me though?' She pokes him in the ribs. 'Were you worried I'd see you differently or something?'

He pretends to recoil at her finger. 'It wasn't relevant. And like I said, this is my dad's place, not mine...' He holds up his hands again, and I realise that if he does this *don't blame me because I've got a rich daddy* act one more time, I'm going to want to slap him. 'Anyway,' he adds, 'once you get past first impressions it's really just a house at the end of the day.'

He stares out at the ocean, almost like Harriet's enthusiasm has just made him see it with new eyes. I notice there's a five-feet tall, all-glass fence at the property line, designed to maximise the view, and a dense and delightful ground cover that looks like a succulent with its shiny green leaves and purple daisy-like flower. I ask him about the enormous rock retaining wall on the other side of the glass, and he explains how the race is on for homeowners on this mile-long stretch of sand to protect their properties from the storms and erosion due to climate change. He's knowledgeable on the topic and he talks about the lengths owners have gone to – some legal and some not.

'So do you have any famous people for neighbours?' Harriet asks, excitedly.

He nods. 'Yes. Loads.' He says it like it's nothing. 'A lot of the Hollywood greats used to live here. Frank Sinatra lived four houses down. Robert de Niro... Charlize Theron walks past here all the time. Goldie Hawn too.'

To keep things real, I ask him if he surfs.

'Yeah!' He seems to welcome the change of conversation. 'I mean, I did. Until I was about eighteen. I'm kinda rusty after all these years.'

All these years? What? All four of them?

He asks me if he can pour me a coffee. I tell him that right now I would probably take it intravenously. We follow him back inside. As he walks around the enormous breakfast bar, I note how he's got a gazelle-like grace to the way he moves that's not something I'd normally associate with a guy his age. 'I still can't believe you grew up here,' Harriet says, slightly chastising, as she perches on a stool.

He shoots her a look that says this is getting a bit tiresome, which is almost cute. 'Can we, like, drop this now please?'

She beams and shoots me one that says *isn't he fantastic?*

He pours my coffee and places the creamer in front of me like he's well used to playing host. I note the way his thick, chocolate-brown hair is cut closely at the back of his tanned neck, and his arms are toned, like a tennis player's. 'My mom and dad divorced when I was a kid,' he explains, directing it to me. 'I mean, I came here a lot. Dad's been here years. But I lived mostly with my mom in the valley.' He stands there beside me, quite at ease. 'Believe me, I'm not some trust-fund kid like the kind my dad writes about.'

I'm a little puzzled as to what trust-fund kids have to do with media franchises, but I don't get to ask because he says, 'At the end of the day, this is Dad's world, not mine. Besides,' he adds, in a final sort of way, 'famous people are just people like everybody else.'

Harriet and I smile. He asks us if we'd like to come sit outside. There's a moment where I stare at him and find myself saying, 'Wow, you really do have enormous eyelashes! Harriet was right.' They are long and curly and so thick, a slightly lighter shade of brown than his lovely hair.

'See.' Harriet chirps. 'Didn't I tell you? They're unreal.'

He laughs. 'Okay, you guys are embarrassing me now.'

As we're about to go back outside I glance again at the open newspaper and the pair of reading glasses, the pushed-back chair.

'Dad's really looking forward to meeting you,' he says, clocking me looking. 'He should be out soon.'

We sit by the fire pit and gaze at the mountain of rocks that rather hinders the view of the sand once you're seated – a problem I find myself mentally trying to fix. We chat about UCLA, his film studies, the architectural landmarks they've ticked off Harriet's bucket list. The Getty Center, Frank Lloyd Wright's Hollyhock House, the home where Frank Gehry lived for most of his life in Santa Monica. Harriet lights up when she talks about her favourite subject, and Aiden seems so captivated as she retells, for my benefit, an experience they've obviously both shared. We sip our coffees. The topic gets around to the Malibu fires and recent mud slides, politics and back to global warming. Harriet and Aiden engage in hot debate, but the heat comes not in their opposition, but from the fact that they agree on so much. His hand, with its slim, artistic fingers remains on Harriet's knee the whole time, and my eyes remain the whole time on his hand. I've always been fascinated by couples who touch each other in public a lot. Rupert was never tactile. Ironically, he once said that when couples are always pawing each other it usually means one of them is cheating.

Then there's a lull. Aiden glances back into the house. 'Dad's finishing up some stuff. He'll be down soon. Promise...' He sends me a look of apology.

'Of course,' I say. In my world people don't keep their guests sitting around waiting for them. 'Haven't missed him for a second.'

Fortunately, we are saved by the bell. Or, rather, Aiden's phone pinging. 'Oh.' He jumps to his feet. 'Brunch is here.' As he strides off back inside, he says, 'Dad doesn't keep much food in the house, unless you want a jar of mayonnaise and a spoon, so we ordered in. Gonna run up and grab it.'

Harriet offers to help but he tells her to chill. After he jogs across the living room then disappears into the lift, Harriet whispers, 'What do you think?'

'Truthfully? I think he's a rude git.'

'What?' She gawks at me. 'How is he rude?'

I throw up my hands and look around. 'Well, where is he? I mean, we've been here forty minutes.'

'Oh!' A relieved smile. 'His dad! I thought you meant Aiden.'

'No,' I tell her. 'Aiden seems like a fine young man, with far better manners than his father. But,' I playfully add, 'I don't really know him. And neither do you.'

Her mouth twists in displeasure.

'I mean, you didn't even know he grew up in a mansion on celebrity beach.'

Fortunately, she smirks. 'Not a bad discovery though! And he didn't really grow up here, like he told you. He lived with his mother.'

Aiden suddenly reappears. He's balancing two large paper bags in his arms, so we get up and go back inside to assist. 'It's remotely possible we've over-ordered.' He nudges them onto the breakfast bar. 'And there's more if you can believe it.'

'Let me come help,' Harriet says, and scampers after him.

As they disappear into the lift, I'm left standing in the middle of the floor trying to resist the urge to set the table or otherwise put myself to good use. But then my eyes are drawn to a huge black and white art print set into an alcove just off the kitchen. It's of a yacht, and a woman who has dived into the water, and all you see of her are her long, sexy legs.

Then a voice says, 'It's called *Splash*, by Riley Harper.'

FOUR

When I pivot, Aiden's father is standing there in a doorway, one shoulder resting against the frame. He's wearing an untucked white linen shirt and faded blue jeans. His feet are bare, one crossed in front of the other, and his hands are stuffed in his pockets. Not bald, bespectacled Bob with the less than desirable facial structure. Far from it. This man is every bit the older version of his son – the same lean build, only with the slight fleshing out that comes with age, the same thick hair, his a little fairer and looking like it hasn't seen a comb in days.

He's attractive. Despite my new determination to loathe anyone with a penis, I register it like a hard clutch in my lower abdomen.

'Oh,' I say. 'Right.'

Green eyes unhurriedly appraise me from top to toe in a way that straddles the propriety line and does something to my central nervous system in the process. 'I got it from a cool store in Venice Beach called House of Spoils,' he says.

'Did you?' For a moment I forget what we're even talking about.

He smiles. I think that's what it is. There's a small sardonic twitch of his lips. I'm trying to drum up something to add about the print, but the longer I don't, the more conspicuous the silence becomes. He doesn't exactly try to break it either. We are held there, the ocean crashing in the distance like a third pulse. And then Aiden says, 'Hey Dad.'

Finally, he moves. 'I'm Frank,' he says, on passing, as he heads to the kitchen, like he's grudgingly taking part in a roll call. No offer of a handshake.

'Dad,' Aiden says, like it's a huge thing. 'This is Harriet...'

I watch him glance at my daughter with the same cool indifference. 'Yes, Harriet. Hello.'

Harriet and I send one another a look. *Hmm...!* Not exactly the welcome of the century. But before she can add anything, Frank says, 'We need to get this food out. Don't want cold eggs.' He roots through random boxes, pulls out a doughnut, stuffs at least half of it into his mouth.

'I'm Moira, by the way,' I say. *You know, just in case you were about to ask.*

'Yeah, I know,' he answers with his mouth full, demolishing the doughnut in two seconds flat. 'Great to meet you, Moira,' he says, like he couldn't give two flying shits. He rustles around in the other boxes, unearths a strip of bacon and snaps a chunk off between his teeth.

I stare at the denim puddled about his ankles, the tanned feet and the white between his skinny toes, and I have this overpowering desire to stand on them and make him howl.

We eat at the L-shaped breakfast bar, so that we can easily look at one another for the scintillating conversation that we don't have. He has ordered a ridiculous amount of food: pancakes, Bennys, French toast, breakfast burritos, avocado toast, sides of everything. Over-the-top extravagance, like one of those scenes straight out of a movie where annoying rich people order everything off the menu just because they can. Thankfully, Harriet and Aiden keep the conversation flying.

Aiden speaks of 'us' as though they've known one another for way longer than the average gap between my menstrual periods. Occasionally I see Frank's big, tanned hand reach out and grab something from a plate. I even hear him stifle a belch.

'So, I understand you're a writer, Frank.' I find it almost excruciating to make the first move, but somebody has to.

The hand going out for a muffin stops for a moment. 'Do you?' he says.

'Dad's a low-key guy,' Aiden says. 'He doesn't like to talk about his success. Do you, Dad?'

Frank shrugs like none of this is worthy of a full sentence.

Low-key might be one word. I have some others.

'Have you written anything I might have read?' I reach for a muffin too, just to fake the illusion of 'I cope with anti-social bastards like you every day and I am chill about it', but I note the slight tremble of my hand.

'Do you read?' He glances my way, and I'm sure that was a smirk.

I stare at the side of his head, fix on the unfortunately pendulous earlobe. 'Hang on... are you asking if I'm illiterate?'

Aiden hoots a laugh but then looks like he maybe shouldn't have, right as Harriet says, 'Mum!'

'Not everyone reads books,' Frank the wanker says as he proceeds to pick blueberries out of a muffin and pile them on the side of his plate, so I'm left staring at a small but rather gross collection of manhandled fruit covered in sticky cake fuzz. 'And even if you do, I don't know you, so how would I know what you might have read?'

I'm about to say *Wow, you just analysed the bejesus out of that one; must have used up all your brain cells,* when Aiden says, 'Harriet tells me you work in mental health.'

I refocus away from the annoying earlobe. 'I was an occupational therapist at a London teaching hospital, yes.' I respond in a tone that says, *not that your dad would care, because perhaps that's just a bit too much real world for him.*

Aiden says, 'Was?'

I don't feel like getting into how, a month before we came to America, I had left my job because I'd felt unfulfilled for a long time, but mainly because I'd been passed over for a big promotion that should have been in the bag. I was feeling extremely bitter and sorry for myself, and Rupert said, 'Look, we have enough savings. Leave. Work out what you really want to do, what'll inspire you. Maybe find something among people who will really appreciate you and recognise your tremendous abilities. Instead of a place that gives a job you'd worked hard for to someone half your age who happens to have a PhD in I Have No Idea How to Function in The Working World. I Just Stayed in School Until I Started Sprouting Grey Pubes...'

Rupert, who loves hanging on to money, was very supportive about me giving up a good salary. I thought it was odd at the time. Now I'm thinking... Guilt?

'Actually, I took a sort of... sabbatical... so I could come here to help Harriet settle into university,' I say. I always knew that word would come in handy one day.

'Ah. Cool,' Aiden says, a little stiffly, and I wonder what he knows about our family, what Harriet has told him, and I hope not *that*. Surely she wouldn't have aired our family's dirty laundry to a virtual stranger.

'Are you missing England?' Aiden asks now. 'Or have the palm trees and endless sunshine convinced you there's a better way of living?' It's a benign question but someone might as well be hammering a stake between my shoulder blades.

'Hmm...' I try to take a discreet breath. 'Believe it or not, I'm actually one of those rare people who doesn't mind the rain. And we do get sunny days in England, you know. Just not all that many of them.' I don't add that the weather, as it turned out, was the least of my problems. But as Gandhi and my therapist friend, Nat, said, nobody can destroy me without my permission.

Aiden smiles. 'I'd love to visit one day.'

I'm hoping we're done now when he adds, 'But you like it here? You must, I guess, given you've stayed on?'

My throat has closed. I have a hard time swallowing the bit of pineapple I just put in my mouth, so I take a drink of water. But when I speak, there's an embarrassing gurgle in the back of my throat that I can't seem to clear. 'LA has been a little different for me to get used to, I admit. But that might be less to do with the place and more to do with...'

My F'd up life?

'...other influences,' I add, with a croak.

I am aware that Frank suddenly turns his big ear in the direction of this comment – just a fraction.

'But I like it because I'm near Harriet, obviously. And I have found some things to love about Santa Monica.' I shrug a little self-consciously. 'Beach walks, cycling the boardwalk, sunsets. Americans are very friendly.' All except one. 'Besides, you definitely feel more cheerful when the sun shines, I will give you that.' I am hot around the back of my neck. Please, Jesus, Mary and Joseph, let this be the end of the interrogation!

'So do you think you'll stay on until Harriet's semester is finished?' Aiden asks.

I unstick my lips and let out another sly breath, only I don't think it's *that* sly because I happen to catch Frank observing me with a certain lazy intrigue. 'You know, right now I'm just trying to get used to the fact that I don't really know what I'm going to do.' I try to smile it off, but it comes out a little quick and defensive. 'I'm just trying to go with... the flow.' I sound like I can't spell flow, much less go with it.

'Cool,' he says, again.

I'm relieved that's over. But then Harriet says, 'Mum's got a lot of thinking to do. Some tough decisions to make.'

The ear turns towards me again.

'Do I?' I send her the stink-eye.

'She's a little cynical about love and relationships right now, and for good reason.' She looks coy for a moment. The air becomes leaden, much like my veins. 'But she forgets that she was actually around our age when she made an enormous decision with her life for a man.'

'Sounds like it might have been the wrong decision though,' Frank finally opens his mouth.

I glance at him, but he's focused on what's on his plate. 'Well,' I reply, a little twitchy now that we seem to be tiptoeing around this topic of life-changing commitments, 'firstly, I'm not exactly sure I did anything *for a man*. That's a little too Tammy Wynette for my taste.' I pick up the muffin again and start pulling the blueberries out, too, until I realise I'm mimicking him, so I put it down. 'What happened was, I made a choice with my life, and no matter what results from the choices we make...' I look at Frank again, who is watching me like he's either going to roll his eyes or burst out laughing. 'I really don't believe in wrong decisions, as you put it, Frank.'

I see the hint of a smirk again. It makes me look away, down to my fingers and the purplish stain on the pads. 'Besides,' I try to say it breezily, 'if I'd never taken this path there would be no Harriet.'

Aiden says a chirpy, 'And we wouldn't want that! A world without Harriet? Oh man! What a loss that would be.' He reaches for her hand again. Not a conscious gesture of show, just an instinctive one. She gives him such an adoring little smile. I stare at them, at the hands, then I look at Frank who is noting me observe these details rather closely. In fact, so closely that I feel like some sort of curtain I was hiding behind just fell away, and I'm sitting here wearing no clothes.

A silence descends. Then Harriet says, 'Speaking of reading... Mum developed a very successful bibliotherapy group in the psychiatric wing of her hospital, didn't you, Mum? Because books can provide therapy to people with depression and other mental health disorders.' She addresses it mainly to Frank, who now has that nonplussed look of a four-month-old. 'Mum, you can tell it best.'

I love her for trying to big me up, and for her valiant attempt to compensate for the shitty manners of her boyfriend's father, but I find myself saying, 'Must I?' Now that I've picked all the blueberries out of the muffin, I've half a mind to put them back.

Aiden says, 'Please, Mrs Fitzgerald, we'd love to hear.'

I try to keep the sigh out of my voice and insist he calls me Moira. 'It was a programme that harnesses storytelling and reading as a support therapy for anyone with mild to moderate symptoms of several mood conditions.' I address a stack of pancakes, because even they probably have more interest in me than Aiden's father. 'And I didn't develop it myself; I was part of a very dedicated team.' Christ. I'm giving my Oscars acceptance speech now.

Frank reaches for his phone, idly scans it, like he's making a show of not listening.

Aiden says, 'That's very cool, actually. A labour of love for an amazing cause.'

'It always sounds way more boring when I try to explain it.'

'You could never sound boring with that great English accent,' Aiden says, then adds, 'Eh, Dad?'

Frank, the scintillating conversationalist, replies, 'That's giving accents a little too much credit.' And then he stands. 'Wanna sit outside? It's feeling a little tight in here.' He heads onto the patio, coffee mug in hand. I watch him from behind. His broad shoulders and hair that could use a date with a pair of shears. The way he drags his bare feet – slap, slap, slap. The way arrogant people walk around their magnificent property when you're a guest who has outstayed their welcome. If you were ever welcome in the first place.

Tight? I want to say. *Like your bottom, perhaps?*

'Can you tell me where the toilet is, please?' I say to Aiden. It comes out sounding like a plea. 'I assume I don't have to take the lift or catch a cab.'

Aiden laughs but I see Frank's ear turn towards the jibe. 'You can walk, yeah,' Aiden says. 'There's about ten of them on this level so you can't go wrong.'

'Ten's tremendous,' I tell him. 'But one tends to suffice.'

As I walk out, I feel a pair of eyes scorching my back.

Finding the toilet is no easy task. I wander down a long, whitewashed hallway that has huge, white barn doors leading to room after room. Every time I open a door – nope, no toilet there either. There are bedrooms, all with windows that give onto the ocean, all sparsely furnished with queen-sized beds, white bedding, a chest, a comfy chair, and a wall-mounted TV. Rooms that look like they're waiting for the family that never arrived. There's a small corner one with big windows and no furniture except for a stool and a telescope. I stare at this for a while. Must be the room where Frank goes to masturbate because he has a home this amazing, *and* he gets to stare at Venus, Saturn and Mars. Then I'm into another slightly larger, windowless one that has an enormous sectional sofa upholstered in lumberjack red and white checks, and a giant red and white wall light like a stick of candy cane; the media room, judging by the enormous TV, and the ceiling-to-floor stack of CDs. There's a leather ottoman with a remote control on it, and an orange wooden chair that seems to have white paint splotches all over it – the kind you might find in a charity shop, that you intend to refinish, but is probably designer and cost thousands. But the best part is the old-fashioned record player and the utterly astonishing collection of vinyl! There must be over a thousand records here. And on the only wall that isn't taken up by records and CDs, there's a giant poster of Bob Seger with a guitar slung over his shoulder, as he stands on train tracks and smokes a cigarette. I'm like a kid in a candy store. I can already see so many of the albums and artists are of my generation. I'm dying to reach out and pluck one from its sleeve, and place it on the turntable, like I might have done when I was fourteen. But I stop myself by remembering I'm actually trespassing, and, who knows, there might even be hidden cameras. Just in case there are, I raise my middle finger to the ceiling. Bob Seger's eyes seem to be looking right at me and smiling through the haze of his cigarette.

Then I am into another room. This one all windows and all view, with a walk-out deck. His room, obviously, judging by the unmade, four-poster California king. Clearly, he sleeps alone, because two pillows are stacked in the centre, bearing the impression of only one head. Opposite the bed, a sofa and armchair sporting blue and white lumberjack checks are arranged around a wood-burning fire, beside which is another telescope with a guy's cardigan hung off it. My eye disappears down a short hallway off the bedroom, at the end of which I spot an inviting giant soaker bath, and... well, hello!

A toilet.

I go in there and stare at my flushed face in the mirror. My dark, ash-brown hair that I colour myself, but recently had chopped, at vast expense, into a trendy 'undone' bob, to mark the new me. Slightly longer than chin-length. Flat-ironed into beach waves, though I can never master those, and end up with these weird iron marks that never come out. My red lipstick that's worn off except for an unattractive line along my top lip. My neck; not quite as firm any more. Green eyes gazing back at me; a few deep crow's feet that I swear Rupert recently put there.

While I'm sitting there peeing and staring at a couple of fluffy white towels left strewn on the floor, and a beautiful framed black and white close-up of Marilyn Monroe as she coyly glances back over her shoulder, I take out my phone, punch *Frank Lewis writer* into Google. The first thing that pops up is a Wikipedia page: Frank Lewis, American Author. And a string of pictures from an era ago. Frank, the young man. Handsome, I grudgingly admit. One of him leaning towards a microphone, lips parted, as though the photographer caught him in the act of speaking. A full-length one of him sitting artfully on what looks like a wooden box in a bare room. A few of him in various stages of contemplation – touching his chin or pressing an index finger to his lips. Then one where he's wearing a striped scarf, with his hair flying away, against a backdrop of what looks to be Central Park. He seems very happy in this one, like the guy who may have nothing, or everything, but he has all that he needs.

And a description:

Frank Lewis is an American author and screenwriter best known for writing the bestselling novel Love for Lara, and the hit motion picture of the same name.

What?

I think I must say it out loud.

I read it again. Nope. It's still there. If I wasn't sitting, I'd fall. *Love for Lara?* The most iconic love story of all time? The gut-wrenching tale of a WASPy trust-fund kid, and a poor, Jewish American drama student who marry despite his father's disapproval, and then she dies? The movie that cemented whatever hopelessly romantic tendencies I had in me for a lifetime? The movie that actually *changed* me? I can still see me and my friends queuing in a huge line outside the cinema, still taste that moment of walking out, ninety minutes later, feeling... How can I put it? Gutted, but oddly uplifted. I didn't know men could love that way, could show their vulnerable side and their feelings like that. I didn't know they even *had* feelings and vulnerable sides. As I sit here with my knickers around my ankles it all comes rushing back. The enigmatic look on his face when he first walked past a room and heard her rehearsing her lines as Blanche DuBois in *A Streetcar Named Desire*. The soundtrack that just punched you in the solar plexus. And that ending. Who could ever forget the most heart-breaking final scene in movie history? This can't be real.

The barefoot, burping, bad-mannered person whose toilet I'm sitting on? *He* wrote *Love for Lara*?

I scan the rest of the Wikipedia entry. It had been a novel first; I had no idea. It says he wrote it when he was twenty-three. It spent forty-five weeks on the *New York Times* best-seller list, was translated into twenty-five languages, and sold over thirty million copies. And he didn't just write this one, either. There are four others, and a link to a *New York Times* article entitled: 'Junior teacher pens the greatest romance of our time'.

Good heavens! I break off a piece of toilet paper and blow my nose so loudly I can probably be heard across the highway.

There are lots of search results for his books: interviews in major newspapers and magazines, reviews, blog posts, banners of his book cover, posters of the movie, pictures of the cast – two of the biggest stars of the day, possibly the world's most famous 'on screen' love match – lines of dialogue that were so timeless and true. I can't look away. In fact, I'm feeling quite comfortable; there's very little reason to leave.

They are still on the patio when I eventually go back out. As I walk over to join them, a very strange thing happens to my legs as I stare at the back of Frank Lewis's head. Since I've been away it seems like he's undergone a personality transplant because Harriet is having a good laugh at something he's just said. And then she sees me approach. 'Mum!' Frank slightly turns his head in my direction, which makes my legs wobble all the more.

Harriet says, 'I was just telling Aiden and his dad that crazy story about how when we landed in LA and walked out of the airport, some guy took your photo because he thought you were famous. And then everybody was hanging around taking your picture and still to this day we have no idea who everybody thought you were!' She chuckles. I'd rather not remember that day for reasons that have nothing to do with mistaken identity, so I can barely crack a smile. Aiden starts speculating about who I look like, naming some cute young actresses, which is charming, bordering on irritating.

'How lovely,' I say. I walk over to the firepit and stand there, awkwardly, like I've taken root. Frank's head is down again, his attention back on his phone. I perch on the end of the seat and there's a moment where I'm dying to say something about the film, about *him*. But then he looks up like he's only just noting my arrival and says, 'We thought you died in there. Hope it's nothing you ate.'

The tiny flicker of whatever embarrassing raptures were about to burst forth from my lips is abruptly extinguished. I could not be more let down. He wrote *Love for Lara* for God's sake; he owes it to womenkind to sit right up there on his giant pedestal until someone commands, 'At ease.'

'Harriet,' I say, trying to keep the completely unwarranted, abject disappointment out of my tone. 'This has been lovely, but I think it's time to leave.'

'Leave?' She sends me the death stare.

'We have places to go, and people to see.'

'Well, we're very sorry you have to go so soon.' Aiden springs to his feet a little too keenly, so Harriet reluctantly follows suit. We're all standing now, except for Frank who continues to be fascinated by his phone. I stare down at the top of his head, almost wishing I'd never read what I just read. There's some discussion between Harriet and Aiden about her staying or coming with me, and them possibly getting together later to play tennis. It seems to go on forever and I continue to stand there, so invisible that I almost don't need to squirm.

Eventually, I walk back into the house. The instant I do, Frank gets up and follows; I hear the characteristic slap of his feet. To think he had guests arriving and he couldn't even put on a pair of slippers. The talentless philistine! When I reach the breakfast bar that looks like forty farm animals ate at it, I reluctantly turn because I'm going to have to say goodbye to him, so best just get it over with. We come face to face. He neither speaks nor emotes, he just looks at me.

'Would you get me my jacket please?' I ask. I can hardly bring myself to maintain eye contact.

'Did you bring one?' His green eyes cast around my face.

'Hmm. Actually... No.'

There's a twitch of his lips which makes me focus a second longer than I want to on his mouth, which is quite a nice mouth, one your eyes would have a hard time not wandering to – if it belonged on a nicer person. Then he says, 'Well, this was a real blast. We must do it again some time.'

It feels like the most attention he's paid me in two hours. I search for an insulting comeback, but none immediately springs to mind.

'Enjoy your leftovers,' I say.

He probably has fallen arches and hard, leathery calluses.

Screw him.

FIVE

I am cycling the beach path towards the Venice Pier. Or at least, I'm trying to. The very best thing about the apartment I'm renting off Airbnb was when the owner texted me and said there were two bikes locked up in the parking garage, and she told me where to find the keys. Up to that point, I hadn't cycled in probably twenty years. But those early morning rides along the Marvin Braude trail from Santa Monica to Will Rogers Beach, or the sunset ones in the opposite direction towards Venice, have become the one somewhat effective way for me to burn off my anger and pain, the one thing that injects a tiny rush of optimism in my veins when I've plumbed the depths of despair. I love it. I love the ocean air, and the rhythmic pedalling, and that sense that everything is overcome-able if you just keep on moving and you don't stand still with your soul-destroying thoughts.

This evening I've got my psychotherapist friend, Nat, in my basket, propped between my handbag and a rolled-up sweatshirt. She keeps toppling over. Not the most effective way to FaceTime. It's imperative I get there in the next fifteen minutes so that when I turn around and cycle back towards

Santa Monica, I'm going to be pedalling into the setting sun. If my timing is off, the whole plan falls apart. Normally this would not be of cataclysmic importance but tonight every minor derailment in life is sending me one step closer to the edge.

'Er... Moira, darling...' I hear her say. 'I'm turning a little motion sick here.'

'Hang on!' I take a bend and swerve to avoid a young couple ambling along with their pit bull, oblivious. I give them a telling-off for being on the bike path then blow by them before they've time to set the dog on me.

'Wow,' Nat says. 'You've only lived there two minutes and you're already laying the law down with the locals. I'm impressed.'

I suddenly feel awful. She's right; I've become a Karen. I almost don't recognise my overstrung self. I decide that if I give up my goal of getting to the Venice Pier and just settle for making it as far as the skateboard park, I can pull over, sit on the sand, and have a proper conversation with my friend that won't turn her nauseous. This is what I do.

'So, I'm not having a very good day,' I tell her.

'Seriously?' she says. 'You look like the most chilled-out soul in the world to me.'

I struggle out a smile. She's lying in bed, propped up with pillows, with a pair of reading glasses on her nose and another on top of her head – her partner Tara is a TV-addicted night owl and has probably nodded off downstairs – and very soon she's probably going to tell me that she's got two pairs of reading glasses and can't find either of them. But instead she says, 'How are you? As in, how are you *really*? I don't feel like I know any more.'

I always find it funny how you can be fine until someone asks how you are, and then it all goes to hell in a handbasket. 'I'm a mess,' I say, just relieved to finally be able to say it. 'One minute I think I'm okay then the next it just hits me that the man I trusted for twenty years has cheated on me.'

I focus on a sailboat so far off in the distance that it appears not to be moving. I must hold it together, be steady just like that boat. 'I still can't really process it, to be honest. Any of it. I go to think about it, about what I'm to do, but all I feel is this weird numbness.' Like it's all sitting there, waiting for me to come to it, to deal with it, but I can't come to it; I can't get there. Every time I try to take steps towards it, it's like I no longer have feeling in my legs.

'Sorry,' my voice wobbles a bit. 'I think I only get in touch with you when I'm about to jump off a bridge, and that's not fair of me.'

'Don't be silly,' she says. 'It was me who FaceTimed you, remember? I was starting to worry you'd fallen off the face of the earth. I don't like it when you go silent on me.'

I tell her I'm sorry again. Back home, Nat and I talk several times a week. We met a decade ago. I'd just moved from the Royal Berkshire Hospital where I'd worked since Harriet was little, to the Royal London Hospital, where I'd exchanged a job that I could do with my eyes shut – but that allowed plenty of work/life balance – for a more senior role in management that required a two-hour commute each day. Nat was an Occupational Psychologist who taught Compassion Training across the NHS, but had a side gig as a marriage counsellor, which she was enjoying more. She became my first proper friend there, and that friendship saw us through her leaving some weeks later and striking out in her own practice, at the same time as walking away from her long-time marriage to Darius to pursue a romantic relationship with a woman – a friend from childhood whom she'd lost touch with for many years; the friend with whom she'd shared something once, something which told her she was different from other girls. A fact she tried to deny by marrying 'the laziest, most advantage-taking man on the planet'

as she once described him (and then she added: 'If you need an
excuse to leave your husband, just make him the most domesti-
cally inept male in the world; no one will ever blame you for it.').
I remember being fascinated that she'd drummed up the courage
to walk away from a marriage that was solid, even though she
routinely put out the wheelie bin way more times than he did,
because deep down she was living someone else's idea of exactly
what solid was. I could not get enough of her dilemma, and the
almost nonchalant way she made it not one any more.

'Have you talked to him recently?' she asks.

I shake my head.

'You can't keep avoiding him forever.'

'Can't I? I think I can.'

'It's been six weeks.'

'Seven, actually. And why do I need to talk to him when
he's just going to say the same thing, isn't he? The same BS.
That nothing happened.' I stare out across the skateboard park.
I like this spot of Venice Beach. It's youthful and buzzing and a
little bit edgy and a little bit dangerous. Problems abound here,
and for the time I'm passing through, mine feel microscopic
compared to all this.

'But you're coming home soon. You'll have no choice but to
face him then.'

'*If* I come home.'

She frowns. 'You've got to come home, Moy. Aside from the
fact that you have your entire life here, isn't there the logistics of
your visa?'

'The ESTA's valid for two years. I can stay here for up to
ninety days at a time, but then I can leave and come right back.'
I coincidentally signed a contract with the Airbnb for three
months, without even realising this.

'Wow. You really *are* contemplating never coming home.'

I tell her that, frankly, I have no idea what I'm contemplating; I'm just surviving, wading through all this confusion one step at a time. I just keep picturing Rupert and me arguing on the beach outside his hotel the morning after we arrived in LA. We'd booked a suite at Loews Hotel for all of us, but after what happened, there was no way I was going to stay in such close proximity to him, so Harriet and I checked in to the Viceroy across the road. I'd truly thought by this point that he'd come clean and admit it. Yet still he was insisting the reason why this Dagmara had said 'I really *need* to fuck you' is because they *hadn't*. That she was just someone at work who had a crush on him. He hadn't realised how serious it was. He was as shocked by the text as I was.

'I feel I'm being gaslit by his continual denial,' I say. 'If he'd just admit he did it, I might be able to understand it and maybe forgive him.'

As I say it, I'm not even sure I mean it, or if it just sounds sensible. I've spent my life trying to be sensible and to see the glass as always half-full, without ever stopping to ask myself, 'Ah, but what's it actually half-full *of*?'

'It's bad enough that the man I've shared a bed with, a life with, might have been intimate with someone else, without knowing he's got so little respect for me that he's trying to actively mislead me.' I pinch the bridge of my nose to make the building pressure go away.

'Cheating's not necessarily about lack of respect,' she says. 'People lie about adultery because their ego won't let them identify themselves as being a cheat. But sometimes they lie to protect the people they love.'

It's one o'clock in the morning in England for her, and I'm sitting on a sand dune in the middle of Venice Beach's crack central; now is not the time for this heavy-duty conversation. 'How are the girls?' I change the subject. 'Have you seen them lately?'

'Girls are fine!' she says, breezily. 'We got together last week. We missed you.'

A few years ago, I joined her lesbian book club, and acquired a wonderful group of supportive friends in the process. 'You didn't talk about me behind my back, did you?'

'Only for about three hours. Then we moved on to some other poor sod whose personal life is far more of a train wreck than yours.'

'Well, I miss you guys, too,' I tell her, forcing out a smile, though my face feels like it's cracking. The weekend after Rupert flew home alone because I told him I needed time on my own, so I was going to stay on in Santa Monica and rent a little Airbnb, Nat rallied all the girls together and threw me a pity party via FaceTime. There was copious alcohol, and similar quantities of outrage and moral support. But since thinking through the fact that my husband may have been a cliché – and in being so, might have made one of me too – I have reeled it in a bit as far as crying on shoulders goes, given them less access to my pain and drama, out of fear they are sitting in a circle across the world drinking wine and talking about me: a pity party I *didn't* get invited to.

'You're a good friend,' I say. 'I don't say it often enough and I certainly haven't said it lately. But I appreciate that you've been there for me. More than I could ever say.'

'You really sound like you're about to top yourself. Maybe you weren't joking.'

To get us off this topic, I tell her about Harriet and the trip to Malibu.

'Wow!' She gawks at me. I think she's going to say it's insane that she can be even contemplating a future with a guy she's only just met, but instead she says, 'He wrote *Love for Lara*? Is this for real?'

I frown. 'It is. But he's a dick.'

'He wrote the most iconic romance of our generation; he's allowed to be.'

'Is he? We differ on that.' I tell her how he virtually ignored me, ate like a pig, how he's so smug and full of his own importance.

'And you fancy him like mad.'

'What? Are you serious? Frank?' I cough up his name like it's a furball.

'Is he attractive? I bet he is.'

'Yuck, no! He walks around with these huge, ugly, bare feet. He's a human yeti.'

I can see she's tinkering with her phone. I try to work out what she's doing. And then a dirty big grin erupts over her face. 'Oh, he is!' She holds up the phone so I can see that picture of him in Central Park, in his striped scarf, with his hair flying away. His appealing smile.

'That was a million years ago. And those years have been unkind.' I waft a hand in front of my suddenly burning hot face. 'Besides, the point of this story was not to talk about that gonk. What am I going to do about Harriet? I think she's serious. I think she really believes this guy is *the one*.'

'For someone who doesn't want to talk about him, you certainly had plenty to say about him.' She's cocking her head and giving me that look she gives – the one that says that so much about my very existence is a contradiction in terms. Then she adds, 'It's perfect.'

'What is?'

'Revenge sex.'

'Huh?'

'A fling for a fling. You and Rupert have been together for so long, no wonder you're chomping at the bit to bonk someone else. So do it if you think it'll make you feel better. Get even, then move on with your marriage. Or not, as the case may be.'

'Revenge sex?' I almost flinch. 'Does anybody actually do that?'

'Some. I counselled three of them last month.'

'So it clearly works, then. If they've still got to come and see you.'

She chuckles.

'You're wrong though,' I tell her. 'My marriage may not have been perfect, but I was never hankering after sex with someone else.' Then I add, 'Not then and not now. In fact, the very thought of getting down and dirty with someone new is horrifying. Stripping naked for new eyes. Navigating someone else's nether regions...'

She holds up the palm of her hand. 'Got the picture!' She shakes her head in affectionate despair. 'So do you *really* think Harriet's serious about wanting to marry this kid?' she asks, once she can stop grinning.

I shake my head. 'I don't know how serious she is about the marriage part. I think she's serious about the being in love part. You should see them. They're so enviably goo-goo over each other.' I hang my head. And I don't even know what I'm more sad about. That Harriet is in love, and I feel like I'm going to lose her. Or because my husband is off cheating, and no one feels goo-goo over me.

'You're going to get through this,' she says, tenderly, reading me like a book. Or like a good friend. 'Remember it's not the journey but the destination.'

I huff. 'Yeah, but this isn't really a destination I foresaw, is it? My daughter hooking up with a guy across the world and maybe making a commitment that no nineteen-year-old knows herself well enough to make.' I certainly didn't know what I was doing when I was just a little bit older than Harriet and signing on for life with someone. 'Me possibly finding myself single at forty-two.'

I tell her I had this crazy, disturbing vision. Us all gathered around the wedding arch that's decked out in bright pink hibiscus while Rupert and I watch our daughter become family with someone else. Rupert's hand around Dag's broad back (not that I know she has one; I just picture anyone called Dagmara as being formidable about the trunk). Aiden's hand around my daughter's tiny waist. And me standing there with no one's hand around me, a piece of driftwood washed up on the shores of middle age.

She rolls her eyes. 'Oh for freak's sake! You're forty-two. You just started the marriage and baby thing really young, so you just *feel* old, but it's not that you actually *are* old. But as you well know, not wanting to be divorced isn't the right reason to stay married. You know what Gandhi said.'

'Can we have one conversation that doesn't involve Gandhi, please?'

'Okay then. I'll keep Gandhi's wisdom to myself. Trust me, you're going to come crawling back and eating out of my hand for a bit of Gandhi.'

I smile, despite very little about this being funny.

'Moira,' she says, in her best pep-talk tone. 'I think you've got enough to focus on with your own problems. I wouldn't get too hung up on the idea that Harriet is going to rush headlong into a future with this guy. That first flush of love is great, and we've all been there; it's a bit like being on mind-altering chemicals. But it doesn't always go the distance. I'd let it ride if I were you. Don't worry about losing her when she hasn't even gone yet.'

'You're probably right,' I say.

'Do you feel better now, pumpkin?'

I nod, over-enthusiastically.

'Good,' she yawns, 'because I'm knackered. I think I need to try to sleep before it's time to get up.'

We sign off and promise to FaceTime again soon and I get back on my way. The Santa Monica beach path never normally fails to put some perspective back in the frame. I always love this phase of the day. Warm enough to wear a T-shirt, but not sunny enough to have to slap on sunscreen. People seem so happy to be alive. I watch dog walkers, and groups doing spin classes on the sand. Another group participating in a boot camp. Teenagers tossing a ball around. Lovers kissing on a wall. But I suddenly feel almost eerily empty, almost bereft, now that my best mate has hung up and is drifting off to sleep on the opposite side of the Atlantic, and I am alone again with my troubling thoughts. I feel so lonely that it almost makes me gulp air. The same inner monologue is back to plague me.

You have to try to believe him for the sake of twenty years of marriage. You've never known him to lie before. He sounded sincere when he said nothing happened.

You totally do not believe the lying sack of shit. Of course he sounded believable. Who wouldn't when faced with having to give up fifty per cent of their net worth?

And just because you've never known him to lie before, doesn't mean he hasn't.

The sun is making its descent. That point where the world is golden, where the palm trees are becoming silhouettes. And then from the bowels of my backpack I hear Ping! I'm thinking it's Nat again with something she forgot to tell me, so I pull over, excited to have my lifeline back. But it's a number I don't recognise. A California area code.

Got your # from H via A. I don't know what your feelings are about all this but let me tell you mine: this business of them being in love and wanting to marry is bullshit. There's no way I'm standing by and watching my son make the biggest mistake of his life.

I read it again in case there's any chance it could mean something other than what it says.

Oh my God, I need a cocktail!

Fortunately, there's a bar a short way down the beach path, so I pedal like the clappers for a few minutes, spot a bike rack, throw my lock around my wheel.

'He doesn't want to watch *his son* make a mistake? What about my daughter? Ugh! Can you believe this man?' I realise I've just said it out loud to the girl showing me to my table, and she's giving me a very strange look indeed. I put my order in for a Moscow Mule before I've even sat down. By the time the gingery, boozy fizz hits my lips I've already banged out my reply.

Hi Frank. It's official. You're an asshole. Thank you for having us for that obscenely wasteful brunch today in your spectacular home which you clearly don't deserve. Please be assured, you and I are very much of the same mind. There are a lot of amazing young women in this world, but unfortunately for all the guys out there, there's only one Harriet – and she deserves so much better than anything you sired.

Oh, and by the way, I've read all your books. Love for Lara was okay, but the rest of them stink. Have a nice life. Moira.

Sent.
Goodbye.
Die!

SIX

I'm still seething as I jam my key in the door. Still seething a couple of hours later when my phone rings.

'Hey, Mum. What're you up to?'

I try to sound the very opposite of someone who has just spent the last two hours chewing the inside of their cheek until they've almost put a hole in their face. 'Oh! Nothing much!'

'You sound terrible. What's wrong?'

'I'm not terrible. I'm fine!'

'Okay. You're worrying me. As in, *really* worrying me.'

I force a smile, my lips resisting all the way. But it stops me from sounding like I'm sucking on a helium balloon. 'I am truly fine,' I say. 'I'm just distracted.' I ask her how her day has been.

'It's been amazing. Aiden and I just played tennis. He just hopped in the shower.' She goes on to say how he helped her solve a complex economics problem that she was over-thinking. 'And you know how he did it? He just applied basic logic. He thought of the obvious. Of course, I totally kicked his ass on the tennis court.'

She finds his outsmarting her endearing. I've never known her idolise anyone before. I'd always hoped that when she did meet 'the one', he'd love her slightly more than she loved him. It had felt safer, somehow.

'So...' she says, like she's doing a drum roll. 'Aiden adores you, Mum. He thinks you're super cool.'

'Thanks,' I say. That means the world.

'You liked him too, right?'

I think of Frank's words about my daughter – *mistake*. So if there's a contest for who dislikes whose child more, then I'm going to win. But taking the hard-line approach in theory is not quite the same as in practice. I try to stifle a sigh but stifling clearly isn't my strong suit. 'It's not about liking him, Harriet. As I told you, he seems like a very nice young man. But you're from very different backgrounds. He grew up in a world of privilege and he's trying to pass himself off as an ordinary guy, and yet you actually *are* ordinary.'

It sounds a bit like the idiot's novel. Rich boy. Poor girl. Marriage...

And then she dies.

Oh my God!

'So, you don't like him because his dad achieved something with his life?'

'I didn't say I don't like him. I said I *did* like him.'

'Oh, well, if this is you liking him...' She *poofs!* I can tell this is going to be one of those conversations, then she adds, 'You just wish you didn't like him, that's the problem.'

I try to appeal to her sense of reason, say it unthreateningly, more like a friend than a disapproving parent. 'Harriet, it doesn't change the fact that you're still a little too young to be thinking of him as anything other than a lovely guy who you can have your first very special dating experience with.'

'Dating experience?' She says it like she can't believe her ears. 'I told you, he's more than that. Much, much more to me than that.' Her voice wobbles with emotion. 'He's the person I want to be with forever.'

Forever. Marriage. The One.

Those words should be stricken from the English language.

I close my eyes for a second and let out a surreptitious breath.

'Why are you sighing?' she says.

I go to sigh again but make a conscious effort to stop myself. I shouldn't have turned this conversation into a lecture.

'Go on,' she says. 'Say what you want to say. I think we need to thrash this out.'

Damn it. I got us into this. I try to think of the least inflammatory way of saying it. 'The only point I'm trying to make, Harriet, is that at this age you barely know who *you* are, let alone who you should be hitching yourself to for the rest of your life. And you won't understand that now, because the years need to rack up before you gain that sort of clarity about yourself – trust me on this.' I swallow a giant lump of my own cynicism – then I'm suddenly so angry at Rupert for turning me into a cynic, for destroying my ability to trust anyone, or myself, again.

'I disagree,' she says. 'I *do* know who I am. And it's true, I didn't expect to fall in love at nineteen, but I'm not going to say no to a life of happiness because it's not your idea of good timing.'

'I get it,' I say, 'I truly do. But I can promise you that a life of happiness is not dependent on you being with Aiden. You're smitten. But you don't think about marrying someone just to try to keep that feeling permanent.'

'Wow,' she says, after a beat, like I might have hit on the acid nerve of truth. 'Look, Aiden's done. I have to go. I don't want him hearing any of this because he'll be very hurt that you feel the way you do.'

Let's not hurt his feelings then.

We make a loose pact to go for a bike ride later in the week.

But by the piss-off-y quality of her tone, I won't bet on it happening.

Once she's gone, I sit there trying to get my head around this other Harriet: Harriet in love. Was I ever like that? I must have been. Surely. Even a teeny, tiny bit like that. It was such a long time ago. I remember meeting Rupert and it being like a stone rolling down a hill. It just kept turning and turning, and even when it ran out of momentum, it somehow still went the distance. But I'm not sure that's the same thing.

Ping!

I think it's Harriet about to take me to task again for something I've said, but then I see that number again.

> SIRED? Is this still a word? I've met a few Brits like you
> over the years. Think because you use olde English
> you're better than everybody else. But putting that aside,
> we do have one thing in common: splitting them up.
> Propose we meet to strategise.

I respond so quickly my phone almost takes fire.

> Meet you again? Not if my life depended on it!

So take that, asshat!

> This is not all about you. It's about my son and your
> daughter. I thought we agreed on at least one thing – that
> there can't be any Aiden and Harriet happily ever after.

Ugh! He's so self-righteous. But he's not entirely wrong. I take a deep breath then type:

> I have zero desire to share another breakfast, lunch or
> dinner with you any time soon or even in the afterlife –

but it's true that we do have the same goal. So in that case, I am willing to meet for any of the above in order to hatch a plan. Moira.

Ping!

Why do you sign off texts with your name? Clearly, anyone texting you knows it's you. And I'm definitely not proposing breakfast, lunch or dinner. Do you hike?

Hiking is my least favourite activity in the world. I loathe it more than life itself.

He sends me a link to a trail in the Malibu Canyon and a pin in a map for where to meet.

See U tmw 6 AM. (Before it gets oppressively hot)

Huh?

SEVEN

'Are you a romantic, Frank?' The interviewer, Darcy Delaney, tries to gently blindside him with her question, but by the way he smiles you sense he saw it coming.

Oh good heavens, why am I watching this? I don't know how I've come across this old TV interview from 2000, or why I even went looking. Clearly, I'm desperately bored and should have spent the evening cleaning my shoes with a toothbrush. But I am glued to the young Frank.

'Probably not in the red roses, candlelit dinners demonstrable ways, no,' he answers. 'I have a good deal of self-improvement to do there. But I believe that at the heart of all of us, beating away beneath every encounter we have with another human being we find attractive, is the desire for a love, a connection, of epic proportions. I think we're always subconsciously chasing that.' He relaxes into the hard-backed chair, rests his right ankle on his left knee, knots his fingers at his chest.

Darcy lets his answer breathe. But her balmy composure makes me unprepared for what she says next. 'So, how do you feel about people reacting with cynicism to your story?'

'Are they?' A pop of red appears on his cheeks. 'The book's sold close to thirty million copies. I'm not sure that's the overarching public opinion.'

Okay. Good answer. Got to give him that.

Darcy smiles a little. 'Well *Love for Lara* is indeed the biggest selling novel of our era. How do you account for the book's phenomenal success? People have written love stories before. Why was this one so resonant?'

He holds his shoulders a touch too high for him to be as relaxed as he sounds. 'I think I lucked out,' he says. 'I think it was timing, like success often is. The nation has been shaken by our President Bill Clinton being impeached for perjury relating to sexual misconduct. People probably just needed something wholesome to latch on to again.'

'But critics haven't responded so well to wholesome.'

'Some critics, I think you mean.'

'Some critics, yes.' She is unfazed by how he carefully corrects her. 'Your story is an unabashed tearjerker. How do you respond to those who call it...' She glances down at her note card, '"Shallow and poorly written"?'

'I don't.'

'You don't have any reaction to that at all?' She remains as soothing as warm bath water, as incisive as a contract killer.

He clears his throat, changes position, rests the other ankle on the other knee. Something in his expression calcifies. The camera zooms in for a close-up. 'Of course I felt it,' he says, diffidently. 'It's hard hearing someone saying you can't write. That's a very different thing to them not liking the story. You have this tremendous sense of unfairness. And then you realise that you've put yourself out there, and, well, you have to take the bad with the good.'

'But it failed to gain a nomination for the American Literary Award. Didn't that hurt?'

He shrugs. 'It's not the first time that a commercially

popular book hasn't been accepted in literary circles as having merit. I am not the first. Fortunately, I don't need an award to be able to look at myself in the mirror, to validate who I am as a writer.'

I smile. Darcy clearly thinks this is a good answer too.

'And there's a movie in the works! How does that feel? And when can we look forward to seeing it?'

He loosens his hands that were interlocked at his chest, his shoulders relaxing. 'How does it feel? Well, it's all a new and remarkable ride for me. As for when it's coming out, that's for the big guys to decide.'

'So *you're* not one of the big guys, Mr World's Bestselling Romantic Novelist?' She might be flirting with him.

'No.' He shakes his head. 'I don't think of myself that way. I'm just a guy who gets a great deal of joy from telling myself a story.'

She smiles and tells him she hopes this is the first of many more.

I wait until the clip ends, then rewind to the part where he talks about epic connection, about how we're all secretly searching for it. I let this tread softly around me, wanting him to be right, and wanting him to be wrong. What if we live a life never having known it? If we silently longed for so much more than that which was given to us, that which we chose?

It's a fascinating question. In fact, now that it's in my head, I can't let it go. Is he right? Do most of us yearn for a spectacular, breathtaking involvement with another human being? Or do we just want to be loved, and to love back? To be found worthy, and to find that worth in someone else?

One thing I do know is... I'm dying to see *Love for Lara* again.

I wonder if it's on Netflix.

.   .   .

It's well after midnight when the film finishes. I have blown my nose and mopped my eyes through an entire roll of toilet paper. I can't believe how it has stood the test of time, how I reacted exactly as I did twenty-plus years ago when I first saw it. How the love story of two fictitious strangers can do this to me. The scene at the end where he allows himself to openly grieve for his dead wife, a young man skipping stones on the edge of a lake, his tears merging with the rain... I realise I've never forgotten it, it's never been far from my heart, even though I've had no cause to think about it for so very long.

After the credits roll, I stare at the last words to leave the screen: *Written, and based on the novel, by Frank Lewis.*

The man I'm hiking a mountain with tomorrow.

A strange fluttering happens in my stomach. It feels like the butterflies, but I decide it can only be gastroenteritis.

EIGHT

'How much narrower does this path get, and where are we supposed to be going? Last I checked, I wasn't born a mountain goat.' I can't believe I'm doing this on only about four hours of sleep.

He strides out ahead. Our feet crunch a syncopated rhythm. Birds chirp brightly in trees. We've been walking for over an hour through what feels like a hairline crack in mountains that are both parched and barren, and oddly beautiful. Small inclines lead to larger ones, a gentle undulation through sunny spells and shade.

'No idea,' he says. 'Never been here before.'

'Huh?' I watch out for those small and wobbly rocks you can easily twist your ankle on. 'What do you mean you've never been here before?'

He stops, turns, plucks his sunglasses off, swipes me up and down with his gaze. 'Hiking's not my thing. I'm a beach guy.'

'So why are we here, then?'

A small smirk. 'Thought you might like to see something instead of just beaches.'

He relocates his glasses to the top of his head, pulls out his phone. He's wearing a slim-fitting, sweat-wicking white zip-up shell, with green and black cargo shorts, and big black trainers that look sturdier than my pair of hot-pink Sketchers. He's not unfit, I am loath to admit.

'According to the map we're supposed to follow the stream the whole way. We're looking for the Bridge to Nowhere.'

It's only 7.45 a.m. but the cloud cover has quickly broken, and I can already tell it's going to heat up. 'If it's going nowhere maybe we don't need to bother?'

'Not as adventurous as your daughter, then?' He strides off again. 'By the way, Aiden never stops talking about her. He's obsessed.'

I gaze ahead to where the shade gives way to a ridge of sun, a dramatic division of light and dark that makes me reach for my phone and take a picture. 'Well, that's his terrible misfortune, poor guy.'

'Why? Is she going to break his heart?'

'No. But he's a guy, so he'll break hers one day, if they go through with this crazy idea of hooking up for life. It's pretty much guaranteed.'

'That's a pretty sexist attitude.'

'I'm a pretty sexist person.'

'Then we better ensure they don't go ahead with this crazy idea.'

We come to a large crop of rocks, and he extends a hand. I take it, and he hoists me up, then just as quickly releases me.

'So, what were you like at Harriet's age, then? Other than a sexist person. Describe...'

I'm taken aback by the question and turn ridiculously self-conscious. 'My memory doesn't go back that far. Probably just like I am now, only with better skin.'

'Harriet's like your husband, then, is she? Is he the tactful one with the brains?'

'He's tactful but he doesn't have a lot of brains.'

Frank picks his way across a stream via a set of stepping stones, and I tightrope-walk the trunk of a fallen tree. We land, virtually together, at the other side.

'What about Aiden?' I ask. 'I'm guessing he's very much like your wife, given he's nothing like you.'

'There's always the possibility he's like neither of us.'

'You're divorced,' I say.

We've reached a flat stretch and I stare at the 365-degree view of dense shrubbery. Only three or four lizards seem to know where they're going. He stops again, takes a breath. 'Rachel died five years ago of a rare autoimmune disease. She was only forty-one. But yes, we were divorced a long time ago.'

'Oh,' I say. 'I'm sorry. That's awful.'

'You were telling me what you were like at nineteen.'

'Was I? I don't think I was.'

'Let's pretend. Or it's going to be a very boring walk.'

'But we came here to craft a plan to split our kids up.'

'I was just trying to be civilised and get to know you a little. You know, given that we're going to be partners in this mission.'

I flex at his choice of words. 'Okay then...' I search for the most interesting layer of my onion to peel. 'Well, I liked to travel. I was really only happy when I was off somewhere. I think I wrote the book on the grass being greener.' I realise that sounds silly given that he really does write books. 'I never went anywhere too far afield though. I mean nowhere I was going to have a mind-altering experience or get kidnapped or...' His mocking laugh cuts me off. 'What I meant was...' What am I even saying? 'Actually, I don't think I *was* all that adventurous at nineteen.'

'And that's a regret?'

'Just an observation.'

'What else was uninteresting about you when you were nineteen?'

I rub my brow. 'Once I answer this, can we get on with

talking about how we can't let our children go through with this hare-brained idea of spending their lives together?'

'I think so.'

'Good. Well... not sure there was much more, really. I wasn't quite as academic, or as driven as Harriet. I got a degree in Occupational Therapy from a respectable university. I thought it would be a steady career and I'd get a chance to help people and do something rewarding. But I never actually bolted up in bed in the middle of the night saying, *Ooh-eeeh! I'm going to be an OT!* It just sort of happened, like a lot of things in life do.'

'But you liked it?'

I note he uses the past tense. So he *had* been listening when I told Aiden that I was taking a sabbatical from my job.

'I did. But it may be time to see what else is out there. Strike out on my own. I've seen a niche in the market.' He doesn't respond to this. 'I should have done it years ago. But I tend to get carried along with things rather than make big changes in my life.' I am panting now. He isn't panting. But that's probably because he hasn't had his mouth open in ten minutes. 'I think I'm done now. I think that's it.'

'It's probably enough,' he says. 'But I believe you're selling yourself short. I believe you are very focused, and you do have passion for something. You want to be self-employed.'

'I don't know,' I say.

'I think you probably do. We usually know more about ourselves than we care to admit.'

'Thanks for the psychoanalysis. You've come a long way from the mute millionaire in the kitchen.'

'Mute millionaire?' He sounds aghast. 'I wasn't *mute*. I was... uncomfortable and contemplative.'

'That's putting a really positive spin on it.'

'And I'm not a millionaire. Not by today's definition. I bought that house sixteen years ago for way below market value.

It was an estate sale and the young kid who inherited it from his father's distant childless cousin had no interest in the property and just wanted to get his hands on some cash so he could blow it all on cocaine. I jokingly lowballed him, no doubt unintentionally contributing to his early demise, and like a fool he went for it.'

'That's a fine hard-luck story. Kudos for ripping off a dead person, taking advantage of his relative, then helping him die in the process.'

He laughs for the first time, a proper, almost infectious laugh. Oddly, it makes my eyes spend time on his face. 'Okay,' he says. 'Back to the reason we've come here. Do you believe two intelligent kids can be convinced they're in love when they've known one another a month?'

'Six weeks, and I don't know. But maybe you should. You wrote the book on it.'

'But that was fiction. As you know. Because you had such high praise for it.'

We arrive at a viewpoint and stare out across the silvery ocean dancing in the light of the sun. 'You were rude,' I say.

'I get that a lot.'

'You sound proud of this fact.'

'Just because it's a theory doesn't make it a fact.'

He dips into his backpack and takes out two beers in cooler sleeves. He flips the top off one and passes it to me.

Some might say it's way too early in the day for alcohol, but I am not one of them. 'You know how to keep a person fed and watered. I will give you that.' I take a sip, welcoming the hoppy coldness. He watches me like he's making something of me that might not be entirely – brutally – unkind. 'Unlike me, Harriet isn't easily put off her goals. I've never yet seen her fail to get what she wants.'

'I don't really know whether Aiden is or isn't easily put off.'

'So, a shit father as well as a preternaturally lovable human being.'

He laughs again.

'Sorry,' I say. 'I think I spoke that thought out loud.'

After sending me a mildly scathing look, he perches on a rock, tilts his head back, drinks. I watch his stubbly Adam's apple slide up and down as he swallows, a domino effect of muscle rippling through his neck.

'You're not entirely wrong about my being a shit father,' he says, wiping his mouth with an arm. 'I was self-absorbed for a long time. Aiden paid the price of that. All those years when I should have been making memories with my kid and concentrating on the now and recognising it for what it was – something eternally in motion, time we were never going to get back – I was looking behind me, and not liking the view.'

I sit on a rock beside him. 'The annoying thing about successful high achievers is that they always spend a lot of time in their own head. So, between them earning millions, and spending the rest of their time in their own head, they seem to screw it up when it comes to relationships.'

He seems to contemplate this. Contemplate me. 'Do you know many of these people?'

'Nope. Only you.'

'Well, I definitely don't match any of that description. Except the fuck it all up part.'

'But Aiden seems close to you.' I study his big, tanned hands, the white crests of his fingernails. 'So I'm assuming you *were* actually present in his life.'

He sends me an honest look; the first I've seen him give. 'Conversation for another time,' he says.

We admire the view for a while. Ocean for miles. Pacific Palisades and Santa Monica in one direction, Malibu, the other, with its multi-million-dollar homes precariously etched into the hills. Then he says, 'What I meant by my earlier comment is that Aiden is a pretty driven guy. He wants a career in the movie biz and he wants to get there without me trying to open doors for him. But I've no idea how he rolls when it comes to his personal life because it's not something we talk about. I know he dates. Maybe not as much as most guys his age, or as much as he should. But he's never asked me to meet a girl before. I will say, he's never talked about a girl like this, or lit up the way he does when he's talking about her.'

For a moment, until I remember this is terrible news, I find myself savouring the way he just put that; the idea of a boy feeling that way about my daughter. Kudos to Aiden for recognising all her amazing qualities. 'Somehow, I'd have thought having a dad who wrote the greatest love story of all time would make it an easy conversation to have,' I say.

'Writers are notoriously horrible communicators. We're more comfortable with silences than conversation. But what I mean is, I love my son and I don't want to undermine his feelings. But I believe he's got a romantic disposition and that's probably going to be his downfall.'

I raise an eyebrow. 'It wasn't *your* downfall.' He clearly made a lot of money out of his romantic disposition.

But he just says, 'Aiden's a pretty cautious and guarded person. He doesn't let everybody in. But he's vulnerable too, and he's suffered a lot of loss in his life at a young age – me as a fully present father, then his mother.' He sighs like this is awkward for him. 'I suppose I'm trying to say that he's met a girl he's impressed with. Her dreams and ambitions might align with his, and he can actually have a proper conversation with her.' He throws up his hands. 'Hey, she's beautiful. And in his emotionally vulnerable state he's probably thinking he's in love. And he might well be. It's not for me to discredit that.' He rubs a hand across his brow. 'The Bible – though, believe me, I'm the last guy to go around quoting the Bible – but there's this passage in it. It says, *Test everything. Hold tight to that which is good.*' He turns his head in my direction. 'It's possible Aiden's holding tight to something that feels honest and true to him, but at his age, and after six weeks, the one thing he hasn't done is tested everything.'

He stands, takes my bottle from me, finishes off the dregs, like he's used to putting his mouth where mine's just been.

'So that's why I'm going to do everything in my power to ensure he thinks hard before he acts. He needs to be entirely sure of people before he gives the best of himself to them.'

People.

We start walking again. I'm not fond of how he has just referred to Harriet as 'people'. Or how he implied his son might not be able to trust her.

'Plus, he's a twenty-one-year-old kid who needs to have some fun. Not saddle himself with some... He needs to see what's out there before he commits to someone.'

Saddle? And – *some* what?

If there were a saddle here, I'd like to hit him over the head with it.

'He's twenty-*two*, I think you'll find.' There is no mistaking my snarky tone. 'And maybe he *is* having fun. Or maybe he knows that all the fun in the world can't come close to what he gets from Harriet.'

'They play tennis and talk about politics and their future careers. Does that sound like a great time to you?'

Ugh! I can't believe someone who sounded so deep in that damned TV interview can be so superficial! Is he Charlie Sheen in *Two and a Half Men?* The hedonistic, single writer lolling around his big beach house with its revolving door of *Playboy* bimbos. Taking nothing seriously. Owning nothing but the stuff that money buys.

'Besides,' he says. He picks up a small rock and pitches it at some coastal sage scrub. 'Aiden doesn't want anything from Harriet.'

The way he emphasises *Aiden* makes me stop in my tracks, and the blood runs cold in my veins. 'What does that mean, if I might ask?'

He peels off his glasses again and looks me straight in the eye. 'Status to live and work in the US. It's obvious that's what this is all about.'

I go to speak but think I might have misheard. 'Wait... You think Harriet might want to marry Aiden for a green card?' This is so preposterous I cannot believe it.

'Everybody wants to live in America. I can't see Harriet being an exception to that.'

'You can't see Harriet...?' My voice has climbed and taken on a note of hysteria. 'But you don't even know her! How can you make a judgement about someone you know nothing about? You've met her once.' The way he's looking at me, with a certain listless composure, I can tell I'm almost wasting my breath; not that this is going to silence me. 'She is absolutely not doing it for those reasons.' I try to cool my jets a little, say it more authoritatively. 'In her entire life, Harriet has never expressed any desire to live in the US and even if she had, this isn't how she'd go about it. My daughter is not a user.' My heart is hammering. How dare he?

'So why do an exchange here, then? She could have gone anywhere in the world.'

'Er... Not sure I really owe you an explanation for why my daughter chose to come to a major international city like LA, to one of the most prestigious universities in the world.' Then I can't help but add, 'It's no wonder you don't write novels any more if your world view is so outdated you'd think she'd do all that just to find a man to sink her hook into!'

By his silence I might have hit a nerve. 'Okay,' he says, 'so let's just suspend disbelief and suppose she isn't wanting to marry him to eventually get citizenship – we still both agree on one thing. They're way too young, and we can't stand by and watch while they fuck up their lives.'

'No, we can't,' I say. 'You are damned right there.' I try to focus on the end goal and not let his comments get to me. 'But we can't exactly snatch them up like they're babies and run them to safety. Or tie them to a chair. And a poorly structured intervention might even backfire. It might make them even more determined to be together. I know my daughter. And I also know she'd not be attracted to a weak-willed guy.'

'Love that word intervention. That's exactly what this is.' He nods. 'We're staging an intervention. So we have to be clever about it. Cleverer than they are.'

'How do we do that?' I ask.

'I haven't the first clue. Have you?'

I think hard for a moment. We are brainstorming right now, so nothing's off the table. Good Lord, Harriet can't marry into this family and have this man as a father-in-law. 'Maybe we just have to do it through careful, kind, compassionate conversation... planting little seeds of doubt in them that'll grow into these giant poisonous poppies.'

I think I'm quite good at this brainstorming thing when I'm motivated.

'You want to poison them?'

'Not poison them *per se*. Just very subtly erode the faith they have in each other, so they'll eventually come to see that they're not suited, and that they've had a lucky escape.'

'Poison their minds,' he nods again. 'Love it. Love the lucky escape part, too.' He looks at me as though he's suddenly discovered I'm a genius. 'That's exactly what I'm going for, as well. Aiden's got to see Harriet as a *big* fucking lucky escape. The mother of all bullets dodged.'

Wait? The mother of all effing bullets? My heart is back to hammering again. *Don't let his nasty comments distract you.*

'So how do we accomplish this?' I ask. Ugh! This man is awful.

'Don't know. I think that might be Phase Two.'

'Phase Two?'

'Of the How to Break Up Harriet and Aiden Plan. We've got the strategy. We just need to think of the tactics now.'

I mull this over. 'There's a risk associated with intervention,' I say, before we throw ourselves too wholeheartedly into this mission. 'Have you ever thought that if you don't support him, he's going to be very disappointed in you? Maybe for the rest of his life. Your relationship might never be the same again, in fact.' *Once he's seen what a nasty piece of work you are.*

'I've thought of that,' he says, unconvincingly – like he's way too lazy to have thought of anything close. 'But it's still better than see him possibly hook up for the long term with her now, and then in a decade realise he's the oldest thirty-two-year-old he knows.'

Wow. He really saves the best for last.

Harriet's going to turn Aiden into the oldest thirty-two-year-old he knows.

I'm not sure I know what to say to that. I am frantically searching my head, but nothing comes.

We have walked in silence for a while. It really does feel like thirty degrees. My crotch is sweating bullets, and my shirt is clinging to my back.

Then he says, 'I think we have to face a grim reality.' He rubs the back of his hand across his brow.

'Which is?'

'I've no clue where we are.'

I'm still smarting from how fiercely he seems to distrust Harriet. Green cards. Bullets. And the oldest thirty-two-year-old he knows. 'This is a joke, right? I mean, you've got a map on your phone.'

'*Did* have. When we had an internet connection.'

'Are you serious? I need the loo.'

He points behind us. 'It was when we left the backbone trail. Remember when I said that we have to head right and follow that creek? I think it should have been left.'

I waft my shirt, to try to let a little air up there. I am pooped too, from my short sleep. 'That must have been two miles back.'

'Or more. There's a road that way.' He indicates another direction. 'And you can solve the peeing problem, by the way. I won't look. Or put you on social media.'

'I can worry about my own bladder, but thanks for your concern. And if you're meaning that road...' I can just about make out a hairline of concrete among the browns and greens.

'The positive is it's downhill.'

I gawk at him. 'There's got to be another solution.'

'Die up here?'

'I don't know why this is amusing.'

'It's not. It's tragic. We never got to the bridge that isn't going anywhere.'

I'm about to say *Why did you even bring me here? It's not like we've accomplished a lot,* when I see it. About five feet ahead of me. Or maybe first I hear it rattle. 'Oh my God! It's a snake!' I turn to stone. Except for my bladder which pretty much goes the opposite of stone.

'Don't panic.' He fixes his eyes on it. 'Though I'm glad you told me it was a snake, as I would never have known.'

'What do I do?' I squeak.

'Hmm... Let's think. You might want to back up slowly and give it some space.'

'Really? I thought it might want to go for a ride around my neck.'

'Not sure if you know, apparently rattlesnakes go for the smartasses first. So, great to have you around, Moira!'

'Do they really bite?'

'I don't know. If I had wi-fi I could google it. But as I don't, we may find out the hard way.'

'Seriously, what am I going to do?' I think I just peed myself. A dribble: that's my story and I'm sticking to it.

'Don't back up too fast. Oh, and watch out for...'

I take one step and trip over a bloody rock. I land hard on my bottom. After a spell of shock, I flip over on all fours, and scramble away. A stone embeds itself in the meaty part of my palm.

'Not your day, is it?'

After he's caused all this fuss, the snake seems to think I'm not worth bothering about and disappears back where he came from. Frank strides over to me, reaches out a hand. I have zero intention of taking it, given this is all his fault, but the hand isn't going away any time soon. Grudgingly, I let him tug me up. He holds on to me a little longer than is necessary, so I snatch my hand away from him. He passes me my bag, which he kindly picked up for me. I dust myself off, pick the stone out of my palm, and look down at my filthy kneecaps. 'Where's the goddamn road?' I growl.

His eyes sweep my face. 'It's still this way,' he says, with a flick of his head.

'Okay. Can we just get there please? And maybe can we just focus on walking and not so much on the talking? I think it might be better that way.'

'Whatever the lady wants.'

'Did you really just say that?' I roll my eyes. 'Yeesh!'

Once we come to the road it's like our problems are just beginning. It stretches off for what looks like many miles without so much as a sign of life.

'Permission to speak.' He holds up a hand.

'Alas, not granted.' I pick a direction based on a glimpse of what I think is the ocean in the distance.

''K then,' he says. 'I won't say it. No need to wonder about the great suggestion I was going to make.'

We walk for about twenty minutes, or it could equally be two hours. My legs have turned wooden. The sun is almost demolishing my sunglasses and I try not to think about how hot I am, and how thirsty, and how knackered. Finally, we see a car coming. As it gets closer, it turns out to be a vintage, Tiffany-blue Bronco that looks like it's being held together by pot and prayers.

'Given I can't ask you if you think this is a good idea, I'm just going to go for it.' He steps out into the middle of the road, sticks up his thumb.

'What?' I gawk at him. He really is doing this. 'We're hitch-hiking now?'

'Unless you have a better idea.'

I wish I did. But I don't. This vehicle looks like it should come with a government health warning, so I'm almost hoping the driver *doesn't* take pity on us, but no; it shakes, rattles and rolls to a stop. Two stoned Sonny and Cher lookalikes peer at us like they're not sure we're real or an apparition. Then Sonny unleashes a welcoming smile. 'Hop on board, bro,' he says to Frank. I assume that means I can come too. We climb in through the back window, try to find a place to perch amidst a rubbish tip of empty food containers, pop bottles, odd shoes, hoodies, twisted thongs, underpants, towels, dog collars, and other detritus of living-out-of-your-car life. By the time we reach the parking lot, I am heady from pot fumes, and my insides are painfully crunched from trying not to impale myself on a surfboard fin.

'Goodbye!' I say to Frank, clambering down then raking in my bag for my car keys. 'This has been fantastic. And here's me thinking we couldn't top our first meeting.'

'I don't know what you're so upset about.' He continues to stand there and watch me as though I'm TV entertainment. 'We've got a plan to break up the romance of the century: we're poisoning them, I do believe. You've seen a side of the Santa Monica mountains you didn't know existed. You encountered wildlife. And then there was me as your own personal tour guide.' He cracks a lascivious smile.

'What can I say? It's just been too much of a good thing.' I pat my trouser pockets, front and back, feeling jittery from dehydration, the bumpy Bronco ride, and suppressed rage. Where the hell are my car keys?

'You look like you've lost something,' he says.

'Haven't you gone yet?'

'Just want to make sure you're okay.'

'I will be. When you leave.'

'Going then...' He starts walking. Back to his sexy little black Porsche. With a click of a remote, it breathes to life.

One more search through my bag and pockets. They've got to be here somewhere. But then a horrible thought occurs. Did they roll out when I fell? That's the only thing that could have happened. They are lying in dirt back up the mountain.

Oh my God. 'Fraaaank!' I holler.

He has opened the car door and slid inside. Now he has closed the car door. Is he deaf? I holler his name again – louder this time. But then I hear the engine start up, the Porsche's trademark clatter and whir. He backs out of the parking space in an arc, rolls up right beside me, looks at me through his window for a long moment before lowering it.

'Erm...' I try to smile a bit. 'Do you think you can give me a lift home please? It seems I've misplaced my car keys.'

He peers at me over the top of his sunglasses. There's a mildly mischievous quality in those annoying green eyes that I try not to pay any mind to. His car has red seatbelts. I mean, whose car has red seat belts? Did he get them custom-made? Who would do that?

He says, 'No, Ma'am.'

In my kerfuffle, I'm not sure I adequately expressed the true nature of my problem. So I tell him again: 'I've lost my keys. I'm going to need a ride home.'

He flexes his mouth into a straight line, stops looking at me over the top of his glasses, takes them off. 'If you say something nice – even something in the vicinity of nice, and you beg a little – I might consider it.'

Nice? After all the things he said about my daughter? I pretend to gaze at the sky like there's a world up there that's endlessly fascinating to me. But it *is* a long walk back to Santa Monica. 'Okay,' I say. 'I really don't think your books stink – though, to be fair, I've only read one of them, so it could be argued that the jury's still out. And I'm sorry I called you an asshole. It's not even a word I use. In England we'd be more likely to say *arsehole* but even then we have a lot better insults than that. So, what I'm trying to say is... I'd be very grateful if you'd drive me back to Santa Monica. Er... Please.'

He fixes his glasses back on his face. 'No, Ma'am,' he says again.

And then he drives off.

He freaking vanishes in a cloud of dust.

NINE

I wait to see if he's going to turn around and come back.

One minute. Five.

Nope. He's not coming back.

I consider my options. Hike back up the canyon to essentially search for a needle in a haystack and risk death by rattlesnake? Not very appealing. Call a tow truck? Years ago, I had a tow truck driver put his hand up my skirt, so I'm not overly fond of tow trucks. Call the rental car agency – who will probably tell me to call a tow truck.

Call Harriet.

I click on our last message string, where I was spectacularly failing to win the award for her number-one favourite person, and decide that, if I call Harriet, I will need some explanation as to why I went hiking when she knows I hate hiking. I am not very good at lying so I give up on the idea of calling Harriet and call an Uber instead.

Thirty-eight dollars to Santa Monica! Highway robbery! But it's not as though I have any choice. While I wait for it to get here – and seethe – I call Frank. The second he picks up, I say, 'Thanks for your kindness. Thanks for being a gentleman.

Thanks for leaving me to die out here in the blazing sun without food and water. In fact, just copious thanks all round.'

He responds by turning up the volume of his classical music. Pavarotti's 'O Sole Mio' blasts my ear hole. I have to hold my phone away from my face.

When it's clear he's not going to turn it back down, I yell, 'Lovely to have a conversation with you. Really great that you're so keen to hear my point of view and you—'

He drowns me out by accompanying Pavarotti in the chorus: 'Laaaaaaaa-laaaaaaa! La *Mio*! La, la, la, la...'

'Oh you're so funny. Yeah, you're so funny and clever—'

'La, la, la, dee, dah. Dum, dum, dum, dee...'

Okay. Might as well sing along with him, then. 'You fuu... cker! Oh la, la, la...! You rotten piece of shit. Dum, dee, dee dee...'

'Sorry, were you saying something?' he turns the volume down. But he doesn't let me get a word in. 'Spectacular ride down the Pacific Coast Highway! Thanks for travelling along!'

Then he turns up his music again and ends the call.

No sooner do I get into my apartment, than I turn back around and walk out again. I'm not even sure what I'm doing, or where my legs are taking me; it's like they have a will of their own. They take me all the way down Broadway to Ocean Avenue. Down the cliffside steps of Palisades Park. Over the pedestrian bridge that straddles the noisy Pacific Coast Highway. Onto the beach path. They take me across the pristine, unpopulated sand, to the water's edge, where there are only a few seagulls strutting their stuff, and a gathering of sandpipers to hear me... scream.

I scream until my throat is razed, until my jaw is locked in agony. I scream like no one is listening. The noise that comes out of me sends tiny long-legged birds flapping into the air.

They fly away in fast formation, keeping low to the water, then disappear in a glitter of sea spray and sunshine.

I just scream the goddamn primal scream. Two months' worth of bottled-up rage and confusion, plus a mere two hours of Frank. And then I feel great. A new flock of sandpipers lands on the sand beside me. They hurry towards the breaking waves with their skinny legs, then scatter away before the water can catch them. Normally I would sit beside them, all of us like birds at church gazing in our meditative state at the ocean. But I feel like my reflecting days are over and it's time to start acting.

I turn around and clamber back across the sand. Back to the beach path where cyclists fly past me obliviously. Back to join the human race again. I cross back over the Pacific Coast Highway footbridge and walk back up Broadway, all nineteen city blocks to my apartment.

I make a nice cup of tea because my throat is still sore. Then I sit down in a patch of sunlight on the sofa, and punch into Google: 'The challenges of growing up rich'.

Oh lovely. There are loads of 'em.

I have a quick read down the list. Get this. They literally *all* apply to Aiden. Freaky, really. As Harriet's mother, it's my duty to ensure she's aware. So I pull up our last text conversation again, type: *Harriet. Just came across this. Love you. Mum. x*

And then I send her a few.

With a little healthy paraphrasing.

1. *Children of successful parents feel an unhealthy degree of pressure to succeed. The pressure can be so intense it can lead to anxiety, depression, substance abuse, even AN INABILITY TO HOLD DOWN A ROMANTIC RELATIONSHIP.*

2. *Children of successful parents may appear normal but they are NOT NORMAL. Nope. Not even a*

> *SMIDGEN NORMAL. In fact, they are the epitome of ABNORMAL.*
>
> 3. *Children of successful parents feel pressure to conform to the expectations of their parents. So if their dad is an irrational, meddling asshole who judges people before he even knows them, his son will be expected to be the same.*
> 4. *Children of successful parents often desire to follow in their parents' footsteps (especially sons and fathers). So while the son might sound like he's pursuing his passion, he's really only trying to do what his dad did, so he's unlikely to have an original bone in his body.*
> 5. *Children of successful parents try so hard to convince everybody that they're not snobs that the very act of humbling-down becomes a reinforcement of how they truly see themselves.*

I make the last one up and am pretty impressed with myself, I must say. I change *children* to *offspring*, just because. Then I press 'send'.

Oh. It's been an oddly productive afternoon.

Cathartic.

It's around two in the morning and I still haven't fallen asleep, when I get a Ping! But it's not Harriet. It's...

Oh no. It's the man who left me in the middle of nowhere to get eaten by mountain lions.

Guess what's in my pocket? he writes, like that little phone call in his car never happened.

Out of date condom?

Try again.

You know what? I think I'll pass.

Your car keys!

I bolt upright in bed.

Found 'em when I got home. My pocket of all places.

His where?

No idea how they got there. Must have rolled out of your bag when you fell. I must have picked them up intending to give them back to you but accidentally kept them. Got an appointment in Santa Monica tomorrow – coincidentally. Want me to drop them off at your place?

Rolled out of my bag? Straight into his pocket? I say a great big, 'Pfiff!' and spray myself with my own spittle.

My hands are shaking when I type: *No thanks! Personal delivery of keys NOT required. Not if it means ever having to set eyes on you again.*

Cool. Just checking.

I wait for more moving dots.

No more dots. *Are you still there?* I type. Then when that gets no reply: *Did you pocket my keys deliberately? You did, didn't you?*

Ah! Dots again.

Why would I ever do that?

Hmm... Why would he, though? And I *do* need my damned keys. It pains me to need anything resembling a favour from him, but I type: *You could give keys to Aiden to give to Harriet.*

Could. But depends how badly you need your car. Won't be seeing Aiden for a while.

Then he adds: *He's too busy having sex with your daughter.* The blood rushes to my face and pounds there. UGH!

Please bring me my keys. And bring your tactics for how we're going to end this unpleasant little romance. It's got to get decided tomorrow.

I shoot him my address.
He replies: *It's a plan, Stan.*

The next day, I hold out my upturned palm, twist my head over my shoulder so I don't have to look at him. He passes my keys through his open car window; they land in my hand. I turn to walk away, get a few steps, but then...

Right as he's putting the car into gear, I rap on his window. He lowers it again, a smirk playing on his lips. 'What can I do for you now?' He takes off his sunglasses, looks me up and down. 'Grocery run? Drop you off at your therapist? Your singing coach, perhaps?'

'What about our mission?' I plonk a hand on my hip, trying not to notice those damned red seat belts again.

'Which is?'

I tsk. 'The Break Up Harriet and Aiden one. Is there any other?'

'Ah!' He nods. 'That one.' In the strong sunlight his eyes look rather more blue than green and I don't like the way they tick around my face and whatever he's seeing seems to be causing him some mild amusement. 'I don't really have one,' he says. 'You?'

'Given you're the one who is so convinced Aiden's marrying a green card grabber, I'm surprised you haven't come with a briefcase, legal documents and a three-ring binder.'

He dips his chin to his chest for a moment, before looking up again. 'I'm sorry I said that. I regret the way it came out.'

My hand is still on my hip. I move it away then plonk it back again for dramatic effect. 'You know, if I'm being honest, I don't really associate you with being someone who regrets a lot.'

He fixes me with his steady blue-green gaze. 'Your honesty means a lot to me.'

'Nice sarcasm.'

'Are we done now?' he says, like I'm a trying three-year-old.

'Done?'

'I'm illegally stopped. Don't want to get a ticket. Maybe you should just invite me in.'

'In? Why would I do that?'

'I returned your keys. It's the polite thing to do.'

'Polite? You drove off and left me in the middle of nowhere. Anything could have happened to me. We're lucky I'm standing here today, actually. It might have been a very different story.'

He sniggers. 'Ha. Ha. Ha.'

'What's *Ha. Ha. Ha* mean? And who would do that by the way? I mean, seriously? Just drive off and leave a vulnerable woman without food, water, transportation...'

'The way you were behaving, something could have happened to *me* if I'd let you in my car.'

'Behaving?' I look at his broad, tanned hand on the steering wheel, the curl of his thumb. '*Me* behaving?'

'I kind of like this, you know.' He smiles. 'The way that I say something, and you repeat it back to me. You've done it four times now.'

'Four—?'

'Five.'

I open my mouth to speak, but now I dare not say a word.

He rests his elbow on his door frame, his red seatbelt straining across his white-shirted chest. 'As it happens, I do have an idea for how we can end this... what did you call it? Nasty little romance?'

'Unpleasant.'

'Yes.'

'Continue.'

The edges of his mouth seem to be trying hard not to smile again. 'I'm going to tell Aiden that you and I have had a little conversation. That you told me that from an early age all Harriet has wanted is to live in America. That you said it's the only reason why she came here to study. That she actually *hoped* she'd meet someone and get to stay.'

The green card thing again! 'But it's not true.'

'It doesn't have to be true. It just has to be effective. Plant a seed of doubt.' He glances me up and down, a little more 'strip my clothes off' this time. 'I'm going to say you told me that Harriet has some mental health issues, and that's why her behaviour can't be relied on. That you wanted Aiden to know, but you don't want him to bring it up with her. The topic distresses her. And if she gets distressed the doctors will have to up her medication.'

'But she's not on medication! You can't say that!' My heart starts to slam.

'I'm going say, Look, son... you were raised to be a kind person, so you should continue to see her, but... find a way to let her down gently.' He observes my gormless expression. 'The *gentle* part is key. Because, you know... because of what happened to her last boyfriend.'

'What boyfriend?'

'The lad in England? That unfortunate business? When the

police had to be involved?' He searches my mystified face. 'What she did.' He upturns his hands. 'Yeesh! Terrible business. Poor guy...'

'W-w-w-w-w-w-w-wait a minute,' I stammer. 'I think it's remotely possible that our tactics to split them up might need a little massaging.'

He puts his glasses back on, turns and stares straight ahead of him out of the window, drums his fingers on his steering wheel. 'Coffee. Upstairs. We can massage.' He turns to face me again, shrugs again. 'My best offer. Otherwise, the plan goes live.'

I point to a parking meter and tell him it's free until 3 p.m.

TEN

We ride the lift in the sort of silence you could slice with a knife. I get out first. He follows me to my door, standing a little too close for comfort while I fish for my key. 'Not exactly a Malibu mansion,' I swipe a hand around once we're inside, 'but I like it.'

He studies me a little analytically for a moment, then he says, 'Very nice indeed.' Though he hasn't even looked.

What is it about having a stranger in your personal living space? Just your person, and his person, barely the distance of a Fisher & Paykel stove? 'Shall we sit?' I say, my tone clipped. 'Get started?'

He doesn't move. His eyes travel up my twenty-feet walls, with their two enormous, stacked windows that look out onto palm trees whose leggy green fronds dance and crackle like party bunting in the breeze. 'How did you find this place?' he asks. I realise I'm clutching my car keys, so I set them down on the round travertine dining table.

I suppose we're back to doing more of the small talk that degenerates into insults and then rage.

'Quite by chance.' I try to loosen enough to breathe. 'I saw a lot of places in my budget on Airbnb that were closer to the water, but they were much older buildings, and most didn't even have in-unit laundry. And then, right when I was giving up hope... up came this.'

I rest a hand on the back of the dining chair, feeling myself waver a little under the weight of his scrutiny. Revisiting that dilemma in any way, shape or form – can I really stay here and rent myself an apartment for a few months, or am I obliged to fly back home with my husband who most likely cheated on me? – is not something I relish doing, so I find myself waffling on...

'Nineteen blocks from the beach – so very walkable. There's a bike lane that goes right down Broadway to the ocean. Also, I'm just a ten-minute walk to Whole Foods and Trader Joe's.'

'You'd have made a great real estate agent,' he says, then adds, 'seems perfect for one.'

It's a harmless observation and not untrue, but there's nothing incidental about the way he looks at me when he says it. Nothing incidental at all.

'What's up there?' He flicks his head to the wrought-iron spiral staircase.

What's this? The Invasion of the Home Snatchers? My vocal cords can't seem to negotiate the words, 'my bedroom', so I settle for, 'Nothing much. Just the, er... the upstairs.'

He tips his head back, feigns great interest in the crystal chandelier and I am almost incapacitated by his suffocating presence. 'Seems a little too cool for you somehow.'

There's a stripe of red across his cheekbones where he must have caught the sun yesterday. That hair of his never seems to look combed. 'Who says I'm not cool?'

'Because I spent a whole morning hanging out with you yesterday,' he smirks. 'Trust me, you're not cool.'

While I flail around for an appropriately insulting comeback, he walks over to my fridge, reaches in, pulls out a beer. What the...? I watch him twist off the top, sink half of it in one go. 'You're not having one?' He wipes his mouth on the back of his hand.

'So good of you to offer. But no.'

My eyes follow him like a moving target as he walks past me, over to my sofa, sits himself down. He sets the bottle on the blond, acacia-wood coffee table, leans back, clasps his hands behind his head. His white cotton shirt strains across his chest, and I have no idea why my eyes shoot to his crotch, but oh my God why did they have to do that? I'm almost certain he saw. 'Do you have any snacks?' he asks, almost a little saucily, like he's throwing out a challenge.

'Snacks.' I slap my temple. 'How stupid of me. I didn't realise we were doing happy hour. I'm afraid I don't have any snacks. I'm just not really a snacky person.' I shrug. 'Sorry.'

He nods, his eyes dropping to my feet in my black flipflops, my pink toenails, which makes me want to curl my toes up to get away from his eyes. Then he says, 'The woman he cheated with was probably a snacky person. She probably wasn't as beautiful as you, or as witty as you, and she couldn't possibly be as uptight as you, but I'd like to bet she kept a ready supply of trail mix for whenever the occasion called for it.'

When I can recover from the fact that he just called me beautiful, I say, 'What makes you think he cheated?'

He picks up the remote and turns on the TV. 'Didn't he?' He clicks onto the big red Netflix logo. Now he's scrolling through my viewing history – *WTF*!

'Maybe it was me,' I say. 'Maybe *I* cheated.'

'Nah,' he says, his eyes not leaving the screen.

My heart is back to hammering again. 'Er... Why is that so hard to believe, if I might ask? That it was me?' I frown. 'And what exactly *are* you doing, by the way?' He's just seen I'm on episode six of *Dirty John: The Betty Broderick Story*. About a wife who murders her cheating husband in cold blood. As well as the damned movie poster for *Love for Lara*. We are both staring at a close-up of the two gorgeous young stars' faces.

I am waiting for him to say something, but, instead, he puts the remote down, looks me candidly in the eye again. 'You seem like an honourable person, Moira. That's why I don't think it was you.'

Honourable. It should be a compliment. It's meant as one, I think. But the word just jumps in line with all the others I've recently supplied about myself: upright, modest, honest. Chump. Laughingstock. Doormat.

He whips me up and down with his eyes again. 'Don't let me be the one with all the great ideas, but we could order some food. You know, given it's after lunch, and you've got no snacks in.'

I don't know where my possibly massive overreaction hails from – I can almost hear imaginary sirens pumping out a warning: *meltdown, meltdown* – but I shoot a finger to the door. 'You know, it might be a really great idea if you leave.' My heart is performing an ungodly hammering. Even my arm is trembling.

'What did I do?' he asks, like he genuinely has no idea.

I continue to stand there, arm outstretched, trying to steady my gaze on the tip of my finger. 'Please,' I repeat. 'I'd really like... I just really need you to go now.' I try to say it as assertively as I can, but my voice is a hot pool of emotion.

He continues to sit there, which makes my adrenaline whoop up a frenzy, a strange push-pull inside me. *Rupert, you bastard. You did this. I am only here, in this strange apartment, in this strange city, with this stranger planted on my sofa, because I can't go home. I can't look you in the eye when I'm so convinced you are lying to me.*

I'm conscious of him picking up his beer bottle, of him standing. There's a very confusing conflict running rife inside me now that it seems he really *is* leaving. He moves past me, making a point of being in no great hurry, the slightly rakish swagger of someone playing to an invisible audience. I keep my eye on my fingertip, but my senses are hyper-tuned to his every micromovement as he places the bottle down on the travertine table.

But instead of heading to the door, he turns. A halting of his course that I'm not expecting. A tingle of energy runs wild down my back as he proceeds to walk towards me until my finger is poking him in the chest – a shocking electromagnetic current that makes my hand fall away to my side.

He takes one step forward closing the distance, his eyes conducting a lazy enquiry of my face. That one step is all it takes.

I have no idea how heat-seeking missiles operate. But I am on him like a human one.

Hands clamping around the back of his head, leg trying to hitch itself to his hips. Kissing his eyes, his ears, his nose, his neck. Inhaling the hoppy, deodoranty scent of him. Tasting the salty tang of his sweat. A new man's taste and smell, not Rupert's. A new man's body with its unfamiliar topography beneath my hand. He makes a murmur of incredulity and pleasure when my hands travel south and I pluck, with ferocity, at his belt buckle. A stopping. Brief, like the relaxation between heartbeats. A chance to turn back that neither of us takes. Instead, he grabs me hard by the waistband of my jeans, yanks my hips into his bulging crotch, pops the top button. It's *him* kissing *me* now. Deeply. Passionately. Probing and consuming me. The sort of kiss that fires nerve endings I didn't know I had. His thumb draws circles around my belly button, dipping in and out, his lips blazing a trail down my throat. I am throbbing between my legs. As though he feels it, he mutters, 'Jesus. Fuck,' and then he rips my zipper down. I suddenly realise that God didn't invent the chaise longue if not to use it, so I push him backward until we fall on it together.

This thing is rock hard.

And the chaise isn't exactly well-sprung either.

He flips me onto my back, easily, like I'm a page he's turning, then proceeds to undress me. My jeans stick and resist as he yanks them down, and I modestly try to hang on to my little white knickers. Once he shakes my last foot free, his eyes home in on my hand clutching the triangle of damp cotton. A smile, like he's decoding new information about me. He plucks my hand away, surprises me by upturning my palm and drawing his thumb along my lifeline, like he's identifying the site of a scar. Then he climbs on top of me, looks down at my face. A question in his eyes. Are we definitely doing this?

I throw my legs around his rib cage.

Yes, we definitely are.

ELEVEN

'So please try to calm down, Moira, and, er, back up a bit...' It's 11 p.m. in England. Nat was on her way to bed. She's wearing her polar bear dressing gown with the 'ears and black nose' hood. In the background the TV has just been switched off. Everything is silent. Except my shame. 'What do you mean you bonked Frank?' she asks.

I was pacing the floor – I have paced the floor for the last couple of hours to the point where I'm sure I must have worn a hole in the hardwood – but I have finally forced myself to sit down. 'Are you truly alone?' I ask her. The last thing I need is for Tara to be earwigging on this.

'Perfectly,' she says. And then I hear the tell-tale squeak of a door being gingerly opened – then closed. 'I am now,' she owns up.

'Revenge sex. Remember?' I say it in a rushed whisper. My eyes shoot to the chaise, but I can't bear to look at the thing without seeing the almost pornographic scene that went down on it, which makes me heat up a thousand degrees.

She looks puzzled at first, then her face drains of all expression. 'Oooh... Wait. You took me seriously on that?'

Our gazes hang together. My heart has just suspended beating. '*Weren't* you serious?'

'Well... er... no. Of course I wasn't.' She gives a little shocked laugh. 'I mean, I *said* it, but it's not like I ever thought you'd do it.' She is studying me like she hasn't met me before, and the fire that is still blazing from Frank's kisses, from Frank being inside me, starts to die. 'What I mean is, you've had three sexual partners in your entire life, Moy. You're super cautious about everything. You overthink things until you're blue in the face. You're just not the person who screws virtual strangers just to...'

'Take my power back? To feel like if he can do it, I can too?' My heart is racing now, all this confusion sloshing around in my head. Nat said it, but she didn't mean it. I did it because... Why did I do it again?

'Hmm...' She grimaces. 'Okay, then.'

That strange expression is still stuck on her face until I almost can't look at her. 'Why do I feel you're judging me?' I say, trying not to sound quite as thrown off balance as I feel.

'I'm not!' She shakes her head, emphatically. 'I'm truly not. Look, for God's sake, I married a good man I didn't love – who I didn't even fancy, not even vaguely – because I was a liar and a coward. Because I was in love with a woman. Because I had fancied her from the minute we met, when we found ourselves in the same class that first day of comprehensive school. And I thought that made me weird, and that it was wrong. And then I left the good man I married, giving him the shock of his life – for that woman. So, I'm hardly one to criticise anyone else's actions. I just... isn't this going to make things more complicated for you now?'

I let that sit there. The bit about me, not the speech about her. Then I say, 'No,' equally as emphatic as she is. 'Not at all. It's possibly the most straightforward thing I've done in my whole life, to be honest.' I had sex with someone I despise. For all the right reasons. What's complicated about it?

She processes this – and me. The new me whom I'd like to think she's just met. 'So, what was it like, then?' she asks. By her jolly tone I can tell she's trying to summon a bit of the ra-ra sisterhood thing, but it comes across as painfully fake.

I can hardly say fast, and – oddly – insanely hot, but totally mortifying at the same time. That I can't stop seeing him, feeling him, smelling him. Every uncovering of a new nerve ending, every touch of his fingers, every bead of sweat that trickled down my chest. Every time his eyes would mesh with mine, that meaningful way that I've never had anyone look at me while they're...

I can't tell her that I can't stop reliving it to the point where my heart is pounding from the memory and I'm so turned on I can barely see straight. So, I say, 'It was fine. The actual act itself was... Good, I suppose.' I try to chirp it out, like you might chirp out something you're not desperately trying to erase, but deep down the reality of it just keeps hammering there.

You had sex with Frank. Your daughter's boyfriend's father. Whom you hate. To get back at your cheating husband. Why couldn't it have been anybody else – animal, vegetable or mineral – but him?

'Right,' she says, brightly. 'So, er, how have you left off with him, then? What happened after you...?'

Covered my crotch with both hands and walked crab style to the bathroom so he couldn't see my bum? Even though he had seen my bum and every other inglorious part of me in broad daylight. While he hurriedly tucked himself back into his shorts. The bathroom door closing at the same time as the apartment one did. Not a word said.

'We had a civilised cup of tea, and a nice little conversation about it,' I tell her.

'You did?'

'We didn't,' I say. 'Not even close. He just left.'

I don't tell her that I've spent the last couple of hours frantically refreshing my messages. That I thought he might have at least texted, even if for no other reason than to say *sorry, that was awkward.* Or, *sorry I got the hell out of there so fast.* Or, *we never did talk about those kids...*

'Well,' she says again. But then she falls silent.

I don't like how she clams up and turns a little rigid and a little unreadable. I know that look. I know what a clammed-up Nat means. 'What is it?' I inquire, with a twitter of dread.

She pulls her hood on, tells me, sorry, Tara switched the fire off and it's freezing in this room. Then she says, 'Moira, I'm going to say this as your friend who cares about you dearly. You're an adult. As I've said, it's not for me to tell you what to do. But I think if you have an affair with Frank, I think it's ultimately going to be a poor decision, one you'll regret.' She lets this breathe. 'Purely unsolicited advice. But I have to say it.'

'But I'm not having an affair.' I'm distracted by the furry friend on top of her head, the black nose pointing into the air; it's like we're streaming the porn channel and the Disney channel at the same time.

She doesn't exactly look reassured. That's when I know she's not done. 'Go on,' I say.

She rolls her eyes back in her head, pulls her hood down her forehead a bit, so now two black beady eyes are staring at me like they're waiting for my reaction. 'Moira, I've got something to tell you, but I don't really know how to tell you, so I'm just going to come right out and say it. Okay?'

Harriet's ominous words just over a week ago. People have to stop saying this to me.

I am held there in critical suspense, when she says, 'Rupert came to see me today.'

I play that back. 'What do you mean he came to see you?'

Rupert is not Nat's friend. Rupert wouldn't pop round to

Nat's home; I doubt he even knows where she lives. Rupert doesn't understand women who aren't attracted to men. Or women who are confident enough to sport a head of very short grey hair at the age of forty. Plus, with her being a psychologist, Rupert thinks she has superhuman powers and can see right into his head.

'He came to the office.'

She clearly sees my astonished face.

'The second he appeared, I told him you're my friend so this would be a conflict, and he had to leave.'

My heart pounds to the point where I might pass out. 'So did he? Leave?'

'Not exactly.'

I press a hand to my mouth for fear I will throw up.

'I mean, he started to talk. It all came pouring out of him. Moy... I think he's just lonely and confused.'

I picture them both sitting there having some lengthy heart-to-heart about me and our marriage. My husband. And my best friend.

'*He's* lonely and confused? You mean he came to see you to tell you that we should all be feeling sorry for *him*?' My voice climbs. I get up and pace around the floor again, go out onto the deck but the sun is too bright, so I come back in. 'He's being manipulative, Nat. He knew you'd tell me, and then I'd pick up the phone, then he'd get to peddle his lies again. Even I can see that and I'm not the marriage therapist. Did he insist nothing happened between them? That he was the victim of some nutter who got the wrong idea about him? He did, didn't he?'

She must be roasting now, because she takes the polar bear off her head. 'You know, this is the very position I didn't want to be in,' she says. 'Torn between the two of you. But yes, he told me nothing happened.'

'Torn?' I repeat.

I try to take all this in but reject it at the same time.

Did she really just say *torn*?

'Wow,' I say, because nothing else will come. There are truly no words. I know it's normal in break-ups for friends to take sides, but only when the friendship was with both parties. How has Rupert even got a seat at this table? 'And you believed him,' I manage to say. 'I think that's what I'm gathering.'

I'm fully expecting her to say, *Of course not!* But she says, 'You know, oddly enough... I think I do believe him.'

My heart gives a series of juddering beats. I sit back down on the sofa, mainly because my legs have turned to jelly.

'I don't think he was lying. Beyond, perhaps, some unwitting encouragement of this co-worker's attention, I don't believe he acted on it.'

When I can't respond, she presses on. 'Look, I've been a marriage counsellor for a long time. Believe me, I know how to spot a bullshitter. I know how people behave when they're doing damage control, and I also know when people are opening up from a place of truth. He said he might have been vulnerable to attention because he hasn't felt you two have been close in a long time. But that's all it was – he was a silly fortysomething fool who was flattered. *His* words.'

'But anyone could say *I was flattered but I never did anything.*'

'I know they could – and they do, all the time. And it's for you to make your own mind up; it's your marriage and your life. But for what it's worth as your closest friend – and a professional – I felt he was being honest.' She lowers her eyes briefly. 'He adores you. I really don't think he was unfaithful to you.'

I am spinning with this new information – and the fact that Nat suddenly seems to know more about the inside of my husband's head than I do. We haven't been close in years, he claims? Then why has he never told me he's unhappy? Then again, when was the last time we sat around and talked about our marriage or our feelings? We're just not that couple.

The idea of him not having cheated tries to override my conviction that he did. Could the text really have been the words of someone who was trying hard to lure a guy into bed – rather than someone who already had? Did I only see what I wanted to see? Was I looking to think the worst of him for some odd reason? Then one little chink in our marital armour and I was off to...

Mount Frank.

I slap both hands over my face and hide. If I never come back out, maybe none of this will be real.

'I think I've heard all I can hear right now,' I tell her. I stand a little too abruptly and gouge my calf with the lethal edge of my coffee table. 'Ow!' I bend over and rub it like I'm trying to start a fire with sticks.

I will not cry. I will *not* cry. Damn it, a tear breaks out anyway.

When I can manage it, I say, 'Nat, no woman would say "I really need to fuck you" to a man, unless she felt she could.' Perhaps in telling Nat this, I am really telling myself. 'That is not flattery. No matter what bullshit he's peddled – and what you have believed – women don't go around saying that to men they work with, unless they are not just men they work with.'

When I'm looking at her straight on again, she says, 'Where the line is, what constitutes infidelity... that's up to you to decide. I'm just offering my thoughts on things. Yes, I was sure he'd had sex with this woman in the beginning. But after talking to him, I don't believe he did.' I'm only half listening. Because I just keep hearing *torn.* 'You're upset with me.' She scours my face. 'I know you are. I'm sorry. I really did try to get him to leave. But short of picking him up and throwing him out myself...'

'I'm not upset at you,' I lie, because I can't take one more shred of conflict with another person right now; not one. But if my best friend's husband – or wife – had come to me with the same bullshit story, I'd have wanted to cause them grievous bodily harm, or at the very least I'd have said *on your bike.*

I go back to rubbing my leg, so I don't have to look at her again. Suddenly everything is colliding in my head. Images of Rupert having sex with some woman called Dagmara, then him looking me in the eye and telling me he didn't do it. Images of me and Frank. Me under him. Me on top of him. Him pushing aside the flimsy material of my knickers with his tongue.

Him not texting, not calling.

I might have to do the primal scream again.

I tell her I'm bursting for a pee, so I have to go. Normally when we sign off, we do our lingering, *Bye! Bye! Bye!* complete with kisses and waves, and we press 'end call' simultaneously, so we disappear together. But right now I click out of there almost before I'm done speaking. Nat is gone, like she never just happened.

If only the past few hours could be so easily erased.

Two hours later, I am still pacing my apartment floor and chewing my fingernails off. So I grab my phone and decide to just march on up to the canon's mouth.

Frank. Moira here. Just so we're clear, what happened was a terrible mistake and it can never happen again.

Hello, Moira there. The thought of a repeat never crossed my mind.

Hmm... Hateful response from hateful man. How could I have expected better?

Glad we're in agreement on that.

He is typing again.

Though it clearly crossed yours. Given you just texted to say it can't be repeated.

I groan.

Didn't realise we had to analyse the ears off it. Just wanted to ensure there are no misunderstandings between us.

None. Sleeping with married women is not my thing.

Not sure I'm loving how this decision to never have a repeat has somehow become *his* decision.

And I don't make a habit of having sex with strange men.

'Strange' being the operative word.

Excellent, then.

Perfect.

This should not detract us from the task at hand, he types after a moment or two.

Fuck off.

When I don't respond, I hear, Ping!

I am staring at an emoji of an aubergine.

I'm confused. Why is he talking about tasks at hand and sending me an emoji of one of my favourite ingredients of Mediterranean cooking?

I google: *aubergine emoji.*

Who knew, but the goddamn aubergine emoji has its own Wikipedia page:

> Social media users have noted the emoji's phallic appearance, and often use it as a euphemistic or suggestive icon during sexting conversations, to represent a penis.

'Ewwwww!' I pelt my phone at the patio door.

TWELVE

'Do you realise, if I marry Aiden, I'm going to have a really beautiful name?' Harriet stands underneath an enormous wooden dining table art installation at The Broad and gazes up at the roof it forms over her head.

Marry Aiden. I just want to cover my head in a blanket and hide until the day I die.

'Harriet Lewis.' She sighs, dreamily. 'It's got a great ring to it I think.'

It suddenly seems fitting how dwarfed she is by this unsettling monument to domesticity. 'Do you remember us once having a conversation about how egregious and anti-feminist you thought it was for a woman to change her name when she marries?' I ask.

'It's not anti-feminist if it's your decision. Then it's empowering.'

I watch her meander around giant chair legs, closing her eyes, like she's dancing a Regency reel to a tune playing in her head. Then she stops interlacing her arms with imaginary dance partners and looks at me. 'So, Mum, you know how I said that after my term ends here in March, I might want to go travelling a bit in North America before I go back to England and take up my summer position at Heatherwick in July?'

I wait for her to go on, conscious that my windpipe is constricting to the size of a runner bean.

'Well, I've had some new thoughts on the matter.'

Oh, please no. Please NO.

'As you know, I've only got three weeks left of my term. And given I don't have to go back to uni in England until September, I thought I might stick around here in LA until June, when Aiden's term ends, and then we might both go to Europe and...'

She comes to an abrupt halt.

'And what?' I prompt.

'Well, you know... just travel for two or three weeks...'

Part of me thinks, well, that doesn't sound too horrendous, then she says, 'We've also been talking about what happens *after* the summer. If we go travelling to Europe, and then I do my placement at Heatherwick... Instead of going back to uni in England, I, er, I might return here and finish my degree at UCLA.'

She drip-feeds it so matter-of-factly that I consider I might have misheard.

'Harriet...' I do a sharp about-turn and take off towards another room, this one full of giant, mirror-polished stainless-steel structures that look like colourful balloons twisted into animal shapes. I come face-to-leg with a menacing silver rabbit and catch a reflection of my own horrified expression staring back at me.

'Mum?' She has followed and is standing beside me so that we are both staring at our freakishly distorted images reflected in the artwork.

I cover my ears with my hands, stride away from her and pretend to read the exhibit description. Suddenly the artist's desire to memorialise the icons that remind us of kids' parties, festive holidays – and the birth of babies – makes me want to slap him over the head.

'What's wrong with my studying here for my last two years?' she asks. 'I can stay on the same student visa, I think. Obviously, I have to confirm that. But if I can't, and we *did* get married...'

Married. Married. Married. Married.

Marrrrrrrried! I inwardly scream.

'Harriet.' I try to tread carefully even though I am so tired of being on eggshells with her. 'You don't marry someone to enable you to stay in a country.' Imagine if Frank gets wind of this plan! All his suspicions confirmed. 'Anyway, I don't understand what's motivating all this urgency. This is not like you. It's not like any nineteen-year-old!'

Is it truly the logistics of long-distance love? Or is there something else lurking at the bottom of this that she's not sharing with me?

'What about how much you loved uni, and your course, and all your friends? Your dream of working for a big architecture firm in London after you graduate?' I pivot on one foot then come face-to-shin with an electric-blue balloon dog that must be twenty feet tall. I'm in art gallery hell complete with demons.

She hurries after me as I trot towards what I'm hoping is the exit. I can tell we're bracing for the showdown neither of us wants to have. 'I still have my dreams! There are top architecture firms here, in LA. Maybe even *more* job opportunities than in London. This is not about me changing who I am as a person. It's about me trying to find a way to have two very important things that I want – two things that I love.' She's imploring me to understand, but I can tell something in her confidence is flagging. 'There's no law that says I have to finish my studies in England. I can transfer to UCLA. Then Aiden and I don't have to be apart for all that time. Otherwise, what happens with our relationship?'

'And who pays for expensive college education in America? Have you thought of that? Your grant was one term, Harriet. One term. Not two years. You have to think practically here.'

A violent flush appears across her chest. 'I know that, and I don't know who pays,' she says, less bullishly. 'We haven't thought through every last detail. But don't worry, it won't be you and Dad. I'll take out a loan or... I'll get a job. Maybe just study part time.' Her neck almost elongates with indignation. 'I'll come up with a solution that doesn't involve you, I promise.'

I cannot believe this is the same Harriet. It makes no sense to me. No sense at all. 'You're doing all this rearranging of your life? You'd consider working full-time while you study – do you know how hard that would be? All so that you can be someone's *wife*? Harriet, think, please...' I implore her to see reason. 'If it's meant to be with Aiden, it will survive two years of you finishing your education in England.' I think of Frank saying that thing about test everything; hold tight to that which is good. 'The best thing you and Aiden could give each other under the circumstances of all this is time.' I scan her fried little face. 'Time, Harriet. Not wedding bands.'

Her face falls. I need air. I spot the door and hurtle towards it. Her feet clack after me.

'You could choose to be part of the solution, not part of the problem,' she snips.

I step outside. Breathe.

'I didn't have to tell you all this,' she continues, her voice evaporating in the din of downtown traffic. 'And maybe if you're so dead set against us, we'll just elope to Santorini or somewhere. Maybe we'll do it, like, *now,* at March break. And then we can stop having this ridiculous conversation! You'd just have to live with it and get on with it, wouldn't you?'

I open my mouth to say... what? I'm not even sure; I don't want to keep railing at her, throwing out practical realities that make me sound so at odds with her.

But then she says, 'I'm happy, Mum. And I'm trying to make the best decisions for myself.' The tip of her nose is as red as her chest. She reaches for my arm. 'Instead of fighting me, can't you just support me?'

No! I hear my inner voice scream. I didn't accompany her to America to have her never come home! She can't marry someone whose father thought she was a green card grabber from day one. At the first sign of an argument, he'll be telling his son to leave.

I get a flash of us going at it on that chaise and I have to stop walking.

Frank, the man I had ill-advised, casual sex with, can't become family.

The sun is beating on the top of my head. I suddenly miss Rupert. I miss having an ally in the pursuit of common sense. Every drama we've ever had with Harriet has been something we have shared. We were parents who were thoroughly on the same page with parenting. All our hopes and dreams for her were the same ones. I massively miss having him to go to right now, having him on side to chew this over. Then I hate that he took what we had and threw it away.

'What about your dad in all this?' I say. 'If you're even vaguely serious about staying here for the next couple of years he's got to be a part of the conversation. Despite you saying you can self-support, there *would* be financial implications for us.'

'No way!' she says. 'He has no right to know a thing about what I'm doing. And if we did get married, well, he's not invited.'

I sigh. 'Harriet, no matter what you feel about him, you can't move to America and not tell him. You can't have a wedding and not invite him.' I can't believe I've just said *wedding* like it's now an event on our social calendar.

She goes to speak but upturns her hands instead. We stare at one another, like we are poles apart and will never come together again. 'Would you want him here?' she asks. 'Say we did marry... What if he brings Dag the Slag? Do you really want to come face to face with the woman who stole your husband?'

I regret ever giving her that name. It was cathartic for two minutes, then it just somehow reinforced the victim status I was determined not to ascribe to myself.

'She didn't steal him, Harriet. He's not a pack of turkey mince on a supermarket shelf. And he's not with her. It was just a flirtation.' I say that for her benefit rather than my own, though it annoys me that Nat's assessment of the situation is still lurking in the back of my mind.

'Because he texts you a million times a day begging you to come home? You automatically conclude it's not still going on?' she says. Now she's looking at me like she can't believe who I am any more.

I start to walk towards the Walt Disney Concert Hall where I've a vague memory of parking my car. Hard to imagine that little over an hour ago we had stood here and marvelled at the originality of the building, and she'd been telling me all about Frank Gehry's vision when he designed it, and she was talking like a sensible, career-driven young woman again. Not like we're in a time warp and have travelled back to the 1950s.

'You still need to tell him if you're truly thinking of abandoning your studies in England to marry a boy on the other side of the world,' I say.

'Ugh!' she grunts but doesn't add anything. We walk a while without speaking. 'You know, Mum,' she says, levelly, when the tension has come down a bit. 'I always listen to you. You're always the voice of reason, and I love that, and I value and respect it... But it's my life. And I could have just as great a life here in America, as in England. I mean, anyone would think I wanted to move to Uzbekistan.' She sounds a little breathless with the intensity of all this. 'And I don't want to have to get dad's *permission*. I don't think he's qualified to know what's best for me. Or you, for that matter.'

Just when I was so certain I knew where I parked, I now realise I have no idea. The street is an assault of traffic, sirens, bad smells. 'Look, Harriet...' I try to keep the angst out of my voice. 'I understand your feelings, more than you might think. And all I care about is your happiness and well-being. But I also think you need to remember your dad still loves you. Nothing he did was about you. It possibly wasn't even about me.'

Nat said people often cheat due to opportunity rather than dissatisfaction. Sometimes it's for self-exploration; to try on a new 'them' or to reconnect with their former single selves. Most of the time it's not because they're unhappy with their partner. Woop. Woop. Makes all the difference.

'That's so pathetic!' she says. 'Now you're just making excuses for him! I mean, how can you say it wasn't about us? It was absolutely about us. We're his family. We're a unit. If he had valued that, he wouldn't have risked losing it.'

I don't know how to respond to this because she's wrong and she's right. If he cheated, then he didn't value us. But I haven't the heart to tell her that we're actually not a unit, that she might just feel that way because she was an only child; the lines that make up the sets and subsets of us got blurred. I can't have her believe that Rupert cheated on both of us; that would make her suffering equal to my own, her self-worth as eroded as mine. And I can't bear that. I can't bear that he could have damaged her as much as he's damaged me.

'Anyway,' she says, 'you've got to promise me that he can't know. You won't tell him anything about me or Aiden.' She clutches my arm. 'You've got to respect my wishes, Mum. If you don't, I swear I'll never forgive you.'

I search her face, those blue eyes that are so much like Rupert's. Before I can speak, her hand falls away from my arm.

'Wow. You're going to, aren't you? Despite everything I've said. Despite what he's done to you...'

'No, I...'

She throws up her hands. 'It wasn't just a flirtation. I mean, he did it, for God's sake. How blind are you trying to be?'

She strides off. I watch her red and white Converses retreat down the pavement.

'I won't tell him,' I call after her. Right now, I will do anything to turn this around. At first, I'm not even sure she's heard. Then she stops.

'You know,' she turns and looks at me. From this distance she suddenly seems so remote, like we are separated by way more than just half a city block in the middle of downtown LA. 'I wish I felt I could believe you.'

This is a gut punch. It almost makes me fold. When have I ever given her cause to doubt my word? This is the most devastating thing I could ever imagine coming out of her mouth.

It lives there – her crashing disappointment in me. Then she says, 'I'll find my own way back.'

THIRTEEN

On the day my wife of seventy-one hours died, she made me make a promise I knew I'd never keep. She said, I want you to live like you never met me. I want you to love again like it's your first.

The opening lines to his novel. It takes me about three hours to read the entire thing. I am in awe of the simplicity of the story, the pared-down prose. I can't stop thinking about it. And then somewhere around one in the morning, that point where insomnia is setting in, and it brings with it that melancholy you managed to fight off during the day, I go to our text thread – first, deleting the damned aubergine – and then I start typing.

Your writing is breathtaking, Frank Lewis; I am in awe of your talent.

Now that I've written it, I realise I loathe him way too much to pay him any form of compliment. So I delete it.

Another hour and I'm still lying there wired and blinking at the ceiling. My mind is back to buzzing with all these dilemmas.

Harriet, and the way she feels so betrayed by her father. How young people see things as black and white, but marriage is a mash-up of so many shades of grey. About what happens if her life ends up being over here with Aiden, and I become the person she FaceTimes, and sees every second Christmas. About Rupert, and what our future would look like if I *did* choose to give him the benefit of the doubt and go home. Me knowing that he may have nobly resisted the temptation of the office hussy, and I threw myself at the first penis I came within two feet of. About doubts and how they try to speak to us, but it's easier to pretend we don't hear.

It's hopeless. I'm doomed to lie awake forever. Is she really considering eloping soon? Is this rushing to start a life with Aiden because she feels so destabilised with what's happening with me and her dad? I remember Nat saying how divorces or separations have almost as big an impact on adult children as on minors. No one wants to envision parents in separate houses, new partners, separate Christmases. No one wants to think their parents are as fallible as everyone else.

I stare at the same giant palm tree outside my window that, a few minutes before sunset, looks like the very cool cover of a 1980s rock album, but during a windstorm takes on an alarmingly bendy quality that makes you think any minute it's going to come crashing through the glass. Right now, it's an unmoving silhouette, hard to discern from the sky.

Then I reach for my phone again.

Frank, Moira here. I fear it's going to take a village to talk them out of marriage. Harriet mentioned the possibility of them eloping.

I don't really know if she was serious, but I press 'send'.

Seconds later, I'm excited to see the three little moving dots.

Moira there. Well, hello...

I frown. That tone's got aubergine emoji slapped all over it.

What does WELL, HELLO mean?

It means hello. And yes, I heard about Europe in June.

I don't think I can let this well hello business drop. But then I remember why I'm messaging him.

No, Europe in June was for a holiday. She also mentioned possibly eloping at March break.

Shit, he writes after a beat or two.

It's possible they actually are in love.

I think of her begging me to support her.

Happened to Ford and Lara.

THAT WAS FICTION.

But a concept you believed in profoundly. You can't write with that degree of emotional acuity without believing it.

I've often wondered what the inside of my own head looks like. Thanks for enlightening.

I roll my eyes.

You're a very hard person to have a conversation with. But what do we do? Seriously.

We could start by repeating the other day.

No, no, no.

I thought you don't have sex with married women?

Not talking about sex. Sorry to disappoint. I meant brainstorming. Our plan...

Ugh! Of course he did.

We've done a remarkable job of that so far. Maybe it's because we really shouldn't split them up?

I don't even know what I'm saying or feeling any more.

Disagree. On some things we are quite in sync...

My mind bounces back to my legs strapped around his ribs, his fingers sinking into the cheeks of my bottom... Oh God. Strike it! Strike it! It's all his fault for bringing up 'fun' along with all these 'well hellos'.

But then he finishes his comment: *but we are not in sync on this.*

I jump up and fling open the balcony door as the air has suddenly become cloying and I don't think I can breathe.

There really are only three options, he writes.

Explain.

Disinherit him. Have him kidnapped. Kill him.

This makes me smile.

Death might be extreme.

So it's one of the other two then.

I yawn. I truly do suddenly feel exhausted. Mid-yawn, another message pops up.

*Tired. Can't sleep. Sitting on the beach, staring at the
moon shimmering on indigo water. It's so quiet out here.
It's why I bought it.*

You bought silence?

And invisibility. Tried to, anyway.

I try to picture him sitting on a deserted beach in the moonlight, at two o'clock in the morning. That stretch of sand right off his property that seems like God only put there so certain lucky rich people would get to enjoy it. His bedroom light on inside his house. Just the very thought of that mellows me and pulls me away from this problem of our kids for a moment.
    Confession? I type.

You think I'm fantastic in bed.

Read your interview in the New York Times. *Saw the
Darcy Delaney one too.*

A pause, then: *Don't recall them.*

You don't recall the NYT *and Darcy Delaney interviewed you?*

No reply.

I thought the Delaney one was outstanding. When she asked if you were a romantic, and you said something about at the heart of all of us, beating away beneath every encounter we have with another human being we find attractive, is the desire for this to be a love of epic proportions... You thought we're always subconsciously chasing that down... It was a fantastic answer.

I don't tell him that I can't stop thinking about it. That the concept just simply won't leave my head.

There's another lengthy pause and then: *If you say so, Ma'am.*

But the book was critically trashed. You told The Times *that it made you lose all passion for writing and all belief in yourself.*

You don't know when to take a hint.

I'm sure you'd be disappointed in me if I did.

Not really! What are you wearing? I liked your pink toes in those black flipflops.

I ignore that.

What I suppose I don't understand is, your novel was a worldwide sensation, so why did you look for your self-worth – and find it lacking – based on what some stuffy

*critics said? People who probably only end up reviewing
books because they're not smart enough to write them?*

The message is read at 2.28 a.m. He seems to fall off the
grid and I wonder if he's not going to answer. Then I hear, Ping!

*You just earned yourself my favourite person of my day
award, Moira Fitzgerald.*

I chuckle.

That's definitely sarcasm!

Oddly, this time it's definitely not.

I'm about to say something like, oh well, thank you, that's
really nice... But another message pops up.

*Done with the trip down memory lane now. Have your-
self a good night.*

Hmm... I respond: *You too...* But when I send it, notifica-
tions have already been silenced.

FOURTEEN

Three days, and no texts from Harriet. And then the ringing of my phone startles me out of a melatonin-induced sleep. For a fuzzy second or two I think I'm still in England in our bedroom that smells of mothballs due to Rupert's fixation on not getting holes in his cashmere jumpers. I turn over expecting him to be there, a softly snoring hump in the duvet, and the next thing I know I've flipped like a pancake onto the floor. Ouch! I grab the phone and press it to my ear.

'Mum! Are you awake?'

'I am now. What's up?'

The wall clock says 10 a.m. Ten a.m.? How did that happen? I tug open the patio door and am met with bright sunshine and a chorus of birds twittering in the palm trees.

'Oh Mum, I don't know where to begin. It's so terrible!'

My world turns still. 'Is it Aiden?' I ask. 'What's he done?'

'It's not Aiden,' she says, through a sniffle. 'It's his dad. His dad just rang and said that if we're really serious about getting married, if Aiden's going to, quote, *make adult choices*, then maybe he needs to take on adult responsibilities and fund his own college education.'

Good grief! It's straight out of his novel. Ford's crusty father disinherits him for getting engaged to someone beneath himself. 'Never in the world!' I say, in my best outraged tone. 'But I'm sure he didn't mean it. He was probably just saying it because, well, he's a bit of a dick.'

'Aiden says his dad never says anything he doesn't mean.'

I can't say I'd find that hard to believe. 'So how does Aiden feel about this?'

'Well, he says his dad can keep his money. He doesn't want a cent from him. He'll pay for his own education. He's got some money from his mother.'

Just like Ford in the book! Life imitating art. 'So... er... how will that work?' While she gives me the details of the plan Aiden has miraculously crafted to fund his own way through the next two years of his life, I bang out a quick message to Frank.

You're going to cut him off financially? I thought we were joking around last night!

He responds instantly.

We took killing off the table. This was easier than kidnapping.

You're not really going to do it, though? Just a threat?

Can't talk. In a meeting with my muse.

He sends a photo of himself sitting on the sand in the sunshine, his bare feet wrapped around a big white coffee mug with 'I Run on Coffee and Grace' written on it in black lettering.

I tune back into my phone call. 'So, I have to ask you, Mum.

Now you've had some time to think...' Harriet's voice quivers with nerves. 'Are you going to support us? Or are you of the same mind as Aiden's dad?'

The opportunity sits there, a gift of an invitation to piggy-back on Frank, the bad guy. 'Harriet...'

That's as far as I get. She cuts me off with, 'Oh wow. Thanks, Mum. Thanks a lot. So you leave me with no choice then...'

And then she hangs up.

FIFTEEN

'I'll show it to you, if you invite me over there.'

Who starts a conversation with that? Frank starts a conversation with that.

'Seeing it once was more than enough, thank you.'

He laughs. 'Ha. Ha. Ha. You're funny, Moira Fitzgerald. But that is not what I'm talking about.'

I fall silent. It's been another three days since my conversation with Harriet and I can't stop worrying about what she might have meant.

'Do you want to know what I'm talking about?' he asks.

Before I can answer that, I hear a Ping!

He has sent me a photo. A photo of...

'That looks like a passport,' I say.

'That's because it is a passport. Aiden's.'

Okay, now I really can't speak. Until I can. 'Hang on... You stole Aiden's passport?'

'Stole might be a little strong. That implies I'm never going to give it back.'

'I don't understand.'

'You're the one who's convinced they're eloping soon. Well... not if he can't find his passport, they're not.'

'So you just took it?' I ask, incredulously. But what sort of chaos is this going to throw them into when the kid goes looking for it and can't find it?

'It was in his room. He's pretty organised. Gets this from his mother. Top drawer. Right-hand side. Along with his birth certificate and some other proof of his existence, and sentimental artefacts.'

I truly do not know what I think of this. Mild horror springs to mind. 'I'm pretty sure you can get a lost passport replaced,' I say. 'That's hardly going to scupper their travel plans. Nice try though.'

'Not in less than fourteen days, which is how long we have until spring break. At least, highly unlikely. I looked online. Even called the passport office.'

'Wow,' I say. 'I think you were wasted on writing romances. You should have gone into crime or thrillers.'

'It's not a crime if you're saving someone from a fate worse than death.'

I scowl at this. Fate worse than death now? Not just the oldest thirty-two-year-old he knows. 'So when he's running around like a headless chicken looking for the thing, you're just going to do... what exactly?'

'Make an oat-milk-mocha-frappa-skinny-chino and go and sip it on the sand.'

I spend the next few days avoiding Harriet. Which is easy, given she seems to be avoiding me. I walk a lot on the beach, and I think a lot. Rupert's texts have dwindled to one a day. A query about where my car insurance documentation is. A long one detailing the hoopla of him trying to get a Lasting Power of

Attorney for his parents. One that simply says *I miss you. Please come home.*

On Saturday – her day off – Nat FaceTimes me while I'm walking around the Third Street Promenade.

'So how is the romance of the century?' she asks.

'What romance?' I think she must be talking about Harriet.

'Yours and Frank's. The second chance romance.'

'I'd hardly call it that. One dip of a toe in the ocean doesn't a swimmer make.'

'What a lovely metaphor for your new life in sunny California.'

And then she tells me there's this course she's come across – an occupational therapist who struck out in private practice and built a business that she then sold for millions, is teaching the ropes to OTs who are looking to do the same.

'You've gone quiet,' she says.

I have perched on a comfy sofa upstairs in Anthropologie and could stay here all day. 'You're cheering for my new life in California, but you're sending me details of courses to get me to come home.'

She chuckles. 'I think the course can be done online. But I do want you to come home, of course,' she says, 'no pun intended. I just miss you.' And then, as I might have expected, she says, 'Have you talked to Rupert yet?'

'Nope.'

She tsks. 'Moy, this is getting a bit bizarre. I mean, surely you must be somewhat closer to knowing what you're going to do?'

'Nope.'

'It's not that hard.' She searches my face. 'If you feel your marriage is over, end it. You don't need him to have cheated to get your official pass out. We know you're a sticker at things, but even stickers know when it's time to walk away.'

'Has he been in touch again?' I quickly add, 'Sorry. I have to ask.'

She looks blown over by a feather. 'Of course not. You think we're going for whine nights down at the local? I mean, come on, Moy.'

I tell her I didn't think so; I really didn't. Then I brief her on the latest goings-on with Harriet.

She cocks her head in sympathy. 'You've got to let her live her life, Moy. You've said your piece. She knows how you feel. She's an adult. Fair enough, a young one, but you've got to leave her to her own choices and mistakes.'

I don't know why this chokes me up. The idea of letting go. Of her marrying young and it going the way mine and her dad's went. 'You made your own mistakes,' I say. Then I add, 'As did I.'

'I did. And life went on. Darius met someone else. My parents accepted me for who I was. Nothing ended up as bad as I feared.' Tears spring to her eyes. 'I've long thought that you have a wonderful, enviable bond with your daughter. Many are not that lucky. I never had that with my parents, and I never had kids to have that myself. But you'll still have that, no matter what Harriet does. You told her that her happiness doesn't depend on marrying this boy but maybe she thinks it does, and you need to let her find out. At worst it doesn't work. Her life will still be long. Think of the terrible fates that befall people. I promise you, Harriet possibly making a mistake by marrying Aiden would not be one of them.'

She's right, I think. She's so very right.

I am the one who has been wrong.

SIXTEEN

Have you heard from Aiden?

I am walking around Whole Foods, simultaneously texting and filling a trolley with things I don't need, only to put half of them back again — and still failing to remember what it is I came in for. Finally, he replies.

Nope. Should I?

Harriet not texting back or answering her phone.

Nothing now. No little moving dots.
I direct my trolley to a less congested corner of the store.

Would you normally have heard from Aiden in a couple of days?

Nope.

Well, I never go more than a few days without hearing from Harriet! I'm worried. It's been almost a week.

Ah. Got it.

Ah got it? Is that all you've got to say?

Question. Do you ever think you're a little co-dependent?

I say, 'Hah!' out loud.

What does that even mean?

Two seconds later my phone rings.

'It means you've become unhealthily enmeshed in each other's worlds. A mother provides her daughter with love and attention but tends to exploit the relationship, fortifying her own needs by living through her child. Like moving from England to LA because her daughter is going to school there for one term. They both grow to depend on the arrangement, despite its dysfunction.' There's a pause, then he says, 'I got that from the internet. Just personalised it for you.'

'At least I don't threaten to cut my kid off from his college fund because some fictitious character in my bogus novel did – then steal his passport. Not sure if I could even find what *ism* that is on the internet!'

Did I really have sex with this man? I mean, what normal person...? I abandon my trolley, abandon the very idea of shopping, and make towards to the door.

'Bogus novel. That's one up from stinking, I suppose. But fair enough. I take it back. You're not co-dependent. You're just on the verge of filing a missing person's report because she hasn't texted you in a day.'

'It's been almost a week! Haven't you heard me?' I burst into

the fresh air. 'Forget it. I might have known better than to
expect any sense, or any help, from you.'

'It's funny because I *never* overestimate you.'

My heart hammers angrily into the silence.

Then he says, 'Just be grateful you know they haven't left
the country.'

'Ugh! You're so helpful. And understanding. In fact, pat
yourself on the back.' I hang up and stomp off down Wilshire in
the direction of my car.

Heard from Aiden

I get his text a couple of days later when, coincidentally, I am
back in Whole Foods searching the hot prepared food aisle to
see what I might pick up for dinner.

Brace yourself... he writes. *They've left the country.*

He picks up on the first ring.

'What do you mean they've left the country?'

'They've flown to Europe.'

I try to think if Europe can mean anywhere other than
Europe. 'But how? They can't have flown to Europe. You've got
his passport.'

'Yeah... I've got his *old* passport. I didn't realise there might
be two.'

'But...' My brain is flapping around. 'You checked, obviously. When you found it in the drawer. You opened it to make
sure it was his, and to obviously check the expiry date.'

Silence.

'You didn't look inside to make sure it was his, and to see if it
was even in date?'

'Who else's was it going to be? Chris Rock's? Of course I
didn't look inside. And I don't ever remember him telling me

that he needed a new one. So why would I need to see if it was in date?'

'Okay, I can't believe this.' I am pacing the floor like a caged animal. 'I seriously can't believe this. You didn't check his bloomin' passport?'

'It was still a better idea than any you've come up with. All the million ideas you had. Oh... Wait...'

'You know what this means,' I say, before pettiness derails us. 'It means they've eloped. Just like she threatened. They've eloped because they have despaired of us.' I drag out those last three words.

Silence again.

'Are you still there?' I ask.

'I'm off to stare at the ocean and smoke a cigarette.'

'But you don't smoke.'

'But it feels like one of those moments,' he says. 'Maybe you should try it.'

It takes me about an hour to compose the right message.

Harriet, I hear from Aiden's dad that you're in Europe!!! Tone is everything, hence the exclamation marks. *How lovely! Surprised you couldn't have just said! But I hope you have a fantastic holiday! You deserve it! Love you! Mum. xx*

I delete 'surprised you couldn't have just said' because it's more than a touch passive aggressive than I want to come across. But then again, she could have just said. So I put it back in and press 'send'.

Two hours later she replies. Two hours! Almost to the minute, which feels calculated. Like she's read all the advice on the internet about how to respond to texts from guys you're trying to dump, and then applied it to mothers. When I read what she's written, the blood drains from my face.

Gutted neither you nor Aiden's dad can be happy for us.
Don't need that negativity around us. Sorry I didn't tell
you but please don't worry about us. We're fine.

Okay. Okay. She said nothing about a wedding. I'm just thanking the gods for this when up pops a photo. One of a white church with a blue dome; the Aegean Sea twinkling in the background. I emit a cry like a hyena giving birth.

I fly out my response.

I'm so sorry I was negative. It's not really how I feel.
Honestly! I hate myself for not supporting you. What can
I do to make this right? Please tell me.

There's silence. I picture them sitting in a Greek taverna drowning their woes in retsina, Harriet dredging up all the times I've let her down over the years. I don't believe there actually are any, except this once, but I expect she's come up with thousands. Then she types: *It's too late.*

No! I fire back. *It's never too late! We can work this out. I am sorry! Truly sorry!*

Wish you'd thought of that before.

I'm not sure what bit I was supposed to have thought of, but I accept it – all of it –whatever she wants to hurl at me, I will own it; guilty as charged. I bite down hard on the palm of my hand. I can see she's typing again.

Very sad how all this turned out. But you're my mum
and I still love you. It's not really your fault that you've
become a very jaded person, I understand.

Jaded? Me?
She is typing again.

Think of us next Saturday.

Next Saturday? What's going to happen on Saturday? Surely not...?

Harriet, can we chat? Can I call you? Please. Not to try to meddle, just to talk.

Dinner plans. Got to go. I love you, Mum. And Aiden still loves his dad. We're just very disappointed in you both.

What can we do? I type, realising that, whether or not he'd want me to, I'm including Frank in this as well.

Nothing, she writes. *Just be happy for us, because we are happy for us.*

'Hello, Moira,' he says, laying on the 'tiresome' tone, when he picks up after the second ring.

'Hello, Frank. Er... Yes...This is Moira here.' I clear my throat. 'I'm phoning because...' I can barely say it as my chest is in a vice. 'I was right. They're getting married in Santorini next Saturday. A week from today!' I give him the rundown of our conversation – calmly, like a sane person, not the co-dependent nutter he thinks I am.

Silence.

'Are you still there?'

'Yeah,' he says tiredly, flatly. 'Well, at this point all I can really say is, go for it, kids.'

I think of Harriet calling me jaded and how I truly don't want to be that person. Of Nat making all the wrong decisions for all the wrong reasons. How – fine – I might have had sex with Harriet's future father-in-law but if a tree falls in the forest and no one hears it... 'Have you ever thought that the fact that we tried to stop them – and failed – is a sign? That they want this because it's right?'

'No. You?'

'No. I mean... Yes!'

It's only now, as I say it, that I realise that I almost – almost – mean it. 'The *New Scientist* says that on average it takes guys eighty-eight days to fall in love, and women one hundred and thirty-four. So Aiden is technically already half way to a normal pace, and, well, the important thing to remember is those numbers are just averages and my daughter is generally sharper and ahead of the curve. She won't thank me for telling you this, but she was potty trained in nine months and knew fifteen nursery rhymes before she even started school. So the bottom line is, I'm not convinced this relationship will be the disaster you're convinced it'll be.' I wait. 'You've gone for real this time, haven't you?'

'No. Still here. Who is the new scientist and why do I care about the dude?'

'It's a publication. I googled it. I was researching love.'

There's another puzzling pause, then he says, 'You were researching love? Do you do any other fascinating things in your spare time? I'm curious.'

'I am trying to talk about our kids and the fact that they might be worth believing.'

'Well, then, Moira Fitzgerald, the woman who researches love, what do you suggest we do? About this and everything?'

'I know what I'm doing,' I say. 'I'm flying to Greece!'

He laughs like he somehow half expected this.

'Look, if they do in fact go through with it, I can't let one of the biggest moments of her life be marked out by how much I let her down.' I'm suddenly galvanised by having a plan. 'You need to come with me.'

He says, 'Whoa!'

'For Aiden.'

'Try to show him I'm a great father? I think that ship sailed.'

'You're wrong,' I say. 'Those ships never sail.'

He doesn't add anything for a bit, then he says, 'They eloped. Moira Fitzgerald, who googles everything, must know that the very definition of elope means they don't want anyone there, least of all their parents.'

'Actually, I believe what you've described is the ancient definition of elope. In the real world in which some of us live, Harriet wouldn't have sent a picture of Santorini and all but told me they're getting married on Saturday if she didn't want me there. So that means it's pretty clear Harriet wants me there.'

'But she didn't tell you until you all but dragged it out of her. It was Aiden who told me they were in Europe.'

'Be that as it may, he'd have had to get Harriet's approval before he'd have been allowed to divulge that to you. And I know my daughter. There's what she says when she's hurt, and what she really means deep down. After nineteen years, I can read code.'

'I'm feeling happier for Aiden by the minute.'

'Oh, I thought I was cynical. You wrote the book on it.' Then I deadpan: 'Oh. Wait. You actually did write the book about a young couple who are so in love that they marry despite his miserable father being dead set against it – and cutting him off from his inheritance. How about that for a case of life imitating art?'

'Life never imitates art.'

'Not according to Oscar Wilde. And I'll take his interpretation over yours, thank you. But can't stop to chat. I'm booking the first flight out of here to Greece to be there for my daughter's wedding. What about you?'

He says, 'Have a great trip.'

SEVENTEEN

I have PTSD just at the thought of getting on another plane.

I try – without drama – to make it known that I booked an aisle seat, not a middle. The freshly minted grown-up with the pink shellac talons pecks away at the keyboard then looks up from under her thatch of black bangs. 'I'm afraid there's no seat selection attached to the reservation, Ma'am,' she says.

'But I only booked last night. I can categorically remember choosing 12C.' At the prospect of having to sit for fourteen hours stuffed into a middle seat, a river of sweat makes its way down my back. I ask her to check again. So as not to sound like a Karen, I compliment her on her impeccable fingernails and hair. She continues clacking away. I wait. And wait. I'm not sure what she's doing. Redesigning the cabin with 3D software?

'I'm sorry.' She looks up, like she's just enjoyed the minor status thrill of keeping me in suspense. 'Middle seats are all we have left. But we can get you one not too near the back, I think.' She smiles. 'Two rows from the toilets. Unless you'd like to upgrade to Business. I can check availability.'

'Do that, please.'

She pecks away at the keyboard again. 'We do have a few available seats. Would you like to do the upgrade for an additional $4,300 one way?'

I pull a taut smile. 'I'll take my assigned seat in economy, thank you.'

She hands me my boarding pass.

I'm trying to balance my weekend bag that's bursting with make-up, hair tools, sunscreens, anti-ageing potions – I didn't have time to think what to bring, so I essentially just brought everything – on top of my carry-on case, and loop the strap over the handle, when I look up and see someone staring at me from the business class line.

He has 'cleaned up' in an expensively cut, but lived-in, tan suede jacket, a white shirt with a firm collar, and blue jeans. My jaw drops open three inches. He waves.

The cute girl at his counter gushes, 'Welcome back, Mr Lewis! So happy to have you fly with us again.'

Frank reads the name tag on her breast. 'Well, April...' He flirts. 'It's a pleasure to be back with you again.'

Athens. Are we really here? I am practically punch drunk with exhaustion. Not so much as a wink of sleep. But that's what happens when you travel stink-class and end up sandwiched between world's biggest talker and world's tallest man who didn't care for me asking him to put his running shoes back on so I didn't have to spend the entire flight wondering if I could smell his feet. For my punishment, he made me 'climb' him every time I needed to get up to go to the loo.

After I dart into the nearest toilet because I've been holding my pee for an inhumanly long time, I stare at my haggard face in the mirror. Baggy, bloodshot green eyes, a brown bird's nest for hair, and the pallor of the recently dead. I contemplate brushing my teeth but decide I can handle my rank breath a while longer. I drag myself back out of there and attempt to get my bearings. The only positive thing is I don't have checked luggage to wait for.

After clearing customs, I'm crossing the concourse towards the exit when I become aware of someone briskly falling into step alongside me. He's walking tall and confidently with his suede jacket slung over one shoulder. Barely a crease in his white linen shirt. 'Oh wow,' I say. 'You look so fresh and well-rested. You even smell good. Like you just stepped out of a Bangkok massage parlour.'

He laughs. 'Well, let me tell you how you look, Moira Fitzgerald.' He scans me up and down. 'You look like shit. If you don't mind me saying so.'

I throw my chin in the air. 'Have a good rest of your day. Safe travels to Santorini!'

A few minutes later, he's still walking beside me.

'As there are no flights leaving for the island before morning, I assume you're staying in Athens tonight, too,' he says. He is so busy looking at me that he's going to trip and bust his lip if he doesn't watch out. I tell him this. He ignores me. 'My hotel's in the Plaka, in downtown Athens,' he says. He digs in his pocket, pulls out his phone, reads the name of a five-star hotel chain.

'Downtown Athens. How very American of you.' We reach the doors and step into a blast of sunshine, and a warm breeze that makes the big blue and white Greek flag in front of us do a happy dance. There's a line of parked cars and taxis on the other side of a road. I start to cross.

'I can give you a ride.'

Something about that phrase makes my stomach do a strange swish-swash. I tell him, 'I'm good.'

'I guess I'll see you around then,' he says.

'But not if I see you first.'

He follows me across the road. There's a confusing line of cabs. Old cars with old drivers, all of them standing outside their vehicles and smoking. Then a couple of suspicious vehicles with younger, extremely attractive drivers who seem overly keen to get our attention.

'I thought ahead and booked a private car,' he says when a shiny limo rolls up.

I nod to an old guy at the front of the line in a flat cap with a roll-your-own cigarette dangling from his mouth. 'Looks like I've got Anthony Quinn.'

'Mr Lewis?' Frank's driver gets out and relieves him of his bag.

I frown. 'How does he know it's you?'

'Because I just texted him and told him I'm walking out of the terminal with a sexy Emily Blunt lookalike in white jeans and a creased trench coat.'

I look around then realise he's talking about me.

He cocks his head. 'Last offer of a ride?'

Can he not keep saying that? 'Last reply. No, thanks.'

My cab driver blows his nose into his hand then reaches for my bag.

'Please...' I shudder, re-routing to Frank's limo. 'Just no conversation, if you can manage it.' I instruct the driver: 'The House of the Rising Sun hotel.'

Frank slides in beside me, his leg brushing mine which detonates a little firework, but it must be my sciatic nerve from all that sitting. 'It's not seriously called the House of the Rising Sun, is it?' He leans in just enough so there's about an inch of distance between our shoulders, looks at me a little rascally, starts singing the famous song in his best mobster voice.

'I do believe that qualifies as talking.'

He just laughs.

. . .

While *some people* might mock it, The House of the Rising Sun turns out to be quite a pleasant little guest house down a sliver of cobbled street in the Plaka, the oldest and most charming area of Athens. The room is furnished for pilgrims, but it's clean and bright. The first thing I do is brush my teeth, then throw myself on top of the bed and make a starfish, letting the small of my back unfurl into the mattress. It feels very strange to be back on this side of the Atlantic. Like the universe is trying to decide something for me. England just a hop and a skip away. My life. My home. My husband. Me here; him there. It's surreal. Yet I feel so many poles apart from him. Like we are two distant planets orbiting the same sun.

The window is open and Greek street life filters in. The sizzle of lamb from a kitchen. The clatter of pans. Something being dropped on a stone floor. A group of men are talking at a café; there's the occasional well-timed burst of laughter. A woman is shouting at her children. All of this to the low and distant pitch of a bouzouki, and a bird somehow making itself heard over the top of it all. Despite it being noisy both outside and inside my head, I fall into a deep sleep. So much so that when I hear a phone ringing, it takes a while for me to realise it's mine.

'Feel like going for a walk, check out some ancient ruins?' he says.

'If I want to see ancient ruins, I only have to look in the mirror.'

He titters. 'We could explore Athens until we drop.'

'Great idea. Will get right on that. In my next life.'

'If you sleep now, you won't sleep tonight and then you're screwed tomorrow for our early flight.' He adds, 'Just saying!'

'How do you know we're both on the same flight?' I get up and stare at my pale face in the mirror, run my fingers through my hair, trying to coax it back into its flat-ironed waves. I still look like a wreck.

'There's only one. Must be my superior powers of deduction.'

My head feels heavy, like my forehead has been cast in cement. The sounds outside the window are different sounds now. A conversation from a kitchen, a man and a woman having a tiff. I don't understand a word he's saying, but you almost don't have to; it sounds like every marriage. The scraping of chairs on a pavement, a restaurant preparing to open, someone skipping through a playlist searching for a particular tune. I go over to the window and stare out. A giant tree with white blossom is making a rather resplendent archway across the alley. Two older men are sitting on white plastic chairs smoking cigarettes. There is an ATM sort of in the middle of nowhere, and an enormous white cat sleeping in a small, cracked, terracotta plant pot.

'What time is it?' I ask, letting the curtain fall away from my hand. My voice is almost swallowed by the vroom-vroom of a nearby motorbike, a dog barking, and its owner yelling at it to shut up.

'Time you washed up and came downstairs. I can meet you at a place called Bar Olympia.' He names a street off Monastiraki Square and explains it's nestled beside the ruins of Hadrian's Library in the shadow of the Acropolis. 'It's equidistant between your hotel and mine.'

'Sounds like you've been out there with a measuring stick.'

'Don't want to have to walk a quarter mile farther than you under the circumstances of our mutual jet lag.'

'You're such a fair soul.'

'Meet you there in thirty.'

.　.　.

As I go searching for Bar Olympia, more random thoughts about my marriage flood in. How Rupert would always recruit other couples for us to hang out with on a weekend; we never really just popped out for a pizza by ourselves, or for a drink down the pub. Getaways were the same. Why would I want to go fossil-hunting with a group of strangers in Boggle Hole just because he read about it in *Science Live*? Or spend a weekend with his tricky best friend and his wife in a futuristic space capsule in the Scottish Highlands? It always felt like he was drumming up unique things for us to do in the company of others, because he secretly knew that if you put both of us together without meaningful distraction, we'd have nothing to say to one another. I think all this with a dull wash of sadness as I round the corner and find myself searching for Frank's face in the crowd.

It's a charming square, really. Pedestrianised, with a giant eucalyptus tree sitting in the centre, its gnarly branches appearing frozen in a bizarre act of gyration, its ancient roots creating treacherous cracks in the cobblestones, like it's grown itself there deliberately to disrupt. There's a grubby white church on one corner, but other than that, the place is teeming with tavernas. Their densely packed patios spill and merge, so you're barely able to tell where one establishment ends and the other begins, if it weren't for the subtle differences in chair colours or table decorations. I spot Bar Olympia almost without looking – and him, sitting on a blue wooden chair at a small table near the taverna's door. He has changed into a sea-foam-green shirt. His head is lowered and he's reading from his phone. As I approach, I get a sudden attack of the butterflies. This is a man I've had sex with. Hot sex with. And we are here, together, in Athens. And I feel like I'm going on a date.

I press my hand to my queasy stomach.

Then I text him. *I'm here.* I'm close enough to hear his phone ping. I watch him reach for it, note the little flex of his lips as he responds.

My phone pings now.

That's a shame. Was having fun without you.

I tap-tap my index finger on the top of his warm head. He startles, smirks, stands.

'You don't have to be a gentleman. We already know you're not one.'

As he pulls my seat out for me, the queasy feeling intensifies. It feels like we've skipped forward in time, decisions are behind me, and I'm living my own future. This is what it would be like to be a free agent. To be – hypothetically – going on a date with a man that my mature adult heart and mind might have chosen. Just to compound this weird feeling, I catch a draught of my own perfume as I sit down. Why did I even put it on?

And then of all the things, he has to go and say, 'You smell good.' He narrows his eyes like he's thinking. 'Kind of like—'

'It's just soap.' I make a grab for the menu, pretend to read it. I'm as a-twitter as the birds up in that tree. *Don't fidget.* I put the menu down again. Force a smile.

He frisks me with his gaze, taps his cheek. 'There's some sleep in the corner of your left eye. It's crusty and a little greenish. Did you forget to wash your face?'

My hand flies to my burning hot cheek. 'If you don't stop giving me the ten-point inspection I might have to sit somewhere else.'

'Violets,' he says, like he's pleased with himself. 'I knew I knew what it was.' When I stare at him blankly, he says, 'Your perfume. It's charming.' He's still giving me his best diagnostic stare.

The young waiter arrives in the nick of time. 'And what are you two lovebirds up for tonight?' he asks, in a 'nudge-nudge, wink-wink' tone.

Frank says, 'Hopefully it's wide open. But I think we'll kick it off with a couple of ouzos.'

'That's it! See ya!' My chair scrapes along the ground. I stride to the farthest point on the patio where there just happens to be a free table. I sit and pretend to immerse myself in a tourist map I took from the hotel, but I realise I've gone into a full-body jitter.

Ping!

Your perfume was razing the sensitive lining of my nostrils. I can finally breathe again. Thanks.

Ugh!

Perhaps the smell is... nose too near own bottom?

If you're going to talk dirty, I need another drink first.

Weak signal. Shame intellectually stimulating conversation must come to an end.

Just when it was getting interesting.

I pointedly hold my phone at arm's length and click off. The cheeky young waiter approaches with two small glasses wedged in the fingers of one hand, and a bottle of ouzo in the other. He sets one of the glasses down, does a dramatic high pour, then gives me a saucy wink. Then he walks over to Frank's table and does the same thing, minus any indication that he fancies him.

I decide to order some mezze and calamari, or this alcohol is going to go straight to my head.

Ping!

This stuff is shit. Why does it look like dirty bathwater?

He's holding up the glass in front of his face and trying to peer through it.

Maybe YOUR bathwater but nobody else's!

I shoot him a sly glance and see he's smiling.

Ouzo is made from anise and fennel oil, I type after a quick google. *When U add water, the oils have a hydrophobic chemical reaction. It's called The Louche Effect. Watch this...*

I demonstrate, like I'm on the shopping network, then watch as the liquid changes from clear to cloudy.

Fascinating. You make a very sexy lab teacher. Got another question for you.

I raise my middle finger, then hear a burst of a belly laugh.

The waiter comes back, and I put my order in. Another ouzo. Food arrives. So does the booze-o. The alcohol quickly hits the spot. I finally manage to release my shoulders from up around my ears.

Who cares if it feels like you're on a date? If the waiter thinks you're here on a dirty weekend? Who cares that you had sex with him for all the wrong reasons when you're married to – er... a cheat – and now you can't take that back? Okay. You care. You care about that last part. But why do you care, specifically? Because it was a wanton act of betrayal that you now regret – because you don't really believe in an eye for an eye, or in coming down to anyone else's shitty level? Or because it was good, and you want it to happen again?

Someone cranks up the music from across the square; there are cheers and squeals; a birthday. I tuck into my *melitzanos-alata* and pitta bread, my *saganaki* with lemon and honey that glistens in the spotlight of the sun... while he has what looks like cocktail-sized meatballs (how very appropriate) and a long, skinny skewer of some sort of meat studded with cubes of peppers. Then he orders five other items and I watch while he devours fifty per cent of everything.

Ping!

How was dinner?

I wipe my fingers on a napkin.

Until you interrupted it? Fantastic.

Want to go somewhere for a proper drink?

Nope.

Possible you'll change your mind on this?

Never.

A long silence, then...

Be fun to tell Aiden and Harriet we're here right now, don't you think?

When I frown, he raises a playful eyebrow. Then he starts fiddling with his phone.

OMG, no! I rush over there, snatch his phone clean from his hand. 'You're not being the one to tell them we're here! This was my idea. I'm the one who's going to break the news, not you!'

'Of course.' He studies me like one of us has come to the zoo to watch the other perform tricks. 'That's exactly how a grown adult would want to go about it. Makes perfect sense.'

I gawk at him, my panic level coming down a notch. 'You had no intention of texting him, did you?'

'Wouldn't say *no* intention. More like very minimal intention.'

He stands, tells me the bill is already paid, and says the sort of blunt, 'Let's go, sparky,' that leaves me with no choice but to follow.

EIGHTEEN

We are leaving a bar that I finally settled on after deciding that half a dozen others were either too loud, too quiet, too young, too touristy, too restaurant-y... and him asking me if I'm always this hard to please. We have watched the sun set on the Acropolis – just because it happened to be there, not because we went looking for a romantic moment – the cool white of the city dissolving to indigo with flecks of gold. We are passing the ruins of Hadrian's Library. A family of four pose for photos on its gently floodlit portico, which blasts me back to holidays past.

The three of us on outings to the seaside where Rupert and I would sit and quietly watch Harriet building sandcastles by the shore. Eating ice cream from glass bowls in the orangeries of stately homes. My life being measured in summers. Where will we go this year? What will we do? Then Christmas. Easter-egg hunts that Rupert was so great at putting together. Birthdays – we mostly celebrated Harriet's, ours didn't feel that important. Guideposts on the annual calendar manoeuvring me through life. An awareness of myself going with the flow of it all, but a dullness I was barely conscious of accompanying me at every step. Each passing year taking us closer to the time when

Harriet would be grown up, married, and we wouldn't be the three of us any more. I try to picture me and Rupert finding our way as a couple, rather than as a family. Us listening to the empty-nester plans of friends and having some cool ones of our own. The one we haven't yet talked about. Because our world has always evolved around her. We made her so much a part of us that there really wasn't an 'us' any more.

Two spindly silhouettes of cats walk single file on a wall. They are almost invisible except for the white flash of their synchronised paws. Athens has come alive now, but a different, more soulful life to the one before dark. Someone is playing the bouzouki off in the distance, a haunting melody I remotely recognise that makes me melancholic. Everything is loose and evolving. Frank picks a random direction, on the hunt for a nightcap. I don't need another drink, but I'm good with walking for a bit. We end up following a moonlit alleyway, sparsely commercialised by day, but at night populated only by the occasional cat; like the street that Athens forgot.

'Can I ask you a question about your book?' I say. I don't know why his beautiful love story comes to me now. When he doesn't reply I say, 'Yes, Moira, I think you can ask him a question about his book. Go right ahead, why don't you.'

He slides his hands into his pockets. 'How about we just forget I ever wrote that damned book?'

'Why have you got a problem with talking about yourself and your talent?' I am swaying a little, the world going a little skew-whiff, the jet lag and drinks catching up to me. 'You're quite a different sort of fellow, you know. Because you *don't* seem to welcome the attention that most people thrive on. It's almost intriguing in a way.'

'Is this "Moira" for shall I compare thee to a summer's day? Thou art more lovely and more temperate?'

I laugh out loud – mainly just glad that I can. 'Okay, that was funny.'

'How about this place?' He nods to a cute little taverna that has two tables outside, both occupied, but one couple looks like they're about to leave.

'Do we really need another drink? I partly think we don't.'

'I prefer the other part of you.'

There is something rascally in the way he says it, and I feel myself blush. 'Let's just walk a bit first. I'm not sure another drink is in my future.'

'We can do that,' he says. 'If you're set on being boring.'

'Okay, so here's the thing that bothers me about your book.' I stop walking and hold up my hands like I'm clutching an imaginary crystal ball.

'Which book, by the way? I have written four of them.'

I tut. '*Love for Lara*. Obviously. Nobody's heard of the others.' I go back to clutching my crystal ball.

'Because you know all these other people in the world, therefore you'd know what they all have – and haven't – heard of. Right?'

'Can we just go back to my question please?' Off in the distance there's a riff of what sounds like church music. Like a midnight mass.

'Why are you doing that strange thing with your hands?' he asks.

The moment he says it, I realise I'm doing a strange thing with my hands. 'Look, when I'm leading up to saying something big, I just need to pontificate properly. Clearly, this is how I do it.'

He shakes his head at me. 'Has anyone ever told you you're the oddest person they know?'

'Just you.' I pat my heart. 'But that's what makes it's so meaningful.'

We start walking again and I try not to do the thing with my hands. Or focus on the suddenly strange and unsettling realisation that I'm walking after dark – and a lot of alcohol – with an

American in Athens with whom I've had sex, and a part of me has just imagined what it would be like to have sex with him again.

We have reached the end of the alleyway and now we're back to Monastiraki Square; I recognise the Byzantine Church. There's a lot going on all at once. Young people drinking, shouting, caterwauling, laughing. 'The thing that bothers me about your book is that from the minute they meet, they seem to not really like one another. They're always bickering. She's always insulting him. I mean, frankly, she's a bitch.'

He tilts his head back and stares at the sky. 'The LA Lakers are playing the Memphis Grizzlies on Friday. I'm gonna miss it.'

'The opening scene when she mocks his wardrobe by calling him Mr Tweedy? It's like she's decided he's rich and privileged and she's out to prick his little smug bubble, only this snarking goes on for the entire book. If you watch the movie – which you probably have, given you wrote it – you'll find they hardly stop sparring until she's hit by the car and then she's dead.'

'It's the third game of the season and I missed the other two, as well. Oh well...' He stops walking. The convoy of young people behind us part and pass around us, their laughter a buoyant wave that quickly recedes. He sends me the side-eye. 'Did you really just say he had a smug bubble?'

The alcohol is making me feel unduly self-important. 'Look, I'm only being this frank with you – Frank – because I know you don't really give a damn what I think. If I thought I genuinely had the capacity to hurt you, you would see a much more reticent side of me right now, I promise.'

This makes him laugh – properly laugh. 'Oh my God, that's priceless.'

We face one another. And perhaps it's the darkness, or the fact that there are no people around us suddenly. Or maybe it's because the floodlit Acropolis has just made another God-like appearance, reminding me of the permanence of everything, and how we, and our imperfect pasts, and our even more imperfect presents, are almost insignificant up against all this history. But the moment, and the way he is looking at me, feels over-the-top intense.

'He likes that about her,' he says. 'She doesn't pander to him like other girls. It makes her interesting. Her insults remind him that he's alive.'

'But he's just a kid. How can he have forgotten he's alive?' Before he can react, I say, 'It was cute in the beginning. But at some point, she has to let her guard drop. She has to expose her vulnerability if they're going to fall in love and be together in the end.'

He puts his hands in his trouser pockets, saunters off.

I trot after him. 'I'm not trying to be insulting. I just wanted to say to them, look, this thing you have... You might think this happens to everyone but it's rarer than you know. Cherish it, because one day it'll probably fade, and you won't get the feeling back once it's gone. And you'll spend years wondering why it had to change, and which one of you was the most responsible for giving up, and then eventually you'll doubt it ever existed in the first place.'

My words almost blow me over. I take a wobbly breath.

'Anyway, that's... er... all I wanted to say.'

'Wow,' he says. 'Some might argue it's enough.'

'What I mean is...' I try to get a hold of myself. *Stick to talking about his book.* 'If they bicker constantly until she's dead, then how can we say it's a love story?'

He turns his face away.

'You're about to tell me to F off,' I say.

'If I did, would you go?'

I find myself smiling. Don't know why.

'Let me ask *you* a question,' he says. 'Did you cry at the end?'

'Are you serious? Of course! Horse tears for days! In fact...' I press my fingertips to my lips. 'I could cry right now just thinking about it.'

His gaze combs my face. 'Then that, Moira Fitzgerald, is a love story.'

I frown. 'But why does one human being have to be left with their heart irrevocably shattered before we can decide if what they had was the real deal?'

'It doesn't have to be, it just is. We have to be confronted with the magnitude of what has been lost.'

'I don't like that,' I finally say. 'If we're not sat there feeling like we've lost something monumental what does that say about the choices we've made?'

He doesn't answer. Every organ is on fire and pumping out of my sweat glands. 'I like happy endings,' I say. 'This messed-up world needs happy endings. If we don't have real life to hold us afloat, we should at least have fiction. People want to escape in a novel, otherwise why read it?'

'Not always. Sometimes people read to feel understood.'

'I don't understand,' I say. All I do know is that this conversation has hit a nerve I wasn't aware existed.

We walk the next stretch without speaking. We pass through a maze of similar-looking alleys; closed store fronts, rubbish bins, cats, a moody streetlamp that brings alive some ancient edifice in the hilly distance. 'I think my hotel is down here.' I suddenly spot the tacky yellow awning, the resplendent tree, the ATM. The restaurant that was opening up earlier is now packed with high-spirited Greeks.

'I thought we were going for a drink,' he says.

'I don't feel like it any more.'

I sense him analysing the sudden but seismic shift in my mood. 'Was it something I said?'

'Nope. Just tired.'

He stands there like he's giving me the opportunity to add something, but I keep walking, conscious that he's not following.

I just have to put distance between me and that conversation.

'Not very nice to just wander off and leave me all alone in the middle of Athens.' He hollers after me. 'Not very considerate of my safety.'

If I try to smile, my face will crack like cement, and I don't want to have a permanently cracked face. 'I think you'll survive,' I say. I remember my dad's words. *Smile, lass. It might never happen.* But it already has.

'If I don't,' he says, 'it's on you. Your conscience, for the rest of your life.'

I don't turn around. I just keep my stiff upper lip and wiggle my fingers in a wave.

NINETEEN

'The flight's delayed!' I do a double take on his whiskered face. 'You look like a human cockerel.'

His hair, particularly the front bit, is standing on end, like there's something sticking in it. Ew! What *is* that? I go to touch it then pull my hand back; I have no idea where that hair has been. He clearly pulled an all-nighter as he's wearing the same shirt – and sunglasses, even though we're inside.

'Something's, er... hanging out.' I point south.

He looks down at his crotch.

'Not there.' I tsk. 'Your bag.'

'Ah.' He zips it open and pushes the dangling sock back in.

'Can't believe we're delayed.' I sigh.

'It's only an hour. I overheard them say it's due to wind. Not sure how they know it'll be less windy in an hour.'

A Greek woman standing beside us overhears. 'First they tell you an hour, then it's two hours, then it's all day, then it's cancelled please come back tomorrow.' She shrugs, gives Frank the lustful once-over then says, 'Welcome to Greece!'

'I could have had another hour in bed,' I moan, suddenly

registering his pallor. 'What *did* you get up to last night? You didn't just go back to your hotel room, did you?'

'I'm taking the fifth on that.' He takes off his shades and presents me with his red eyes.

'Yikes!' I peer closer, our noses almost joining. 'I think you've got conjunctivitis.'

'That's just the whisky.' He slides me an unscrupulous grin.

'Well, how late did you stay out? And who were you with?'

'I don't know, *Mom.*' He puts his face in my face again, so close that I do a little jump back. 'Think it was way past my curfew.'

I start digging in my bag. 'I'm going to be civilised and read my Kindle. What about you?'

He fixes me with a stagnant stare. 'I'm going to be civilised, too.' He turns to the Greek woman who seems overly interested in us. 'Is there a bar here by any chance?'

She puffs up with importance. 'No, sir. No bar. Not here.'

'I think she's lying,' he says. 'I'm off to find one. Hair of the dog.' He glances me up and down, slackly. 'You coming, Mother?'

'I'd rather pour hot tar down my throat.'

'I think you should give that a try.' He walks off.

Our fellow randy traveller gawks after his rear end like she's ravenous and it's a hamburger.

Ding-a-ling! Ding-a-ling! Ding-a-ling!

I'm trying to get into this book. *His* book. *Moon on River.* Can't he leave me alone? I go to pull out my phone to tell him precisely this, but then I realise it's a Ding-a-ling! not a Ping!

WhatsApp.

The only person I ever WhatsApp with is Harriet. I fill with a mix of excitement and terror. But when I look at my screen, I am staring at Rupert's blue eyes. The mischievous little overbite smile.

Rupert's a bit old-fashioned when it comes to technology. He doesn't use video-chat apps. Or... he didn't. I swallow the urge to puke at the thought of him having video sex with Dagmara. I swipe up and reject the call.

Now there's a *whoosh* sound! A message notification. I tell myself not to read it, but I'm too curious.

Switched to WhatsApp. Tired of sending texts you ignore. Thought you can ignore me in a different medium.

There are more whooshes, but I click off without reading them. But the dilemma surfaces again. How do I tell him I'm here in Greece, and betray Harriet, just when I've crossed the world to make things right with her again? And how do I *not* tell him that his only daughter is getting married in Greece on Saturday, and he could hop on a plane and be here in a few hours?

Hop on a plane and be here in a few hours?

I try to picture what *that* would look like. Him. Me. Frank. And my stomach turns queasy again.

Frank comes back an hour or so later. I tell him they just announced it's delayed until noon now. He parks himself beside me, stinking of stale booze. 'If that woman's right and it ends up being cancelled, then we lose a day to find them.' Today is Tuesday, I remind myself.

He unscrews a bottle of water and downs the contents in one go.

'Comments?' I say to the side of his head.

He burps. 'None.'

His face is flushed. 'I can't believe you're not finding this annoying,' I say.

He wipes his mouth on the back of his hand. 'It can't be easy being you.' He pelts the empty bottle at the bin.

'Actually, it's very easy being me, thank you.' I pick up my Kindle again and attempt to read. It is still surreal to me that we came together to stop our kids from getting married, yet here we are – plan epically failed – en route to witness them do just that. 'Don't you just hate it when they tell you it's the weather that's causing the delay and yet, look, nothing's blowing. Not even a leaf on a tree. I mean, can you see one moving?' I might as well be talking to myself.

He finally stares out of the window. 'No. But that's because there aren't any trees. There's just an airport runway. Anyway, thought you were reading.'

'But if there *were* trees... And the book is not all that gripping.' I glance at him to see he's giving me a very strange look indeed. 'I'm not trying to be insulting, but maybe it's all okay for you. You're used to having copious time on your hands. No book deadlines. No place to be except in your lovely mansion on the ocean. Maybe it's easy to just let these things roll.'

'I think that should be your epitaph.'

'Huh?'

'Here lies Moira. She wasn't trying to be insulting.'

I give him my best blank stare.

'But as you mention real life. Well, let's talk about that,' he says. 'So, you've run away from England and, if I'm to read between the lines, from your husband. You're hiding out on the other side of the world purporting to be helping your daughter settle into a semester of college – help she doesn't need. And you engage in almost non-consensual sex with a virtual stranger, then try to pretend none of it happened. What were we saying about real life? Remind me again?' He leans in again, so the distance between our faces closes significantly; in fact, it makes me go cross-eyed. 'Growing a little fuzzy...' He gently tap-taps a finger on my temple.

'Non-consensual?'

'I believe it was you who mauled me then threw me onto a piece of furniture.'

'What?' A giant heat wave rushes over me at the very memory of what happened on that chaise.

'If we have a re-run,' he raises an eyebrow, 'I'll point out the exact part where the line gets blurred.'

It takes me a moment but then I grin. But then I realise I am not supposed to do that.

Do. Not. Smile.

I discreetly blow air up to my forehead.

'Looks like it's cancelled.' He breaks the bad news when I get back from the loo.

'What?'

'They just announced it.'

'Unbelievable!' I throw up my hands. 'Did they say why?'

'Think someone checked the trees and discovered it's still windy.' When he sees my face, he adds, 'No, they didn't say. I was just chatting to our Greek friend.' He points to the woman who is eating an apple while still giving him a lewd stare. 'Nothing we can do about it. Just chill and try to see the bigger picture.'

'The bigger picture didn't include us being stuck in Athens tonight. What if it happens again tomorrow? I can see this becoming a Greek Groundhog Day. They're getting married in four days' time – remember? And we don't even know where they are. We're literally just about to drop a pin on the map of Santorini and assume with a bit of luck that they might be where it lands.'

Oh dear. Look how far we've come. I can't believe that I'm now actually panicked at the thought of *missing* their wedding.

He stands, reaches for his bag handle. 'How about we

shelve that prospect, Miss Bright Side Finder, and consider a worst-case scenario instead?' Then he puts his sunglasses back on. 'Anyway, she said cancellations never happen two days in a row.'

I perk up. 'She did?'

'No. I made that up.' He nods to my luggage. 'Come on. Let's get out of here... Go find some trouble we can get into.' When he says *trouble* he whips his eyes the length of me and smiles.

Given I can't exactly stay here, I trot after him.

TWENTY

The House of the Rising Sun is full.

He responds to my text with a selfie. He is lying on his perfectly made bed with his ankles crossed and his shoes on. I can only see him from the knees down.

Sorry 'bout that. Sucks.

Is that all you can say?

I'm just typing that he's an asshole – though it's starting to feel like old news – when my phone rings.

'I thought it would be easier just to talk rather than engage in one of our mammoth text sessions.'

He sounds very chilled out. How I intend to be, in my next life. 'What do you have to say?' I ask.

'Is that "Moira" for hi, it's great to hear from you again?'

I touch my hot, sweaty neck. 'Frank, I'm sorry, I'm not in the best of moods right now. I've got an accommodation problem. For some mysterious reason there are no hotel rooms on Expedia tonight unless I move miles out.'

'You've got a lot of problems, admittedly, but a room for the night isn't one of them,' he says, brightly. 'You can stay here.' Then he adds, 'Not here. In my room. There is no way I would condone that. But... in my hotel.'

'Lovely. But I can't afford a five-star palace, thank you.' The downside to taking on an Airbnb for three months, and leaving a well-paid job, is that I'm already practically bankrupting us.

'Not asking you to pay,' he says.

I am quick to say, 'That's kind, but I can't be a charity case.'

'It's not charity when it's family.' There's a smile in his voice. 'I mean, when you think about it, we're practically related, aren't we? Relatives who actually have sex with one another. The best kind.'

'Ew! That is so disgusting! I can't believe you've just said that.'

'It's one night,' he says, after a moment or two. 'And it'll save a lot of hassle with us getting to the airport tomorrow. Please let me do that for you.'

It's true that it *would* save a lot of hassle to be staying in the Plaka. 'Well... Okay. That's very kind of you.' I tell him I will accept.

'Excellent.' The smile is back in his voice again.

'Oh, and one more thing,' I say, before we hang up. 'If you're going to put your feet on a lovely bed that's not your own, you should at least take your shoes off.'

He just laughs at me.

My room has an amazing view of the Acropolis. All I can do is stand and gawk at how the majestic limestone rock, home to kings and mythical gods, stands serene and proud against the blue dome of the sky.

Does your room have the same view as mine?! I text him, still a bit overcome that he's done this for me.

Should do, given it's next door.

I blink. *Next door?*

I told the young receptionist that you're a close friend. I guess she took close literally.

I experience an ungodly rush of panic at the thought of a door separating our two rooms. But there are such things as locks. So I simply say: *Well, thank you again. I appreciate it.*

He responds: *Meet you downstairs in 10 so we can go find an early dinner or something?*

I type: *Sounds like a plan.*

He is standing by the main entrance, checking his phone. He has changed into a pair of loose beige trousers, and a white T-shirt, with a light jacket looped over his shoulder. I am assailed by a memory. My nipples against the soft hair of his chest. Him moving slowly in and out of me in breathless strokes. Him saying, *God, you're so hot,* saying it so instinctively that he might have just been thinking aloud. Me not remembering the last time anyone called me that. But something about the power of suggestion just let me go with it, let me find that confidence in myself. I perform a slow exhale.

As I approach, he looks up, and I feel myself flush from the crown of my head to the tips of my toes. 'Nice...' he says, giving my turquoise dress with the white daisy print, and trench coat, the once-over. 'Beautiful, in fact.'

Next, he ushers me so that I go first through the revolving door. Then he slides right in behind me, into the same tiny, confined space, so we're like standing spoons. I give the door a firm push, then we perform an awkward two-step shuffle in time with the moving glass. Despite me trying to ensure that no part of our anatomies ever makes contact again, we bump and graze in a routine that wouldn't be out of place in *Dirty Dancing*.

'You're wearing that perfume again.' His breath is like a little draught near my ear.

At the first crack of an opening, I bust out onto the pavement.

'So, you're the one who's been to Athens before, Moira Fitzgerald. What are you burning to revisit?'

The question blows dust off an unpleasant memory. 'None of it, thanks. Not big on revisiting the past. I prefer new experiences.' I pluck my sunglasses off my head and put them on, still a bit shaken from that moving door. 'Let's just walk and see where we end up.'

'A fine idea.' He falls in stride. 'And something we have in common. I'm not big on revisiting the past either.'

We wander for what feels like a long time through a changing stage of the day, through a maze of narrow lava-rock streets, each one ending with either a café, an *ouzeria*, a spice shop, or a *gyros* shop with various fragrant meats twirling on rotisserie spits. We turn corners, slipping from sun to shade. Food smells. People smells. Drain smells. Flowers from a nearby vendor's stand. Cats hunch on steps, some napping, while others watch the world go by, their skeletal frames perched on the branches of cypress trees. A tired-looking mother feeds her kittens, and we stand and watch.

'What happened last time you came to Athens?' he asks. 'You kind of have to tell me now.'

I try on a smile. 'How about I ask you one instead. Have you travelled anywhere in Europe?'

'I never leave my actual house, remember.'

'Ah yes. Your monument to your vast success on the sand. I

forgot that.' I'm warm, so I take off my trench and loop it over my shoulder like he's doing.

'I have been to Europe,' he says. 'Once. On a book tour. Well, twice if you count the time my dad took me to Paris while he was conducting his affair.'

'Affair?'

'Yup. I was fourteen. It was supposed to be a guys' trip of the cultural enrichment kind, but he'd parked his mistress in a hotel around the corner from ours and was gone all night and eighty per cent of the day.'

'He just left you on your own, and went off with a woman?' I scope out his face to see if he's being serious.

'Yup! He flew her in especially for the occasion. I followed him one night. I recognised her from the flight out; a stunning, flamboyantly dressed Jamaican girl. And coincidentally she was on the return flight, too.'

'You're kidding!'

'If only.'

I stare at our footsteps landing in sync on the ancient cobblestones. My white plimsolls and his well-polished tan loafers. 'I have a story I could tell you about unsettling discoveries on aeroplanes, but it's best I don't.'

'I already like your story better than mine.'

'I don't think either of them are very good.' My brows pull together, that horrible, horrible memory circling and trying to land. 'So, what did you do with all that time to yourself in Paris?' I ask.

'Lay on my big bed in my very expensive hotel room, ordered beer, and watched porn.' He smiles, ruefully. 'That's what I mean about only having been to Europe once. It was hard to count that first trip.'

I tell him that, while I doubt my father ever did anything as extreme as that – mainly because we didn't have the money for him to be hauling girlfriends to exotic destinations – I was pretty sure he wasn't faithful. That my mother chose to just crack on with it, maybe in semi-denial; I will never know. I still remember some of her eye-rolling expressions when he'd practically fallen off a restaurant chair while gawking at another woman's legs. *Boys will be boys. A cat can look at a canary...* The arguments, the content of which usually consisted of lines I had to read between. Everything muffled, angry ellipses, things that went unsaid because I was there, a young teenager, listening, absorbing, the reluctant witness; the curse of the only child.

I'm telling him all this when a moped suddenly appears out of nowhere. Frank swiftly pulls me into him. It's jarring at first, because I actually feel the draught of my near-death experience. So maybe that explains why I stay like this for a little longer than is necessary, huddled into the warm space between his arm and his chest, into the soft and firm lines of him.

'Let's not talk about bad parents and just try, ourselves, to be better ones,' he says. He releases me but my body retains a disarming muscle memory. I make a note that I must try to get nearly knocked over by a moped again. Ideally in the near future.

'What else shall we talk about then?' I say, buoyantly.

'I don't know.' He frisks me with his gaze. 'But I don't want to talk about me any more.'

'Well, I don't want to talk about me, so what does that leave?' I spot a basket of lemons outside of a small grocery shop; ginormous, gnarly, deformed things and I pick one up. 'Look at these...'

He picks one up too. 'They look like they could rob graves and feed off corpses.' He runs his thumb over the pockmarked skin, and I'm reminded of his thumb on my stomach, trailing just north of my panty line until it disappeared inside. Then he holds the lemon out for me to smell, and I realise I almost need something to resuscitate me. I push his hand away with a firm,

'No thanks.' Then I try to chirp, 'But what about the second time you visited France? The book tour?'

He puts the fruit back in the basket, with a little snort of amusement. 'Done talking about me, remember!'

'Please. Come on.'

He sighs. 'Eight countries and seventeen cities in nine days. It was mad. Exhausting. Not to be repeated. And, as it turns out – haha! – it wasn't!'

'You didn't want to stay on anywhere for a day or two? Catch your breath?' Since he saved me from death by moped, we are walking a little closer, our arms more than occasionally making contact – but it feels tame compared to an invitation to sniff a lemon, so I am okay with it.

'It wasn't really an option. I had a wife and fourteen-month-old back home and I'd already been away from them for too long. I could hardly go jack off and travel like I didn't have a care in the world.'

'It sounds a bit unromantic. Couldn't they have come with you?'

'It wasn't meant to be romantic. It was work.'

Before I can say, *I didn't mean it that way,* he says, 'People never think writers work. The biggest misconception: they just sit around in their jammies watching daytime TV and waiting for inspiration to strike.'

'And masturbate a lot.'

He sends me the side-eye. 'Well, there's some truth to that one.'

I chuckle. He tries not to. But then a great big smile appears anyway. I like the sight of it so much that I want to keep on making him do that. Until I think *what's wrong with me?* I'm a married woman in the middle of Athens with a strange man I had a one-night stand with – never to be repeated – and I want to make him smile? Am I for real? 'Okay, so I'm picturing this book tour... You... Young, fit, not entirely horrible to look at...'

'I was pretty horrible.'

'I've seen worse.'

'The compliment's too gracious. I don't think I can handle it.'

We turn onto a street that seems to have a disproportionate number of closed-down shops with graffiti all over their shutters, and a church whose steps look like they've become a dumping ground for the city's rubbish – all ironically beautified by strings of fairy lights that form a twinkling canopy for us to walk under. An older lady dressed in black drags a rolling shopping bag past two guys strumming bouzoukis on a bench.

'So there you are on your book tour... not entirely horrible-looking. You've written this amazing love story that's broken hearts the world over. Destroyed my chances of ever meeting a boy who can live up to Ford...'

'Of course. Let's make everything all about you.'

'You're sitting at a table in a very big room and there's a huge line-up of horny females, and they're all clamouring for a flash of eye contact, a touch of the hand from the visiting American author *god*.'

'Very few women manage to bring up horny and masturbating within five minutes while they walk the streets of Athens by the way. I salute you.'

'Thank you! I'm just skilled, what can I say.'

He laughs hard and I feel like a puppy whose owner has just applauded him for taking his first pee outside. A couple of Greek girls are walking towards us. The observe us like we're infectious and they want to catch some of what we have.

'So what did you do – this young, not entirely horrible-looking, but married literary sensation – with all that panting, throbbing female sexual energy?'

'Signed books. Smiled. Masturbated. Went home.'

I squawk a laugh. He is watching me like he's taking great pleasure in this. 'It was a serious question,' I berate him.

'It was a serious answer.'

We come to a stall that's practically capsizing with sun hats, sandals and Aegean seaside souvenirs, and I pull a hat on, and pose for his approval. He shakes his head. 'All I was trying to say, obviously badly,' I return the hat to the stand, 'was that it must have been an utterly mind-blowing experience for a young guy, that's all.'

'It was. But just so we're clear, that was all that got blown. Minds.'

When the corners of my mouth slide up again, he says, 'If we're being serious, Miss Dirty Mind, it was surreal. Truly. To everyone else I was this famous writer. To me, I was still just this kid who had written a book—'

'And a movie.'

'Yeah. The book always gets eclipsed by the movie, but the book came first, remember that!' He says it proudly, like a father pushing his kid up the line so he doesn't miss out on the free ice cream, and there's a spark, a vivacity about him when he talks about his novel, that I haven't seen before. 'I felt like a giant imposter. I'd gotten the dream, but it felt like I was dreaming it.' I can tell he's a little in awe of his own story, and I find that surprisingly touching. We stop in sync again and look at one another. 'I was the teenager who never put his hand up in class. The one who went through life thinking that because I rarely said anything, everyone must assume I had nothing to say. Then there I suddenly was, thrust into the limelight. I was no longer just a writer. I was the person behind a highly commercial piece of intellectual property. I had to step up and give people the Frank Lewis they needed me to be, and I didn't know who the hell that guy was.'

'But you don't sound like you actually wanted what you got, though. You don't sound like it made you happy.'

By the way he shuts down, I think he might not respond. Then he says, 'I was grateful. I knew I was lucky. But the thing is...' His expression darkens. 'It was the best thing I could ever have imagined happening to me, and it was the worst thing that actually *did* happen to me.'

Hmm... Interesting. I'm dying to say *how so?* But something in his demeanour shuts this down, so I decide I'd better not.

We come to another standstill, and I realise this might be the slowest walk around Athens that two people have ever undertaken. But then we hear someone call to us. A young guy is sitting on the ground by an easel. His clothes are torn, and he's missing part of his right leg. He asks if he can sketch our portrait. I instantly tell him, 'No, no, no! We are *not* a couple.' The guy narrows his eyes and says, '*Hmm...*' as though he doesn't believe me.

Fortunately, Frank tells him thanks, but sadly neither of us is carrying any euros. The guy very sweetly offers to do it for free. I make sure to haul Frank off by the sleeve, before he gets any ideas about agreeing to it.

'You were saying,' I prompt, as we move along. I'm dying to go back to this. 'Why was it the worst thing that happened to you?'

I think he's going to answer but then he says a slightly aloof, 'Story for another day.'

We reach Monastiraki Flea Market, cut a path through the crowds. 'I suspect all your stories are stories for another day, Frank.'

He doesn't correct me. Instead, he says, 'Drink?'

TWENTY-ONE

Six missed calls from Rupert, dating back a day or two. I spot them when Frank goes to the bar to order a bottle of wine and some mezze for us. Another flurry of texts, and messages on WhatsApp.

I'm inclined to have a peek, but Frank is coming back from the bar, so I put my phone away.

'If you tell me about what happened last time you were in Athens before you have a drink, I can assure you the story will come out better than if you're shitfaced,' he says.

The place is dimly lit. An Athens version of a dive bar. A place where secrets are spilled, and everything's wiped clean in the morning. I don't want to talk about it yet find myself saying, 'It was years ago.'

'Once upon a time...'

'We'd come away with our friends, Sarah and Dan, for a holiday.' I stare off at the memory. It's fresher than I thought. 'We were sitting in a taverna. Across the room there was another party of four – two couples. One of them, a man, kept looking over. Like we were more interesting than anyone at his table.' Then I add, coyly, 'Or *I* was.' I can still picture his face.

The darkest of brown eyes. The roman nose. The thick, brushed-back, brown hair. 'It was very strange. I felt an almost unsettling draw to him. It went on for a full two or more hours, this business of us quietly tracking one another...' I smile. 'At one point I got up to go to the toilet. And he followed me.'

Frank's face is rapt and I try not to let it distract me.

'We met at the communal hand basins. We both washed our hands without a word between us. Just standing there with that intimacy of performing something personal alongside one another. And then, before he walked out, he looked at me and asked me my name. And he told me his was David.'

'And?' Frank's voice cracks a little.

'And that was it. We exchanged nothing more than names, yet it felt like we'd exchanged our whole life stories. Our entire respective disillusionments and disappointments.' This is turning me absurdly emotional. 'I remember how when I told him my name was Moira, he performed a very slow nod, like he was processing what might have been if we'd led some other life, if we weren't trapped in our existing ones.'

'Wow,' he says.

I tell him how that same trip – it was a very strange trip indeed – I saw a look pass between Sarah and Rupert, just a split-second's eye contact across a restaurant table that I just as easily might not have seen, that made me see our friendship and my marriage in a new light. And it was almost like those two events coming in the same short span of time were trying to tell me something. 'Does it sound like a pitch for a new novel?'

'Not fully formed yet. Needs more detail. What did you do about it?'

I stare into my wine glass like it's a crystal ball that, instead of seeing the future, helps you rewrite the past. 'Nothing. I couldn't prove anything. They'd have probably said it was all in my mind.'

'Was it?'

'No.'

'So you never challenged him? Or your friend?'

'I wanted to, believe me. My whole life I've had a pathological dread of being made a fool of.'

I tell him it started with my cheating father, then was compounded by my first 'boyfriend' who kept standing me up. How he'd arrange these dates, then never show. And still I kept going back. Basically, he took my self-esteem and wiped the floor with it, but still I let him even though I knew it was wrong. I was so attracted to him that I was determined to have my fantasy of him no matter what shame I had to endure.

'There was a point in my life where I vowed I would never tolerate any man who didn't deserve my loyalty. I mean, my self-inflicted humiliation over a guy who wasn't worth it could be put down to youth. But my mother's? I mean why did she stay all those years?' I have often tried to make sense of it. 'Did she do it for me? And then I grew up and time passed and maybe she decided it didn't matter any more?' I shake my head, a mental picture of them assailing me. 'They sit there in their retirement, looking all benign and cosy, yet you know there's all this murky history between them. I mean... Why?'

This is what will happen if you choose to believe Rupert, I think. *You will grow old together, and it will sit there between you until it is nothing more than your shared experience, rather than any sort of stain on his conscience.*

I realise I've gone off on a tangent, but Frank seems quite fine with it. 'So yes, to answer your question, I thought about confronting them. But once you make an accusation you can't walk it back. There were two marriages, three kids, involved. I didn't want to turn Harriet's world upside down. And maybe, you know, maybe it helped me understand my mother a bit more too.'

A canary-yellow building catches my eye through the window, a black and white magpie perching on its corner. I watch it for a while. 'Maybe it really was just an unacted-on attraction. She was my close friend, and he was my husband... People can't help who they're drawn to, only what they do about it.'

'Do you always believe the best of people?'

'No. But does any good ever come of automatically assuming the worst?'

He doesn't say anything. I am overly perturbed by his silence. 'I was attracted to the man in the restaurant enough to think about him for quite a while after. And in the end, it didn't mean anything.'

'I disagree. I think it meant something or you wouldn't have remembered it all these years.'

I stare at my hands clasped too tightly on the table in front of me. 'Poor guy will never know the hornet's nest he disturbed!'

Frank doesn't smile. I can't even bring myself to, either.

'I will say this... What I saw between Sarah and Rupert made me question a few things, I suppose. All those dinners at each other's houses. All those intimate conversations Sarah and I had shared about our marriages...' Then I finally say it. 'How happy Rupert and I truly were. That bloody holiday was the very first time I'd consciously asked myself that. And once it came into my mind, it's sort of been lodged there ever since.'

I am feeling, absurdly, like I could cry.

'It shook me up on some level. I'd never really thought that you can love the person you are married to but grow to realise that love can mean something different to what you first thought. That you can be with someone who never feels out-and-out wrong for you, yet you can wonder, in your heart, if you were meant for someone else. I'd never really intellectualised compatibility or desire before.'

He lets that sit there, his silence, his contemplation, bestowing too much weight on it. I don't tell him how I have walked through my married life feeling a bit flat. Sometimes wondering if other women occasionally felt this way about their choices. Telling myself it's probably normal but a part of me saying, *is it?* Is it really?

'The holiday ended up being a disaster. Dan got shellfish poisoning and ended up in hospital the very same day as their daughter Greta was rushed into A and E in England with appendicitis. We stayed with Dan. Sarah went back home.'

'And what became of your friendship?'

'Not a lot. The following summer, Dan got offered a job in Singapore and they moved.'

'Did you stay in touch?'

'Oddly, no.'

The years have closed back in, making me realise that suspicion has the longest half-life of any emotion. It is nigh on impossible to eradicate it from your system. 'Not sure why I'm telling you all this,' I say. 'Can we change the subject?'

'Of course,' he says.

'That second bottle of wine wasn't as good as the first.' I hiccup and link him as we teeter down the street. 'But it was better than the third.'

He sends me the side-eye. 'I thought the fourth bottle went down the best.'

I frown. 'We didn't have a fourth.'

'A lost opportunity.' His eyes drop to my hand looped through his arm.

'To be clear,' I say. 'I am only linking you because I am severely intoxicated and I'm terrified of falling, blacking my eye, and having to show up at our kids' wedding looking like I tried to beat someone up, only they won.'

He laughs.

'Oh my God,' I say. 'Are we really about to go and crash our kids' elopement?'

'I don't know if that's exactly what we're doing. For starters, we don't know where the venue is. And if we text them, and they're still mad at us, they're unlikely to tell us.'

I think of the white church with the blue dome. 'Santorini isn't that big. It's not going to be *that* hard to find them. Besides, you write romances, so you of all people are bound to be able to find them for us.'

'*You* are the one who wanted to come here, remember... Way I see it, we can rent a moped and go scoot around the island, find that church – or some other church. They must have made some sort of reservation. We can take the priest aside.'

'Are we back to poisoning people again?'

'Nah. With this one, we pay him off. *There's your money. Now you don't marry them.*' He catches my incredulous expression. 'Hey, everybody has their price. Even clergy.'

The insane thing is, I truly don't know if he's playing with me here. 'I hate to scupper the plan,' I say, 'but I'm not even sure Harriet would want to marry in a church. She's more spiritual than formally religious.'

'Aiden, too. He hates religion.'

'She's never more at peace than when she's with nature. The beach, the marvel of the natural world... *that* is Harriet's church.'

'Same with Aiden. I worry about that a bit with him. That one day he's going to wake up and realise that you don't solve the problems of the world, or even your own, by inviting the universe to do the guiding.'

'But maybe they're right and we're wrong. Maybe we should all try going with the flow of life rather than trying to control it at every step.' Then I am clearly drunk, because I say, 'Maybe they really are meant for each other.'

He smirks. 'There is one more consideration.'

'There is?'

'It's entirely possible that a wedding in Greece is not considered valid in America. That they have to make it legal back there. And it's possible that neither of them has thought of this – because the universe would never send them such a bureaucratic complication.' He raises an *aren't-I-clever?* eyebrow. 'So what we do is, we keep this quiet until their first big fight. You know, not one of the petty little disagreements that end in make-up sex. But *the* great big mother of a fuck-you, we're done, you are dead to me fight. Then we present them with it. Our little well-timed gift to them. The news that they were never legally married at all.'

'Wow.' I try to process all this. 'You don't mean that,' I say, though a part of me thinks that if such a situation were to occur, and their vows were not legal in America, then maybe this really *would* be the universe looking out for them – not me and Frank.

'Hey,' he says, 'maybe I do...' He nudges me. 'I mean I'm the dude who stole his out-of-date passport. I had to disable then reactivate an entire high-tech security system in my home, to the tune of several hundred dollars, so he'd never be able to prove I went into his room. Would you put anything past a guy like me?'

'I would not,' I say.

TWENTY-TWO

'Walk for a while, or head back to our rooms?' He poses it like a tantalising invitation.

'Eighteen thousand steps.' I peer at my phone's Health app. 'And if you could measure talking in steps, I'd probably triple that. So I think that might be enough walking for one day.'

'Funny, I'm not tired.' He nudges me again. 'Come on... Let's wander dark streets and stumble upon floodlit ancient ruins until morning.'

I find myself indulging that pleasing picture of us for a while. My life taking on a scene from a movie, and me granting myself permission to be the main character in my own story.

'Think about it,' he says, when I have fallen silent, the precipice sort of silent. 'We've come all this way. We might never be here again like this. You can't just quit and go to bed.'

A part of me is egging the other part on to do it. But, untimely as it is, melancholy has wrapped its cloak around me again, this strange tug between opposing forces that always seems to be going on inside of me, without my ever really knowing what those forces are. Except that one is probably Rupert. I look up at a smattering of stars crowning the floodlit

Acropolis, wishing that if the universe had a flow right this second, it would kick in and I could attempt to glide with it. 'It's possible I'm actually insanely envious of my daughter, you know,' I say, apropos of nothing. If you've never experienced it, one way to deal with that is to deny it exists. Maybe that is why I was so down on her love story in the beginning. Ugh! What a weird confession. Freud would have a field-day.

'Explain,' he says.

I settle for saying, 'The absence of complications that she clearly must feel.'

'That's just called being young.'

'She's prepared to change everything about her life for love.'

'And that's a good thing how?'

'Never said it's a good thing. Just saying, for Harriet, it's that epic thing you once talked about that we're supposedly all chasing down.'

'Is it,' he says quietly and rhetorically, like something I've said has just moved him.

I link him again. Need to. For stability. Don't want to twist an ankle. 'Do you have, like, any idea where our hotel is?' I am suddenly insanely tired and don't want to talk about love and all that crap any more.

'If I say yes, then we're destined to go back to our separate rooms. If I say no, then we have to wander dark streets and stumble upon floodlit ancient ruins until morning.'

It hangs there. The invitation. Possibilities dancing. Mine for the taking. Quickly evaporating.

'I do know where our hotel is,' he says, when I am silent for too long. 'As well as God granting me the serenity to write the world's most crapped-on romantic novel, I also have the most finely tuned sense of direction.'

'Well, that makes one of us.'

You should have walked all night through Athens with him. The thought just blindsides me, makes me catch my breath. But we keep on walking. Moving farther away from the tantalising prospect of that with each step we take.

We arrive back at the hotel. Shuffle into the same slice of moving door. Did the space get smaller? He is so close behind me that I can feel the infrared radiation of his body; there is no air. 'Er... I don't think we're moving,' I tell him, standing painfully still again.

'Oh yes. Right. You forgot to push.' He reaches an arm around me, gives the door a little start. I could not be more conscious of what it would feel like if he touched me, than if he just did. We do the silly shuffle again. Then we arrive in the lobby. The pretty girl behind the desk wishes us *kalispera* and coyly keeps track of us crossing the marble floor.

Inside the lift, we are offered the inevitability of the sliding door. 'Which floor are you on?' My voice is so giddy I hardly recognise it as my own.

'Same as you. That's why I only pressed one button.'

'Oh. Right.' I might be blushing. 'Good to know I can safely go to the moon with you in charge of the rocket.'

'It might make for an interesting adventure.' His body is too angled towards mine now. Everything about him is angled towards me too much.

The door slides open. 'Here we are.' My voice quivers.

'One small step for mankind.' He gestures for me to step out ahead of him.

'Gentleman.'

'Not really. Just wanted one last glimpse of your ass.'

We come to a halt in front of a wall. 'I'm this way.' I indicate right.

'The funny thing about having rooms next door is... Me, too.'

We start walking down the narrow hallway, which seems to go on for forty minutes. I have never been so conscious of the practice of placing one foot in front of the other, and of having no idea where it's leading. I point to a door, a flurry of nerves loose in me. 'I think this one's mine... 606. Almost the antichrist.'

He smiles. 'I like your mnemonic technique.'

'All that wine brings out your advanced vocabulary.'

'I could say something about what else it brings out, but I'm not going to.'

I turn to face my door. He is so close to me that I can feel the draught of his breath on the nape of my neck again, like a contactless kiss. I am back on that chaise, the short, sharp shock of how in tempo we were, of how he managed to turn something arguably quick and dirty into some sort of extravagantly close communion that could easily become a compulsion to me.

I dig in my pocket for the key card which doesn't seem to be there. Shit. Damn. Where the hell is it? I pivot, wave the piece of plastic. 'Found it!'

'Pity.' His gaze hooks, hardcore, onto mine.

Heat rushes to my face, and a very different heat rushes somewhere else. 'Got yours at the ready, have you?'

'If you mean my key...' He brandishes his piece of plastic.

'Perfect.' I purse my lips, let out a surreptitious breath. 'We have the necessary tools to access our own rooms.' I turn my back to him and aim mine at the keypad – twice. Both times, it flashes red.

'Maybe you just need to...' His arm is reaching around my body again.

'Green!' My hand is poised on the handle. 'Well, then... Goodnight.'

'Goodnight,' he replies, but he doesn't move. Not one inch.

I stare into the door, wondering why I haven't yet gone inside. *You're not allowed to kiss him again, no matter how critical to your existence this feels right now. You are still married, even if that feels like an improbability right now. Plus, you do not need more complications. Frank = more complications.*

I turn, slowly, try to resist my own momentum, almost as though my will and my body have different ideas. His eyes bore into mine again; then they buzz around my face like he's attempting to communicate complicated thoughts. I try to read him, but I can barely read myself.

'It's possible I may be suffering from a case of analysis paralysis,' he finally says. He looks a little cowed by his own admission.

'What do you mean?' My eyes drop involuntarily to his mouth, my brain launching into a tumble of over-thinking. But I want to know. I want to know what he means.

He looks like he's on the brink of explaining, like the words are poised there if he can just give them one small nudge over this awkward hump. But then he says a rather rueful, 'Explanation for another day, Moira Fitzgerald.'

I feel it like a tiny puncture wound. More than tiny. Instead of opening up, he has shut us right down. 'Why do you always call me by my full name?' I try to sound upbeat to mask my crashing disappointment.

'So I can keep you straight from all the other Moiras I know.'

'I thought that might be why.'

I need him to go. Badly. I need him to go like my life depends on it. But still he stands there. And still I find myself waiting. And then he does something I'm totally not expecting. He lowers his forehead to mine, just presses it there, warm skin to warm skin, mutters a quiet, 'Damn.'

When he looks up, I save us both from ourselves. I say, 'Goodnight, Frank.'

And he says, 'Goodnight, Moira.'

TWENTY-THREE

'I don't think all that drinking was a very good idea, Frank.' I struggle down the ramp, feeling almost as tipsy as before I went to sleep, a gust of wind lifting my skirt, my feet landing on Santorini soil.

We're here! The airport is in the middle of what appears to be nowhere, no hallmarks of the postcard Santorini. Instead, flat volcanic earth as far as the eye can see, with sparse clusters of white, square structures, like sugar cubes that astronauts have left on the moon. We look around for a moment, at the bluest of gemstone skies, a wash of island promise, and I brim over with excitement.

'There's really only one solution, Moira.' He stares at our surroundings like a cinematographer scoping out a location.

'If you say hair of the dog...'

We troop through the terminal to a taxi. I tell the driver to take us to Firostefani. If I know Harriet, she's going to want to be somewhere romantic but less touristy so she might be in Imerovigli – the iconic, whitewashed, sapphire-domed town built on the highest point of the caldera cliffs. We can walk to it from Firostefani, but we won't feel like we're breathing down their necks.

'When should we let them know we're here?' We have already decided that cycling around looking for churches is not the way to go. I am positively giddy with the idea of announcing our arrival to them now.

'Soon,' he says. 'Or maybe never.' When he sees my astonished face, he adds, 'Look, I think we need to get ourselves into town, find a room, get our bearings, *then* we'll text them.' He winks. 'Maybe get a small beer in the sunshine? Drum up a plan?'

I feign outrage. 'Anyone would think you're terrified to tell them we're here!'

'Hey, just saving the best for last.'

The cab tips us out – almost literally – at the main square. Where did the sun go? We stand under an angry canopy of cloud and take stock. Before us is a buttermilk-coloured church whose bell tower punches the sky like a giant, three-tier wedding cake. Ordaining the cliffside, white buildings merge with pastel, their walls draped with cerise bougainvillea, their views bowing onto the spectacular caldera. Nothing moves except for a gusty Greek flag and a cat who hurries across our path.

'This is where a bit of forward planning would have come in handy.' I park my wheelie case in front of my feet. 'Good thing it's low season, so getting a room shouldn't be a problem. We'll probably have our pick of the town.'

'What do you say to that beer?'

'I say we should secure our accommodation first.'

'Because all the empty hotel rooms you just talked about are clearly going some place, and then there'll be none left?' He plucks off his glasses. He looks as green as he looked when he stumbled out of his hotel room this morning.

''K, alky pants,' I say. 'If we go for the beer now, then you're going to stop talking about having a beer, right?'

'We can take that theory for a spin. No promises, though.'

We walk the pebbled street that etches a trail along the cliff-side, with its jaw-dropping view into the blue, passing a few closed shops selling jewellery and souvenirs, a pharmacy, and a coffee shop populated by older men. I don't know if it's the combination of the shitty weather, or the time of year, but not everything appears to be open. 'This looks like it used to be a restaurant before the apocalypse,' Frank says, as we stop in front of a taverna with an empty menu stand outside.

Just when I'm thinking there truly is no sign of life, we are suddenly surprised by a voice. '*Kalimera.*' A stocky, bald man, with a disproportionate amount of facial hair, appears out of nowhere and inspects us – not exactly an open-arms welcome.

'Where are all the tourists?' I ask. 'This place is a ghost town.'

He throws a hand to the sky. 'Wind. Rain. More wind. More rain. Tourists go somewhere else.' He grins, revealing teeth that belong in the Natural History Museum, and says, 'Spain.'

Frank asks him if he's open, and he says, 'If you here, we open.' He directs us to follow him down the path, telling us that if we want more things that are open we should go to Fira, the main town, a fifteen-minute walk along the cliffside. He shows us to a table that perches on the edge of the caldera some four hundred feet above an indigo Aegean Sea; still beautiful even on a cloudy day. 'Today no charge for the best view in the house.' He gives us his blindingly black smile. Frank orders two Greek beers. The owner says he will come back and tell us what's on his menu. I imagine him going inside, calling upstairs to his napping wife and telling her she'd better shift it because they've got business.

'It's annoyingly perfect.' Frank looks around us in awe. 'I almost want to spoil it just to know that someone can.'

'Annoyingly perfect. Maybe you should write guidebooks? I see a bestseller in your future.' I tell him what I read: that some say Santorini is the lost city of Atlantis, the legendary kingdom that plunged into the sea when it was at the peak of its power, disappearing without a trace.

'So no metaphor there, then?' he says.

I smile. I immediately open my phone's camera and snap some pictures of the white confectionary houses, the occasional one painted lemon or pale green or pale pink, clinging to the side of the rock, the steep, stark incline to the sea.

'Have you noticed that since the advent of the smart phone, no one can ever just enjoy the moment the old-fashioned way?' He is studying me like I am now way more interesting than the view.

'Nope. Oddly, I have not noticed that.' I start recording a video, steadily panning the camera. 'Can you move your big fat head out of frame, please and thank you?'

He slumps sideways. 'Has anyone ever told you your descriptive powers rival Hemingway?'

I play it back for him. 'Look, you totally ruined the view.' This calls for a selfie. I dash around to his side of the table, crouch behind him, my warm ear touching his warm ear. 'Say feta cheese.'

He says, 'Oh Jesus,' instead.

I sit back down and admire my handiwork.

'You're going to send that to Harriet, aren't you?'

'Maybe.'

'But not now.'

'I'm not?'

'Nope. So put the phone down. Like a good girl.'

This makes me cackle. But I do put the phone down. Our beers arrive. '*Yamas!*' the owner says. Cheers!

I sip it and already feel a little less hungover. This is nice. I close my eyes, take a long slow breath in. When I open them, he is looking at me in a way that makes me say, 'What?' I glance at the phone in his hand. 'Did you just take a picture of me?'

'Why would I do something like that?'

'Give me your phone then.' I hold out a hand.

'Come and get it.' He sends me a rascally smirk.

'I am not going to do that. I am not a child, like you.' I feign great interest in my fingernails.

He says, 'Ha. Ha. Ha.'

Ding-a-ling! I'm convinced he just texted me the picture, but then I realise this is a Ding-a-ling, not a Ping. Rupert's face again. Why all this urgency? Did the universe let him know I'm so very close to home – geographically, at least?

'Who is it?' Frank asks.

'Nobody important.'

The owner comes back out and sets down small plates of food for a couple of cats, then he reels off our menu options. Moussaka straight from the oven. Greek salad. Grilled calamari in lemon sauce. English chips. Frank says, 'Are all of them a possibility?'

My phone rings now. The old-fashioned phone call. I look at the screen. The familiar blue eyes. I put it in silent mode, turn it face down. Next, he'll be sending up a drone.

Frank is watching me almost forensically. 'Is that nobody again?'

'Yup.'

'Question.' He cocks me a curious look. 'Why isn't he here, if his daughter's getting married?'

I roll my eyes back in my head, not really ready for this. 'That's a very long story.'

'We've got time.'

When I just stare silently across the water, he says, 'How did you meet, then? You can surely tell me that part. We could begin at the beginning, where the least challenging fiction starts.'

I watch a ferry blazing a solitary trail to somewhere other than here. The sun is suddenly trying to break out. We do have to eat before we contact Aiden and Harriet. Something in me uncoils.

'I managed a bar in my last year of university.' I can see it in my mind's eye, the way you always see the moment where your life's path was being carved out in front of you, but you didn't know it at the time. 'I was serving a group of guys. One of them – the cute one with a mop of curly black hair – kept looking over. Later, one of my busboys said the cute one wanted to take me out, and he'd asked him to give me his business card. I looked over, but they were just walking out the door. The cute one glanced back and smiled.' The memory makes me smile now. 'I'd just read a fascinating book about love at first sight, and I remember thinking, hmm... does that ever happen in real life? Or is it a just concept that songwriters and novelists sell to us, so they can make millions and we're left chasing a figment of their imagination?'

He is listening to me like he's utterly captivated. 'What did you do?'

'Well, I was intrigued. So I rang him.' I try to ignore his rapt expression. 'He was bright and funny, and we agreed to go on a date. When I showed up...' I throw up my hands. 'It wasn't him, was it? Not the cute one. It was one of his mates. Someone I could barely recall.'

He beams. 'Hate to say it but I kinda saw that coming!'

'He was a little nerdish and uptight. But he had amazing blue eyes, like the Maldives on a human face.' I loved Rupert's eyes. 'He'd just taken over his dad's estate agency and regaled me with stories about selling homes to the rich and famous.' I smile. 'Rupert can be very entertaining... We went out for a year. I had to come off the pill due to medical reasons, then I fell pregnant.'

I stare across the water again, think how best to phrase it. 'The thing was... up to that point, you know, he was great, and it was comfortable, but I wasn't sure I'd spend the rest of my life with him. But then the decision somehow felt made.' I meet Frank's eyes again. 'I don't know if I felt like I belonged with him in the way I imagined you should feel you belong, if you're committing your whole life to a person.'

'But you could have always terminated? We always have choices.'

'Could have. But I suppose once I got over the shock that I was going to have a baby when I was barely out of university, I quite loved the idea of being a mother.'

He nods, like he's making something of this. After a studied pause, he says, 'So before, when we talked about this, you said the first time you questioned how happy you were with him was when you wondered if he had something going on with your friend. But sounds to me like you knew he wasn't right for you even before you married.'

I'm a little taken aback by this unsolicited evaluation of my marriage. And by how he seems to be banking everything I tell him, like we're in some sort of therapy session.

'What's happiness, anyway?' I say. 'Unless you're actively *un*happy, then you're probably happy enough.'

'That's a pretty low bar. You were a little young to settle.'

'It didn't feel like settling. It felt safe.'

'Safe?' He says it like it's an obscene word.

'By the time I met Rupert, I think I'd decided, on some subconscious level, that I wanted a guy who would never mess me around. A guy who would always show up for me, the way I would show up for him. And I thought that guy was him.' I lower my eyes for a moment. I almost can't handle the way he is looking at me – like he feels sorry for me. 'Rupert was a good husband. He really pulled his weight with Harriet when she was little, so I could pursue my career as soon as I was able. We were equals in every possible regard, and he's easy to be with.' I shrug. 'Maybe there was no extraordinary passion. But we weren't on the emotional rollercoaster that comes with that, either.'

I tell him how I've seen some married couples who are so into one another that they're riddled with distrust and jealousy – not a way I'd want to live.

His silence is really bothering me. I meet him firmly in the eyes. 'If you don't adore them with everything you have in you, then they don't get to have that power over you. And that was partly why I was so worried for Harriet. Because of how much she seems to adore Aiden. I worried that might come back to bite her.'

'This conversation is starting to trouble me. Don't think I can take any more.'

I give an ironic huff. Fortunately, our food arrives.

'Maybe I'm just not a romantic like you,' I say, popping a hot chip in my mouth. 'Mr Beating Away Beneath Every Encounter Is The Desire For A Love of Epic Proportions. Maybe I'm just too practical.'

I dig into the luscious moussaka, thinking about the lies we can tell ourselves. How could I ever admit that if I've missed out on anything, it's that sense of true connection with a man? Not just the sex. Not really the soulmates thing, either. Just one of those feelings buried deep inside you, that your day-to-day life conspires to help you ignore – but occasionally the profound undeniability of it hits you. You were not in love. You were capable of feeling so much more.

As if he can mind-read, he says, 'From everything I'm learning here, I think you're in denial about yourself.'

'In case you're wondering,' I say, after an overly long silence, trying to inject a note of levity into my tone. 'I *did* sometimes wonder how my life might have been different if the other guy had shown up.'

He is staring at me, steadily. No smile. 'Do you always have to make light of things the second you've expressed a serious emotion?'

'Do I?' I throw it back a little bit defensively.

He turns his focus back to his food. 'There's something I need to remind you, though,' he says. 'You may not have been in true, passionate love yet, Moira Fitzgerald, but your life probably isn't even half over.'

I stare at the burnt cheese stuck to the edges of the white bowl, stare until it blurs, and I cannot make out what it is any more.

'I think I'm going to text Harriet,' I say.

TWENTY-FOUR

'Why the sudden rush to text Harriet?' Frank asks.

'No rush!'

'You're doing it again.'

'Huh?'

'Running away to your safe space.'

'Don't be ridiculous. And can you please stop analysing me? If I needed a shrink, I'd probably pick one with better credentials than you.' As if to prove a point, I drop my phone back down onto the table with a little more gusto than I intended.

But now is actually *not* the time to text her. Not while I'm feeling so unhinged by all this conversation. He is watching me like shrinks do – or at least the ones I've seen in movies – when they just want you to keep blowing off steam so they can make their money really, *really* easily.

'If I don't call her now, can we please talk about something else?' I say.

'Must we?' He cocks his head. 'I rather like talking about how your entire life has felt like a compromise.'

'Thanks a heap. I feel so much better now... Let's pay up

and go and find accommodation,' I say, pulling my bag onto my lap and diving in there almost headfirst in search of my wallet.

The hotel we decide on is an iced white confection that clings to the caldera, all several luscious layers of it unfurling to a hot tub and a small infinity pool that consorts with the sea and the sky. When I hear the price of the rooms, I almost have a heart attack. Oh well! One more Herculean charge on the credit card, but in for a penny, in for a pound, as my mother used to say. I am wiped out suddenly after all that soul-searching and stuffing my face, so tell him I'd like to take an hour's rest and we can reconvene later and decide what we're going to do about tracking our kids down.

The room is sparsely furnished in blond wood and marble. Everything is white. White walls. White rugs. Simple white louvre blinds dress two dramatic floor-to-ceiling windows that give onto a swathe of sapphire sea. The bed is a pouffy, pillowy white perfection. All of it conspires to be purely hypnotic which makes me nap longer than I intended. When I next check my phone it's almost five-thirty. I text him and we agree to meet downstairs.

When I go out onto the pool deck, he is gazing out at the water. He has his jacket on, because it's chilly, and his hands in his jeans' pockets. I register every nuance of him standing there in the fading light, hard, almost pivotally, in the pit of my stomach. Then he turns, looks me over appreciatively, and smiles.

'Should I text her now, you think?' I stroke a skinny tortoiseshell cat who comes to greet me, abandoning her perch at the bottom of an enormous flight of steps that leads all the way back up to the street. 'I was thinking I'll just say, Harriet, look, we have a gift to deliver to your hotel if you will please send me your address. Then... Ta-da! The gift will be us.'

Frank seems to mull this over. 'That's a pretty big thing to spring on her – on them. I mean, what if they're seriously pissed?'

The cat meanders around my ankles, tickling me. 'I hadn't really thought of that possible downside,' I say.

'Why don't we take a walk around town for now? We have to eat. You never know, we might bump into them.' He pulls his jacket tighter around his body. 'You know, given it's freezing, and we are probably the only four tourists on the whole goddamned island.'

'Because that *won't* be less of a shock? Bumping into them on a deserted Greek island when they think we're four thousand miles away? No surprise at all there!'

He titters. 'I think this clearly illustrates we haven't got a clue what we're doing. So let's just walk and not care. For now.'

'So what's happened to your marriage?' Frank says, when we have climbed the steps and are back onto the street. 'You kind of have to tell me now.' He is a little breathless. 'Was it to do with the absent fireworks?'

'Oh, we're not back to this?' The sky is now striated with red and orange. Below us, patio lights start popping on. I stop and catch my own breath for a beat and watch a ferry on its way to Crete that barely appears to be moving. 'Nope. Not the fireworks. As you get older, those things matter less anyway.'

'I disagree. They matter more.'

I tug my trench coat around me, glad I put on my merino wool hoodie for an extra layer. 'They burn out in most relationships.'

'But who wants most relationships? And what about the ones where they never do?'

'If we can stick to the facts and do less of the philosophising, I might tell you,' I say. We randomly head uphill towards Imerovigli because it's closer than walking into Fira. The streets are eerily deserted, except for the odd tourist in a hoodie or windbreaker.

I tell him about the aeroplane. When I get to the part about how the text pops up, then seconds later the plane starts barrelling down the runway and then we're stuck there for the next twelve hours, he says, 'Jesus Christ. I mean... Wow. How did *that* go?'

'Well,' I say. 'I've had less turbulent flights.'

We stop and look at one another. The wind catches my hair and I try to hold it down with one hand. 'Somewhere over Iceland he finally admitted he'd had an "inappropriate flirtation", but that was all it was. Harriet said, "Well then, if nothing happened, let's just check his phone."'

'Oh no!' he grimaces. 'I think I can see where this is going.'

My eyes are watery from the wind.

'At first he was, like, "Fine! Here it is!" But then when I was, like, "Okay. Give it here, then..." he was all, "I'm not going to let you see it on principle. Not because there actually is anything to see. I just have this massive problem with you not believing me."'

'So you tried to pry it out of his hands?'

'Close. Things got a little heated. The flight attendants said that if I continued to behave in an unruly manner I'd be taken to another section of the plane and "restrained".'

He gasps. 'They were going to handcuff you?'

'Stuff my mouth with British Airways socks? I wouldn't have ruled it out.'

We get to the top of the hill and look back at the view: Santorini preparing to sleep. Inky sea merging with inky sky. The cliffside structures, a stark white by day, are softened in the glow of the warm light of living rooms. I realise I am recounting this story like it's someone else's. 'What got me was the flight attendant was so in sympathy with him. I remember him apologising for *my* behaviour – to a stranger.

But he had no intention of apologising to his wife about his own.'

'I am, like, totally hating this asshole. Just so you know.'

I smile, a mirthless stretch of a few taut muscles. 'The worst part of all this was that Harriet was caught in the middle. She'd always looked up to her father, and then she learned he was the very cliché she despised.' Like I once did with my own dad.

I tell him that's why she wants nothing to do with him, and why she wouldn't want him here.

'That's brutal,' he says, 'and understandable too.'

We decide to search for a bar or a place to grab a snack, but nothing seems to be open and clomping around in the wind is starting to wear.

'It's funny because he'd mentioned her a few times. *Dagmara thinks. Dagmara says...* I remember thinking who died and made this Dagmara person the Oracle?'

'Didn't you ask him about her?'

'No. I truly just thought she was a colleague.'

'Moira, who never thinks the worst of people.'

I tell him about my conversation with Nat.

'So this makes you believe him? Because your friend said you should?' He scowls. 'I'm not sure it was her place to weigh in on whether he was being honest. Seems that was a bit above her pay grade.'

'No,' I say. 'I respect her opinion on most things, but I think she's wrong on this.'

I realise I'm sharing all this with him simply because I just like telling him things.

'So that's why you decided to stay in Santa Monica,' he says. 'Not because you couldn't bear to be apart from your daughter. But because you couldn't face going back to him.'

I nod.

'And now?'

'And now I don't know,' I say.

We come to a small, cobbled square, not much here except for a giant tree, a bench in the centre, and two tavernas that look very 'local'. The one with the more visible windows seems to have a lot of people in it, as though the few tourists around have all made their way to the same sign of life. 'Do you think they could be in one of these?' I ask him. 'Oh God, they might be.' I press a hand to my stomach.

'Don't care. I'm heading in. I'm freezing.' He strides to the more obviously populated one.

I grab his arm. 'You can't barge right in. What if they're in there?'

'Then I'm the surprise that pops out of the pudding,' he says.

'Let me look in the window first.' I scoot ahead of him.

'Look, if you want to case the joint and bring in the sniffer dogs, be my guest, but I'm going in before I perish to death.'

I walk past the window exactly how I used to do it in central London. In those posh parts of Kensington and Chelsea where rich homeowners seem to deliberately leave their lights on with no window coverings.

Walk straight on with purpose.

Slight turn of the head.

Quick dekko out the corner of your eye.

Return focus to the path ahead.

'Not there!' I tell him. 'Let's try this one.'

Unfortunately, this one's windows are eighty per cent covered with net curtain, leaving only a sliver up top to see in. There's a giant tree almost concealing the door. If I am to see in there, I need to be seven feet tall.

Unless...

I quickly take off my trench coat, stuff it into his hands.

'Can you give me a little nudge?' I ask, when I've managed to climb one tree-limb up – and one human limb – and am running out of nerve. I knew I wore jeans and running shoes for a reason.

He is standing at the bottom. *My* bottom.

'If you're not strong enough to *get into* the tree, you're not strong enough to *stay* in the tree,' he says. He goes on standing there staring at my ass. I know this because I am looking back, and his head is almost up my...

'Thanks again for everything!' I try not to look down again because if I did fall I'd be right on top of him – not like that would be a first. 'I always climbed trees as a child.' I try another leg up, try to avoid my merino wool hoodie snagging on a branch. 'No kid is allowed to do this any more. I tell you, it's a dying art.' I am panting.

'There is indeed a lot of artistry to this,' he says.

I glance back again and he's still gazing up between my legs and smiling.

I can finally see past the damned curtain. Cosy couples. A few families. Tables of *saganaki* cheese going up in flames. A long one full of raucous Germans who sound like they're at a football match. I hang on for grim life.

'No Harriet and Aiden,' I say.

Now I just have to get back down.

'Might be easier to just call them,' I tell him, when I land back on the ground with an ungainly thwack that I feel in my kneecaps. 'Less damaging to good cardigans.' I show him the enormous hole in my hoodie and pout.

'Maybe after we eat, and warm up?'

I cock my head and pretend to give this thought. 'Er... no. We can't keep putting this off.' I huddle beside him under the canopy of my mate the tree, conscious of him watching me tinker with my phone. 'It's why we came here,' I tease. 'Remember?'

I dial her number.

'Hmm... That's odd. Her phone's off.' I frown. 'Harriet's phone is never off. Why don't you try Aiden?'

'I thought you were the one who wanted to break the big news?'

'Ah yes. Forgot that part.'

He smiles. 'Look,' he says, 'they've probably got better things on their mind than food. My guess is they're probably entirely unfindable right now. Unless you're a bed bug.'

'Please. Not that again.'

'It's what I'd be doing if I was young, here and in love. Wouldn't you?'

I cock my head and study him. 'Frank. I hate to break the bad news, but we will never again be young, in Santorini and in love. How's that for a sobering thought?'

He casts a languid gaze across my face, a tender quality suddenly lighting his eyes. 'Two out of three wouldn't be bad, Moira Fitzgerald.'

TWENTY-FIVE

'So what happened to *your* marriage, as we've covered mine?'

I have tried Harriet's phone three more times and it's still off. We are walking back down the hill, as neither of those tavernas could seat us right away. We vaguely remember that we passed a rather less inviting-looking place on the way up that may, or may not, be open.

I glance at him when he doesn't answer. 'What?' I say.

'Nothing. Just... this is not *you show me yours, I'll show you mine*.' He says it fake-cavalierly.

Something about his attitude stops me in my tracks. 'What does *that* mean?'

He shrugs. 'It just means some topics are not on the table.' Then he says, an almost taut, 'Sorry.'

He walks on, leaving me still standing there processing this. 'What happened with your book success then?' I trot after him. 'You said it was the best thing that happened to you – but also the worst. Surely you can at least tell me that.'

He pretends to sigh a dramatic sigh. 'Seems the lady doesn't take no for an answer.'

'The *lady*?' I catch up to him. 'Is this for real? You're seriously *not* going to tell me?'

'I'm not going to tell you,' he says, with finality.

Wow.

We reach that viewpoint again. But not before passing a couple of cold-looking tourists who ask us if there's a restaurant open anywhere. We point them in the direction of the square and Frank tells them there's a bit of a wait.

'I don't think I want to go to dinner any more,' I say when they get past us, their bodies rounded to fight the wind. I plonk myself on the wall that has a precarious drop right behind it with no safety barrier. The kind of death trap that would be illegal anywhere but Europe.

'What's wrong?' he asks, like he genuinely has no idea.

I feel like I'm bracing myself for a massive overreaction. I want to stop it, but the other part of me just wants to let it rip. 'You can't say you have a story for another day and then not tell me. Not after I've poured out all that personal stuff about my situation – about my whole damned life.'

He looks at me rather despairingly. 'Come on. We have to eat. Tonight would be ideal. Not sometime next week.'

'Go on your own,' I say. I can't bring myself to look at him. 'In fact, you know what? Forget it. Even if you told me, I wouldn't listen.' I cover my ears with my hands to make my point.

He does that *Ha, ha, ha* thing of his again, which suddenly inflames me so much that it makes me want to push him off the cliff.

'Okay now you're being a child.' He is watching me like he's unsure about me. 'You're cold and you're hungry and we're supposed to be trying to find our kids. We're not talking about anything until you've eaten.'

'Oh, you care about me, do you? You care about my well-being?' I lean back from the hips, outstretching my arms like wings, feeling a prickle of daring in the soles of my feet.

'Don't do that, please.'

'Why not?' My coat sleeves flap with the wind. I hate my behaviour, but I'm powerless to stop it.

'You can fall. Seriously. People do that in movies and they never fall, but in real life they end up quadriplegic, so don't do it.'

I lean back a little farther and get another attack of the tingles. There's a moment where I wonder what it would be like to do one fatal skydive, that glorious feeling of flight before you realise you're seconds away from ending your own existence. 'So you do care,' I say, a fraction more serious this time.

He closes his eyes briefly, then says a quiet, 'Yes, I care.'

It crosses my mind to lean back a little farther, but even I know when to stop.

He strides over and snatches my hand. He yanks me up so that I almost fly into him. My heart slams as his hand stays clamped around mine, a flare of desire in his eyes. I think he's going to kiss me. Every atom of my existence is convinced of it, is drawing to it; I can almost already taste it. We are so on the brink of it that I am almost fully lost to him. But then he says, 'You need to sort your shit out.' His eyes register my surprise for a beat – or three. Then he lets go of my hand.

I don't even know what part he's specifically referring to, but a tidal wave of disappointment washes over me, almost wiping me out. 'Because I asked your advice,' I say, my voice tremoring with my injured pride. 'Because, clearly, you know so much about marriage and relationships. Because... why? Oh... wait! You write about it, rather than actually live it. Or I should say you *used* to write about it. But you don't any more.'

He turns and shoots daggers at me, the wind whipping our hair around our faces. I pluck mine out of my eyes. My heart hammers, a thousand regrets filling the stiff silence.

When I can get hold of my emotions, I say, 'You can't see me with no clothes on, and then listen to me while I bear my soul and give me nothing in return.' I try to say it levelly, but I am almost choking on the echo of my own despair.

I search his face for some sign of understanding – something. Anything. But he just stares an inch past my head, gazes out across the caldera. Stoic. Intractable.

'Definitely got no appetite now!' I barb.

He suddenly snaps out of his pensive stupor. He turns and strides off down the hill.

'Where are you going?' I ask his back, watching his long legs, the angry bounce of his shoulders.

'To eat, Einstein,' he says. 'Sorry you're not coming.'

TWENTY-SIX

I follow him into the restaurant, because, yeah, I'm hungry too. Harriet and Aiden are not in this one, either. It doesn't take a genius to know this, because there is literally no one here besides us. Frank orders two rakemelo, which the waiter tells us is a grape-based spirit heated with honey and a cinnamon stick 'to warm you up,' as the guy says.

When he sets two menus down then leaves, Frank says, 'I'll tell you, if you want. But prepare to go off me in a big way.'

'That's okay,' I say. 'I was never on you, so it shouldn't be a problem.' And then I repeat what he once said to me. 'Begin at the beginning. The place where the least challenging fiction starts.'

And so he does.

'Meet young Frank...' He slides the cutlery to the side to stop himself from playing with it. 'Twenty-three. First year as a high school English teacher. Small town. Young wife. Baby on the way. Kid's born. We call him Aiden after Rachel's Irish grandfather. It's not always easy. There's young couple struggles. Not much money. Grown-up responsibilities on inexperienced shoulders. Frank works long days teaching, then coaching hockey, and on the side, he's writing a novel.' He upturns the palms of his hands. 'Flash forward two years. Book's published. They move to a bigger house in a better neighbourhood. Get a part-time nanny so Rachel can go to graduate school. Frank could afford to give up teaching but the job's a part of him now. Plus, by keeping this aspect of his old life, he gets to keep it real.'

I can't look away from the picture he's painting, rather enchanted by how he's talking about himself in the third person.

'Movie rights get sold. There's talk of him writing it. Then it isn't just talk. He suddenly has agents, managers, and he's taking three months away from his family to write in a log cabin in Tahoe that the studio leases for him. Next his kid is three-and-a-half. They've moved to an even bigger house. His wife finished graduate school. And then...'

I am hanging on his every word.

'A seventeen-year-old student makes an accusation against me.'

'Accusation?' I'm sure he must see my head almost fly back in surprise.

'Sexual harassment.'

'Oh.' My eyes drop to the untouched basket of bread between us. 'Wow.' Those words write themselves out in my mind.

When I look up again, he is studying me closely. 'You want to ask me if it's true.'

I flounder at first. 'I don't know, Frank... I suppose it's the natural question.'

He nods, like he's absorbing this. 'She was a just a flirty kid. Hangs back after class, asks thoughtful questions, blushes a lot.' He smiles almost tragically. 'I was her high school English teacher. I wasn't *that* much older than she was, and yet I'd written this book and movie and it was a *love story*.'

I search his face, my mind buzzing in all corners.

'I was headed into a bar for a buddy's thirtieth. It was a

Saturday night and I rarely went out without Rachel in those days. We were in line to get in, and, next thing I knew, she was there – this kid – with her friend. She was all *Hello, Mr Lewis...* She'd clearly been drinking. They were wearing provocative clothing and a lot of make-up. I barely recognised her at first. Then she asked if I could get them in.' He looks almost bewildered; the past has become present again and the dilemma has closed back in on him. 'I said no, you're underage, and even if you weren't, I'm not that guy who has pull with doormen. So they left. About a week later, I got called into the head's office. Two police officers were waiting to speak to me.'

My heart flares. 'What happened?'

'I was suspended, had to retain a lawyer. Publisher dropped me. I was still contractually committed to being on the promotion circuit for the movie studio, but then somehow this got out and, naturally, all these questions started to come up.'

A woman walks by the window with a three-legged mutt struggling behind her. 'Had you actually been charged at this point?'

'No. And nor was I. But it was the whole "no smoke without fire" thing, wasn't it? At the merest hint of scandal, people were prepared to believe it was true. Because, as we well know, in ninety-nine per cent of these situations it *is* true. The guy *has* done what the woman is accusing him of.'

I search for outrage or anger, but his face has lost all expression.

'The parents lawyered up. There was the very real possibility that, even if they couldn't charge me with anything criminally, there might be a civil case and I could stand to lose everything financially.' He drags a hand across his mouth. 'It was rough. It made the local media. My wife could barely leave home without comments and glances. People painted crude messages on the side of the house. I even got a death threat in the mail.'

The waiter comes by, takes our haphazard order because we haven't paid the menu much attention.

'Anyway,' he says, when the guy leaves, 'the kid's best friend ended up coming forward. Apparently, it was common knowledge that she'd had a crush on me. After I didn't help them get into the bar, she'd told this friend, *I'm going to make him pay*. So the investigation was dropped, and it all went away. From a legal standpoint, anyway.'

'She wanted you to pay? But you hadn't done anything!'

'I guess that was why.'

I try to get my head around all that he's saying. I wonder how I missed this online. I suppose if I'd googled him more extensively, and not got side-tracked by one or two fascinating articles... 'So, was there an apology? Did your publishers take you back?'

'Apology? No. Like I said, it all just blew up then died a death.'

'What happened to your teaching?'

'I never went back to teaching. The whole thing... it was a very bad experience for me. I should have come out of it stronger, looked upon the whole thing as character-building, but I felt wronged, and it changed me on some level.'

I think of that younger man being interviewed by Darcy Delaney. The guy who had the world at his feet. Who'd wanted to keep teaching because it kept him humble. And then it all comes crashing down.

'I wrote a few other novels, but they weren't my best work – as you correctly observed. After all that shit had gone down, well, I had some problems writing the sort of story that came naturally to me.'

'And your marriage?'

'It was the end of us.'

'She left you because of the scandal?'

'No. I left her.'

I must look confused.

'She asked me the one question you were about to ask. She said, "Did you do it?"'

'Wow,' I say. I realise I'm saying a lot of wows. 'You left her because she doubted you? That seems a little extreme, surely?'

'Maybe to some. And maybe it was. Like you just said, it's the natural question. And it is, of course – from strangers, but not from your wife. Not from anyone who knows you. Really knows your integrity, your moral code.'

I stare at the plate of grilled sardines glistening in greenish olive oil that the guy popped down in front of us.

'I tried to get past it. Told myself I was just being hard on her because I was angry at the situation in general. But I just kept seeing her face when she asked me. That mix of accusation and dread. She feared I was that guy.'

I try to imagine people saying that your husband is the monster in the room, and you longing to discredit it, to take him at his word – but fearing being that woman who lets the whole of womankind down by taking the side of a dangerous predator. I don't know what to say.

'I stayed a couple more years. But in my heart, I couldn't think of her in the same way any more. I just kept coming back to the same thing. She'd been prepared to believe the worst of me.'

'Good grief. This is so sad!'

He scoops up a sardine on a hunk of bread, but the bread doesn't make it to his mouth; he sets it down on his plate. 'I did my best to be a stable part of Aiden's life, but the reality was he grew up in a broken family and there was a lot of bitterness in the subtext of everything. His mother never quite forgave me.'

'She stayed in love with you?'

'I can't get inside her head,' he says, a little too quickly. 'She met someone else. They were together eleven years – almost up until she became ill. But Rich wasn't the best stepfather to

Aiden. I think he resented him because he was the product of this first relationship that cast such a big shadow.'

'Because the book was based on Rachel. You were the love of each other's life.' I had suspected it. Mainly because Ford felt so real to me. I felt he was writing something he knew.

'Yes,' he finally says, almost like he hasn't said it at all.

He has turned pale. When I think we're leaving it there, he says, 'Part of me thought that if I'd never written a book about a young woman who dies, then maybe Rachel might still be alive. She didn't die in her twenties like Lara, but she still died young. Forty-one.'

'But that's crazy! It's not like it was some self-fulfilling prophecy.'

'But life did imitate art in a way.'

'I thought you said it never does.'

'Maybe I was just hoping.'

There is a lull now and I find myself trying to digest all this. Is this why there doesn't seem to be anyone else in his life? Because he couldn't get over his scar?

'Years later, I mean we're talking over a decade, I received a letter through the publisher of *Love for Lara*. It was from a Joanne Levarre. The name meant nothing. Turns out Levarre was my old student's married name. She apologised for making a false allegation against me. She said, if it was any consolation, her life had been ruined by it too. She said she'd thought we shared a special friendship and that she was in love with me. She said she'd had therapy for years to try to work out why she'd done it. She said she was a maladaptive dreamer.' He raises a wry eyebrow. 'You'll have to look that one up. Anyway, she had two kids and a divorce behind her, and she said it was actually her therapist's idea that she should write me a letter of apology, in an effort to finally move on.'

'That's amazing!' I feel so exonerated on his behalf. 'Did you write back? Did she leave an address?'

'She did. But I didn't.'

I think about what I would have done. The possible down-side of triggering further communication. And, besides, what was he going to say? Thanks?

'How did reading it make you feel?' I ask.

He huffs, mirthlessly. 'Surprised, obviously. I think there were times over the years when I'd managed to doubt myself. Had I unwittingly encouraged her feelings? What could I have done differently? In a way I felt like I'd been vindicated. I wanted to hold it up and say, see, I wasn't that guy you all so quickly assumed me to be. I wasn't the entitled asshole, the sexual predator that seems to be everywhere we look these days... Of course, no one would have cared at that point. Prob-ably no one ever did care. In the grand scheme of things, it was a small story that came and went and made no impact on anyone's life – except mine.' Then he adds, 'And Rachel's and Aiden's, and my parents' of course. And anyone else who went to bed with a ball of puke sitting in the back of their throat wondering if I really was that guy.' He looks at me as though he's properly seeing me again. 'Then I felt bad for her. She was a kid. It had haunted her for a decade. It took some guts to say she was sorry. I had no desire to trigger any sort of communica-tion with her, but I didn't really hold it against her. Not when I thought about it.'

'I doubt I'd have felt as charitable.'

He cocks his head. 'You know what, I bet you would have. We all make mistakes, have some wrong we'd like to make right.'

'Not one that damaged someone else's marriage and career.'

He looks at me with that note of tenderness back in his expression again. 'A maladaptive dreamer, if you want to know, is someone who spends an unhealthy amount of time engaged in elaborate daydreams that impact their ability to live their daily life. Often those daydreams are of a romantic nature.'

I stare at his patient mouth, the twelve o'clock shadow that disappears beneath the collar of his white shirt, his kind eyes. I try to put myself in the shoes of a young girl confronted with a young Frank, and I think, yes, I could see how someone could become maladaptive over you.

'So, if you could live it all over again, would you have stayed with Rachel?' It's a bold question but it's out now, like the new intimacy between us.

He tilts his head back, gazes at the ceiling. 'Oh man, if I could live the years over, I think I'd have liked to have reacted differently, maybe not be so led by my principles. When you're in your twenties you hold yourself and the world to a higher standard. It's the perspective that comes with time that makes you re-see things... But no. I don't think staying with Rachel would have been the right choice because, ultimately, we are who we are, and we can't change our values. Not the fundamental things. Not what makes you tick as a human being.' A brighter look crosses his face. 'Besides, I'm a fuck-up, and it's probably best that no one else had to be exposed to that on a daily basis.'

'I disagree. I don't think you're a fuck-up. Not at all.'

'Thanks.'

'Go on... You're thinking, *that's because you, yourself, are a fuck-up, so you're hardly one to judge.*'

He laughs, not quite a proper laugh, but I'm glad I managed to make him do it. 'You may need to get a higher opinion of yourself,' he says. Then he adds, 'But I like that you said that. I like it very much, Moira Fitzgerald.'

We eat. We leave. We head back down the hill in the direction of our hotel. I find myself in a state of extreme reflection. We are walking closer after all those intimate revelations. His left hand is so near to my right one, like a body part has just decided to put itself there on the off chance that someone might want to take a hold of it. I have never been more conscious of a hand.

'You married young, Frank. I married young. And look where that got both of us,' I say, quite out of the blue. 'Do you think if our marriages had been spectacular successes, we'd have been so against Harriet and Aiden?'

'I don't know,' he says. 'They're not us.'

'But maybe we thought we weren't us when we were their age.'

'Don't let your experience turn you into a cynic.'

'That's rich,' I say, 'coming from you.'

He turns his head and I see the edges of his smile. 'I'm rooting for one of us. I'm a lost cause, so it's all on you.'

We've arrived back at the hotel. I'm anticipating he's going to say goodnight, but instead he raises an eyebrow and says, 'Hot tub?'

TWENTY-SEVEN

'I might just take off my clothes right here,' I say.

When he looks pleasantly taken aback, I qualify: 'What I mean is, this day has gone on forever. If I go up to my room to change, I might never come back down.'

He nods. 'You do that. I'm gonna go up and change.' And then he takes off across the patio.

The water is wonderful after the cold night air. The floodlit pool is the only object calling out a shape against the indigo sea and sky. Off in the distance, a lone beam from an oligarch's yacht cuts through the darkness, perhaps on its way to Mykonos, and the winking lights of Imerovigli pepper the cliff-side, a little constellation of existence that reminds us we are not alone. I try to relax and concentrate on the feel of the hot water gently rolling against my skin, but now I'm stricken with unease.

Even though you've just had very a serious – arguably castrating – conversation with him, and you're feeling closer to him because he's confided in you, being in a hot tub in your underwear with Frank is probably a very, very bad idea. In fact, there's hardly a probably about it.

I'm just about to run for the hills when I hear, 'Well, hello.'

When I turn, he is standing there in his white towelling robe brandishing two bottles of water like the fairy godfather. Something about him is a tiny bit apprehensive, or maybe that's just my imagination.

'I asked the Lord for beer, and he answered with these instead.' He sets the bottles down on the ledge, shrugs off the robe, and comes and stands right beside me, his bare feet inches from my shoulder. My eyes do a lightning sweep of his body. Even though I have touched him and kissed him intimately, the one thing I never got to do in our passionate frenzy was to just let myself appreciate the sight of him with no clothes on.

He's fit. Not quite Daniel Craig when he walked out of the water, but his shoulders are big, his waist narrow, and his legs are strong. He lowers himself in, and the temperature in this thing seems to go up two hundred degrees, making my face blaze.

'Mmm...' He tips his head back, his left arm grazing my right one, an electric tingle travelling down my spine.

'You could sit over there you know.' I indicate the opposite side. 'It's not like we're expecting ten more people.'

'Why?' He slides me a lazy, amused look. 'I like being near you.'

I stare at the defined little hills and valley of his top lip, the patient, good-natured way that mouth flicks up at the edges. That mouth that I have kissed. That mouth that has explored my most private of places.

'This is nice,' he says.

Oh, it was, I think. *It really was.*

And then my other voice barges in:

Don't romanticise him. He doesn't want a married woman any more than you need to be a married woman who wants him right now. This is not the solution to anything. Nat is right.

Besides, he may hold women to impossibly high standards. At least Rupert never did that.

His left arm is now fully pressed against my right, like we are of one arm, like our skins have sought the other out. Every inch of me is on fire, my pulse pounding in my temples.

'I'm shrivelling up,' I say. 'Might not last long.'

'I can't say I've got that same problem.'

'Oh God.' I close my eyes.

'Oh God, what?' There's a smile in his voice.

'You know something?' he says, right as I'm aware that my crotch is actually throbbing because of this arm resting on mine. 'You've got a lot of freckles on your chest, but not a single one on your face.' He is sweeping my decolletage like I am enchanting to him. 'Did you get that laser stuff done? Have them blasted off the surface of the earth?'

'You have such a colourful way of describing things, Frank. It must be the writer in you.'

He just moved his hand. The back of his knuckles just made accidental contact with my thigh. The air is gridlocked in my chest because he isn't moving his hand away. The hand has not moved.

'It was just my roundabout way of saying they're charming.'

'Very roundabout. But thanks.' I try not to concentrate on the fact that I can still feel him inspecting my entire epidermis, his eyes like hot pulses of curiosity on my skin. And I remember how his warm mouth explored places no man other than Rupert has explored, igniting me in ways that Rupert never has. The way I have longed to feel, without ever allowing myself to dwell on its absence.

'*You* are charming, by the way. Not just your freckles.' His voice has taken on a disarmingly tender quality again.

'Well... thanks... For the, er, plethora of compliments.'

'Pleth-or-a,' he repeats.

The hot tub is going to be a very bad idea. A very bad idea indeed.

I close my eyes again, and I'm hit with a flash of myself on top of him, how he so naturally positioned my hips to better have an orgasm – a tiny adjustment, like a bolt coming loose by vibrations. How it worked. How Rupert would never have thought of that. How our lovemaking always lacked a bit of artistry, lacked soul. We never stared deeply into one another's eyes when we were engaged in the most intimate act two people can engage in. Our eyes rarely met.

'And you know what else you are?' I hear him ask. His thumb absently moves against my leg so that the entire area south of my navel is now buzzing and pulsing like a thousand cicadas have begun nesting – or starting a war.

About to spontaneously combust with longing?

'No, Frank. But I think you're going to tell me.'

'You're caring, and kind, and fun. And funny, and fair, and something else...'

'Near naked?' About to pounce on him?

'Well, there's that. Which is pretty epic.'

His tone tells me he's trying to be serious, so I try to pull my mind back from the graphic hot tub sex scene writing itself in my mind.

'But also,' he says, 'you didn't ask me if it was true... The rumour about me.'

It takes me a moment to process that he has taken us back to that. 'Didn't I? I think I did.'

'No. You said it was the natural question for people to ask. But you didn't ask it.'

'Hmm... Well... I don't know why I didn't. I mean, you seem like a decent person to me.'

Didn't he once say those words to me?

'But of course, as we said, lots of guys who appear decent are the very opposite.' He is listening like he wants me to go on, so I do. 'It's just a feeling I have about you, I suppose. I'm obviously not right all the time about people. But my instincts are generally my sonar in a black ocean, so I try to trust them.'

'I like that,' he says after he tries it on for size. 'I like it a lot.' And then he surprises me by saying, 'Thank you for thinking that way about me.'

The oligarch's yacht shimmers in the distance, its white lights changing to blue. Our arms remain together, a companionable silence between us. Some of the sexual tension has diffused but has been replaced by something equally as beguiling to me. 'I also want to tell you that I'm sorry,' I say.

'Sorry?' He looks puzzled.

'For making that comment about you not writing any more. The fact that you...' *Had a hard time writing the stories that came naturally to you. So now you don't write at all.*

He cuts me off with a quiet, 'It's okay.'

We let this settle, then I say, 'You wrote an incredible novel full of emotional honesty about the woman you loved. I think that's the most unique and wonderful thing anyone could do.' The intimacy of our conversation makes me yearn to lean into him. To smell him, taste him, to imprint with him. To let myself be that woman I was in his arms.

'Thank you,' he says. Then, after a lull he adds, 'She gave me a hard time when we met because she thought I had a high opinion of myself... Unwarranted, of course.' The tell-tale smile of someone retrieving a memory that never went to its final resting place, and probably never will.

'Just like Ford in *Love for Lara*.'

'Just like Ford,' he says.

'No one will ever write a book about me,' I say, almost tragically, though it sounds a little self-serving, like I'm fishing for something.

'How do you know?' He is looking at me in a certain open-ended way.

'I suppose I don't know,' I say.

A black cat trots along the ledge of the floodlit swimming pool, and I wonder where he's going so purposefully. To a rendezvous with a secret feline friend?

'Was there never anyone else?' I ask, and I feel his bicep twitch against my arm. Every nerve in my body has become wired to his.

'Never really met anyone else. Never really looked, I suppose.'

'But hasn't that been lonely?' I stare at his handsome face in profile. I suddenly want to know everything there is to know about this man. I am craving it like I crave air.

'I'm not a monk,' he says, mildly scathing. 'But I guess after a time you just get used to being mostly on your own. You get into the habit of dwelling in your own head.'

'How is that healthy though?'

He turns and meets my gaze. 'Never said it was healthy.'

'No online dating?'

'Too old-fashioned for that.'

'Younger women?' I tease.

'Nice skin. Not enough life experience.'

'So you're not a cliché then?'

'I strive to be anything but a cliché.' He looks at me candidly. 'I had one long relationship. Five years. More a friendship with benefits. Maybe a touch more.'

'What happened?' I am loving this back and forth.

'Just ran out of conversation, I guess.'

I think about me and Rupert. How most of our conversation is either about Harriet, or what we've got lined up to watch on Netflix. Have I ever talked with a man the way I am talking with Frank? I think I know that answer. I think that answer is no.

'I wasn't really looking for a big commitment,' he says. 'And I didn't want to just have people come and go in Aiden's life.

And then time just passes so very quickly. The older you get, each year seems to consist of fewer than three hundred and sixty-five days.'

'So true,' I say. Sobering and true. I pull a face. 'I'm not sure I'd want to marry again, either. Having to learn a new person's history, navigate all those gaps in his knowledge about mine.' I catch myself saying something I don't even know is correct.

'You'd just do casual relationships?'

'Hmm... Not sure I'm a casual sex sort of person. Knowing me, I'd fall in love.'

I realise what I've just said.

He catches on to it quickly. 'But you don't believe in being in love, remember?'

'Don't I?' I smile rather ruefully. 'Oh yes. You're right. I forgot.'

After a contemplative spell of our gazes hanging together, he says, 'I've had casual sex, but I'm not really a casual person...'

The way he leaves it there makes me want to pick up the ball, but I don't know where to run with it.

And then he says, 'Moira, I...'

He is looking at me so intently that I find myself hanging there, in almost excruciating suspense.

'Tell me,' I say. I want to say, *Better yet. Don't tell me. Just kiss me. Kissing me will make up for all the difficult things we might struggle to say.* But he just searches my face – searches and searches – like he's running outcomes in his mind. The tension is so thick I cannot defuse it.

We are back in Athens. Back outside that hotel room door.

'Look,' he says. He is nodding to himself like he's just flipped a coin only to find it's the same on both sides. 'Whatever my selfish desires... I'm not the kind of guy who tries to take what might not be available.' He tips his head back, closes his eyes, and my eyes run the length of his throat where I long to kiss him. 'What happened between us in your apartment... That wasn't about me, was it? That was about him.'

It's too blindsiding. The question. The way he is looking at me. My eyes tick around his face, what I'm on the brink of saying already cancelled by the time it's taking me to say it.

'Got it,' he says, curtly, flat.

At his reaction, I fill with a something akin to panic. I'm about to say *No! You haven't got anything!* But then his phone rings.

We process its arrival like it dropped from outer space.

'Aren't you going to get it?' I ask.

'Nope.' He sits there stiffly, his mouth set in a hard line. Then he surprises me by hoisting himself out of the tub in one swift movement. His phone is still ringing. He reaches for a towel and starts drying himself off with his back to me.

'It might be Aiden,' I say.

He tugs the towel across his shoulders. 'Fuck it.'

The strength of his reaction makes me bolt back.

His phone stops ringing.

Mine starts.

I stare at my bag lying on top of my clothes, too far out of my reach, an unsettling feeling brewing in me.

'Aren't *you* going to get it?' He wraps the towel around his waist. Then he looks at me with so much hostility that it almost takes my breath away.

What the hell just happened?

I am almost too paralysed to move. But then the ringing stops.

His rings again.

Our eyes meet, joined in the same thought: something is wrong.

He picks his phone up from the chair. I see the slight frown. 'It's Aiden.'

Something inside of me just falls away and my heart start a

furious beating. 'What is it?' I clamber out of the tub, as he is saying, 'Hello, son.'

The cold air slaps me to my senses. I grab a towel, clutch it to me as I stand there shivering in my sodden underwear. I can hear Aiden's voice but not what he's saying.

'Okay...' Frank latches onto my eyes, holds them while he tells Aiden that we're actually here in Santorini, that we came to surprise them.

But there's no pleasure in his voice. This is not a man who is letting his son in on a fun big surprise.

'What's going on?' A wave of dread climbs my gullet; that sickly sensation I've had so many times in the course of being a mother; the knowing with certainty what you can't yet know. 'What is it?' I press.

I'm so cold, my jaw has gone stiff, and my teeth are chattering. I reach for my wool hoodie but am too stressed to remember how to dress myself.

'We'll be there shortly,' he says to his son. He clicks off. There's a brief hesitation where he seems to take in the trembling mess of me.

'Please don't panic,' he says, 'but Harriet is in the hospital.'

TWENTY-EIGHT

I don't really know what happens next, or in what order. I go upstairs and throw on dry clothes. The front desk guy calls us a taxi. Maybe it's island time, or because it's 10 p.m., but we seem to wait an eternity for it to arrive. *Argument. Harriet missing. Pneumonia.* In the taxi, flashes of dark sea and structural white go by, all of it dazzling me.

'Stop torturing yourself,' he says. His hand on the seat seems to instinctively slide towards mine, but his baby finger stops just shy of my own. 'She's going to be okay.'

Pneumonia.

Missing.

While I was half naked in a hot tub, thinking how much I wanted to join every part of my body with the man who was in there with me, my daughter was lying in a hospital bed? This is so awful I can hardly bear to think about it.

Aiden is waiting for us at the entrance. He is pale and drawn, his hair all over the place, dark circles under his blood-shot eyes; nothing like that self-assured young man I met in Malibu. More like a kid who's just realised that adulting is overrated.

'Dad!' He steps forward into Frank's embrace.

I watch them hug, Frank's solid, spontaneous embrace. He's a good dad; the thought just travels to me. No one hugs their son like that if they're not a good dad. When they pull away, Aiden turns to me and his face blazes red. 'I'm very sorry, Moira. This is all my fault.'

Fault.

'What happened?' I ask, pinning him to the ground with my gaze.

It takes him a moment, then he says, 'We had a big fight. She was really furious with me, and she took off.'

'When was this?' I glance at Frank who won't meet my eyes.

'Last night,' Aiden says. 'She took off and she was... she was gone all night.'

'What the hell do you mean she was gone all night?'

Frank says, 'Hey, maybe we should chill and maybe sit down.'

'I don't want to chill and sit down,' I throw back. 'I want to know why my daughter was out all night.'

Aiden looks horribly out of his depth. 'Like I say, we had a fight. I went looking for her. I... When she came back this morning, she was cold and hungry, and she had this terrible cough.'

'I need to speak to a doctor.' I search around. The small waiting area has only a few people in it. A kid nursing his arm like it might be broken. His mother tinkering on her phone. An elderly Greek man and his wife. A teenage girl holding a puke bucket. 'Harriet had pneumococcal meningitis when she was nine,' I say. 'She was very, very sick and spent two weeks in hospital.'

I remember the girl guides' weekend. The headache, stiff neck, confusion. Me rushing her to hospital and the young doctor almost making light of it. Me saying no, no, no, it's not just some virus. Rupert beside me, little more than a bewildered bystander. His words: *Darling, the doctor thinks she's fine.* But then they did the tests I insisted they do, and she wasn't fine.

Frank puts a hand on my lower back, tentatively, then takes it away. 'Don't start jumping to conclusions. We'll hear what the doctor says, and if we're worried, we'll get a second opinion.'

We.

I stare helplessly into his eyes, longing to take his comfort, but at the same time, conscious that I am not entitled to it. The doctor walks through a set of doors. 'Mr and Mrs Fitzgerald.' He looks straight at Frank.

I tell him I'm Harriet's mother, but this is *not* her dad.

Aiden says, 'And I'm Harriet's fiancé.'

Frank says, 'She's right. I'm just Frank.'

The doctor looks puzzled, but then addresses me. 'Okay, Mrs Fitzgerald... We did a chest X-ray. Your daughter has pneumonia. We have her on a strong antibiotic, giving her a little bit of oxygen and some rehydration. You do not need to worry too much. She will be fine.' His tone is all smiley-faced emojis and a big, yellow thumbs-up.

I search his expression. 'Fine? That's it? But... you don't realise... Harriet had pneumococcal meningitis when she was nine. Is this going to turn into—' I try to rush it all out because I can tell we're his brief pitstop on the way to somewhere else.

He cuts me off with a nod. 'She told me.' He places a firm hand on my arm. 'I understand your concern. But the two are not related. Having pneumococcal meningitis as a child did not make her more susceptible to pneumonia on her holiday to Greece, nor will it impact her recovery.'

'She got pneumonia just from being out all night?' Frank asks somewhat sceptically.

The doctor shakes his head. 'Not exactly. Though she is not the first tourist to underestimate how fickle the weather on Santorini can be in March!' He smiles at us again. 'Most likely she was exposed on the plane, or in a restaurant. Then maybe she is a little run down, a little stressed, her immune system a little low, and... bam! She winds up in the hospital in Santorini.' He looks at me again. 'We gave her a stronger antibiotic just because of her medical history, just to be cautious, but there is no reason to worry. We will keep her in overnight to help her breathe better, but tomorrow most likely you can come and get her.'

'She can't breathe?' I say, almost breathless myself.

I feel Frank's hand on my back again. The doctor is still smiling. 'She is fine,' he repeats. 'You might want to give her a day or two before you travel home. Coughs on aeroplanes these days... But she will be feeling better on the antibiotic very soon.'

'And how long before she's fully back to normal?' Aiden asks.

The doctor says, 'The lungs are like a sponge soaking up all that bacteria.' He makes a grabbing gesture with his hand. 'So before all that cleans up properly... Four to six weeks.'

Aiden's says, 'Oh, man.' And he looks at his feet.

'You want to see her?' He asks it like he's a tour guide seeing if we'd like to visit the ruins.

'Yes,' Aiden and I say together but I flash him a look.

The doctor starts walking and we're supposed to follow, but Frank touches Aiden's arm and says something I don't hear. Then Frank says to me, 'You go see Harriet first.'

I try to send him a thank-you with my eyes, but his gaze falls away.

Aiden says, 'Please just tell her I'm really, truly sorry, and...' He lowers his eyes, possibly so I don't catch the tears in them. 'Tell her I love her.'

This is all my fault...

Frank pats Aiden on the shoulder and says, 'She will, son. She will.'

In her room, Harriet is propped up with pillows, attached to oxygen and an IV. Her face is ashen and her eyes red from lack of sleep. She looks smaller somehow, stripped of the vitality that is so my daughter.

'Mum?' She scopes me out, frowns. 'Wait a minute... Am I dreaming?'

I push a rogue tear from my cheek, force a smile. It reminds me of when she used to have nightmares as a kid and didn't recognise me at first when I crept in to comfort her. 'No, love. You're not dreaming. I'm here. Frank and me. We came to surprise you for your wedding.'

I don't know whether it's a processing thing, or because right this minute she's incapable of showing joy, but she just looks at me blankly. And then she bursts into tears.

I hug her. I kiss her clammy forehead. She cries and wheezes, and then makes a stoic effort to right herself and blow her nose. I perch beside her on the bed. 'I'm so sorry,' she says. 'I'm just so sorry.'

She upturns her palm to meet mine, and I'm blasted back to ten years ago when I sat by her hospital bed and did pretty much this same thing. For hours. Days. Me and Harriet. My parents. His parents. Rupert was always dropping in, hurrying out. Showings. Closings. Got to dash. Grimace. Leave you to it then.

'You have nothing to be sorry about,' I tell her. 'You haven't done anything.'

She is staring at a fixed point on the bed cover. Her dark hair hangs lank around her shoulders, her crown slick with grease. 'I'm just sorry you came all this way,' she croaks. 'We're not getting married, so you both wasted your time.' No sooner are the words out than she does an ungodly wheeze that makes the others pale into insignificance, and panic ignites my every last nerve. I am assuming she means they are no longer getting married given they've had some sort of fight but then she says, 'Mum, we were never getting married. Not here in Greece, not this weekend. I'm really sorry. We were both just so mad at you guys that we just wanted to get away.' She hangs her head for a second or two, while I try to make sense of what she's just said.

'There was never going to be a wedding in Santorini?' I hear my own bemused voice. 'You were never eloping?'

'No.' She shakes her head, her cheeks reddening. 'When I said that bit about *think of us this Saturday*... I'm sorry. I knew exactly what you'd assume. I suppose I just wanted to...' She frowns like she's going to cry again. 'I wanted to reinforce that I am an adult and you don't get to control me.' She says it firmly. As firmly as you can when you're wheezing. 'But it's beside the point anyway, because I'm so annoyed at him!' It comes out in a rasp of nerves and emotion which sets off a full-blown coughing fit. 'Ow...!' She cuddles herself around her middle. 'It hurts like billy-o.' Her dad's favourite expression that manages to make him sound both posh and like a relic from another era. Harriet used to mock him for it, then adopted it herself. 'Is he still here?' she asks. 'Is Aiden still outside? Did he tell you what he did? How he *betrayed* me?' She lays that word down like cement with a trowel. 'I don't want him coming in here! I don't want to talk to him or even set eyes on him.'

'Of course not,' I say, my heart sinking. The bastard must have cheated on her. She hacks again, and the rattle of her chest is almost more than I can stand to hear. 'He's not coming in. Don't think about him right now. You never have to see him again. Don't get upset. Please, Harriet.'

Her eyes are streaming, and she wipes her face with the back of her wrist. I spot the box of tissues and pass her a handful. 'I can't believe I trusted him! I can't believe I saw him as this upstanding human being.'

I am boiling with anger. Aiden – the rat standing outside with his father, acting like he loves my daughter – has betrayed her with another girl. I'm going to kill him.

'Please don't think about what he's done right now,' I

implore her again. I just want to hold her and make all this go away. 'I can promise you he's not worth your tears.'

And he'll be dead soon, so there's that.

'I know.' She presses a hand to her side.

'Shush...' I stroke her leg on top of the blanket. 'You're going to be okay. We're going to get you better. We're going home.'

How could he stand there and ask me to tell her he loves her? Ugh! The worm! The wriggling, slimy human tapeworm stuck in someone's colon.

'I promise you, Harriet, this feels massive, but you will get past this. And when you meet a real guy, *the* guy who would never consciously hurt you, you'll realise you dodged a bullet, that this was a necessary part of growing up, and a valuable life lesson.'

She nods and sniffles, a little of the angst subsiding.

By seeing I've been able to comfort her, even in the smallest way, I puff up like a silly, sad superhero. 'You're an amazing young woman. I am so very proud of you.'

She doesn't answer.

'You trust me on this, right? That it's all going to be okay?'

'I trust you,' she says, unconvincingly, and then she struggles out a smile. 'I trust you because you're my mum and you're the one person who genuinely wants nothing but the best for me.'

Yes. To the power of a million.

But so too does Rupert. I'm going to have to call him. What am I going to say?

Her brows pull together again. 'I'm so, so sorry. I can't believe you and Frank came all this way...'

Frank. It suddenly occurs to me that if I'm going to despise Aiden, I have to despise Frank; he's the cheating cad's dad, after all. I think of our time together these last couple of days, the shared confidences, the easy way I can talk to him, and I don't know why, but I suddenly feel horribly unprepared to have to despise Frank.

'Let's get you out of here tomorrow and we'll work out what we're going to do,' I say. 'Maybe we'll spend a few days here, just you and me in a lovely hotel.'

'Okay,' she nods. 'This all feels like a mess. All my stuff is in America but right now I just want to go home.'

'Your term is finished now. You *can* go home.' I squeeze her hand. 'But let's sort all that out later. Let's just get you feeling better first.'

A bubbly young nurse comes in with medication. '*Kalispera*, Miss Harriet!' Her arrival resets us like a breath of fresh air. Harriet responds to her banter like a reflex, takes the pills.

'Mum,' she says. 'It's late. You must be tired. I'm really, really sorry again. Why don't you go and get some sleep.' I'm sure she knows I need permission to stop being a mother hen. 'I'd like to listen to my music and then try to rest.' We agree that I will return first thing in the morning.

Once I reach the door, I turn and wiggle my fingers in a wave. 'Say hi to Frank,' she says.

In the taxi back to the hotel, which the very kind hospital staff called for me, I check my phone. One message from Frank.

Aiden's wiped. He's gone back to his place to try to sleep.

Aiden is wiped. Oh, poor Aiden.
I text him back.

Just on way back to hotel now. I suppose Aiden has told you there never was going to be a wedding in Greece. They weren't eloping.

I wait a while then I see the dots.

Yup!

I wait for a snarky comment. But instead, he types: *How is Harriet?*

Not great, I reply. *Glad they're keeping her in overnight.*

I wait to see if he's going to ask how I am. But after a minute or so passes, he writes: *Let's hope she's a lot better tomorrow then.*

Once I decide that's the end of the communication, I turn my mind to Rupert. I am going to have to call him. But it's so late now that I decide to save that job until tomorrow.

TWENTY-NINE

Frank and Aiden are sitting on the same side of the table when I go down for breakfast, with a couple of coffees in front of them.

'How was she last night?' Aiden asks before I've barely sat down.

He still looks exhausted, like he might have had the same sleepless night as I did.

'Well, she's not very bloody good, is she.' I can barely bring myself to look this boy in the eye.

'Coffee?' Frank chirps.

When I don't respond, he pours me some from a big pot.

I stare out of the window. During the night, all I could think was this is all my fault. I was the one who encouraged her to do a study term in America; Rupert thought it cost too much. I was determined to help her have what she wanted, as though by doing so I'd win the favourite parent award. It's like I was using her to redress some unarticulated balance between Rupert and me; one that probably only I was aware of. And look at the price we've paid.

'You need to tell me what happened,' I say to Aiden. 'All of it.'

He looks like he barely has energy to sit upright in a chair, let alone have *the conversation*. As he wipes a hand across his mouth in a gesture of anguish, I can't help but note his fit arms and upper body, the even-toned complexion – the damn eyelashes – and I completely understand how Harriet could be so taken in by appearances. How she would falsify feelings. How she would desire everything she saw this person representing. And how other girls would, too.

'Let me help you,' I say. 'You cheated on her. And I'm probably going to kill you.'

Frank says, 'Whoa! That's a bit extreme! Maybe you need to hear what Aiden has to say first, rather than put words in his mouth.'

He sends me daggers. I've never seen him so riled; it's like we've suddenly gone onto different teams and we're each in it to win it.

'I don't know why you'd conclude that, Moira.' Aiden looks bewildered. 'There's no other girl.'

I'm about to speak but Frank says, 'Aiden's not that guy.'

I roll my eyes far back in my head. '*Every* guy is that guy.'

He rolls his now.

'It had nothing to do with any other girl,' Aiden asserts. 'I'm not like that. That's not how I conduct myself.' He says it like the very idea is some sort of affront. Clearly, he's a very fine actor.

'Well,' I say. 'That's not what Harriet told me.'

His dark eyebrows draw together again and he shoots a glance at his dad. 'She said I had someone else?'

'Yes.' My heart hammers. 'She... didn't exactly use those words... But...' I can't help but note in my peripheral vision that Frank is watching me with an expression that says, *Uh-oh! This is about to go Moira-shaped.*

Fortunately, the waiter appears and asks us if we'd like to order breakfast. He lists what's on offer – Greek yogurt and honey, omelettes, *pitarakia*, which he says are hot pies made from *mizithra* cheese... I stop listening after that. Frank orders for us.

'You were busy explaining,' I say to Aiden.

After a very uncomfortable intermission, he says, 'I contacted her dad.'

My head whips back. 'What?'

'I found his email and I wrote to him. Despite knowing she didn't want him to know about us, or about her plan to maybe continue studying in America, despite knowing she kinda hates him right now. I did it anyway.'

Rupert's attempts to get in contact – WhatsApp! Now it all makes sense. My eyes slide from Aiden's face to Frank's. 'Back up,' I tell him. 'You contacted her dad?' It wouldn't be hard. Rupert is very findable online and, even if you didn't know he was Harriet's father, you would after you saw his picture. The same blue eyes, the infectious little bunny smile. 'But why?'

Aiden wipes a hand over his face. 'Look, I know he's not a great guy. I don't really know what he did, but...' His cheeks redden again. 'Okay, that's not entirely true; I know a bit about what happened. But he's still Harriet's father. I didn't think it was right to keep something like this from him – that his only daughter was seriously considering finishing her studies in the US, because of me... that we might live together, even get married...' He meets me directly in the eye. 'It felt wrong to me.'

'So you took it upon yourself to meddle in a family matter that had absolutely nothing to do with you?'

He's already shaking his head. 'No. That wasn't my...' He says it uncertainly, as though he's only just this minute gaining perspective on his own actions. 'The way I saw it was, Harriet isn't going to hate her dad forever, and if I do end up being part of the family, I guess I just didn't want it to start out this way.' He drags a hand over his mouth again. 'I just wanted to say, hey, hi... I'm Aiden Lewis and I'm the guy who's in love with your daughter, and I care that, whichever way we move forward, we just kind of do it properly.'

He holds my eyes with an almost admirable intestinal fortitude. 'Plus, I thought that, maybe in a strange way it might help get some communication going between them. She's really suffering because of all this. Despite her maybe telling you she hates him, and her blocking his calls and everything, it's hurting her very much. Because she doesn't hate him...' He searches my face, and then his dad's. 'She wants to be there for you, Moira. If you're not talking to him, then she's not talking to him. That's the way she is. She's loyal. But, well, it's killing her.'

I'm not sure I'm loving how Aiden is reeling off my daughter's personality traits – as though I don't know them. 'So I believe that's the very definition of meddling,' I say.

I hear Frank mutter a very quiet, 'Give him a break,' which I choose to ignore.

Aiden visibly swallows down his gumption. 'I know it was wrong what I did. But if anything, I thought I was being honourable.'

Honourable? What twenty-two-year-old kid bangs on about honour? *I'm the guy who's in love with your daughter...* Does Gen Z even talk this way? It all feels a little 1940s. But then I realise it's exactly because he's got old-fashioned values that Harriet fell for him. She was never going to tolerate a bloke who couldn't show up for his dates.

Then, as though it needs any adding, he says, 'Harriet definitely didn't see it that way, though.'

'No,' I say. 'I expect she didn't.'

I glance at Frank who is carefully monitoring me.

'It's not particularly admirable that you disregarded Harriet's wishes,' I say to Aiden. 'But I'm very glad there wasn't another girl.'

I can almost feel Frank thinking, *Are you going to do the right thing and let it rest now? Or are you going to be Moira and gnaw on his flesh until you penetrate bone?* Then I just find it plain odd that I can read his thoughts at all.

Something else occurs to me. 'How did she end up being out all night, though? I don't understand.' Then it lands. 'Ah... Of course. You told her.'

He takes another quick sip of his coffee. 'I did. Keeping it from her felt wrong in the end.' He clears his throat. 'She was furious. I've never seen anything like it. She stormed out...' He shakes his head, clearly reliving the memory. 'I went looking for her. I searched all over. I went back to the hotel a few times in case she'd gone back. The next thing I knew it was three in the morning. And then I was freaking out.'

I gawk at him – at Frank too, who swiftly looks at the table-top. 'Why didn't you call me?' I ask.

He looks momentarily exasperated. 'I thought you were a world away in LA. What were you going to do from all that distance? The only purpose letting you know would serve would be to make you worry.'

'Of course I'd have worried!' I stare at the warm cheese pies that have just arrived and are giving off an appetising smell, if only I felt like eating. 'But I would have done something. I'd have called the police. A young woman out wandering a strange country in the middle of the night... Why did you think that was okay?'

Frank finally speaks. 'He didn't say it was okay.'

'I don't know,' Aiden answers me. 'All her stuff was here. I knew she'd have to come back at some point. I didn't really think—'

'Exactly. You didn't think. I mean, when *were* you going to contact the police? At noon the next day? When was an alarm bell going to go off in your head?'

Frank holds up the palm of his hand. 'Okay, maybe we're done with the Spanish Inquisition for now.'

'Spanish Inquisition?' I shoot him daggers, my pulse flicking hard in my temple.

'You're right,' Aiden says. 'I should have done something. When she came back, she was coughing pretty badly. I made her some hot food. But it just seemed to get worse real fast. I googled the symptoms and said, look, I think we need to take you to the hospital.'

'And the rest is history!' Frank chimes in, like he's officially had enough.

'What's your problem?' I'm surprised how savagely I turn on him. 'This is *my* child in the hospital, not yours. Do you really think I have no right to ask how she got there?'

He doesn't immediately respond, just holds my eyes, wordlessly, for a spell or two. Then he says, 'I understand that part. And I get why you're upset. But you don't need to attack my son. It was hardly all his fault.'

I play this back. The words, plus the scathing tone. 'Except for the fact that it was your son's actions that started all this!' I can't believe how insensitive he's being. Aiden sits there so obviously uncomfortable with us talking like he's not there.

'I think he's made the point that he's sorry,' Frank says. 'He should have respected her wishes about her father. But he didn't make her run off and stay out half the night in the cold. You can't pin the pneumonia on him.' He throws up his hands and says a spiky, 'Sorry!'

My jaw practically drops to the ground. When I recover, I unleash my sarcasm on him. 'Wow. You make a great point. No one could have said it worse. So, thanks for that.'

I look away, sharply out of the window.

When my heart stops thrashing and I can say it calmly, I say to Aiden, 'Harriet might wear her emotions on her sleeve at times, but she's not a drama queen. All her life this has been what she does when she's hurt or angry. She disappears.' As a kid she'd hide in the small cupboard behind her dad's desk. We'd pretend to look everywhere for her – everywhere except there – to let her have her secret little space. As a teenager, when friendship dramas or exam pressure got too much, she'd take off into town and could be gone a whole day, yet she never came home with any purchases; she'd just been wandering around, finding her balance again. 'Disappearing is how she works through things. You don't know this about her because you don't know her.'

'I'm sorry,' Aiden says again.

Franks holds up the palm of his hand. 'Son, you've said sorry enough. Moira has more than made her point. This stops here.'

Great. Now I'm being refereed. Or parented.

I'm sure this is not one of my finer moments. I'm sure there's a better way to behave. But I stand up sharply, my chair scraping along the ground.

Frank says, 'Where are you going?'

And I say, 'Oh, fuck off.'

THIRTY

When I go back to the hospital, Harriet's doctor breaks the news that her breathing isn't quite where they want it to be, so they're going to keep her on oxygen one more day.

When I go into her room, she is sitting up reading her Kindle. 'Have you heard?' she asks, like it's the end of her world. 'I'm not getting out today!'

I tell her I know. I give her the cheese pie I took from breakfast. Then I tell her I know what happened with Aiden. 'I understand you think he betrayed you, but he was trying to be a good guy. He realises he didn't go about it the way he should have.' I touch her hand. She draws hers back.

'Well, nice to know whose side you're on. Maybe you, Frank and Aiden should go off and be one big happy family.'

'Okay, now you're being a child. I'm not taking anyone's side. I'm trying to be fair. He didn't mean any harm. He thought he was doing the right thing. He's very upset.'

'I'm gutted for him.'

She sounds so much like me. 'You've made your point. Believe me, he gets it. So, it's time to move on from this now.'

My God, I sound like Frank. Who knew I would end up advocating for Aiden instead of wanting him to take a long walk off the face of the earth?

She looks disappointed in me. 'What else do you suppose he'll disregard my feelings over? Make a decision based on what's best for him rather than for me?' Her chest rattles. 'Like you once told me, I didn't really know him. You were right. And now what I do know, I don't like.' She hard-stares out of the window. I can see the bubble of a tear in her eye, can almost feel her willing it not to fall.

'Then you have to talk to him,' I say. 'Either tell him it's over or give him another chance.'

When she doesn't answer, I say, 'Harriet, Aiden is not a doormat. He's not an extension of you. He's an educated, proud, opinionated individual. I don't think you'd be attracted to him otherwise.' I search her face for signs I'm getting through to her, but she won't look at me. 'You're going to have to take the good with the bad with that. And – honestly? I really don't think you want to break up with him over this. You don't have to commit to spending the rest of your life with him, but I'm not convinced ending things with him is what you really want to do either.'

She shoots me the side-eye. I've seen this look a million times and I know exactly what it means; she's coming round to my way of thinking.

After a time, she says, 'I don't know.'

'When you're feeling better, you'll probably see that this is not the end of the world – and maybe not the end of you guys.'

She fiddles with the edging of the blanket. After a long silence she says, 'If I just forgive him, just like that, what message does that send? That all he has to do is wait a day, then everything will be back to normal?'

'Talk to him,' I tell her again. 'Give him at least that much of a chance.'

I am clearly good at giving out relationship advice, but not so good at taking my own.

The side-eye again. 'He can pop in later if he likes.'

When I taxi back to the hotel, I do what has to be done. I text Rupert.

> *Harriet in hospital in Greece. Thought u might like to know. She's going to be fine. She got a cold and it turned to pneumonia.*

I perch on the end of my bed. Reaching out to him, after three months of avoiding him, gives me that same rush of dread as the day I stood on the beach in Santa Monica and told him that I wasn't going back to England with him. That fear of him saying something to weaken my resolve, guilt me into going back to him. Time should have eliminated that worry. And yet here I am with the same fear.

Fifteen seconds later, my phone rings.

'Finally!' he says. 'At long sodding last she contacts me!' He sounds almost breathless. I can almost feel his heart beating down the line. 'You thought I might like to know? Like I'm just some sort of... random human being, instead of her father, the person who helped bring her into this world? You thought I might like to know?'

I open my mouth to speak, but he isn't done.

'You didn't tell me our daughter might not be coming home. Didn't even tell me she had a serious boyfriend! You don't answer any of my calls. You rent yourself somewhere to live on the other side of the world. You didn't even tell me when *you're* coming home—'

'I did,' I say. 'We said three months.'

'No, Moira, *we* didn't say three months. *You* said three months. You said you needed time to think. I never agreed to it. You just left me with no say in the matter...' He sounds so wounded, like his pet gerbil just died. 'It's absurd. I mean, who just decides not to come home?'

'Someone who thinks her husband is screwing someone else, maybe?'

Silence. Then... 'Not this again. You're doing this to me *again*?'

I seethe. 'Of course, let's make this all about you. Here's me thinking your first question might have been how is our daughter.'

'Of course, that's my first question!' he says, in exasperation. There's a contrite beat, then, 'How is she?'

I try to put my anger aside, and just focus on Harriet. I tell him briefly what happened. I say I flew out because I thought they were getting married. I tell him I know Aiden contacted him, and all hell has broken loose because he did that.

'Good grief!' he says, when I'm done. 'This is a nightmare.'

I can picture him mussing his hair. One of those quirks of his where he does it for so long while he's thinking about something, that it goes from being a cute affectation to making him look like he's got a head lice infestation.

'You should have told me,' he says, a bit calmer. 'I mean, I get some stranger calling me with an American accent saying he's in love with my daughter, and that they want to be together to finish their degrees... She can't have known him more than two minutes.'

'Six weeks.'

'How do you fall in love in six weeks?' He shakes his head. 'And you kept it to yourself? Not a single message? I've been trying to call you for days! Couldn't you have picked up? What if I was dying? If I'd been hit by a truck? Or your parents. What if I was ringing with bad news?' He takes the stridence out of his tone again. 'How d'you think this makes me feel, Moira? How is that either normal or reasonable conduct?'

He's right in that I didn't once consider bad news. But I say, 'Under the circumstances, I don't think you're the person to talk about reasonable conduct. I mean, who shows up at Nat's office to flog their sob story? Someone you barely even know?'

'It was my last-ditch attempt to get through to you! How else was I supposed to get around the stonewall?'

My heart hammers, and as messed up as it is, I almost feel a little sorry for him. 'I rang about Harriet,' I say. 'I didn't ring to fight.'

'Who is fighting?' His voice quavers. 'In fact, why don't you ask yourself who is stoking all of this? Because I think you'll find it's you, not me, Moira.'

'Stoking?' Did he say stoking? I get up and walk to the window. A young couple is standing on the pool deck, gazing out at the caldera. They take a moment to kiss. I watch them, let it bring me back to some sort of baseline. 'I am not stoking anything,' I say, calmly. 'I'm reacting the only way I know how, and the way any woman would.'

There is no venom in my tone, only sadness. I am sadder than I thought I had capacity. Rupert and I became a sinking ship, and a part of me – the skipper, the sticker – wants to tow us to shore. Because on some level that is what I've done my whole life; I have navigated us away from trouble, steered us around the iceberg without even calling out that the iceberg is there. A tiny part of me still thinks it might be easier to fix what's broken than to build a new boat.

For some crazy reason my mind flies to Frank. It flies there, and it locks there for a time; it takes me right off course.

Out of the window, the young couple are making a move. I watch how he holds her hand and leads her to the steps, how she briefly dunches his bicep with her head. The honesty of them. Second chance romances, to use Nat's term, are way more complicated than first love.

'Are you still there?' He speaks into the radio silence.

I tell him that I am. There is another choked silence. Then he says, 'Everyone is asking where you are. Even the postman. Can you imagine? The bloody postman thought you might have died.'

I can tell he's overcome with emotion, which makes me press my head with the heel of my hand.

'I didn't cheat,' he says, soberly. 'I have told you that a thousand times. I want you to come home, Moy. I *need* you to come home. Nothing's the same without you.'

I rub a hand around the back of my neck, the tension has me in a vice. I think of what Aiden said about Harriet suffering because of all of this, more than she will admit. Deep down, is she secretly rooting for me to forgive him? Am *I* going to be the one who is the bad guy, if I don't? But then I hear a little voice inside my own head. *Recommit, and there goes the rest of your life...* I picture my parents. The benign little couple in the living room, watching *Coronation Street* together in practically the same chairs for forty years. My mother, lobotomised by her choices.

'I'm going to fly out,' he says, unsurely. 'I need to see Harriet, and you and I need to talk.'

My mind darts to Frank again. Our unfinished conversation in the hot tub. My need to set the record straight. 'No,' I hear myself saying. 'That would be a terrible idea. Harriet needs to get better. If you come, you're going to upset her and that's the last thing we should be doing right now.'

I wait. *Please, please don't say you're coming or I'm going to implode.*

'Alright then,' he says, after an agonising moment. 'If you really think it's going to make things worse, I won't.' I can hear the little-boy-lost quality in his voice.

Oh, thank God. Thank you, God.

'But promise me you'll keep me in the loop and that you'll at least think about coming home, given you're already only a few hours away. So we can sit down and have a proper conversation, face to face.'

'I promise I'll keep you in the loop,' I say.

THIRTY-ONE

I take a big breath in, then let it out. 'Okay,' I say to Frank. 'Telling you to F off might have been a tad extreme.'

He cocks his head. 'Er... you think?'

'I was upset.'

'No. You were *mean*.'

I plonk a hand on my hip. 'I will not own mean. I will – if I'm being pressed – admit that you were right; Aiden didn't cause Harriet to get sick. Harriet's hot temper, that she clearly must get from her paternal grandmother, caused her to make a poor judgement. So I was wrong in saying what I said, and when I'm wrong I admit I'm wrong.' I mutter under my breath, 'Unlike some people.'

He just stares at me, his eyes combing over my face, my collarbones, my decolletage, and I think I see his mouth twitch like it wants to smile. 'Have you eaten?' he asks.

I tell him, yes, no, maybe. I have no idea what time it even is. I tell him what I really feel I could use is a drink. More than anything in the world. A drink, and to breathe.

. . .

'Are you furious at me for dragging us across the world for a wedding that was never going to happen?' I ask.

We have wandered in the direction of Fira and found a little place to have a drink. Raki and honey, warmed. The most perfect marriage in the world. It's still cold but the wind has died back.

'Furious is a little strong. I just view it as one of your quirks.'

'So I'm not perfect then?' I tease. 'Is that what you're saying?'

'You're a person with a lot of heart and a lot of passion, that's what you are,' he says, almost too seriously.

I let that settle for a moment or two.

'So do you think Harriet's going to forgive him?' he asks.

'Don't know,' I say.

'Do you hope?'

'Do you?'

He seems to ponder. 'I guess the fact that this has brought Aiden so much pain tells me that it can also bring him so much happiness. And that's the way it goes, I suppose... Love.' He looks at me meaningfully. 'Pain and great fulfilment. One, you can only hope for; the other keeps it all real.'

We talk about the pair of them for a bit. Share stories about their triumphs, their foibles, their childhoods, how they started to navigate being adults. 'I can't believe we worked so hard to split them up,' I say. 'They *do* seem like they're meant for each other.'

'Look at it this way. If they stay together, it'll be us they have to thank.'

I frown. 'How do you make that out?'

'If they'd never come to Greece to get away from their cynical old parents, their feelings for one another wouldn't have been tested.' He observes me with a rather wistful expression on his face. 'Out of great suffering comes great certainty.'

Not sure that particular adage applies to me.

'I hope she forgives him,' I say. 'If someone has been a special part of your life, occupied a place in your heart, well, life's too short not to try to put it behind you and move on.'

He raises a wry eyebrow. 'Wise words,' he says – as though it's the least wise thing he's ever heard.

Later, when we get back to the hotel, he asks if I want to go in the hot tub again. The memory of our last time in that thing is still all too searing. But he puts it out there like a peace-offering, so I tell him I'm going to my room to make a quick call to check on Harriet first, that I'll see him back downstairs in ten minutes.

He has already climbed into the water when I arrive. I slip my dressing gown off and quickly climb in beside him in my black bra and pants set, the closest thing I've got to a bikini. The water is divine. I tilt my head back, shut my eyes and try to let it soothe me.

When I look at him, his eyes are trailing a path of longing down my throat.

'Why does life have to be so complicated?' I say, apropos of only my thoughts. My shoulder is pressed up against his shoulder again.

'It doesn't,' he says. 'That's the thing.'

I tell him about my phone call with Rupert, that he still claims he didn't cheat, not sure why I'm bringing this up now.

After a beat, he says a sarcastic, 'Awesome.'

'Just updating you,' I say.

I think he's not going to add anything, but then he says, 'You're going back to him. It's obvious. I get it.' His flesh no longer presses against mine. His tone says he doesn't get it at all.

'He wants me back.' I'm almost trying to be deliberately exasperating and I don't know why I'm doing it, why I'm playing this game.

His eyes drill into mine. 'Who wouldn't want you back? And why does it have to be all about what he wants?'

'Why do you dislike him so much?'

'Why *don't* you?'

My turn to be silent now.

'You suspect he cheated with your best friend years ago. You've pretty much got it in writing that he cheated with someone now.'

'What's your point?' I say it almost languidly, almost like this is conversational sport. I just like batting this back and forth with him.

'My point is, how many times does he have to appear to have cheated before you believe he did? Does all this not tell you something worth listening to?'

'Maybe I'm just bad minded.'

'That's right. Maybe the problem is you.'

We let that sit. The weight is back in our silence again. Hot tubs are not exactly the place where we bring our best selves.

I stare at the reflection of the moon on the water. 'I've always had trust issues,' I say. 'Even when I was a kid. I used to fear dying. Not the actual death part. But the point where I'd be lowered into the ground. I was, like, what if they close that lid and start throwing that soil on top, and I'm not actually dead?'

I realise I'm trying hard to make him smile, but he's not going for it.

'So you're afraid of living and you're afraid of dying. So where does this leave you?'

I play that back, and frown. Am I afraid of living? I hate that I'm wondering if there's a grain of truth in that.

'Because of your cheating father, and your loser first boyfriend – and now your shitbag husband – you no longer trust men, but what's worse is you don't even trust yourself. That little voice has told you for a very long time that you're not happy, but you've convinced yourself that, so long as you're not actively *un*happy, you've probably got all you should expect.'

I'm amazed he always remembers everything I tell him. When it's put like that, it does make me sound lame. I think of Nat when she was leaving the sham of her marriage. How she said, 'There's never a good time to tell someone it's over. You've got to just do it; do the hard thing.'

'So what about you and your trust issues?' I say, before my frustration with myself makes me slide into a downer. 'How about we turn the surgical spotlight on you? I mean, are you going to continue to not let anyone get close in case she lets you down just by being human? Are you going to keep using having to parent Aiden as an excuse? I mean, he's not a child now. You can't fuck him up. And, you know what? You should be proud of the fact that you never did.' I am almost out of breath, but I have to say it. 'When are you going to stop using everything that happened to you as a giant excuse for not fully living your life and for squandering your talent?'

I try not to focus on how he looks at me like I just shot some kind of arrow a millimetre from his heart. Or how I started this whole conversation almost for sport, and now we might be going to war again.

'This isn't about me,' he says. 'We weren't talking about me.' And then, after a barbed beat, he adds, 'And why would you care anyway? I'm just the guy you had sex with to get back at your husband. Remember?'

He says it so accusingly that I almost rear up from the water. 'Wow,' I say. 'You really don't let anything go, don't you?'

'Deny it then.' He turns to face me, and I'm surprised to see the longing blazing in his eyes again – and anger, raw anger. 'You can't deny it, Moira, because you know it's true.'

I open my mouth to say: *But back then in my apartment, I knew nothing about you. How could it have possibly been more than what it was when you were a virtual stranger to me?* But he's on a roll.

'Moira, who doesn't do casual sex, had no problem doing it a few weeks ago. No problem there, boy!' He seems to check himself, then adds a quieter, almost empty, 'What happened in your apartment was Moira having no problem with casual sex at all.'

I've got a head rush. My head is literally swimming, a thousand protestations lining up to get out. Instead of attacking me over no-strings sex, shouldn't he just be grateful he got it? Isn't sex without attachment and commitment most men's dream? I go to say all this, but then we hear, 'Hi, Dad.'

No sooner does Aiden appear, than Frank hoists himself out of the water in one swift movement like an Olympic hot-tub leaver. Aiden seems oblivious and perches on a sun lounger. 'The good news is she doesn't want to kill me any more.'

'And the bad?' Frank's voice is torqued with suppressed emotion. He pulls on his dressing gown, while I sink lower under the water in my underwear, until I'm basically just a floating head.

'Don't know if it's bad, actually.' He throws back his head and yawns. 'I don't know what we're going to do about... well, about anything at the moment.' He directs the explanation to me. 'Harriet seems really confused about what she wants.'

Frank says a quiet, 'Seems to run in the family.'

'She's super tired right now,' Aiden continues. 'Hopefully she'll feel better in the morning.'

Frank asks him if he's eaten. Aiden says he had something hours ago at the hospital. Frank says, 'You must be starving, then. We should get you a proper meal.'

'Yeah, okay,' he says, 'I wouldn't say no.' He shoots my floating head a look. 'Do you want to come, Moira?'

'You guys go,' I say.

Neither of them makes a move which makes it impossible

for me to make one either. Then fortunately Aiden says, 'Dad, can I use your bathroom first?' Frank fishes in his pocket, gives him the key.

When he disappears inside, I wait for Frank to look at me, say something, anything to give me a chance to redeem the moment, but there is nothing except pivotal silence.

Finally, I say, 'Can you hand me my dressing gown, please?'

He holds it out to me, deliberately staring off in the opposite direction. I scramble out, take it from him. My undies have glued themselves to every crack and crevice of my anatomy. As if he is unable to resist looking, he turns. His eyes map every contour and elevation of my body until my legs are almost quaking. And then he looks away again, rather deliberately, like a snub.

'Can we talk?' I plead, strapping the belt tightly around me. My voice is soaking with emotion.

'Don't think there's anything more to say.'

'There might be, if you'd ever let me get a word in.'

He stands there rigidly, refusing to look at me.

'Well...' I go on anyway. 'You've sold yourself quite a little narrative about me, haven't you?' Ridiculously, I could almost burst into tears.

'Unlike you,' he flashes me a hostile glance, 'I sell myself only what's true.'

'Ready!' Aiden comes back right as I'm trying to thrust my feet into oversized towelling hotel slippers. I can't see them for my blurred vision. 'Are you sure you don't want to come with us, Moira?' Aiden asks.

Frank says, 'She doesn't. Moira's going to her room.'

THIRTY-TWO

Fortunately, I don't see Frank at breakfast. When I psyche myself up to text him, I get no reply. On my way out to see Harriet, I run into Aiden cantering down the steps.

'Have you seen your dad this morning?' I ask.

He says he hasn't heard from him, that maybe he's sleeping in and he's going to knock on his door now. I tell him I'm heading back to the hospital to see what time they're going to release Harriet, and that I'll catch up with them later this afternoon.

When I get back around 11 a.m. – they said Harriet can get out at 4 p.m. after the doctor sees her – I'm half expecting Frank to be lying on the pool deck because the sun has finally managed to break out and it's almost warm. But there's not a human being in sight, only cats occupying various patches of sunshine. I knock on his door, but he's not in his room. I put my ear to the wood, listen. No sign of life. Feeling more than a bit defeated, I go into my own room. Housekeeping has been so I try lying on the bed, try to surf Apple News, but I can't focus.

I text him again: *Are you angry with me?*

I add some other stuff about how I didn't just use him for

sex, but then I delete it. Then I sit there waiting for the little moving dots. Checking and checking. Nothing. Finally, I grab my denim jacket and wander back down to reception, where I ask the guy at the desk if he's seen any sign of Mr Lewis today.

'Ah yes,' he says. 'Mr Frank. He asked about jet ski rental. I send him to see Nikos at the pier.'

Jet ski rental? I ask him how I can get down to the pier and he tells me where to go to take the cable car.

I spot him right away, the only person out there on the water. He's standing on the shiny white and yellow craft, in his white T-shirt and navy shorts, taking the waves like a pro. I watch him for a while, but he just performs the same repetitive loop, the same turn at either end that kicks up a frothy wave on the one that was slowly fading. Behind me, the jagged edges of the caldera draw my eye up some four hundred feet of the cliff face, to the towns on the rim, etched in white like a French manicure. Frank looks so insignificant out there among all this, a solitary speck of energy and matter.

I walk to the end of a short jetty, and on one of his circles back I holler, 'Frank!' He doesn't seem to hear me, so I shout a little louder. Still, nothing. I wait for him to come back again, and then I start hooting and jumping up and down.

I have no idea if he sees me. But suddenly he throttles it. The craft takes off like he's Superman on steroids, its nose shooting into the air. A wheelie. His body is almost parallel with the water.

'Frank!' I scream, thinking, Jesus, he's going to kill himself. 'Please slow down!'

But the engine revs and roars. He circles in a doughnut. Then a doughnut inside of a doughnut. Some might say it's just a guy out there showing off for the only person watching him, for a woman. But I know different. This isn't a performance;

this is psychotic. It's reckless. I can't watch, and I can't look away.

'For Christ's sake, Frank...'

My voice has run out of power, and I'm hit with another ridiculous urge to burst into tears. What to do? I could rent a jet ski myself, blaze out there... And do what? I've never been even ten feet close to one, let alone ridden one. I could run for help. Nikos at the pier. I'm just deciding that both sound like poor options when...

There's an ungodly splash. Like a pod of giant whales just landed from Mars.

He has flipped the jet ski upside down. He disappears beneath the water.

I wait for him to pop up. My eyes dart around almost convulsively. But I can't see him.

I can't see him. Where the heck did he go?

I search the surface of the water, yearning for any sort of sign. There's nothing. Not a single indication of anything living beneath the slowly calming surface.

He is gone, just like Atlantis.

'Frank!' I shriek.

I don't know how you know these things, but when he hasn't popped back up after I've just tried to count to five, all my instincts say something's very seriously wrong. I am a nervous swimmer. I love looking at the ocean, but not necessarily being in the ocean. But I dive off that jetty. I dive off that thing and I don't even stop to think whether the water is deep enough, that I could break my neck, or drown. I am off that thing before either reason or common sense can weigh in. I am dropping down, down, down, the water filling my ears, my nose. The cold... Oh, the cold. I flap and flail, my dress billowing with my hair. My denim jacket is up around my neck, weighing me down and restricting my movement. I have to fight to get my head above the surface. I am gasping, wrestling with all this

damned fabric, but I make it. Somehow. My head pops up. Air.
I realise I'm alright. For hell's sake, I shoot a glance around and I
still can't see him.

He's dead!

A tremble riddles my limbs now. My body is shutting down
in shock. I tread water, try to keep my head above the surface,
but a cramp is building in my right foot. I tell myself that
panicking is not helping. I mustn't panic.

Don't panic.

Do not panic.

Okay, panic.

'For God's sake, Frank, you fucker! Where the hell are you?'

No sooner do I almost give myself an aneurism from how
hard I'm screaming, than... his head pops up. It pops up and...

It damned well looks straight at me, almost like he knew I
was there all the time. Like he did this deliberately.

He did. He deliberately did it to freak me out. The realisation takes a while to sink in. We are but fifty feet apart. He
doesn't smile, doesn't wave, doesn't say, hey, I'm okay. He just
keeps his eyes anchored on me – firmly on me – while we both
tread water in the blue silence, the jet ski's black hull bobbing
behind him like a dead whale.

Then in one swift movement he flips the jet ski the right
way up. He scrambles on board from the back. There are a
couple of sticky tries of the engine before he gets it to start up.
He potters around in a circle, like he's trying the thing out, like I
am not there again. Then it occurs to me: oh my God, he's going
to drive off and leave me, just like he did that day on the hike.

But instead, he turns its nose to face me, and after another
suspenseful moment or two, putters over. I am shivering, and
the cramp that was forming in my right foot now has me in its
grip. Right when I could almost shout out with the pain of it, he
is there, reaching out a hand. I stare at that hand, the wide
expanse of it. The blondish hairs plastered down, salt forming

thin white cracks on his skin. He thrusts it at me again. He still hasn't said a word. Nor have I.

I grasp it, and he pulls me up. I am shivering and shaking. There's nowhere for me to stand that's far enough away from him, so I have to clutch him around his waist.

'Frank,' I say, my teeth chattering. 'That was a very, very cruel thing for you to do. You selfish sod, you almost gave me a heart attack.' I cling on to him for dear life, so I don't fall off the back of this thing.

He doesn't say a word. He just goes, 'Hmph.'

I don't even know what that's supposed to mean.

The jet ski rental place is fortunately pretty close. I stand there under a tree, hugging my shivering body, while he returns the thing, tells the guy about his minor mishap – the edited version. In the taxi, we don't speak a word. It's absurd.

When I can't stand his silence any longer, I say, 'I could have died out there. Just so you know. I got a cramp in my foot. You can die from cramp in the water.'

He doesn't answer, just makes a point of turning to look at me – scathingly. When I think it's possible he's literally never going to speak to me again, he says, 'You can't die.' Then he scoffs, 'Nice try, though.'

He stares straight ahead now, and I glare at his ear. 'You absolutely *can* die,' I assert. 'You can one hundred per cent die. Google it.'

He *Phuf!*'s. Then to make sure I've heard it, he *Phuf!*'s again.

'Er... what does *Phuf!* mean?'

He deliberately stayed under that water. He deliberately tried to get me to think he wasn't going to come back up.

'It means you can't die from your foot going into a cramp in the water, you idiot.'

Now *I* am the idiot?

If he *Phuf's!*'s one more time I will open this door and *Phuf* him out of it. But he must decide that he's done now. I catch him doing a small smirk, then he turns and stares out of the window.

We arrive back at the hotel. We get out like two drowned rats. Our feet slap-slap like flippers down the steep steps to the pool deck entrance.

The place is deserted, just like before. Except for one person who is standing with his back to us, staring out to sea. At his side, on the ground, is a mid-sized brown leather travel bag. It's the luggage I recognise first. His battered, beloved old bag from his boarding school days – the very one his father used during his.

'Rupert.' I hear the mortification in my own voice.

THIRTY-THREE

Rupert's eyes slide from me to Frank – to the bedraggled state of us.

'What are you doing here? How did you...?' I start, then stop.

'Find you?' His eyes linger on Frank for an instant too long. 'I was texting you and you weren't answering, so I asked someone at the airport where the island hospital was.' His voice gets progressively slower and flatter as he speaks. Then he adds, 'And I'm here because Harriet is my daughter and I decided you don't get to tell me what to do.'

He's wearing his pale pink trousers and navy-blue and white polka dot shirt. And he is looking at me in a way that says everything he ever knew about me has just been called into question.

'You've seen Harriet?' I pull out my phone and see there's actually a bunch of missed texts from her.

He nods. 'I have. I didn't need an appointment. Didn't have to contact her secretary.' I'm about to say, Oh, must we do the sarcasm? When he adds, 'Funny, I imagined you'd be by her side, given she's, you know, lying in a bed attached to machines and drips.' His gaze rolls over Frank again, then returns to me. 'Bit of a case of the pot calling the kettle black, actually... Isn't it?' Then he says to Frank, 'Who are you, by the way?'

'It's not what you think.' I don't say it defensively, but I wish I hadn't said it at all.

Frank says, 'I wish it was what you think.'

Rupert suddenly appears to be on the brink of an explosive reaction, but it never quite materialises. 'My God,' he says in horror. 'He's an American.'

I tell him Frank is Aiden's father.

'Ah.' He hangs his head like the wrongly accused in the dock and who has just been issued a life sentence. 'I see...' When he eventually looks up, he meets me squarely in the eye again. 'So *this* is why you've wanted no communication in three months. Because you've been getting it on with the dad.'

Frank says, 'Whoa! Easy there!' Then adds, 'Fucker.'

'No,' I tell him. Perhaps it's because I know I *did* get it on with the dad that it comes out so lamely. 'That's not the reason at all. This is... er... this is nothing.'

It's only once I've said it that I realise how it sounds. I shoot a glance of regret to Frank, but he won't look at me. Instead, he says, 'She's right. It's really nothing.'

The wind suddenly kicks up – like it only went away for a couple of hours to mess with us. I have never experienced anything so bizarre. I am standing between two people, one who represents the almost entirety of my past, and the other who is probably nothing more than my intoxicating present. And I should be pulled, as though they each have hold of a hand, and my arms are almost coming away from my body, yet I am leaning in one direction. One direction. I cannot speak, cannot even think another thought, for fear it will break the force of gravity.

'Well, this is fun.' Rupert picks his hair off his face, his shirt sleeve flapping like a sail. 'I've always wanted to come to

Santorini during an EF5 tornado with my wife and her boyfriend.'

Frank shoots back, 'Hey, my son's the boy. I think you'll find I'm a man.'

Rupert says a curt, 'Glad you clarified that.'

I listen to them like they're a game of ping pong. Rupert's face has turned unhealthily red, and I remember again that this is the man I've shared most of my adult life with, and I feel a bit bad for him.

I'm still standing beside Frank. And Rupert is still standing on his own over there. I can't bring myself to walk over to him, but I take a step forward into more neutral territory.

'Anyway,' he is saying to Frank, 'I would like to spend some time alone with my wife right now, if you don't mind. You know, *my* wife, not anyone else's. What about you, Moira? Would you like to express an opinion on it?' His blue eyes make contact with mine, the slight bunny quality of his teeth, that I used to find so endearing, made all the more mammalian by the fact that they're chattering with the cold, like he's grinding down fibrous vegetation.

Frank says, 'Yes. Let's hear Moira's opinion on what she wants right now. I think that would be a great idea.'

'Yes,' Rupert chimes in, like he's a willing participant in ganging up on me – as though this is all *my* fault. 'Who would you like to be with right now, Moira? Your husband whom you've been married to for twenty years? Or your lover whom you've known for all of two minutes?'

His pomposity almost pushes me over the edge. 'For God's sake,' I groan. 'I told you he's not my lover.'

Frank says, 'Sadly.'

Rupert calls him an insolent Yank. He takes a step forward, peacocking himself up for the punch he must believe he's really going to swing, until he realises he's never swung one in his entire life, so maybe best not to start now.

Frank gives a mocking laugh, then starts walking across the pool deck and I want to run after him. As though he hears my inner panic, he says, 'Going to leave you to it, Ma'am.' His wet clothes are still clinging to his body, his white T-shirt outlining his flanks, the navy shorts revealing the hair stuck down on his legs. He sends us a curt salute. 'You know where I am if you need me.'

'Need you?' Rupert scoffs. 'Why would she need you? Her life is in some sort of jeopardy, is it? By being with me, the man she's married to?'

Frank turns, rubs the back of his head, tiredly. 'Rupe, I'd let your wife decide her own needs at this point, if I were you.'

Rupert bigs himself up again. 'You know what? Fuck you, and the horse you rode in on!'

Frank throws up his hands. 'What did the horse do?'

'I'm going to take a shower,' I say to Rupert when we go upstairs. I don't want him here with me in my room, but he followed, leaving me little choice. I walk into the bathroom and lock the door. I remember we used to joke about never locking a bathroom door in case someone banged their head or had a stroke in the bath. Now, both those options feel preferable to the idea of him maybe walking in on me and seeing me naked.

First, I park myself on the toilet lid and read Harriet's three messages.

Dad's here! Did you know? This whole thing has become a shitshow!

Are you there? Did you know he was coming?!

I'm not mad. You don't have to hide from me.

I text her back and tell her my phone was accidentally in silent mode. A harmless lie, I suppose. I tell her how I urged him not to come, but he was so worried about her.

It's okay, she writes back. *No worries. I'm fine. Suppose we had to see him at some point!*

I tell her I'll see her shortly, and then I run the water until it's almost too hot and stand under it for what feels like forever.

When I walk back into the bedroom, he's unpacking his bag, laying out shirts and jumpers and neatly folded rolls of underwear on top of my bed. Rupert is the only man I've ever heard of who folds his knickers.

'You can't stay here,' I say.

He appears to process this. 'Why not? It's your room, isn't it? We're paying for it, aren't we?'

'Maybe. But you can't stay in it.'

There's a bewildered silence. Then he says, 'Well, where am I supposed to go?'

I tell him there are plenty of hotels around. Besides, when Harriet gets out this afternoon, she might want to stay here with me. 'There isn't room for three of us,' I say.

He kicks up a big 'I'm hard done by' protest, but I tell him I'm going to dry my hair, get dressed, then I need to get some lunch.

He stands there clutching a ball of socks. 'Well, do you think I can at least come with you for food? I haven't eaten since four a.m.' As if on cue, his tummy rumbles loudly and he grimaces.

'Okay,' I say. But I tell him he has to wait for me downstairs; I just need him out of this room.

He starts putting his clothes back into his travel bag.

I walk back into the bathroom. I hang onto the sides of the hand basin, stare at my chalk-white face in the mirror, my bloodshot green eyes. I am riddled with tension, until I hear the click of the door.

. . .

We go to the same taverna Frank and I went to last night. A young Greek guy – perhaps the son – looks Rupert over like he's a speck of fluff, as we walk in. Rupert orders a beer and chicken souvlaki. But I suddenly can't face food, so I just order a tea. We talk about Harriet, and I tell him my suspicion is that all this urgency about suddenly wanting to live on the other side of the world is motivated by her not wanting to be on the scene while our marriage falls apart.

He pecks away at the corner of the beer bottle's label. 'But that's not happening now, is it? I mean, you're coming home.' He says it like he's so sure of it – sure of me.

'Why would you assume that?' I ask.

He stops mutilating the label and looks up. 'But you have to come home. I mean, where else are you going to go? Back to America?'

I tell him I haven't thought it all through yet.

His face drains of its colour. 'But... You can't go back to America. You can't legally work there.'

'OTs are sought-after in the US,' I say. 'I'm sure I could get a work visa. Or I could work on my business plan.' Then I add, 'Besides, I'll have half the proceeds of the house.'

'The what?' He almost coughs up his beer.

'Why wouldn't I? I worked hard for twenty years. I paid half the mortgage. Maybe it's time to cash out, reap the rewards of my investment.'

His eyes almost pop out on stalks. 'Well, I can promise you that half the money from the house won't get you very far!'

'Should be okay when you factor in the maintenance support.'

His jaw hangs open. To wound or be wounded; there's got to be a better way.

'You can't divorce me, rip me off just because—'

'Rip you off?' Anger makes my heart pound.

'Sorry.' He sighs. 'It was a proverbial...'

'Rip you off?' The couple next to us look over. I tell him I need to go to get Harriet, that we're done here.

'Please don't just get up and leave.' He puts out a hand to stop me. 'Besides, I want to come with you to bring Harriet back.'

'I need to see her alone,' I say, reaching under the table for my bag. Then I say it one last time. 'Rip you off.'

'Moy...' He stands, glances helplessly at his abandoned food. 'It was an unfortunate choice of expression.'

I start walking to the door. He hurries after me. 'I'm not bothered about who gets the house or how we divide the money. I don't want you to leave me. I'm very unhappy without you. My life isn't the same.'

My heart is empty except for a rogue, fault-line crack of profound sadness.

'No matter what you may think of me... I want you to give me another chance. I *need* you to give me another chance, Moira. Please.' His hand reaches for my arm.

I clearly have one more in me.

'Rip you off,' I say again.

'I want you to watch something.' He is hurrying after me up the street.

'Go away!' I say, quickening my pace. 'What part of "we're done here" do you not understand?'

He catches up to me. 'Will you watch this, please?' He sounds out of breath.

I stop while he fiddles with his phone. What on earth is he doing?

The wind is back. It seems to spot you stepping outside and

performs a massive encore, in case you'd forgotten how much you'd missed it.

'Here.' He thrusts his phone under my nose, the screen facing me. 'Please. I wasn't going to show it to you. Only if I really needed to. But this might... This might help clarify things.'

I find myself staring at the face of a woman. Someone around my own age. Overly made-up. Lipstick too pink. Eyeshadow a 1980s frosted baby blue. Unblended blush on the apples of her cheeks. 'Who's this?' I ask, no longer knowing if my life is real or make believe.

He blows out a big breath. 'Dagmara has a message for you.'

I must need a smack to my senses. He presses play. In an Eastern European accent, the talking head says, 'Hello, Moira. This is Dagmara. I want you to know that nothing happened between your husband and me. Nothing. Okay?' She stiffens, shoots a glance off camera like she's looking for approval, and then the video ends.

I gawk at Rupert like he's sprouted a second head. 'Are you bloody kidding me? You had your girlfriend record a message for me? What are you, nuts?' I start walking down the street. He bullets after me again.

'She's not my sodding girlfriend. She just told you the truth! *Nothing happened!*' He grinds the last words out. 'If you had listened to her entire message, which I edited, because I knew you'd have a short attention span, you'd have heard her say that she knew I was married, yet she decided to make a play for me anyway. That she wasn't proud of it – ashamed, actually – but—'

'Get away from me, you freak!'

I think I'm walking the wrong way, so I turn to go the other, and then...

A guy appears out of nowhere and grabs Rupert's arm. The

young Greek guy from the restaurant. 'You left without paying,' he says.

Rupert looks up at him. Way up. 'Who are you?'

The big guy says, 'In Greece, food and drink not free.'

Rupert stares at the enormous hand gripping his arm. 'Look, if you don't remove that thing...'

'You're going to do what?'

Rupert looks to me for help. I have a horrible feeling he's about to stammer – a childhood affliction that got almost entirely stamped out with years of speech therapy. '... Cause a lot of trouble for you with your boss. That's what I'm going to do,' he adds.

The big Greek guy doesn't move his hand. Instead, he leans into Rupert's ear and says, 'Thirty-five euros.'

Rupert almost squeaks. 'Thirty-five? That's highway robbery! We only had a beer, a tea and a shitty souvlaki.'

The guy leans on him again. 'I would pay it and shut the fuck up, if I was you.'

Rupert digs in his pocket then hands over two twenties. The guy takes the money and turns to go back inside. Rupert shouts, 'Wait! What about my change?'

I suddenly realise what direction my hotel is in and start walking.

I hear his feet hurrying after me. 'No change! Can you believe this? Disbelieved, divorced, and almost left for dead by a Greek bouncer. How does this stuff happen to me?'

I try to walk quicker but the wind pushes me back. I hug my arms to my body, my hair lashing my face.

And then he says, 'He called me Rupe. No one's called me Rupe since I was at Eton.'

It takes me a moment to realise we're not still talking about the Greek bouncer. I stop, turn, look at him. His nose is running down the right side, a bubble poised on his nostril. 'His name is

Frank Lewis,' I say. 'He wrote the world's most romantic movie, and novel, and he lives in a beach house in Malibu.'

'What's that got to do with him calling me Rupe?' he asks.

'Nothing.' I pluck my hair off my face and hold it down. Beneath us, the grey Aegean Sea whips up in a frenzy. This island suddenly feels like the place where nineteenth-century poets meet grim deaths.

'He didn't really write the world's most romantic movie and novel, did he? You were just saying that to be...?' He gives me his best puzzled look. 'Actually, why *were* you saying that, if I might ask?'

'Because it's true.' I tell him he wrote *Love for Lara*, and I tell him he's a good guy. Then I say, 'I think you're missing something.'

'Talent, perhaps?' He upturns his hands as though appealing to me for reason. 'Fame and fortune? An ability to seduce you with my words? Yes, Moira. Clearly, he's got all of that, and I've got none of that. So that makes him worthy of you, and me not worthy of you...'

I shake my head. 'No. Your bag. You must have left it in the restaurant.'

He looks down at his empty hands. Then he says, 'Faack!'

THIRTY-FOUR

In the taxi, on my way in to see Harriet, I hear Ping!

Frank.

He has finally replied to the text I sent him this morning. The *Are you angry with me?* text.

He writes: *No.*

Harriet is looking brighter now, perhaps because she knows she's getting out of here in an hour. We talk about her dad's visit, and she says she hasn't got the energy right now to go on being angry with him.

'I think we maybe have to talk about going home,' I say, as I perch on the end of her bed. I have to start looking into booking flights and getting airline credits for our US ones.

'Oh,' she says, flatly, and stares off across the room.

'I know it's not what you want to hear,' I tell her, 'but the doctor said it could take up to six weeks for you to fully recover. We can't risk you going back to America and having some sort of relapse and needing health care, and us learning that the insurance sees it as a pre-existing condition and denies it.'

I try not to see her face fold. 'It's all so practical. Insurance, pre-existing this and that. Gah... It leaves so much out.'

'I know,' I tell her. 'It doesn't mean forever. But for now, we'd be best to run home to the safety of the NHS in case we need it.'

'But what am I going to do about all my stuff? I have to pack up my dorm. Everything's still over there. Yours too.'

'I know.' I tell her I can probably extend my Airbnb lease for a bit until we work it all out. 'We can find a way for one of us to get back there to pack up once we get home and get you fully better.'

'So you're going back to Dad?'

I can't quite read her tone. She doesn't exactly sound aghast or disparaging, which makes me wonder if it *was* what she wanted deep down. If Aiden was right. 'Harriet, right now, I'm going back to England because it's my home. Yours, too. For now we just have to crack on with it for practical reasons, and do the best we can.'

She doesn't add anything, just stares off across the room again. I know she's grappling with the fact that this has big consequences for her and Aiden.

'I've made a mess of everything, haven't I?' she says.

I frown. 'Mess? No.'

'I have. You're just too kind to let me have it.'

I want to stay in the moment, but I find myself staring an inch past her head, picturing Frank and me treading that water. When he went under then popped back up – unlike the lost city of Atlantis – his eyes holding on to mine. His eyes forcing me to confront all the things that neither of us could say.

'Mum?'

'Sorry.' I try a smile.

She smiles too now. 'I just want to say thank you for always being there for me. For being you.'

I struggle not to choke up. 'Don't be silly.' I give her a cuddle. 'I'll be there for you until my dying day, and even longer if I can swing it. That's what mothers are for.' I tell her I'm going to text her dad and Aiden and they can come in, and then we can get her out of here.

'You won't miss California?' she asks as I pull out my phone.

It sounds so final. I suddenly see my beautiful loft, the palm trees, my beach walks, my sunset bike rides. My favourite place for coffee and cake. All the things I've started to love without knowing I was loving them. All the things that weren't mine to want in the first place. 'Yes,' I say. 'Of course. But I don't belong in America.'

And I see Frank. How can I not see Frank blazing in my mind's eye? I think of the easy way we can talk. His libidinous way of looking at me. His kindness when he said that thing about getting Harriet a second opinion, even though he was angry with me; how he took charge like he cared – not like he felt he had to. How we connected sexually, like I've never known before. How he lives a million miles away. In a country where I have no status beyond that of a tourist.

Not mine to want in the first place.

We manage to act like civilised human beings as we escort Harriet out of the hospital and into a people-carrier taxi. The only person missing is Frank, who doesn't respond to my text asking if he wants to come with us. Perhaps it was thoughtless of me to suggest it.

When we arrive back at my hotel, Harriet decides she'd like to go on with Aiden, to theirs. They go on in the taxi, and Rupert gets out with me.

'Here we are again,' he says. The unspoken lyrics to a song beat there, only we're not happy as can be, nor are we good pals enjoying jolly good company.

''K, then,' I say, and I turn to head down the hotel steps.

'What? Where are you going?' He sounds slightly exasper- ated. 'Can't we go for dinner, given we didn't exactly eat any lunch? You're surely not just going to go off and leave me to my own devices?' He's practically whimpering like an abandoned puppy. I tell him, look, sorry but I'm insanely tired, that this has felt like a month in one day, that I'm going to take a nap and then maybe we can turn out later for a bite. As soon as I suggest maybe getting together later, I regret it. But I tell him I'll text him.

I stand and watch him as he walks up the road to his hotel. There is something remotely metaphorical about seeing him go on his way. Something vaguely astonishing to me to think that this moment could be marking out the point where our lives go off in separate directions, even if I do have to return to England. I watch him until he disappears through a door. And then I disappear through mine.

I text Frank when I get back to the hotel, telling him we all disbanded and I've gone back to my room. I'm lying on my bed, asking myself would a guy really get the woman he'd had sex with to go on camera and deny having had sex with him? Surely they'd both have to be certifiably mad? So maybe he didn't screw her.

Then Frank replies.

Do you want to go get some raki?

I type back: *The liver is willing but the flesh is weak.*
The dots come instantly.

Meet your liver downstairs in ten?

I smile, wishing I could feel something other than utterly joyless.

.   .   .

We wander downhill again, towards Fira. The commercial centre is bustling but lacks charm; we search around for a bit trying to find some. I tell him I'm going to have to change the return portion of my ticket and go back to England with Harriet. I explain my insurance fears if Harriet goes back to the US before she's fully better. About how my first consideration has to be her. I wait for him to comment but he stays silent.

'It's a big consideration for us,' I say, when I can't handle his lack of response any longer. 'Maybe it wouldn't be to you, but a denied insurance claim could bankrupt us.'

'Sure,' he says, noncommittally.

I decide to let it drop because I don't want us to end up in an argument.

I am more desperate than ever for a drink now, though. In answer to my prayers, I spot what looks like a tiny bar down a sliver of a cobbled side street. A big black cat sits on the corner like he'll usher us into a speakeasy if we just give him the right nod.

The door is actually locked when we get up to it. 'Oh,' we groan together. I throw up my hands. 'Fate is telling me I should maybe just head back to my room,' I say. I am feeling churlish.

He frowns. 'Don't believe in it. There's what you make happen and what you don't.' He grabs my hand a little roughly, draws me back down the alley to the main drag. We pass a buzzy commercial strip – three or four shops selling all manner of gold jewellery, a tacky souvenir shop hawking casts of Greek gods, a vendor smoking outside. Between them, a kiosk emits the scent of rosemary and charred meat.

The smell is so tantalising, I am suddenly ravenous. We order two lamb *gyros* – tender, fragrant shavings on a bed of cold tzatziki, sweet tomatoes and onions, wrapped in a soft pitta with a few chips fresh from the fryer sticking up like flags, and we devour them standing against a wall.

'Tomorrow is Saturday,' I find myself saying, when we start walking again. 'The wedding day that wasn't.'

He huffs, mirthlessly. 'All that scheming. Putting our worst selves forward.'

'You didn't really have to rejig your entire security system so Aiden wouldn't ever be able to prove it was you who nicked his passport, did you?'

'Would I lie to you?'

I settle for shaking my head. But then whatever little bit of humour I have managed to muster quickly drains out of me.

'Stop worrying,' he tells me. When I frown, he says, 'She's going to be fine. Aiden will take good care of her. You can pretty much bet he's going to be the world's best boyfriend now.'

'How did you know I was thinking about Harriet?'

'Because I know you.'

I contemplate this. The idea of being known by him. How much pause those four little words can give a person.

'I wish we were off this damned cold island,' I say.

'Well, we will be soon enough.'

We meet eyes, for a long time, drawing out the unsaid.

'I feel a complicated conversation coming,' I say. 'Can we not talk about deep stuff right now? We always talk about deep stuff.'

'What other stuff is there to talk about?'

'There must be something.'

'Maybe for some people. But that's not how we're wired.'

We.

'We could talk about our favourite colours, or our recurring dreams,' I say.

'Do you have recurring dreams?'

'Just the one where I'm on safari. I'm sleeping in this tiny tent and this massive lion decides he's going to maul me, and I have to keep dodging this enormous paw coming down.' I do my best lion pawing someone to death impersonation. 'And I'm

caught between feeling like I'm outmanoeuvring him, and
knowing it's a challenge I won't win.'

He shakes his head at me.

'Silence, then,' I say. 'Silence is golden, remember.' We
resume walking. My hand close to his hand, like a conversation
in itself.

He looks at me, wistfully. 'Any silence shared with you is
pretty good, Moira Fitzgerald.'

It's the blast of loud music off in the distance that we hear first.
Voices and laughter. Rambunctious. Fun.

Frank hears it at the exact same time. 'Hmm. What's going
on? Shall we go see?' Somewhere in the last little while he has
taken hold of my hand. We follow the pied piper, a winding
trail through unpopulated alleyways, around wind-blasted
corners. Past cats, and then an elderly man and his son fixing
the ripped blue and white awning above his doorstep, the son
trying to snag a hold of it as it billows like a sail. It looks like it's
really all just houses, sugar cube after white sugar cube, but the
music and the voices are growing louder. It would be defeatist
to turn back now.

Then, suddenly, around a bend... here we are. Into a square
that has a single restaurant jammed between two enormous
cypress trees strung with fairy lights. A throng of people, maybe
a hundred of them. Guys in suits. Gorgeous girls in glamorous
dresses and stilettos. Older couples seated at tables, smoking.

'A wedding!' I chirp when I spot the bride and groom.

'Jesus,' Frank says. 'Someone needs to warn them not to
do it.'

'By the looks of things, it might be too late.' We hang back
by the tree, trying to be inconspicuous.

The groom and his three groomsmen are performing their
version of the Zorba the Greek dance. Arms outstretched and

hands on shoulders, they step slowly at first in six-point formation to the assertive strum of the bouzouki; well-timed kicks and
dips, they jump and turn while the crowd claps to the thrum of
their steps. The pace picks up; the steps become more complicated. The groom throws himself into the dance for all he's
worth. It all builds to a frenetic climax along with the clapping
and cheering.

Someone spots us. A Greek lady in a purple taffeta dress.
Her face bursts into the biggest smile and she boogies over to us
with arms wide open. She tells us she's Sophia, the groom's
mother. Stavros is his name, and his bride is Athena. She asks us
ours, then asks if we're married. I say, 'No,' right as Frank says,
'Very much so.' He sends me the saucy side-eye.

'Join us!' Sophia gestures to the floor. She takes hold of
Frank's hand and starts tugging him. He looks back at me and
fakes a cry for help. Sophia parts a sea of outstretched arms,
hands gripping shoulders, and deposits him bang in the middle.

Frank throws his hands up at me, shrugs.

Sophia starts teaching him the nine key steps of the Greek
dance, counting them out – one, two, three, four. The crowd
makes way for them, not seeming to mind the American inter-
loper who has pretty much zero sense of rhythm. Sophia takes
great pains to see that he does them properly, until he can take
them from the top and perform them seamlessly on his own.
Some of the older folk at a nearby table wave me over but I
laugh them off, and hope that's the end of it.

But then I am spotted by the man himself. The groom is
bounding towards me, his charm and enthusiasm as over-
whelming as his frame.

'Welcome, English tourist!' he says. He's handsome. His
smile is genuine, and he smells of strong cologne. He drops a big
arm around my shoulder and says, 'I think your husband is
missing you!'

Before I can muster up an objection, I too am led to the

dance floor. But instead of giving me a lesson, he hands me off into Frank's arms. 'Do you like Greek music?' he asks, dunking a big hand on Frank's shoulder now. Then he leans in and says, pretend-privately, 'At Greek wedding we have to play Greek music for all these old dears, but English music is my favourite!' His face is bright and shiny from sweat. His English is excellent. 'Wait!' he says. 'I have a song for you... I'm going to play a song for you, okay.' He takes off, looking very purposeful.

I grit my teeth and say to Frank, 'If it's Lionel Ritchie I'm going to lose the will to live.'

He beams. 'My money's on Michael Bolton.' Then he croons, 'How am I supposed to live without you...'

'Please God, no!'

Stavros has bounded over to an enormous sound system. One of his drunk groomsmen tries to clamber onto his back. A moment or two later, and Stavros has shut down the Greek music, and everyone who is dancing, stops. Practically kissing the microphone, he says, in his best *I fancy myself as a radio broadcaster* voice: 'I want to take this moment to play favourite English song.' He turns and addresses us. 'For very special, very beautiful English couple...'

I plant my face in Frank's armpit. The song starts up. A long musical intro with a hard, pulsing beat that gathers frenetic speed. I don't recognise it. And by the knit of his brows neither does Frank. We wait a bit longer.

But then...

Oh. My God.

It is no longer unfamiliar. Not unfamiliar at all.

It's horribly... Horrifyingly...

'*I Touch Myself*?' I shriek. 'By the bloody Divinyls?'

Ground, swallow me up!

Frank throws his head back and laughs. 'Oh boy! What were the chances? I haven't heard this song in thirty years!' I have never seen him find anything so amusing. He snatches hold of my hand. 'Okay. Let's do this, baby.' He spins me so I go flying to the end of his reach, then he draws me back hard against his chest, twirls me lavishly under his arm. The crowd erupts in cheers. It's definitely a catchy song – if you don't know what the damned lyrics are. The groom is really digging the dirty chorus, shaking his imaginary maracas above his head, throwing his pelvis at it for all he's worth.

I try to dance and pretend it really isn't a song about a woman having to play with herself every time she thinks about her fella. But it takes some serious delusion.

'I think she wrote it just for you,' Frank says and launches a big smile. 'She did, didn't she? Admit it. You're practically singing all the words.'

'This is the most mortifying moment of my entire life,' I say, with gritted teeth, when I land back against his chest.

He laughs. 'How did you get to be such a prude?' His hand grips my hot one, and he twirls me again.

'Do you suppose they were a one-hit wonder?' I ask. 'Please tell me yes.'

Once Frank has exhausted his two-trick-pony moves, we eventually give up trying to stay in step, and Frank just holds me and rocks me in his arms.

'If you tell me it's got two more verses I will end my life,' I say.

Frank flicks his head at the groom who is still having a great time getting it on with himself. 'Stavros isn't going to run out of juice any time soon.'

We chuckle.

Dance of shame done. We say goodbye to our new friends, then meander our way back through the tight maze of tiny streets, the music and laughter fading behind us, replaced with the high-pitched buzzing of cicadas. 'You do know I'll never be able to hear that shitty song again without thinking of you, right?' he says.

'Good job it doesn't come on the radio very often, then!' I say, my cheeks still flaming with embarrassment. Then I add, 'Do you know I've never actually seen *Zorba the Greek*?'

He squeezes my hand. 'Nice deflection!'

I try not to smile.

But then he stops. 'Are you serious about not having seen *Zorba the Greek*?'

I pretend to frown. 'I am.'

'Well, then, we must remedy that.' He pulls out his phone. 'You need a little cultural enrichment,' he says. 'Especially after that dose of public humiliation.'

We seem to have meandered back to the main square. Frank stands still, engrossed in his search. I watch his big, tanned hands, the neat half-moons of his nails, the expression of concentration on his face. ''K. Found it.' Instead of passing the phone to me, he draws me close, so I have to tuck into him. He presses play.

The scene begins with Alan Bates standing on a beach and saying to Anthony Quinn, 'Teach me to dance.' And Anthony Quinn says, 'Dance? Did you say dance?' And he rips off his suit jacket, rolls his sleeves up, and says, 'Come on, my boy!'

And the rest is history. Or it is to everyone who has seen the movie.

We watch the short clip of them frolicking to their own made-up steps on the sand. Then Frank clicks off.

'It's priceless!' I trill.

His gaze combs over my face. 'The movie's about finding joy in even the most trying times, Moira.' Then he smiles. 'Just to put you in the picture. Because you haven't seen the whole thing.'

His hand drops away from my shoulders and finds my

waist. A negligible distance travelled, but it feels like an earth-quake affecting several continents.

'I like that,' I say.

'I like it too,' he replies. And I have no idea what it is we're agreeing on.

'It's been a very weird day,' I say.

We have arrived back at the hotel. Something about the peaceful view from the pool deck, literally nothing moving except for the reflection of the moon on the water, makes us pause there before going inside. Something is building, brewing between us. I can sense it. But I can't shake it free.

And then he looks at me and says, 'Moira...'

'Frank.' I get in there first because I can't stand the gravity in his tone, in his expression. 'I thought we were only doing light conversation. I feel this is not going to be light conversation.'

'I thought we decided we have zero capacity to do light conversation.'

I stare out at the cliffside, at the pink, blue and white fondant hotels and houses that are as surreal to me as this situation, almost. All these crucial threads just seem to end in such complicated knots. The fact that I am here in Santorini, and Rupert is here in Santorini. But I am not with Rupert. I am with Frank. But I am not really *with* Frank. And God knows what I am with Rupert. I can hardly process it all.

'Go on,' I say.

This time, I know we are not back in Athens outside that hotel room door. Frank does not have analysis paralysis any more.

Nor are we back in that hot tub where he's trying to work around saying the thing that's bugging him.

Whatever he's about to say is not going to be difficult for him.

THIRTY-FIVE

'Look...' he says.

His eyes are bolted to mine, but there's a subtle disconnect behind them; like he is here almost fully, except for the part of him that is gone.

'It's not for me to help you make your mind up about the rest of your life. I barely know what *I'm* doing, let alone what *you* should be doing.'

The way this comes out, so bluntly, so on point, almost blows me off my feet. 'But—'

'I'm being very straight with you here, Moira. Whatever you might be thinking, or wanting, I can't offer you a life to replace your current one. I can't put myself in that position.'

No, no, no. What? Did he really just say that? *Position?* A thousand no's, and then a thousand more. Where did this come from?

The blood drains from my body. He is scouring my face, so much conflict and consternation in his eyes that I have to look away; I have to try to breathe.

Did he think our earlier conversation about me having to go back to England was my way of fishing for him to offer up an alternative? 'Frank,' I say, trying not to get overly het up, determined to make my point as succinctly as he made his. But my voice is wobbling with dismay and hurt pride. 'Let's get one thing very straight. I want nothing from you. I am not asking you to give me a life. I do not expect any other person in this world to give me a life. Only *I* can give me a life.' I prod my chest with my index finger. 'Only me.'

Didn't succeed on the not sounding het up part!

'Irrespective of the fact that I have to go back to England right now for practical reasons, I am very much aware that I have a life in England, and I don't have a life in California. Even if I wanted to, I can't stay there for anything other than small snatches of time. I have no right—'

'To the life you might want? So you settle for one you don't.'

He almost sounds like he's contradicting himself. I am so damned frustrated and confused.

'That might be over-simplifying,' I say.

'Sounds like it's you who's over-complicating.'

His hand goes to my face, his fingers curling to cup my jaw. And I don't know if he's going to kiss me or if he wants to comfort me, but I move away from his touch. I cannot have him touch me right now. The rejection registers hard in his eyes.

'This is not easy for me,' he says. 'But what I'm trying to tell you is that...'

But he never does tell me.

He never says it because we hear the most ungodly thud.

A body has just comes tumbling down the huge flight of steps. It lands hard onto the pool deck, almost right at our feet. Like a beautifully dressed sausage.

'Rupert?' I almost can't believe my eyes.

My husband struggles to his feet. He stands there, partly stupefied, rubbing his arm, like he's come to tell us that war has just broken out – but now he thinks he may just have had a nightmare.

'What the hell?' I gawk in horror at this clown before me. This clown I'm married to. And then it dawns on me. 'Were you...?'

'Spying on us from behind bougainvillea bushes?' Frank finishes.

Rupert dusts off his trousers, tries to tug his jacket back round the right way. He looks me guilelessly in the eyes and then he says, 'You didn't text.'

The three of us stare at one another, for a moment. My heart seems to skip beats at this man, this idiot, who lies to me about cheating, shows me videos of his girlfriend, and tumbles down flights of steps, like he's turning my life into a slapstick comedy. Then he says, bashfully, 'I wasn't spying on you. Truly. I... I slipped.'

Frank sniggers. 'You were spying, dude. C'mon! Might as well just admit it.'

Rupert smoothes down his hair. 'I happened to be passing by,' he says. 'I was on my way to... to...' He makes a point of looking directly at me. 'I was on my way to ask you if you wanted to go to a late dinner, actually. Given you hadn't texted. And then...'

'You thought you were going to see some action,' Frank finishes.

I'm waiting for him to add something very Frank-like, such as *Hey, you and me both...* but he just stands there silently assessing the situation, looking like it's not one he wants to find himself in at all.

And then he says, 'Right. I'm fucking out of here.'

I want to say or do something, but I am stunned into silence and inaction. Rupert arriving and Frank leaving is not how it's supposed to go at all. Rupert and I watch Frank walk across the patio towards the hotel door. Frank doesn't even look angry; he looks neither in a hurry to leave, nor a hurry to stay. He looks like a guy who really doesn't give a damn any more.

As he opens the lobby door, not even glancing back over his shoulder, Rupert gives a flick of his wrist, and says, 'Scoot! Go on. You're almost there. Yes. Excellent. Lovely. Keep going.' And when Frank disappears around the door and it closes, Rupert chirps, 'Have a jolly good night!'

In my room, after I tell Rupert that I've had dinner already, and he needs to go and F off and maybe buy a pack of Elastoplast for the one-inch gash on his forehead, I pore over events of the past hours, days, of the last three months of my life, staring into the unmoving ochre blades of the ceiling fan.

The thought just comes to me, unbidden. That clearing in your head of all the wool that makes everything so tangled. Frank might have just acted like he doesn't give a damn. But Frank does give a damn. Frank gave a damn when he pretended he'd drowned, because he needed to know my reaction. He gives a damn when he listens to me so intently and remembers every word I say. When he shares intimate revelations with me. When he gets frustrated because I struggle to see the very thing that is staring me in the face.

Frank gives a damn. A very big damn, in fact. I see it now.

And I see something else. It rushes at me: that moment of clarity about myself.

I realise I am not confused any more. Far from it. I am acting now, not reacting. I might not have authored this particular chapter of my own story, but I'm taking the red pen and I'm deciding what gets cut and what gets to stay.

So I phone Rupert.

He picks up after the first ring.

I tell him I want to make something very clear. I tell him I am not coming back to him. I will return to England, for Harriet, and because I really have no choice in the short term, but I will be starting divorce proceedings immediately. I tell him

I don't believe him. I never believed him. I'm sorry he chose to keep on bullshitting me. But the crazy part of it is, it doesn't even matter any more. This isn't about him any longer. This is about me.

I tell him we shouldn't share this with Harriet until we get back to England; we should let her enjoy her remaining time with Aiden. I tell him that if he tries to come to my hotel to have a conversation with me, I will call security and insist I don't know who he is.

I tell him that's actually not too far from the truth.

I don't wait for him to say anything. I hang up, and then I power down my phone.

And then I walk down the hall to Frank's room.

I know the scene I want to write next. I don't care how it fits in with the ultimate ending.

I care – hugely, magnificently – about now.

THIRTY-SIX

When I tap on his door, the knock is so quiet it's almost like I'm hoping he won't hear it.

'Well,' he says, when he opens up, raising a nonchalant eyebrow to mask his surprise.

He is wearing a white T-shirt and navy bed shorts. I don't know why the sexy sight of him in his sleepwear, the soft, soapy scent of him, his mussed hair, almost takes the resolve out of me, almost makes the red pen hover again. *How can I be intimate with this man and then have to walk away? How can I do this to myself?*

'Don't get the wrong idea here,' I tell him.

He glances down at my white cotton tank and red tartan PJ bottoms. 'How could anyone possibly get the wrong idea about you showing up at my bedroom door at two in the morning, braless?'

In my haste, I forgot to put a dressing gown on. I stupidly cross my arms in front of me, scan his sleepy face, his rumpled hair. 'Did I wake you?'

'It's two in the morning. What loser would possibly be asleep at this hour?'

'Basically, you were out for the count, weren't you? I can totally tell.' I reach out and touch his hair; I can't help it.

'My mother used to do that to me,' he says, with a very straight face.

I pull my hand away. 'So that's a passion killer right there, then.'

His gaze coasts across my collarbones, wanders down my cleavage, then he meets my eyes again, and says, quite seriously, 'Very little about you, Moira Fitzgerald, could dampen my passion.'

'We didn't get to finish our conversation,' I tell him. I need to get this out before the proximity of him can throw me further off course. I say it in my best no-messing tone. 'There's a couple of things I need to set straight...' I clear my throat. 'First of all, I'm not here because I'm looking for a life with you. There's not even the remotest chance I'd consider walking away from a marriage, straight into a relationship with someone else. I'd have to be insane. And if you think that about me, then you're the one who's insane. This is real life we're in. Not a Julia Roberts movie.'

He beams, but I plough on anyway.

'I don't fear being alone, and I don't need someone to save me.' I have to focus on his ear, rather than on those eyes that are brimming with affection for me. 'There. I've said it.'

'Are you finished?' he asks.

'I am.'

After a slow sweep of my face, he says, 'Might we be talking in circles again?'

I nod. 'We might.' And then I find myself adding, 'But the thing is, I like going round in circles with you.'

'I like it too,' he says, quietly. 'It's pretty mega, is what it is.'

This warms me until I am almost melting.

'What was the second?' he asks. 'You said there were a couple of things you wanted to set straight.'

'Oh.' I look down into the negligible space between us. My tartan PJ bottoms, and his navy shorts. Our bodies so close to touching. The gravitational pull I almost can't resist, of my pelvis towards his. The almost dizzying memory of us in my apartment. The 'match to gasoline' of my finger making contact with his chest.

'The second is... Do you want to ask me in?' I say it before I can lose my nerve. 'One last night before we both go back to our lives?'

'I do,' he nods. His gaze performs a lazy wander down my neck, the way his lips once did, the way I long for him to do again. 'Very, very much. In fact, pretty much more than anything in the world.'

And yet he doesn't move.

His eyes search my face again, that expression back in them that I want to hold there and just keep seeing. The warmth. The affection. The passion. But also some uncertainty.

'Moira,' he finally says. 'I need you to really have thought this through – what you're doing here. Because I will say that if I let you in here right now, I'll be incapable of continuing to be a gentleman.'

The snort is out before I can stop it. 'You know if you wrote that line in a novel it would be universally panned, right?'

He tries not to smile. 'This must be why I no longer write novels. I save my cheesiest self for real life.'

'Well, then...' My eyes drop to his ridiculously kissable Adam's apple. 'I think you need to stop analysing everything, and just let me in.' Then I add, 'So I can get acquainted with your cheesiest self...'

His kiss is something I fall into behind a closed door. It is hot, yet equally tender. We merge like two streams flowing into the same river. I cannot get enough of his mouth devouring mine. The bulk of his sexy shoulders. The damp heat under his hairline. The feel of him growing hard against my thigh.

When he mutters, 'God, I've wanted you so much...' his voice rasps against my throat and I almost taste the tiny vibration. 'I want you.' He repeats it like he could be arguing with himself.

'I want you too!' It comes out in a gush, like it's life or death for me.

He groans at this and whips my tank top off over my head. My breasts are in his hands, and I inhale sharply. We are off on a collision course with various items of furniture, him steering us towards the bed while I practically try to climb him like a ladder. Hands and kisses landing imperfectly, and wherever. When we bump into the bedframe it halts us, and we catch our breath. His eyes plunder mine, an electric search of my face, while he lifts his hand almost languidly to play with my hair, letting the strands slip through his fingers.

The space where he'd just been sleeping is still warm from his body as he lowers me gently into it, my hips raising so he can peel off my PJ bottoms. I have his heat underneath me, and I want it on top of me, but for a moment, all he can do is stand there. His eyes caress the contours of my naked body like he wants to know me by heart.

And then he says, 'You are beautiful, Moira Fitzgerald. And right now, I'm about the luckiest guy in the world.'

THIRTY-SEVEN

Harriet texts me.

Aiden texts Frank.

We hear the joint pings barely seconds apart as we lie there lost in one another's faces, in a swathe of sunshine, our heads propped up by our arms. Frank's cheeks are flushed from sleep and sex.

I read mine:

Meet you downstairs at 10 for breakfast? The five of us.

He reads his:

Hey dad. What you up to this morning? Gonna meet Harriet's dad and hopefully her mum at 10 in your hotel restaurant. You in?

We say a joint, 'Oh God.'

. . .

We convene on the patio because it's finally warm enough to sit outside. Me. Frank. Rupert. Aiden and Harriet. I cannot look Frank in the eye. For the life of me, I just have to pretend that he's not there.

'So this is nice, then.' Rupert spears a lemony potato. By his ebullient demeanour, anyone would think all was well in his world. 'All of us together, like a family.' And then he adds, 'Plus Frank.'

Today Rupert is wearing the reverse of yesterday: a pale pink shirt and navy-blue trousers. And because he clearly didn't want to risk winning any fashion award, he has knotted a navy-blue cashmere jumper over his shoulders. By contrast, Frank has on jeans and the same white T-shirt from last night that I peeled away from his body and slid over his head while I kissed an uncharted trail across his chest and down his stomach; an unending path to a destination that turned him to putty in my hands.

'But speaking of Frank,' Rupert continues. 'When will you be heading home to America?'

Frank slowly drags a spoon around his Greek yogurt. 'No plans, Rupe, but thanks for asking.' After a beat he adds, 'Might do some travelling.' He licks the back of the spoon, and an incandescent blush blasts my face. 'England's a six-hour flight from here, huh?' He finally meets my eyes, like he's throwing out a challenge.

Rupert says, 'Four, actually.'

'Four actually.' Frank's eyes stay bolted to mine. 'Hmm.'

He places the spoon down on his plate and I stare at that spoon for a very long time. Anything to avoid looking at him again.

Rupert starts waffling on about the Greek islands he's been to, the ones he'd like to go to – and he's even got a lot to say about those he couldn't give a damn about. When there's an uncomfortable lull in the conversation, Aiden stands, places his napkin on the table. 'Well, I think I'm gonna walk off this break-fast.' He pats his non-existent stomach. 'You coming, Dad?'

Frank sits back in the seat, knots his fingers at his chest. 'I'm good.'

Aiden hovers there. 'Dad, I think you should come for a walk.'

Frank is studying me like he's revisiting personal things he knows about me. I stare at his fingers, the white T-shirt that fits snuggly across his lean waist, remembering those solid shoulders against my hands, remembering a lot of things, and I discreetly blow air up to my own face. 'I think you should go for a walk,' I tell him.

'Okay,' he says, after a beat, with a solid message in his eyes. 'Walk it is.'

Aiden drops a quick kiss on Harriet's lips and tells her he'll see her later. They seem cute with one another again. I watch as father and son saunter across the bright white patio towards the steps where Rupert nearly fell to his death. And then the three of us are left with our own company.

'How was UCLA?' Rupert says, cheerfully. As though Frank never came, and Frank never just went. As though Harriet just went to America, and came back from America, and nothing happened in between. As though I didn't just tell him our marriage is over last night. He returns to spearing his potatoes.

Harriet says, 'So fantastic that I'm going back just as soon as I'm fully better.'

Rupert looks from Harriet to me, his fork frozen in his hand.

I'm thinking, *Please Harriet, let's not do this here. My consti-tution almost can't take it.* Then Rupert says, 'Aiden seems like a very fine young man.'

She goes to answer but takes an ungodly coughing fit instead. I have to dig in my bag for some extra tissues.

'That is ghastly!' Rupert nearly lifts from his chair. 'Darling, we need to get you home so you can see a real doctor, not a Greek quack. That way you can be around people who love you and will take care of you.'

'I was around people who love me and would take care of me,' she says, when she can manage. 'Mum and Aiden.'

'That's not fair,' he pouts. 'Very hurtful, actually.'

'Because you never hurt people, do you, Dad?'

'Are we really doing this again?' he asks.

Harriet says, 'Did you think we were just going to have a civilised conversation? Act like none of this happened?'

Rupert says, 'I'm ever the optimist.'

'Ceasefire, please!' I rap my knife on the table.

Rupert says, 'Hear, hear.' Then he rolls his eyes in that slightly effeminate way he has of doing, that he might have learned from me. I can't help but stare at the large chunk of potato that has missed his mouth and is languishing in the hammock of his jumper sleeve.

'Are you guys getting back together?' she asks.

Rupert quickly says, 'Of course.'

At first I wonder if he's just following the orders I gave him last night about us not discussing this with Harriet until we get home. But the way he bluntly meets my eye tells me something different.

'You are?' Harriet directs this to me.

'We're not,' I say. 'I didn't want us to talk about it here, but as you have asked. You have a right to know.'

'Okay this is seriously messed up.' She looks askance at both of us. 'How can one think you are, and the other think you're not?'

Rupert says it's a fascinating question but, unfortunately, he badly needs to pee. When he trots across the patio and disappears behind a door, Harriet says, 'What's going on with you and Frank? Are you sleeping with him?'

Another tidal wave of heat rushes over me again. 'What? With *Frank*? Good heavens, no!'

'Oh my God, look at your face!' She throws a finger at me. 'You *are* sleeping with him.' She screws up her face in distaste. 'You're having sex with Aiden's dad? Ewwwww! That is so...' She can't even finish. She just settles for shaking her head. Then she croaks, 'Is this why you're not going back to Dad? Because you're now with Frank? Or were you never going back to Dad? Is Frank just...' She throws up her hands. I open my mouth to say something, but she cuts me off. 'Is Frank just a sex thing, or are you in love with him?'

It's as though the tables have turned again. I'm the shocking teenager, and she's the disapproving parent. Rupert must do the fastest pee in the world because now he's walking over to us, smiling like it's a brand new day. 'Shush!' I say to Harriet. 'Please. Not now.'

But before he's even sat down, Harriet says, 'I think you two need to get your acts together.' She looks from me to her dad, then back to me again, staring hard at me like I'm a colossal disappointment to her. 'Are you staying married, or are you getting divorced? You should listen to yourselves. I mean, seriously...' She presses a hand to her ribcage, winces a bit. 'You guys are making me ashamed to call you my parents. This is colossal crap.' She stands, throws her napkin down on the table, and then she walks off coughing, and still clutching her side.

Rupert stares solidly into the tabletop. I think he's going to say something profound, or even try to gaslight me again. But he finally looks up and says, 'So Frank has facked off, and so has Aiden. Am I supposed to pick up the bill?'

'You're leaving?' I stare, slightly mystified, at the half-full carry-on case on top of Frank's unmade bed, the heap of shirts and the toiletry bag waiting to go in it. Our flight back to Athens isn't for two more days.

'Yeah.' He sends the suitcase a look like it's annoying him. 'Thought I'd head back a day early. Got some things to do.'

I am not clear if he means he's just getting off this island a day early, or if he's actually heading back to America a day early. Either way, my soul seems to depart my body.

I can't offer you a life to replace your current one. Can't put myself in that position.

There's not even the remotest chance I'd consider walking away from a marriage, straight into a relationship with someone else.

Of course. We had what I asked for. One glorious night. But now we're the proverbial rock and a hard place; neither is going to change its position.

He gestures to the armchair. Not exactly an ebullient welcome but I go and sit. 'How's it going for you?' he asks, glumly, tiredly.

I stare at the rumpled sheets, the wet towel tossed on it. 'It's gone better.'

'You and your Greek vacations. Next time you need to pick a different destination.'

I want to snigger at this, but my heart is breaking in two. 'You might have a point there,' I say. 'What about you, are you ever coming back to Santorini?'

He hisses. 'Jesus. Never.'

Our gazes hang together. Finally, when the torture goes on too long, he says, 'Look, whatever it is that's been happening all this time...'

'Was beautiful,' I finish for him. I avert my gaze out of the window, to the water where I can see shadows of islands that might not even exist; they could just be some sort of illusion, like maybe all this has been. 'I don't regret it. Not one minute.' When he doesn't add anything – this thing he does, this infuriating habit of his – I say, 'You could add something, you know. You don't just have to blithely fuck off and leave me feeling so...'

'What is there to say?' He regards me rather mournfully. 'People who tell you they don't regret things the way you just said it, are usually putting it down to an episode of lapsed judgement.' He cocks his head and looks at me quizzically.

And I don't know if this is a test again, like playing dead in the water. Or if it's his way of taking the easy road out. The one that bypasses all signs that point to commitment.

Then of course I know. I know that I will likely never know.

I look him in the eye and say it steadily, and clearly, 'It may have started out as a lapsed judgement back in my apartment that day, but it will never, ever, be a regret.'

THIRTY-EIGHT

After much back and forth on the topic of itineraries, Harriet and Aiden decide to stay on in Santorini for one more week so she doesn't have to travel while she's hacking up a lung. Rupert returns to London for a conference. And I get on the blower with my best mate.

I tell Nat I'm here in Santorini. I tell her everything that's happened. I tell her that Frank flew back to Athens yesterday, and, for all I know, is probably boarding a plane back to LA right this minute. That we have essentially said goodbye.

And I tell her I'm distraught about it. I should never have let him go. I'm a huge idiot.

Once I let her get a word in edgeways, she says, 'So when you went off to his room, you never told him that you'd just told Rupert it was over? That you've left your marriage?'

'No.'

'Why not?'

'Isn't it obvious?' I'm aghast. 'I mean, it's obvious. Obviously.'

'Of the many things it is, I can promise you it's far from obvious,' she says.

My heart quickens a bit. 'Well, I mean, I was hardly going to knock on his door and say, "Right then. Just gave Rupert his marching papers. Now let me sink my hook into you."'

'So right now he is still under the assumption that you're probably going back to your marriage?'

'I have no idea what assumption he's under,' I say.

She tsks. 'Insane. But we can analyse you later... Back to the problem at hand. So you don't know for sure that he's changed the Athens to LA portion of his flight to go back today? You haven't been in touch?'

'No,' I tell her. We haven't talked since we said goodbye. Since I sat in my room in a full-on panic, because he was standing outside waiting for his taxi, and there was more I wanted to run downstairs and say to him, but something kept holding me back; something wouldn't let me do it. Then it was too late.

'So, for all you know, he might just be hanging out in Athens for his last night? He might just have needed to get the heck off that island.'

'Possible. I didn't attach a tracker to his suitcase.'

'And you're now flying home directly from Santorini, tomorrow? Correct?'

I tell her that, yes, I spent an insane amount of time on hold with the airline but eventually I cancelled the return portion of my trip to LA and got a credit. Then I booked an easyJet flight from Santorini to London that leaves tomorrow.

'So what happened to your flight from Santorini back to Athens? Did you cancel that too?'

I realise that in all the booking and cancelling, and getting credits, I actually forgot to cancel my Santorini–Athens flight. 'Er. No.'

I hear a smile in her voice when she says, 'Well get your arse to Athens, then. And, please, when you get there, tell him you've left your marriage.'

· · ·

The House of the Rising Sun is not full. I know this because I get my arse to Athens.

They even give me my old room. As soon as I put my suitcase on its little hammock, I text Frank the view from the window. The one of the tree that forms a canopy across the alleyway, and the oddly placed ATM. My heart pounds, not sure what his reaction will be, given we've already said goodbye once. Or if he'll even reply.

But two minutes later, I see the moving dots.

Don't tell me you checked back into that shithole.

I grin.

Is that "Frank" for Well, hello! Delighted to hear you're back in town?

Are you really here? he writes after a beat. *That's not an old picture?*

I tell him I really am. Which must mean he is still here, too.

There are no more dots.

My heart sinks. Oh my God, he's annoyed. He was trying to get a million miles away from me, and here I am, legging-it after him. My life *is* a Julia Roberts movie. Die a thousand deaths and cringe a thousand cringes!

And then I see the dots. I swear I'm holding my breath to bursting point. But then up comes:

I have nine hours before I have to be at the airport. How about we wander dark streets and stumble upon floodlit ancient ruins until morning?

. . .

'Let's try a new direction.' I tug his sleeve towards a different alleyway that branches off from Monastiraki Square.

'I like new directions. Why take the same path because it's familiar?'

'If there's a hidden message there, it stinks, thanks.'

He says, 'Ha, ha, ha.' Then he holds out his arm for me to link it.

'Knowing our luck, this one will lead to a dead end.'

'I don't really believe in luck, Moira Fitzgerald.' I feel his arm flex through the thin fabric of his shirt. 'Like I once told you before. There's what you make happen, and what you don't make happen.'

'Can we just have a normal conversation, not a loaded one?'

He reaches for my hand that's looped over his arm, massages my knuckles with his thumb. 'We can. For tonight, we can do anything you say.'

And so we walk and we don't talk for a while. We just enjoy Athens in the early evening. Wandering without wondering where our steps are going to take us. Same Plaka. Same grey sky. But not same us. As luck, or chance, would have it, we even round a corner and encounter the very same portrait artist who is missing part of his leg. He is sitting on the ground with his sketch pad and pencils. Frank digs in his pockets, pulls out a roll of euros and walks over to him. I hang back and observe them as they engage in conversation. Then Frank waves me over. 'Afrim says he won't accept my money unless he draws us.' He holds up his hands. 'Don't shoot the messenger!'

'Ugh!' I roll my eyes. The very last thing I want is portraits and last pictures. Too morbid.

'Afrim insists.'

I roll my eyes. 'Well, if Afrim insists...'

We perch on a crumbling wall, touch our heads together;

my warm temple pressed to his warm temple. I try not to overly focus on the feel of it there. Afrim works swiftly, with broad sweeps of the charcoal. I pretend to be an engaged subject, but all I can think of is the press of Frank's head against mine, its micromovements as he breathes or speaks, the way my warm ear nestles against his warm ear. The way this cosy little communion doesn't faze us.

Then Afrim is finished. 'Look at this work of genius!' Frank turns it around to show me.

I stare at our charcoal likenesses, my head tilted against Frank's straight one. Frank's eyes staring straight at me; mine staring off into a daydream. After we've paid Afrim and said goodbye, I say, 'I look like a bloody wombat, but it's a good one of you.'

'I disagree.' Afrim has rolled it up and placed it in a protective plastic sleeve. Frank has tucked it proudly under his arm. 'I think it's just us, exactly as we are.' Then he nudges me. 'Besides, the beauty of wombats has long been underrated.'

We walk on and find a place for dinner. 'Just wanted to say,' he says, as we roll out of there at 10 p.m. Frank has to be at the airport by 4 a.m. 'I'm glad they don't have direct flights to London from Santorini.'

'But they do,' I say.

He is smiling before I can finish.

'You knew that,' I say.

'I knew that.' He nudges me. 'You just wanted to have one last meander around Athens with me, didn't you?'

I search for a witty comeback, but at the thought of last meanders, melancholy tugs the corners of my mouth down. 'Maybe I did,' I say.

'If I was a gambling guy, I'd bet you're going to miss me.'

'I never said I wouldn't miss you.' I stride out a little ahead of him so he can't see my face. 'I'm always going to be curious about when you're going to start writing your new book about a fantastic, enigmatic, impressionistic, sadomasochistic, illogical English woman.'

He laughs. 'Hey, who says I haven't already started?' He catches up to me, snatches my hand. 'It's possible that I might need something to get the inspiration flowing, though...' Before I can say anything, he pulls me in for a kiss. My lips part. My hands find the back of his head. My fingers burrow into his hair. It is deep and long and familiar. As familiar as my childhood. As familiar as summers. As warm as the sun on sand. Knowing this might be the last time I kiss him threatens to bring on a bawl-inducing meltdown, so I try to push the cognitive dissonance away and just inscribe it into the very fabric of me, save it for a rainy day. But then...

It comes out of nowhere. A downpour that bursts through deceptively benign clouds. Merciless drops like daggers on our faces.

'Oh my God!' I shriek. We are soaked in seconds. 'Run!'

'Where to?' He pelts after me, giving a disbelieving laugh.

I glance around. Where are all the tavernas and shops when you need them? I can only see houses. Pink houses. Yellow houses. Drab, compared to Santorini houses. Wrought-iron balconies. Plant pots. Shutters at every window and door. Then... a doorway under a narrow awning. A step. I make a leap for it, avoiding an already-oceanic puddle.

'I knew I'd be punished for wanting one more day with you!' I say, glad that the shock of this has saved me from my maudlin self.

He springs onto it after me, catches me around the waist again. 'Careful. You just said something pretty massive, and you can't take it back.'

And then he is kissing me again. His warm mouth devouring my cool, wet face. The rain, almost biblical, plink-plinks on the small roof above us and rushes in torrents into drains. In the distance, car horns blare, like their team just scored a goal. But I can only concentrate on Frank's skin between phases of my eyes opening and closing. Frank's eyelashes, long and fair. His warm hand cupping the back of my head. His urgent lips. I am hot and freezing, shivering and melting. I am alive, and unaware of anything outside of this moment. It's the longest, most thorough kiss anyone can do in public that travels to all poles of my body, that trickles down my spine and collects in my groin until my knees almost buckle.

When he comes up for air, he says, 'Damn.' He closes his eyes, presses his wet forehead to mine like he did that day outside a hotel room door. I can feel his heart hammering. Or maybe that's my own.

'No more analysis paralysis,' I say. 'Good.'

He plucks a strand of my hair that's stuck to my cheek, picks it off with almost surgical precision, then cups my face in his hands. I'm certain he's about to say something monumental, but then he freezes for an instant then pats his chest. 'Shit,' he says, looking down at our feet. The rolled-up portrait is lying in a puddle on the ground. 'Oh no.' He bends to retrieve it. I watch as he carefully slides off the soggy sheath, then sets about unrolling the paper which sticks where it has buckled quite a bit.

'Oh dear,' I say. The rain obviously managed to penetrate the plastic, causing the charcoal to run. He has miraculously got away with just a smudge on his forehead, but my face is streaked with ghoulishly long, black drip marks, like tears.

'Get rid of it.' My reaction is over-the-top but for some stupid reason looking at my charcoal likeness makes me remember what he said about his novel. About how it's only a love story if you cry at the end.

'Come on! It's not that bad.' He blows on it to dry it, but the damage is done. 'It's just a few imperfections. I kinda like the raw version of you.'

'Seriously,' I say. 'Can you make it go away, please?'

'It's easing up a little,' he says, after he has rolled it back up and put it back in its sleeve. 'Let's make a go of it.'

He's right. It's coming down in a glittery, silver shower now, so much quieter, almost poetic. Everything feels like it's returning to where it left off. Except, perhaps, me.

'I think that might be a little café across the way. What do you say?' His hand that was just calling out the curve of my waist, takes my hand.

Next, we are dashing across the road. I'll remember this, I think. In years to come, I will remember us dashing in the rain, in a way that might have been entirely forgettable if we had just walked.

The café is one of those charmless family-run places that serves the sort of lethal coffee only locals drink, plus slabs of North American-style pizza, and cheese pies that sit on a warming tray all day; one of those places that's just been there forever, that's a little bit of this culture, and a little bit of that; a place that has imprinted itself into the fabric of the city. The two outside tables sheltered from the rain by a rusty, retractable awning, are occupied by elderly Greek guys who are smoking roll-ups, drinking ouzo, and putting the world to rights. They stop talking and watch us as we walk in as though we are drowned tourist rats who are of great interest to them. On seeing us, the young guy behind the counter reluctantly stubs out his cigarette and indicates for us to sit anywhere. No one's inside, so it's wide open. Frank still has hold of my hand which I am powerfully conscious of not wanting to change.

'It never rains in Athens. You know that?' he says. His cheeks are rosy. He looks young – almost like the guy in that photo in Central Park all those years ago.

Looking out at the ground, you'd think a pipe had burst. 'We definitely won't forget this, that's for sure,' I say.

He looks at me with such plainspoken intensity that I have

to steady my breath. 'Believe me, Moira Fitzgerald, I don't need any memory trigger.'

No.

'You're cold.' He sees me shiver. 'We need *rakomelo* to warm us up,' he says to the young guy who is wiping down our table with a grubby, oversized cloth. When the glass dries, Frank carefully sets our bedraggled portrait down in the centre.

They are playing English music. The Four Tops' 'Can't Help Myself' ends and Louis Armstrong's 'We Have All The Time In The World' comes on. Frank cocks me a look. 'Of all the songs in all the gin joints...'

I love this song. I love this song so much, but right now I think I hate this song. We hold eyes as we listen to Louis sing about the one thing we don't have: time. The words make me undergo a strange rewiring, until I have to stare hopelessly out of the window at the rain-splattered street. The waiter brings us *rakomelo*. It is lovely and warm, and I wrap my fingers around the little carafe. Frank sips his, and I'm aware of him observing me as I sip mine, conversation eluding us, until Louis is done torturing us.

And then he says, 'I'm going to tell you something. And I might be going out on a limb here, but I'm going to say it anyway...' He gives me a moment – or gives himself one. 'You can love two people, but you can only be in love with one.'

I focus on his hands that are patiently crossed on the table-top. *Now. Do it. Tell him you told Rupert you're not going back to him. Don't be so worried that he'll think you're trying to ensnare him. Just do it. Say it.*

I stare at those hands for an unseemly amount of time. The words don't come.

'I know what I want,' I say, instead. I slide my hand across the table, not quite touching his. 'I want to go on wandering dark streets and stumbling upon ancient floodlit ruins – until morning. Can we do that, please?'

'Okay,' he says, unreadably.

And that is pretty much what we do. We wander around the streets of Athens for three hours or perhaps more, until it's time for him to head to the airport. At some point – after more than a little persuasion – I finally convince him to dump that ruined portrait of us in the bin.

It feels more than a little symbolic.

THIRTY-NINE

I set my bag down in our hallway, and greet Tiddles, who makes figure of eights around my ankles. I take a moment to process what it feels like to be back. No Harriet just yet. And, because he's away at the conference, no Rupert for tonight, either. No stale cooking smells hanging in the air. Only the lavender detergent our cleaner uses, and an overripe banana stinking in the fruit bowl. I go upstairs. Normally I unpack immediately. But right now, I just lower myself onto our bed, and lie there with my arms stretched out like a starfish and think about my last few hours in Athens.

His flight leaving at 6.10 a.m., mine at 9.00. Us tiredly making our way back to the hotel at dawn, so he could collect his bag. Him telling me I should try to take a nap. Me agreeing but knowing that I was unlikely to become Rip Van Winkle any time soon.

'I'll see you, then…' His parting words. The kiss that would have been on the lips if I had not awkwardly moved my head, because I wanted to remember our last kiss when it wasn't our last kiss. I didn't want last anythings; not the last time he touched me, or the last time his eyes met mine.

After he walked away, and I'd watched him, he suddenly stopped, turned. 'Do what your heart is telling you,' he said, apropos of nothing. 'It's not selfish. It's your life. You're entitled.'

He didn't say *Please come with me*. He didn't even say, *Let's stay in touch*.

I spend the better part of the afternoon wandering around Marks & Spencer's food hall filling a trolley with groceries.

Rupert texts right as I'm driving up to our door.

Did you make it home?

I stare at that word 'home'.

Back, yes.

There's nothing, then I see the three dots. What pops up is not what I'm expecting.

Thank you.

Wait... Thank you? I am too exasperated to do anything other than sigh. Next door's lad, Ian, walks up the garden path in his school uniform and waves like he might have just seen me a day ago or last week. I wave back.

Conference wrapping early afternoon tmw. Should be home by 4 p.m.

I just ignore it. Before dinner I text Harriet and she tells me all is okay.

Still coughing but less hacking and my ribs don't hurt!
It's sunny here now!

I remind her to keep warm anyway, especially at night, and to not take her minor improvement for granted – and that she's not supposed to consume alcohol with the antibiotics. She responds with a big thumbs down. I smile.

For my dinner I open the bottle of red I bought and cut off a big slab of cheese. I take them into the garden with a pack of oat crackers and some butter.

I eat way too much of the cheese, and half the pack of crackers, munching through the lot and not really tasting it. Before I know what I'm even doing, I'm scrolling through my camera in search of that photo I took of him, the one that preceded the video where I told him his big fat head was in the way. The instant I find it, the breath catches in my chest.

Frank.

I'm still staring at that picture a good while later, still replaying that video and freeze-framing it at the point where his face erupts into a laugh, when a text pops up.

Frank!

Home.

Just that one word.

The reality of him being more than five thousand miles away hits hard, the blow softened slightly by my pleasure he's texted. I think about how to respond, settling for *Good flight?*

At the sight of the moving dots I am giddy like a teenager.

Slept a chunk of it. Watched a couple movies. Feels odd
to be back. Like I've been gone longer than a week. You?

It's almost impossible that it was only a week. I type: *For me too.*

I send him a photo of my patio, my wine glass, and the two-thirds empty bottle of red.

He responds with: *Nice view. Your night is my day, and my day is your night.*

He sends a picture of himself outside of LAX, his sunglasses on top of his head, his eyes a little bloodshot, and the sign to Uber and Lyft behind his head.

Never sent a woman a selfie before! First time for a lot of things with you!

Looking at his smile makes me smile.

Not true. I've seen your legs from the knees down.

His feet on the hotel bed.

My second, then.

I chuckle.

The man in the Malibu mansion lives under a rock.

I did until I met you.

I stare at this, every single neurotransmitter turned in the direction of this comment.

The moving dots again.

Walking to get an Uber. Beautiful SoCal afternoon!

He's happy to be home; the exclamation mark is everything. If he'd put three dots after it, I might have thought he was trying to say, Beautiful afternoon, if only you were here...

Safe travels home to Malibu, I write. When he 'likes' it, and there are no more moving dots, I find myself sliding back into a blue funk.

The Ping wakes me up.

Good evening.

Frank again!

I push a sleeping Tiddles off my stomach and sit up. He has sent a picture of the ocean by moonlight.

Good morning! I respond. I glance at the clock. Almost 9.30 a.m.; 1.30 a.m. in LA.

Just taking a beach walk. How was your sleep?

I picture him walking under a canopy of stars at the water's edge. Alone. The ocean feeding his soul. Because that's really all he needs.

Not great. Couldn't get my head to settle down...

Will he know why?

No more dots. I stare at my damned phone, panicking.

Just when I'm on the brink of despair, up comes another Ping!

Just walked back indoors. How's Harriet?

I imagine him striding onto his patio, past the firepit where his chairs are arranged, entering his kitchen. The place where I first set eyes on him when he commented on the picture of the boat and the woman's sexy long legs shooting out of the water. *Splash!* I believe it was called.

I tell him she's okay, that Aiden is taking good care of her.

That's great, he responds, after a minute or two.

The conversation is drying up. I don't know what else to say to hold him there.

But then up pops a photo. Me, in profile, staring out at a setting Santorini sun. I don't have any memory of him taking it, but I look serene and content.

Not bad. Considering you didn't get the subject's approval.

He responds.

I have another one that wasn't exactly approved of...

I find myself hanging there in a silly state of suspense. I don't know if he's deliberately keeping me waiting but...

'Oh no!' I actually say it out loud.

Our portrait! Me with my ghoulish 'tear-stained' face. Or, rather, a photo of it lying on his Carrara marble breakfast bar.

What??? How????

Made the cab driver reroute on way to airport. Reeks like garbage but I'm going to frame it.

I chuckle, despite the fact that this is terrible, just terrible.

You can put it in your bathroom beside Marilyn Monroe.

That's the plan! Wait. How do you know what's in my bathroom?

I'm about to confess that I snooped the length and breadth of his house, but then I hear something. The purr of Rupert's engine.

He said he'd be back before 4 p.m. Not 9.30 a.m.

I quickly type to Frank: *Wild guess*

I can hear Rupert having a word with Kevin, our neighbour, who will be on his way to work, them laughing.

Another Ping!

I haven't been able to stop staring at it.

A key in the door. Rupert's voice. 'Moy?'

I can't think of what to type fast enough. The lull feels too long. I see the dots again.

I have no right to text you any more. Tell me to stop.

Rupert's voice again, a little more assertive. 'Moira?'

My heart thrashes. Rupert is on his way up the stairs now. I can hear his heavy footfall, the familiar squeak of a loose board on the sixth rise. Then he walks in the room. 'You're there.' He says it like he might have expected me not to be. His eyes go to the phone in my hand.

'So are you,' I say. 'I thought you were coming later?'

'I decided to sneak out before breakfast.' He greets the cat who has now jumped off the bed to say hello to him. He stands there, awkwardly, then he says, 'Bursting for a pee.' He throws his jacket onto a chair then walks into our en-suite. He pushes the door closed, but it stops part way so I hear him relieve himself.

I stare at Frank's message. *Tell me to stop.* We are back in that café. With all the time in the world, and no time at all.

I quickly type: *Don't stop.* The small Swoosh! of it sending gets drowned out by the flushing of the toilet.

'Are you alright?' Rupert comes and stands by the bed. 'Not like you to sleep in.' There is genuine concern in his voice.

'I'm fine,' I say.

I swipe out of messages, click my screen off.

FORTY

I'm not fine.

Not freaking fine.

I'm far, far, far from freaking fine.

Frank hasn't texted again. This feels like the end of my world. Harriet comes home and Aiden goes back to California. Her cough is really no better. I pay for one more month's rent on the Santa Monica Airbnb to buy us some time until we can work out who is going back to get our stuff. Rupert is pissed off: 'If you're only going back to America to pack up all your belongings and Harriet's, why can't you just stay in a hotel for two nights? Why are you wasting all our money on a month's Airbnb?' he says.

At least he said *our* money.

Harriet reconnects with some of her friends. Despite her telling me she fully supports me leaving her dad, I don't see much of her, so we don't really get to talk about it. Rupert goes to work, and Rupert comes home from work. When he comes in, I go out. To the cinema. To a café. To a quiet pub where I can sit in a corner and nurse a drink. Anything to avoid being under the same roof as him at the same time.

I relocate to the spare bedroom, moving all my clothes in there. But that mattress is a relic we should have replaced years ago, and it gives me an ungodly backache. So I move back into our bedroom – given *he* won't sleep in the spare room – erecting a barricade of pillows down the centre, so we're clear that we each have our own half. I lie awake for hours listening to him snoring, playing it all over in my mind – how Frank and I met, that hike, our conversations, how he kisses me, how he caresses me, how he makes me come.

The second week brings the full-on realisation: Frank isn't going to text again. He texted that time to tell me he was back in America, then to show me that he'd unearthed our portrait from the rubbish bin. Those texts were not a continuation of us; they were really just an extension of goodbye.

I pull up our last messages so many times it's not funny. I activate the message bar and stare at the winking blue cursor. But then I click off because – what can I really say that's going to change anything?

By the third week, I am so drained from all the over-thinking that if he showed up at my front door, I don't think I'd even have energy to walk to the foot of the stairs to greet him.

On Tuesday night, I go out with Nat. In a bar around the back of the train station, I tell her that this entire business of looking at flats I might be able to afford to rent on my own, trying to decide if I should attempt to get my old job back, leaving the house every time Rupert comes in, is just so exhausting. The logistics of setting up life as a single person is almost enough to make you want to go back to him even if he's committed mass murder. I tell her I can't believe we ever bought a house with a double vanity in the en-suite bathroom. Because when Rupert stands there beside me flossing his teeth, I've got to watch bits of food fly out of his mouth and stick to the mirror. And, I mean, how can I have been married all these years to a man who shaves his forearms?

She smirks. 'So you think Frank doesn't have stuff stuck between his molars?'

I pull up his picture. My favourite one of him I took before the video. 'How could this guy's teeth possibly be a breeding ground for oral bacteria?'

She shakes her head in affectionate despair. 'Yup. I'd also rather have sex with him than with Rupert – and I'm not even into fellas.'

I try to smile but pull a duck face instead.

'Moira,' she says, almost impatiently. 'You've been back three weeks and you still haven't called that lawyer whose number I gave you. You moved out of the marital bed then you moved back into it.'

I throw up my hands. 'It's a case of sleep there, or give myself scoliosis.'

She shakes her head at me. 'Why isn't it him who is doing his back in? Or him looking at flats to move into?'

I tell her we had the conversation, but he said he's not moving out because he's not the one who thinks there's a problem with our marriage. I tell her that rather than him gaslighting me, he seems to be gaslighting himself.

'I don't know why you're being so passive,' she says.

'I'm just a laggard,' I tell her. 'I got that on my report card when I was in junior school.'

'That was thirty-five years ago.' She shakes her head in despair. 'You know what I think? I think you've been leaving Rupert for a lot of years. You might have been leaving him from the moment you met him.' She lets me digest that. 'I also know from years of professional experience that when a person suspects their partner of adultery they don't run away for three months to decide if their marriage is worth saving. Nor do they jump into bed with someone they say they don't like – for whatever reason they tell themselves they're doing it – when casual sex is not part of their code.' Before I can protest, she says, 'I think you were waiting for Rupert to open some sort of door for you to leave. And the second you saw a crack, a glimmer of light on the other side, you wanted to explore what it would be like out there...'

She searches my face with so much understanding in her eyes that I find myself agog to hear what she's going to say next.

'I think that in Santa Monica you were trying out what life would be like if you did leave him. And I think somewhere in there you've figured out that it wouldn't be half bad.'

'Wow,' I say. 'It's a good job you don't charge by the word, or I'd be bankrupt.'

She doesn't smile, so I say, 'He told me he has nothing to offer me, remember? He can't put himself in the position.' Ugh! I still hate those words.

'But he also said it wasn't for him to help you make your mind up about your marriage – and he was right; it wasn't his place to help you with that one.'

'He doesn't trust anyone enough to commit to them again. He's had one semi-serious relationship since his wife died. He doesn't want something deep and meaningful.'

'But he almost killed himself on a jet ski because you all but admitted that having sex with him in your apartment meant nothing.' We hold eyes. 'As if that's not convincing enough,' she adds, 'he told you that you can love two people, but you can only be in love with one... I mean, how much persuading do you need to see it for what it is?' She searches my face almost in despair of me. 'He's in love with you.'

A hot tear rushes down my face. 'It's just too many mixed messages,' I hear myself repeat my old refrain. Even I don't fully believe it any more.

'There are no mixed messages here,' she says. 'He's been very clear. He wants you to take responsibility for your own decisions – and your own heart. But if you do... he is there waiting.'

Can she be right?

'You know there are a bunch of regrets that people have when they're dying,' she says. 'Depending on which source you read there's about ten of them or about thirty. But you know what the main one is?'

I shake my head.

'It's not having the courage to express their true feelings, speak up for what they want. So they settled for mediocre existences while they know in their heart that their life could have been so much more.' She studies me sympathetically. 'If you love Frank, tell him. Put that stubborn pride and fear of rejection aside, and go all in. Because he was right. This is your life. *One* life, that's all we get, Moira. And you have a lot of it left. So don't be that person who always looks over her shoulder at what might have been. For heaven's sake, don't be that person. Be braver than that. Please.'

She flags down our waitress and orders two more drinks.

FORTY-ONE

'I'm not going to spend the next two years studying in America.' Harriet says it matter-of-factly when I walk in the door. 'I'm staying here to finish my degree as planned.'

I park myself on the edge of the sofa.

'What happened?'

I knew she and Aiden had FaceTimed this morning, but they FaceTime every morning. I'm thinking she's about to tell me it's over, and I suddenly feel so horrible. All that disapproval, all that determination to split them up... Is it the only thing I've succeeded in, out of all this? I projected my fears onto two kids who shouldn't have had me trying to tell them that their feelings weren't true.

She beams. 'We're going to do the long-distance thing, Mum! We think it's incredibly romantic!'

She is watching my face, but she really isn't seeing me. She's seeing the path of her life meandering exactly the way she wants it to. 'We'll commute between terms. Maybe Christmas he'll come here, maybe next year I'll go there... We're going to do something really fun next summer, like, a proper trip somewhere! Maybe Australia and New Zealand.' Her excitement is palpable. 'He's going to come here this summer, Mum. While I do my placement at Heatherwick. We even thought that we might rent a place for a few weeks in central London. If we can find somewhere we can afford.' She puts it out there carefully but unequivocally. 'I'll be closer to work. And he gets to hang out and maybe do some research for a film idea he has.' She beams again, some tears filling her eyes. 'We're going to make it work, Mum! He said the very thing you once said. That if we're meant to be together then we will survive being apart for two years. And he thinks we will. He thinks we are.' And then she adds, 'And it goes without saying that I do, too.'

'So you've fully forgiven him, then?' I tease. 'You don't worry that he might meet someone else? That you might, too? Two years is a long time.'

She coughs, reminding me that she's still fragile. 'Mum, I'm not threatened by other girls. And as far as him having to worry about me, well, yes, I wanted to kill him not so long ago, but I've never met a guy I've felt this way about before, so there's absolutely no reason for him to think he's got competition lurking around the corner.'

She sounds so beautifully practical and like a modern fairy-tale princess, all at the same time.

'Well, that's wonderful, then,' I say.

Later in the evening, while Rupert is in the toilet with the newspaper, I type a text to Frank.

I miss our conversations.

I wait two minutes. Two hours. Two crushing days.
No reply.

FORTY-TWO

Today I had a consultation with Nat's lawyer. And tonight, I'm warming up a Marks & Spencer Dine In Meal Deal for Two, only I'm going to eat both portions. When Rupert comes in, I'm most of the way through a second slow-cooked, Korean-style spicy chicken thigh, but I'm not really tasting it. I was thinking about Frank kissing me forever on that step in the rain. Of him moving inside me on that hotel bed, his eyes plundering mine. Of our deep conversations. And I was trying to work out which I loved more, and which, if I had to choose, I'd settle for living without. If our life just consisted of endless hours sitting by the beach and talking, without anything physical, would I still feel like everything I had was exactly what I needed? And then I thought who would even need the beach? The beach is actually superfluous. But what if we had zero emotional connection, but endless repeats of that amazing sex?

So when Rupert says, 'I need to talk to you,' it takes me a minute to realise 'you' means 'me'.

'What do you want to talk about?' I ask.

He comes and stands by the table, clutches the chair back. 'Him.'

I've never known a pronoun carry such weight of cells and water.

Then, after a suspense-filled spell, he says, 'Last night in bed you called out his name in your sleep.'

'Did I?' I say, a little taken aback.

His face turns almost scarlet. 'Actually,' he clears his throat. 'That's er... not... entirely true. You didn't actually call out his name. You didn't actually call out anything for that matter.' His hand falls away from the chair back. 'What I'm trying to say is that I keep lying there waiting for you to. You know, I keep lying there wondering if he's the last thing on your mind before you fall asleep, and the first thing when you wake up. I just keep...' He clears his throat. 'Sorry. That was really pathetic of me. I don't know why I said it.'

I say, 'You once called out Dagmara's name in bed.'

His face drains of all expression. He goes to speak. Nothing comes at first. Then he says, 'That's actually... That's actually bullshit, isn't it? I mean, I never did that, did I?'

'You sound uncertain.'

He turns even more violently red. 'Look, I didn't really invite this conversation to play mind games.'

I stare at him unseeingly for a moment. 'Rupert,' I say. 'I went to see a divorce lawyer today.'

He starts to shake his head before I'm even done speaking. 'No,' he says. 'I will not let you leave me. You can't do this.' When I don't answer and we are silent for a very long time, he says, despondently, 'Is there anything I can do to maybe change your mind?'

'Be honest with me,' I say. 'You owe me that. I don't care about you sleeping with someone else. I care about the three months you've tried to mess with my head.'

He listens closely, turns his ear towards me in that way he'll do when he realises it's time to smarten up and pay attention.

'I didn't,' he says. He starts shaking his head again. 'I didn't sleep with that woman.'

He is shaking and shaking and shaking that head. And then the shaking turns into a nod. 'Once,' he says, so quietly that I almost don't hear.

He meets my eyes now. 'I slept with her once.' He frowns like his admission is going to make him cry. 'I didn't intend it to happen. I didn't intend to lie to you about it. I don't know why I...' His voice fades away. He manages to add, 'I regretted it...'

He stares unblinkingly at the floor, and I see the glisten of tears in his eyes. Then he clears his throat, looks up at me again. 'And you slept with Frank, I'm assuming.'

'Yes,' I say, conscious that my reaction to what he's just told me hasn't yet arrived. Or if it has, then it was a soft landing. And then I add, 'And I *did* intend it to happen. And it felt right. And I am in love with him.'

FORTY-THREE

They call it the June gloom. It's the band of cloud and fog that sets in during the night and often kicks around until the middle of the next day. The 'marine layer' they talk about that whitens out the world and makes the sand blend with the ocean, the ocean merge with the horizon, that obliterates the mountains, and turns people into pencil pops of the colour of their clothing. It has burnt off by the time I drive out to Malibu, so that when I follow the secret path that residents don't want you to know is there, down to the sand, I can clearly see the parade of homes that line Broad Beach, shielding this rarefied mile of oceanfront from those of us who don't belong here. I walk straight into the water. It's as cold as I remember it, and makes me say, 'Ah...!' I stand there letting it rush and ripple around my ankles until the shock of it subsides, noting the curious way the sand, which seems so solid underfoot, is swiftly dislodged with the retreating tide, leaving everything teetering and uncertain.

I walk along the pebble-free sand, the soft filter of the sun at my back, a little jetlagged still. Several mansions down, I think I see it. I recognise the enormous rock retaining wall, the glass railing, the dense ground cover with its shiny green leaves and purple daisy-like flower.

I pull out my phone, type my very simple message: *You stopped.*

Three minutes later – long enough for me to worry he's going to ignore this one too – I see the little moving dots.

Texting you? Yes. Thinking about you? Never.

I let out a huge, held breath.

How do I know you're not just saying that because it's the gallant thing to say?

Because I'm not that gallant. We discovered that. Remember?

A wave breaks over the tops of my feet. I stand still, letting myself feel it. All of it. The sun on my back. The moment.

Didn't you once tell me that you don't have sex with married women?

The little dots don't appear immediately. But then:

It's complicated.

I start walking down the sand again, getting a little closer to his house.

Tell me.

I see the dots, but this must be a long reply.

I told you I'm a romantic. Going to bed with a married woman – even one possibly on the brink of leaving her marriage to a cheating schmuck – never sat well. I only wanted you when you were sure about me, not when you were still deciding.

But you broke your own rule.

There's a pause, then:

If you were here, I'd tell you why. But it's probably best I don't.

I have moved down the beach like a piece of driftwood, washed up right in front of his house. Of the many places he could be, searching for bridges to nowhere, or riding around in his Porsche, he is sitting there on a patio chair. He has his back to me, his knees are spread and he's leaning forward with his phone in his hand. There's an open laptop in front of him on the ledge of the fire pit.

Then my phone pings again.

Guess what? he writes. *Our song came on the radio the other day.*

I think he means the Louis Armstrong one, but he says, *the one we danced to.*

I slap a hand over my mouth. By craning my neck over the hump of rock, I can see him side on, see the edges of his smile.

Guess what else? he writes.

Go on.

When I got back to the US, I did a small mathematical calculation. I worked out how long it had been since I first met you, to our last night in Athens.

I am held there in suspense, then he writes:

Six weeks.

Oh my God. It can't be.

You can't be in love with someone you've only known six weeks: my words to Harriet.

What are you doing right now Frank? I type.

I get such a kick out of watching him as he replies.

Well Moira... you might not believe it but I'm sitting outside writing. You'd be proud of me.

Are you really? I am trying to picture that. A book by any chance?

He tilts his head back for a moment, looking quite happy with himself.

An idea that might turn into a book.

How can I climb these rocks without killing myself? I have a mental picture of me almost getting to the top then slipping, falling to a squealy and inelegant death.

What's it about? I ask.

He rubs the back of his neck.

Hard to get into over text.

My heart is flying. A rush of daring zinging in me.

If I were there, would you tell me?

If you were here... among a lot of things I'd do... yes, I'd
probably tell you.

Looks like I'm doing it then!

I place one foot on a big boulder and hoist myself up. One large step. Success! Then two... I reach the top, convinced that any second now he's going to sense my presence and the whole surprise will be blown. But his head stays lowered, his attention glued to his phone as he waits for my response.

'It's a shame I'm not here, then,' I say.

There's a nanosecond where nothing happens, then his head turns sharply in the direction of my voice.

'Hello, Frank.'

He shields his eyes with a hand. There's a beat, and then he says, 'Moira?'

I scamper down the other side of the rocks, jump onto his patio. 'Ta-da!' I fling my arms into the air like I'm hoping for a round of applause.

He says a thunderstruck, 'What the fuck?'

He doesn't quickly snap out of his surprise, which is funny.

'I've got two things I have to say to you,' I say, determined to not let his face, the disbelieving way he is looking at me, throw me off course. 'Just so we're *abundantly*, *uber* clear... Firstly, I may have left my marriage, but I'm not looking to jump into a relationship with someone else. I still don't fear being alone, and I'm still not looking for anyone to save me.'

His face remains as serious as a face struggling to be serious can be.

'And second?' he asks.

I don't know if I can say *I love you.* Not without him saying it first.

Instead, I say, 'So... what's this book about? I think you're obliged to tell me – now that we know I'm here.'

He gets up from his seat, like his brain suddenly

commanded his body, takes tentative steps towards me. He's wearing an untucked white linen shirt, and faded blue jeans, like that first day in his kitchen. And his feet are bare.

'It's about a jaded, middle-aged writer, and the woman who makes him believe in something again.'

'And does it have a happy ending?' I ask.

'I don't know,' he says. 'You tell me.'

A LETTER FROM CAROL

Dear reader,

Firstly, I want to say a huge thank you for choosing to read *Second Chance Romance* – I really hope you enjoyed it. If you want to keep up to date with all my latest releases, you can sign up to my newsletter at the following link. Your email address will never be shared and you can unsubscribe at any time.

www.bookouture.com/carol-mason

You may know me through my other bestselling women's fiction novels. *After You Left* was a Kindle Top 100 e-book in 2017. It was the novel that relaunched my career. Several other women's fiction stories followed that one, all which I loved writing, all of which are close to my heart.

But like many things in life, once in a while we're itching for a change. A new direction. For me that restlessness came in early 2021. We were going through the whole Covid misery. Positivity was thin on the ground. I wasn't feeling my usual optimism about things. I was feeling the pressure to get on with writing a novel, but I just couldn't muster up any enthusiasm for the more 'serious issues' type of story I'd written before.

And I'd started watching some good old classic romances, and romantic comedies. I was rediscovering the joy of laughter, and the zing of witty one-liners. Characters we believed, and rooted for, whose lives lacked something crucial, who were transformed by love.

Then I bolted up in bed (almost) and said *I want to write a romantic comedy!* But one that was also a very warm and touching love story. I knew how it would begin, and I knew how it would end, but I had no idea about the other 80 per cent. And that's pretty much what happens with all my novels. It makes for a rollercoaster of a writing experience – but helps me write in the moment.

I'd always been drawn to writing humour. And I'll let you in on a secret. The very first novel I wrote, when I quit my job at thirty-two to give myself a year to get published, was a romantic comedy/chick lit story. Sadly, I submitted it to literary agents at the end of chick lit's huge wave of popularity, and they told me that while it was a great read, publishers wouldn't touch it with a barge pole – they were hungry for more serious women's fiction now. So that's what I then pivoted to, and *The Secrets of Married Women* came out of that.

So you could say that *Second Chance Romance* brought me full circle. And here's the thing. Have you noticed there are lots of romantic comedies that feature females finding love in their twenties? While I can appreciate these stories, I can't always relate to them. I wanted to write a book that would resonate with readers who have had their first love and are maybe onto their second – or maybe they are a bit older and haven't yet met 'the one'. Readers who still want edgy humour, and vibrant, imperfect, quirky characters, but plots that might reflect their lives, or their hopes and aspirations, with characters who might be a mirror of themselves. So I decided to make Moira, my main character, forty-two, and about to undergo a massive upheaval in her life. And then she finds love when she least thinks she wants it again.

And I set it in Malibu and Greece. Greece because – c'mon! – who doesn't want a love story set in Santorini? And Malibu, because my husband and I have an apartment near there and I've got to know the area very well, and I am fascinated by the homes of the movie stars and the super-rich that line the sand there. So I thought, hmm... my leading man is going to live in one of these homes. But I didn't want him to be a businessman or an actor, so I decided on a writer. A writer of the world's most famous romantic movie and novel who is, oddly, a cynic about love. And a woman who hates him – at first.

I love being a writer. I love nothing more than seeing a book go out into the world and thinking it might bring pleasure to a reader, give them an escape, a chance to swoon and laugh. I am a hopeless romantic myself, but I'm also a realist – so I want my stories to feel realistic. If you can believe it, then you can feel it deeply. And if I can take you somewhere in your imagination, and in your heart, then that makes me very happy indeed.

I also love hearing from readers. I choose my social media carefully. You'll find me most active on Facebook because I love the interaction I get there with friends, so please do follow my author page there if you'd like to get to know me better. I will do my best to entertain and give you a glimpse into a writer's world. I'm also on Instagram. My website is a good place to check for my other books, and news – or to contact me directly. I will always do my level best to answer your emails.

Best wishes,

Carol

www.carolmasonwriter.com

facebook.com/CarolMasonAuthor

instagram.com/carolmasonauthor

ACKNOWLEDGEMENTS

I began writing this book in early 2021. We were doing the Covid thing, and the 'work from home' thing. I remember my world felt small, and the smallness never-ending. I was aware I had to start a new novel, but I was feeling so very uninspired. Then I started watching classic movies and romantic comedies again. Ones I hadn't seen in years. *Something's Gotta Give. My Best Friend's Wedding. When Harry Met Sally. As Good As It Gets...* Something about the quality of the writing, the humanity, the honesty made me think, 'I want to write a book like that!' An uplifting, romantic story that's funny, contemporary, timeless and true. I had the bones of an idea, but I had absolutely no idea how hard that was going to be to pull off! Two years later, after countless drafts and incarnations, I finally had something to go out with.

I signed with a new literary agent, Laura Bradford. Thank you, Laura for having faith in my story. Then I signed a two-book deal with Bookouture and began working with my excellent editor Lucy Frederick. Lucy, Richard King, and the team, saw what I was trying to do with this novel and gave priceless feedback to help me get it right. I am enormously grateful for that push, and your insight. And I'm delighted to be part of the Bookouture family.

Writing can be lonely work. But I have some fantastic friends who cheer me on. Whether it's for being there to bounce ideas off, or for the boundless positivity and encouragement you give me, I'd like to thank, in particular, Stefany, Suzannah, Julie, Alison, Robyn and Bob.

My husband, Tony, listens to me rattling on about my novel/career more than any person should have to. So I have to thank him for his endless patience, advice and support – and for never once telling me it was time to get a real job.

I will be forever grateful to my parents for my grounded, happy childhood. There was always a song from a bygone era on the record player, and a black and white film on a Sunday afternoon. I'm sure that's what gave me my romantic disposition, and what helped me write this novel. Thanks, Dad, though you are gone. And thanks, Mam; at ninety-four you are still an inspiration to me.

PUBLISHING TEAM

Turning a manuscript into a book requires the efforts of many people. The publishing team at Bookouture would like to acknowledge everyone who contributed to this publication.

Audio
Alba Proko
Sinead O'Connor
Melissa Tran

Commercial
Lauren Morrissette
Hannah Richmond
Imogen Allport

Cover design
Emma Graves

Data and analysis
Mark Alder
Mohamed Bussuri

Editorial
Lucy Frederick
Imogen Allport

Milton Keynes UK
Ingram Content Group UK Ltd.
UKHW031653170724
445742UK00004B/132